A
Convenience...

More than a practical marriage…?

Three passionate novels!

In September 2007 Mills & Boon bring
back two of their classic collections,
each featuring three favourite
romances by our bestselling authors...

AT HIS CONVENIENCE...

Mistress of Convenience
by Penny Jordan
A Convenient Husband
by Kim Lawrence
A Convenient Marriage
by Maggie Cox

BRINGING UP BABY

The Baby Plan by Liz Fielding
Her Royal Baby by Marion Lennox
Her Boss's Baby Plan by Jessica Hart

At His Convenience...

MISTRESS OF CONVENIENCE
by
Penny Jordan

A CONVENIENT HUSBAND
by
Kim Lawrence

A CONVENIENT MARRIAGE
by
Maggie Cox

MILLS & BOON®
Pure reading pleasure

*First published in Great Britain 2007
by Harlequin Mills & Boon Limited,
Eton House, 18-24 Paradise Road, Richmond, Surrey TW9 1SR*

AT HIS CONVENIENCE...
© by Harlequin Enterprises II B.V./S.à.r.l 2007

*Mistress of Convenience, A Convenient Husband and
A Convenient Marriage were first published in Great Britain by
Harlequin Mills & Boon Limited in separate, single volumes.*

Mistress of Convenience © Penny Jordan 2007
A Convenient Husband © Kim Lawrence 2001
A Convenient Marriage © Maggie Cox 2003

ISBN: 978 0 263 85524 1

05-0907

*Printed and bound in Spain
by Litografia Rosés S.A., Barcelona*

MISTRESS OF CONVENIENCE

by

Penny Jordan

Penny Jordan has been writing for more than twenty years and has an outstanding record: over one hundred and thirty novels published, including the phenomenally successful *A Perfect Family, To Love, Honour & Betray, The Perfect Sinner* and *Power Play,* which hit *The Sunday Times* and *New York Times* bestseller lists. Penny Jordan was born in Preston, Lancashire, and now lives in rural Cheshire.

Don't miss Penny Jordan's exciting new novella *Bride at Bellfield Mill* – part of the anthology *The Widow, the Waif & the Foundling,* out in November 2007 from M&B™.

CHAPTER ONE

'Wow, will you look at that? His Royal Highness and the industrialist everyone swears is not up for a knighthood. And don't they look cosy together for two people who are supposed to be sworn enemies.'

As Suzy struggled to hear the voice of Jeff Walker, the photographer from the magazine they both worked for, over the noise of the busy launch party, she heard him saying excitedly, 'I've just got to get a shot of that. Come on.'

This was her first month on the magazine, and immediately she followed him.

She had taken a couple of steps when she heard him saying bitterly, 'Hell! He's got Colonel Lucas James Soames with him. Ex-Commando, Special Forces, hero, and hater of the press!' he explained impatiently when he saw Suzy's uncertain frown. 'Despite the fact that a female reporter with a certain British news team practically dribbled with lust every time she interviewed him during his last campaign.'

Suzy tried to look as though she was up to speed with what she was being told, but the plain truth was that she knew nothing of Colonel Soames. Already unnerved by the photographer's comments, she looked round discreetly, but was unable to spot anyone wearing any kind of military uniform.

She knew she ought to be grateful to her university

tutor for recommending her for this job. He had been so enthusiastic about it, telling her what a wonderful opportunity it would be for her, that she had felt she would be letting him down if she didn't accept the probationary position. But after nearly a month working on the political affairs desk of the cutting-edge City magazine Suzy was beginning to suspect that she had made a mistake.

Maybe it was the fact that she had been out of the swim of things for so long whilst she nursed her mother through the last two years of her life that made her so uncomfortable about the methods the magazine adopted in order to get its hot stories. She had certainly felt immeasurably older than her fellow students when she had returned to university to complete her degree.

'I'm sorry—' She began to apologise uncertainly to Jeff. 'I can't see the Colonel.'

But she could see a man several yards away, who stood head and shoulders above every other man in the room—or so it seemed to Suzy. She was transfixed, every female hormone in her body focusing on him with an eager interest. Her mouth had gone dry and her heart had started to pound unevenly. The fact that he was standing alone, somehow aloof from everyone else, only piqued her interest further.

She had the most unexpected and dangerous urge to go up to him and make him... Make him what, exactly? Acknowledge her presence? Talk to her? Tell her that he was experiencing the same heart-wrenching, sanity-undermining, wholly unfamiliar need to be with her that she was experiencing for him? Was she going crazy? Her legs had gone weak and her heart was racing. She didn't know whether it was shock that was running through her body with mercurial speed or excitement. Her? Excited by a man? A stranger? She was too sensible for such stuff. Too sensible and too wary!

Determinedly she started to look away, but he had turned his head, and her heartbeat went into overdrive whilst a surge of explicit and bewildering arousal and longing raced though her. Longing for a man she had only looked at? How could that happen?

And yet Suzy couldn't help watching him. He wasn't looking at her, but past her, she recognised. However, whilst he did so, Suzy was able to stare at him and greedily absorb every tiny physical detail. Tall, dark and handsome went nowhere near describing his full male magnificence. He was more than that. Much, much more! Suzy could feel her whole body responding to just about the sexiest man she had ever seen and was ever likely to see. Her heart gave another small nervous flurry of thuds when he turned his head again, as though he knew that she was now looking at him. He was now staring straight at her, imprisoning her almost, so that she felt unable to move!

She felt as though she was being X-rayed—and that there wasn't a single thing he didn't know about her! Pink-cheeked, she realised that his incisive gaze had finished sweeping her and was now fixed on her mouth. She felt her lips starting to part, as though they were longing for his kiss. Hurriedly she closed them, her face still burning.

His eyes were a shade of intense dark blue, his skin tanned, his hair so dark brown that it was almost black. His profile was that of a Greek god and, as though that wasn't enough, Suzy was forced to acknowledge that he had about him that indefinable air that whispered into the female ear *sex*. And not just any old kind of sex either, but dream-breaking, heart-stopping, mind-blowing wonderful sex! In fact the kind of sex…

Somehow she managed to get her wayward thoughts under control just in time to hear Jeff telling her curtly, 'You're going to have to distract the Colonel's attention whilst I get my picture.'

'What?' Suzy asked, anxiously scanning the crowd packed tightly around the Prince.

'Where…where is he…?'

'Over there—next to the Prince and the Secretary of State.'

Wildly Suzy looked from the photographer's face to the man he had just indicated. *The* man. *Her* man…

'But…but you said he was a colonel. He isn't in uniform.' She was stammering like an idiot—behaving like a woman who had fallen passionately in love! Now she *knew* that she was crazy.

'Uniform?' Jeff's voice was impatient, contemptuous of her ignorance. 'No, of course he isn't in uniform. He isn't in the Army any more. Where have you been? He works on his own, freelance, providing a bespoke protection service for those who need it. Not that he needs to work. He's independently wealthy and well connected; his father was the younger son of an old county family, and his mother was American. He's ex-Eton. Cut his teeth in Northern Ireland and got made up to Major, then was decorated for service above and beyond the call of duty in Bosnia—that's when he got his next promotion. Like I just said, he isn't in the

Army any more but he still does the dangerous stuff—acting as a personal bodyguard. He's in great demand on the ''I'm an important person and I need a top-class protection service'' circuit. Visiting politicians and heads of state, et cetera.'

All this had been relayed to Suzy in a grim whisper, but now suddenly Jeff exclaimed excitedly, 'Look at that! Get that picture and I won't ever need to work again. Yes, you stay right there, baby,' he crooned to himself, before commanding Suzy, 'Come on! You'll have to distract the Colonel so that I can get this shot.'

'What? What am I supposed to do?' Suzy asked anxiously, and she looked to where the Colonel was standing casually in front of the two men, screening them from interruption.

Jeff gave her an exasperated look. 'Why the hell did they land me with you instead of someone who knows the ropes? I've heard that Roy has only taken you on as a favour, and because he likes your legs—he probably interviewed you imagining what they'd look like wrapped around him.'

Suzy struggled not to let Jeff see how upset she was by his comments. Her boss's openly sexual and often crude remarks to her were just one of the reasons why she was becoming increasingly unhappy about her job.

'You're a woman, aren't you? Go over there and do what comes naturally!' Jeff grunted, before pushing his way through the crowd, leaving Suzy to follow him.

Do what comes naturally! Oh, yes, she could quite easily do what came naturally with Colonel Soames... A thrill of dangerous emotion spiked through Suzy as she looked into the face of the man who was now

standing right in front of her. He was, Suzy acknowledged, quite definitely the sexiest man she had ever
seen. Those broad shoulders, that handsome face!

She was beginning to feel seriously alarmed by her
reactions to him! Her friend Kate was always scolding
her, telling her she didn't get out enough, and now
Suzy thought she might be right. To be affected like
this, to react like this simply at the sight of one specific
man... She closed her eyes, willing herself to be sensible, and then opened them again.

What was it about a man in a dinner suit? What was
it about *this* man in a dinner suit? Well, for one thing
he was wearing his with an unselfconscious ease that
said he was used to doing so, and for another it fitted
him somehow as though it were a part of him. What
had he looked like in his dress uniform? In combats?
A tiny shudder ripped through her.

And as for that tan and those teeth...teeth that she
was sure gleamed nearly as white as his shirtfront! And
she was sure there were real muscles beneath all that
tailoring as well.

Out of the corner of her eye she saw Jeff glowering
at her. A little uncomfortably Suzy took a deep breath
and stepped forward, a muddled plan of action forming
inside her head. A smile of recognition at the Colonel
then a brief apology for having mistaken him for someone else. A few seconds' work, but long enough, she
hoped, for Jeff to get his picture.

Gritting her teeth against the knowledge that this
kind of behaviour was quite definitely not her style,
Suzy ignored the nervous churning of her stomach and
stepped forward.

And then stopped! One step was all she had taken—
so how come she now had her nose virtually against
the Colonel's pristine white shirt? How had he moved
without her being aware that he was doing so? When
had he moved? Suzy wondered frantically. In less than
a blink of the eye he had somehow gone from standing
a couple of yards away to being right in front of her.

Suzy's sensitive nostrils started to quiver as she
breathed in a discreet hint of cologne, underwritten by
something very male and subtle that sent her self-
control crashing into chaos.

He reached out and took hold of her arm, his grip
firm and compelling. Suzy could feel her blood beating
up around his encircling fingers as her body reacted to
his hold.

Like someone lost in a trance she looked up at him.
An instinct deeper than any thought or action seemed
to have taken control of her, and she was powerless to
do anything other than give in to it. The navy blue gaze
fastened on her own. Her heart jerked against the wall
of her chest, and the polite social apology she had been
about to make died unspoken on her lips.

In a haze of dizzying desire Suzy felt her gaze slide
like melting ice cream from the heat of his eyes to the
curve of his mouth. Her whole body was galvanised by
a series of tiny tremors and she exhaled on a small,
soft, female sigh of wanton pleasure.

Without knowing what she was doing she lifted her
free hand to trace the hard, firm line of his mouth—to
see if the flesh there felt as erotic as it looked. But then
her hand dropped to her side as another even more
pleasurable way of conducting her survey struck her.

She had to reach up on her tiptoes in order to press her mouth to his, but the hand holding her arm seemed somehow to aid and balance her. The busy hum of conversation in the room faded as her lips made the discovery that just touching his mouth with her own was opening a door for her into a whole new world.

Blind and deaf to everything and everyone else around her, Suzy made a soft sound of pleasure deep in her throat. An aching whisper of female recognition.

Closing her eyes, she leaned into the male body, waiting hungrily for the Colonel to return the pressure of her lips, to part them with the swift, hard thrust of his tongue, to share with her the devouring intensity of need and longing that surged through her.

As she sighed her pleasure and hunger against his mouth she felt its pressure, his kiss heart-joltingly male. One of his hands slid firmly into the thick softness of her red-gold curls whilst the other pressed into the small of her back, urging her body closer to his own!

Suzy knew she was not very sexually experienced, and what was happening to her now was way out of her league! The way his mouth was moving on hers— firm, warm, knowing—the way his tongue-tip was laving the eager softness of her lips, was rewriting the logbook of her sexual history and adding a whole new chapter to it!

Lost in the rapture of what was happening to her, Suzy pressed closer, caught up in a cloud of hormone-drenched fantasy.

This was it! This was him! Her dragon-slayer and protector, the magical lover she had dreamed of in her most vulnerable moments. The hero she had secretly

longed for all her life in her most private dreams. Her
soul mate.

Suzy ached to tell him how she felt, how filled with
delirious joy she was that he was here, how…

She gave a small shocked gasp as suddenly she was
being pushed away.

Confusion darkened her eyes as she looked up at
him, at a loss to understand what was happening until
she saw the way he was looking back at her.

Instantly her joy was replaced with pain and despair.
Shock gripped hold of her with icy fingers as she recognised the anger and loathing in the navy blue gaze
boring into her.

'No!' She heard herself whisper the agonised denial,
but it was no use. There was no mercy or softening in
the hard, contemptuous gaze. Her whole body felt as
though it was being drenched in shame and humiliation. Her soul mate? He was looking at her as though
she were his worst enemy!

Anger, contempt, hostility, Suzy could see them all
glittering in his eyes, before they were hidden away
from her with a blank look of steely professionalism.

What on earth had she done? Why had she done it?
She had made a complete and total fool of herself!
What stupidity had made her resurrect that idiotic old
dream of a soul mate? She'd thought she had had the
sense to recognise it had no place in reality! It was a
dream she had clung to for far too long anyway, like
a child reluctant to relinquish the security of a worn-
out teddy bear.

Her face was burning painfully—and not just because of the way he had looked at her. The shaky,

sickly feeling invading her was surely a form of shock, a physical reaction to an emotional trauma. And she *was* traumatised, she admitted unwillingly. And not just by the Colonel's contempt and dislike!

Her own feelings had left her even more shocked and distressed…

She could feel his concentration on her, but she refused to look back at him. Because she was afraid to? Somewhere inside her head she could still feel the unspoken words 'I love you' banging frantically against the walls of their cage, like a tiny wounded bird desperate to escape. But Suzy knew they could never be set free. They had to be kept imprisoned for ever now, to protect her own sanity and self-respect!

'"*Down and Dirty* magazine."' She could hear him reading the name-badge she was wearing. 'I should have guessed. Your tactics are as cheap and tasteless as your articles.'

Savage pain followed by equally savage anger spiked into her heart. Illogically she felt as though somehow he had actively betrayed her by not recognising the person she really was, by misjudging her, not caring enough to recognise what had happened to her.

'I think your friend is waiting for you.'

The curt words were distinctly unfriendly, his voice clipped and incisive, and the look he gave her was coldly dismissive. But deep inside her Suzy could still feel the hard pressure of his mouth on hers.

Shaking, she turned to make her way towards the door, where Jeff was standing, an impassive bouncer holding his arm—and his camera.

Jeff's face, she saw with a sinking heart, was puce with temper.

'What the hell do you think you were doing?' he demanded once Suzy reached him. 'I told you to distract the guy, not eat him!'

Red-faced, Suzy couldn't think of anything to say to defend herself. 'Did you get your picture?'

'Yes! But if you hadn't been so busy playing kissy-face with the enemy you would have noticed that one of his gorillas was taking my camera off me! Good, was he? Yeah, I'll bet he was—after all, he's had plenty of experience. Like I said, during his last campaign a certain news reporter really had the hots for him. He's got quite a reputation with the female sex, has the Colonel. A killer instinct in bed and out of it.'

Suzy was beginning to feel nauseated, disgusted by what she was hearing. And even more so by her own idiotic gullibility. She couldn't understand her reaction—never mind her behaviour. She must be going crazy—and certainly her friend Kate would think so, if Suzy was ever foolish enough to tell her what had happened.

Kate and Suzy had been at university together, and Kate had kept in touch with Suzy when she had decided to drop out of her course and go home to nurse her mother through her final illness. Kate was married now, and with her husband ran a very successful small, independent travel agency.

Kate was constantly urging Suzy to enjoy life a little more, but Suzy still had debts to pay off—her student loan, for one thing, and the rent on the small flat she had shared with her widowed mother for another!

Thinking of her mother made Suzy's greeny-gold eyes darken. Her mother had been widowed before Suzy's birth, her father having been killed in a mountain-climbing accident. It was Suzy's belief that her mother had never got over the death of the man she loved, nor ceased blaming him for having died.

As she'd grown up Suzy had been the one who cared for her mother, rather than the other way around. Money had been tight, and Suzy had worked since her teens to help—first with a paper round and then at whatever unskilled work she could find.

Suzy remembered now that Kate often said she had an overdeveloped sense of responsibility and that she allowed others to put upon her. She couldn't imagine Colonel Lucas James Soames ever allowing anyone to put upon him, Suzy decided bitterly. If anyone were foolish enough to turn to him for help or compassion he would immediately reject them!

Suzy tensed, angry with herself for allowing the Colonel into her thoughts. And yet running beneath her anger, like a silent and dangerously racing river, she could still feel an unwanted ache of pain. Fear curled through her with soft, deadly tendrils. Why had she had such an extraordinary reaction to him? She wasn't that sort of person. Those emotions, that fierce rush of sexual longing, just weren't her! She gave a small shudder of distaste.

It was an experience she was better off forgetting—pretending had never happened, in fact!

And that was exactly what she intended to do!

Luke studied the schedules in front of him. Meticulously detailed plans for his upcoming work. The

Prince had hinted that he would like him on board for his permanent staff, but that kind of role wasn't one Luke wanted. Perhaps his American mother's blood was responsible for that! He had never been someone who enjoyed mundane routine. Even as a boy he had liked the challenge of pushing back boundaries and continually learning and growing.

His parents had died in an accident when he was eleven years old. The Army had sent him home to his grandmother and the comfortable country house where his father had grown up. His grandmother had done her best, but Luke had felt constricted at the boarding school she had sent him to. Even then he had known he would follow his father into the Army, and the happiest day of his life had been the day he had finally been free to follow that ambition.

The Army had been not just his career but his family as well. Until recently. Until he had woken up one morning and realised that he had had enough of witnessing other people's pain and death. That his ears had grown too sensitive to the screams of wounded children and his eyes too hurt by the sight of thin and starving bodies. He had seen it happen too many times before to other soldiers to hesitate. His emotions were getting in the way of his professionalism. It was time for him to move on!

The Army had tried to persuade him to change his mind. There had been talk of further promotion. But Luke had refused to be swayed. In his own mind he was no longer a totally effective soldier. Given the choice between destroying an enemy and protecting a child Luke knew he could no longer guarantee he would put the former first.

And working for His Royal Highness was definitely not for him! Too tame after the demands of Army life. Although there were some similarities between the two! He started to frown. Female reporters! He loathed and despised them! They were a hundred times worse than their male equivalent, in Luke's opinion. He had seen at first hand the damage they could wreak in their determination to get a story. A shadow of pain momentarily darkened his eyes, and the newly healed wound just below his hipbone seemed to pulse.

And as for the lengths such women were prepared to go!

His mouth hardened. So far as he was concerned Suzy Roberts and her ilk were as contemptible as the rags they worked for.

Reporter? Scavenger was a more appropriate word.

He turned his attention back to his paperwork, but, maddeningly, she would not be ejected from his thoughts.

What the hell was the matter with him that he should be wasting his time thinking about Suzy Roberts? That auburn hair and the way her gold-green gaze fastened on him must have addled his brain.

Had she really thought he was so idiotic that he would be deceived by that obviously fake look of longing she had given him? That equally fake tremor he had felt run right through her body when he had touched her? And as for that faint but unmistakable scent he could have sworn he could still smell...

Angrily he got up and strode across the room, push-

ing open a window, letting in an icy cold blast of air.
Perhaps the unintentional celibacy of his life over these
last few years had suddenly begun to affect him. But
to such an extent that he wanted a woman like Suzy
Roberts?

Like hell he did! But the sudden tension in his groin
told a different story.

It was late, and he had a business appointment to
keep. Finishing what he was doing, he made his way
from the office to the privacy of his own apartment,
automatically watching and checking as he did so.
Once a commando always a commando—even when
he could no longer…

Suppressing thoughts he did not want to have to deal
with, Luke walked into his suite and headed for the
shower.

Stripping off, he stepped into it, the hot needle-jets
of water glistening on his body as he moved beneath
the shower's spray. The light fell on old scars on his
chest, and the newer one low down on his body.

Having finished showering, he stepped out onto the
marble floor, padding naked into his bedroom to extract
a pair of clean white boxer shorts from a drawer. The
phrase 'going commando-style' might have a certain
sexual edge to it when used to describe the choice not
to wear any underwear, but from his own point of view
weeks, sometimes months of living in the field, in one
set of sweat and dirt-soaked combats had given him a
very different take on the matter! To anyone who had
experienced desert combat conditions the luxury of
quantities of clean water was something to be truly
appreciated.

CHAPTER TWO

Six months later

SUZY paused and studied the sleek yachts clustered in the harbour of the small Italian coastal resort. Two women walked past her, expensively groomed and wearing equally expensive designer clothes. Suzy had dressed as appropriately as she could for this luxurious resort, in white linen trousers and a brief sleeveless matching top, with sandals on her feet and the *de rigueur* sunglasses concealing her eyes, but no way was she in their league—and no way was she made for such an exclusive resort.

She had tried to tell Kate as much when her friend had announced that since she and her husband could not take up the week's holiday they had been offered via their business they wanted to give the treat to Suzy instead.

'Oh, no, Kate, I couldn't possibly accept your generosity,' Suzy had protested.

'It isn't generosity,' Kate had retorted. 'You need this break, Suzy. You've been through a lot these last few years—nursing your mother and then losing her, working every spare hour you had to finish your degree, and then that awful job you had!'

Suzy had sighed. 'I shouldn't have handed in my

notice, really. My tutor had been so kind, getting the intro for me, I feel so guilty.'

'You feel guilty?' Kate had exploded. 'Why on earth should you? You said yourself that you hated the way the magazine worked, its lack of morality with regard to how it got its stories and everything. And when I think of the way that slimy boss of yours tried to behave towards you! If anyone should be feeling guilty it's them, not you, Suzy! I'm surprised they're allowed to get away with treating you as they did. You know my opinion—you should have reported them for sexual harassment!'

Just listening to Kate's words had been enough to make Suzy shudder a little.

'It wasn't as easy as that, Kate,' Suzy had reminded her. 'For one thing I was the only female working there. No one would have backed me up.'

Hearing the strain in her friend's voice, Kate had shot her a quick look of concern before continuing, 'Suzy, I know how strong you are, and how independent, but please just for once put yourself first. You need this break. You need time to relax and reflect, to pick up the threads of your life and weave them into a new pattern. You need this breathing space! I want to do this for you and I shall be very hurt if you refuse.'

Put like that, how could she refuse? Suzy had acknowledged ruefully. And besides, there had been enough truth in what Kate had said to make her see that her friend was right.

She still shook with anxiety and nervous tension when she thought about the scene in the *Down and Dirty* office the day she had handed in her notice. The crude insults her boss had hurled at her still made her face burn with embarrassment and loathing.

'You aren't leaving—I'm sacking you,' he had told her furiously. 'No jumped-up little nothing is going to mess me about!'

He had then claimed publicly that he was sacking her because she had offered him sex in exchange for promotion—but privately told her he would rescind his claim if she agreed to go to bed with him.

Her flesh still crawled at the thought.

Roy Jarvis might be the magazine's editor-in-chief, but so far as Suzy was concerned he was the most morally corrupt man she had ever met. And her opinion was not just based on his attitude towards her, but on the way he ran the magazine and obtained its articles. Roy Jarvis's reporters were told to let nothing stop them in their pursuit of obtaining a story. She had been like a fish out of water in such an environment.

And Kate had been right, Suzy acknowledged unhappily now. She *did* need some time out to reassess her life. And her emotions.

Suzy closed her eyes and tried to swallow past the hard ball of pain and misery lodged in her throat. Panic prickled over her skin as she fought against allowing herself to think about the cause of her pain.

Instead she switched her mind to more easily dealt with issues. The difficulties of the past few years, then the misery of realising she was in a job she hated, and working with people whose morals she could never accept, never mind adopt, had all affected her. But she still needed to earn a living—somehow! And giving in to Kate and accepting this holiday was not, in her opinion, going to aid that.

No, but it might stop her from dreaming about a man she should have forgotten.

And this pretty Italian fishing village, perched precariously on the steep sides of a small bay, was surely a perfect spot in which to chill out and ground herself, to assess her own ambitions and think again about her original desire to become an archivist, perhaps. Her tutor had scorned her ambition, but Suzy had a deep longing for the cloistered quiet of such career.

Skirting the pretty harbour, with its chic and very expensive restaurants, Suzy headed for the steep path that led to the top of the cliff.

Half an hour later she had reached it, and she paused to study the magnificent view and to take a couple of photographs to show Kate.

Another hill rose up a short way along the path, and Suzy headed for it, wondering what lay beyond.

Its incline was steep, and she was a little out of breath when she finally made it to the top. She gasped, her eyes widening in delight as she looked down into the lush valley below her at the stunningly beautiful Palladan villa at its centre. She just had to get a photo of it to show Kate and her husband.

Rummaging in her bag, she found the small digital camera Kate had insisted on lending her.

'If you get any really good pictures we can put them on our Web site,' she had announced when Suzy had tried to protest.

The camera was obviously expensive, and Suzy had said as much, but Kate had dismissed her concern, shrugging it aside as she reassured her, 'It's insured—and if you do lose it—which I know you won't—then we shall replace it.'

Dutifully Suzy had photographed everything she thought might be of interest to her friend, and she knew that Kate would love this wonderful villa in its beautiful setting. From her vantage point Suzy could see the layout of its formal gardens within the high walls surrounding them, and the lake that lay beyond with its picturesque grotto.

Carefully she focused on the villa, pausing for a moment, as sunlight glinted on the metal casing, to stare in bemused awe at the sight of four imposingly large men in military uniform heading for an even equally imposing large black Mercedes, almost hidden from view beyond the entrance to the villa. What an impressive sight! She had to get a photograph of it—and of them! Who on earth were they?

On his way across the courtyard—having escorted the private security officers who had arrived to check out the villa without giving any warning, and against Luke's strict instructions, to their huge Mercedes with its blacked-out windows—Luke froze as he caught the unmistakable glint of sunlight on metal. Automatically he reached for his binoculars, training the powerful lens on the steep hillside above the villa.

He had done everything he could to avoid having to take on this commission, but pressure had been put on him, via his old commanding officer and certain other people, and reluctantly he had given in—although not without first enquiring grimly why on earth MI5 operatives could not be used.

'Because it is so sensitive, old boy,' had been the wry answer he had received. 'And because we don't have anyone in the field of your calibre.'

Reluctantly Luke had bowed to the pressure he'd been under.

Making sure that the Foreign Secretary was able to conduct a very politically sensitive meeting with the President of a certain turbulent African state, without either arousing the curiosity of the press or certain factions within the African state required optimum vigilance. And why on earth anyone had ever thought it a good idea to conduct such an exercise so close to a popular Italian resort—visited by the rich and famous and followed there by the paparazzi—Luke had no way of knowing.

Of course he had tried to initiate a change of venue, but he had been overruled.

A smooth-talking suit from MI5 had announced that no one would suspect that the Foreign Secretary would be seeing anyone political whilst enjoying a holiday with his children.

Children? Luke had baulked furiously at that point. No matter how many reassurances or platitudes the MI5 suit might choose to utter, this was potentially a dangerous mission.

The African President was insisting on bringing his own private guards with him, and he was a man who was obsessed with a fear of betrayal—both at home and abroad. If things should go pear-shaped Luke did not want to have to worry about two young children as well as their father. He had said as much to Sir Peter Verey when they had been introduced, suggesting that his children might be better left with their mother.

'My dear chap,' had been Sir Peter's drawled response. 'I wish I could oblige, but you see my ex-wife is insistent that they come with me. Thinks I'm not doing my fatherly duty and that sort of thing.'

Luke knew all about Sir Peter Verey's ex-wife. She had left him for a billionaire industrialist who had little liking of his predecessor's offspring, with the result that she had placed both children at boarding school.

Luke frowned as he swept the hillside for whoever had been responsible for that telltale glint.

The resort less than a couple of miles away seethed with celebrities and minor continental royals, all of whom seemed to be followed by their own pack of predators, feeding off them as if they were carrion.

It didn't take Luke's trained eye long to find its quarry—in fact, he reflected in disgust, it did not need a trained eye to spot her at all. She was standing there openly photographing the villa. She? Luke frowned as he studied the familiar features. Suzy Roberts! It was as little effort for him to conjure up her name as it had been for him to recognise her face. Suzy Roberts, reporter for *Down and Dirty* magazine. Automatically he swept the area around her to see if she was on her own, before focusing on her once again.

She looked thinner, paler—and what the hell was she doing standing in the strong sunlight without the protection of a hat when any fool could see that she had the kind of delicate skin that would burn?

How on earth had she got wind of what was going

on? The editor of the magazine she worked for got his
stories by trawling in the gutter for them.

Luke's mouth compressed. The gutter, maybe, but
then Roy Jarvis did specialise in 'revealing' the failings
and vices of those in power, as well as breaking some
extraordinarily sensitive news stories. Someone was
supplying him with his information, and Luke knew
that if he had been in charge of finding out who it was
the leak would have been stopped a long time ago.

Luke refused to believe that anyone could have got
through his own rigorous security, but he was not the
only person who knew what was happening. Somehow
Roy Jarvis had been given a tip-off about the upcoming
meeting, and he had obviously sent Suzy Roberts to
find out what she could and confirm the story so that
he could publish it. After all, a reporter like Suzy had
the extra assistance of her sexuality to help her get her
story—and she would have no qualms about using it!

Lucas had seen it happen over and over again in the
theatre of war, and of course he had already discovered
for himself that there were no lengths Suzy Roberts
was not prepared to go!

Silently Luke slipped out of the villa grounds, moving quickly and stealthily towards his quarry.

Oblivious to the danger, Suzy pushed her hair back off
her face. The villa really was a gem. She paused to
admire it again before lifting the camera to take another
shot.

Luke, who had circled up behind her, waited until
she had raised the camera before making his move.

As Suzy focused the camera he reached for it…

Someone was trying to steal the camera!

Instinctively Suzy turned round, and then froze in shocked disbelief whilst Luke took it from her.

'What are you doing?' she demanded as soon as she could speak.

Lucas Soames—here! She could feel the colour leaving her face and then surging back into it. Her heart was thudding in panic, and she felt as though she was trembling from head to foot. Emotions she had assured herself she had totally destroyed were taking a frightening hold on her, threatening to swamp her.

Frantically she tried to ignore them, to focus instead on what she should be feeling. These emotions had no right to exist. Lucas Soames meant nothing to her, and one of the reasons she was here on holiday was to make sure she was fully recovered from whatever it was she had experienced six months ago.

Willing her physical reaction to him to subside, Suzy demanded sharply, 'Give me back my camera!'

Her eyes widened as she watched Lucas delete the pictures she had just taken.

'No!' she protested, trying to snatch back the camera, to stop him ruining her photographs.

Luke reacted immediately, fending her off with one deceptively easy movement that kept her at arm's length from him, his fingers locked around her wrist as he finished what he was doing.

Despairingly Suzy closed her eyes, trying to blot out the physical reality of him in an effort to protect herself. But almost immediately she realised her mistake. Deprived of sight, she felt all her sensory receptors focusing instead on the feel of Lucas Soames's hand around her wrist—the texture of his flesh, the powerful strength of his grip, the coolness of his skin against the heat of her own. Weakening thrills of sensation were running up her arm, and she could feel the frantic jump of her pulse.

Panic and desperation speared through her. 'What are you doing?' she demanded, the sound of her voice raw and frantic in her ears as she recognised her fear and the reason for it.

What was it about this man that made her feel like this?

Luke studied her silently, assessing her behaviour and her reactions. She looked convincingly both distraught and distressed, and he mentally applauded her acting talent whilst cynically wondering how many victims she had honed it on.

Ignoring her anxious question, he asked one of his own. 'Why were you photographing the villa?'

His response caught Suzy off guard.

There was something about the coldly intense way he was watching her that unnerved her, and Suzy felt a shudder of apprehension run through her body. Stubbornly she fought against giving in to it—and to him!

'Why shouldn't I?' she shot back. Antagonism towards him was a far safer emotion than that dangerous and overwhelming surge of longing she had experienced the last time she had seen him. Don't think about it, she warned herself frantically. Don't remember. Don't feel…

Seeing him then had been like having the clouds part to reveal a miraculous space of blue sky and a dizzying vision of heaven. But things were different now, she reassured herself fiercely. *She* was different now!

Taking a deep breath, Suzy gave a deliberately nonchalant shrug before saying, 'That's what people on holiday do—take photographs.'

Her body language was flawless, Luke acknowledged grudgingly. Not by so much as the flicker of one of those ridiculously long eyelashes of hers was she revealing the fact that she was lying. He could feel his temper starting to rise. Immediately he checked it, alarmed that somehow she had managed to pierce the shield of his professionalism.

'On holiday?' He gave Suzy a comprehensive and cynical look. 'Oh, come on—you can come up with something better than that, surely?'

Just looking at her now—anger sparking her eyes to brilliant gold, flushing her cheeks with heat—anyone other than him would have believed immediately that she was a woman righteously defending herself from an unwarranted attack. But he knew she had to be lying, given who she was, and sure enough, as he continued to watch her, she was unable to continue to return his gaze.

What was Lucas Soames trying to say? Suzy wondered frantically. Had he guessed how he had affected her? Did he think she was nursing some kind of desire for him and that she had followed him here?

Her face began to burn again. If he did then she was going to make sure…

'Nice camera.' Luke interrupted her thoughts, adding assessingly, 'Expensive too.' Still nervously on edge,

Suzy told him stiffly, 'It isn't mine…it belongs to a friend.'

Luke could see the discomfort and the guilt in her eyes—but, to his own irritated disbelief, the knowledge that he was right to be suspicious of her made him feel more angry than satisfied. Determined to stamp on such feelings and destroy them, he responded coldly, 'A friend? So, Roy Jarvis is a friend now, is he, as well as your employer?'

Her employer!

Suzy shook her head.

'I don't work for the magazine any more,' she told him quickly. 'I…I left.' Even saying the words was enough to bring back the unpleasant memories, and she had to swallow against the bile of her distress.

'Oh, come on. You don't really expect me to fall for that, do you?' Luke demanded unpleasantly.

'It's true,' Suzy insisted fiercely. 'I no longer work for the magazine. You can check if you don't believe me!'

Her eyes were more green than gold now, Luke recognised. Reflecting her passionate nature? He frowned, irritated with himself for allowing his attention to be distracted from the professional to the personal.

'Oh, I have no doubt that officially you might have left, but it isn't unheard of for your boss, your *friend,* to use underhand methods to get what he wants. He has sent you here to work undercover—which is, as we both know, why you are up here photographing the villa and spying!'

Now cynicism had joined the cold disdain icing his

voice, and Suzy decided that she had had enough. Not allowing him to finish, she interrupted him hotly.

'That's ridiculous! Why on earth would he send me to do that? It's the resort that is full of the glitterati, not this villa, and as for my agreeing to spy on anyone—I have my own moral code!' She gave him a bitingly scornful look, but her glare might have been directed at an invisible shield for all the effect it had on its intended victim.

'Very affecting.' Luke stopped her. 'But you are wasting your breath and my time with this unconvincing show of innocence. I know exactly what you are, remember? I've witnessed your professional reporting methods—and your *moral code*—at first hand,' he reminded her grimly.

A telltale crimson tide of guilt and misery flooded Suzy's face. Illogically she felt not just humiliated by his words but emotionally hurt as well.

How could he say something like that to her? Hadn't he been able to tell that she had kissed him because of her own overwhelming need to do so and not for any other reason?

Unable to stop herself, Suzy discovered that she was reliving the feelings she had had then. Anguish filled her. Did he really think she was the kind of woman who would do such a thing for any other reason than because she simply had not been able to stop herself?

The very thought of what he had implied disgusted and nauseated her, and she burst out defensively, 'That wasn't—I didn't—I did it because—'

Abruptly Luke stopped her again. 'You did it because you thought it would be an excellent way of providing a firescreen for your companion—yes, I know that!' he told her grimly. 'Unfortunately for you it wasn't very effective.' He paused, and then added curtly, 'And neither was the kiss!'

What the hell was he thinking of? Luke asked himself savagely as his comment fell into the silence between them and he was forced to remember the kiss they had shared. A woman as experienced as this one must have felt his body's arousal, and gloated over his response to her. Any minute now she would be reminding him of it and challenging him to deny it. And there was no way Luke wanted to be dragged into that dangerous and unreliable ground.

Yes, he had responded to her. He could not deny that! Yes, he had for a split second in time experienced the most extraordinary physical longing for her, and the most extraordinary emotions. But that had been a momentary weakness, quickly controlled, and of no lasting or real importance whatsoever!

'What did Jarvis tell you to do—apart from take photographs?' he demanded sharply, steering his questions back in the right direction.

Still grappling with her own feelings, Suzy told him angrily, 'He didn't tell me to do anything!'

Her anger must somehow have heightened her senses, she decided, because suddenly she was aware of the musky male scent of Lucas Soames's body. She could see the sunlight glinting on the fine dark hair of his muscular forearms. Her heart somersaulted and then attempted a cartwheel, crashing into her chest wall as it did so. She willed herself to drag her gaze away from his body, but somehow it was impossible to do so. The white tee shirt he was wearing, although not tight-fitting, still revealed an impressive breadth of shoulder and chest. Something dangerous was happening to her, and she seemed powerless to stop it.

Suzy began to panic.

The back of her head was burning from the heat of the sun. It was making her feel slightly sick and dizzy—or was it the intensity of the navy blue gaze, the shock of her own emotions that was responsible for her malaise?

She couldn't give in to such feelings, Suzy warned herself frantically. She must not give in to them! She must think of something else! She must get away from here—get away from here and from Lucas Soames, and the sooner the better. If she didn't leave, if she was forced to stay, she was terrified that she might be trapped into saying something that would betray how she felt about him. How she *had* felt about him, she corrected herself. Taking a deep breath, she searched for the right words.

'I'm sorry if you feel you can't believe me,' she began politely. 'But I assure you that I am telling you the truth. I do not work for the magazine any more and no one from it is responsible for my being here! Like I just told you, I am here on holiday!'

She was picking her words too carefully for them to be genuine, Luke decided.

'On holiday? Alone?' he challenged her softly. One dark eyebrow rose tellingly, and Suzy was hotly conscious of his merciless and unkind gaze sweeping her face and then her body.

'I needed time on my own...to...to think...'

She had to get away from him!

'Time on your own? A woman like you?'

The razor-edge contempt in his voice made her face burn, but before she could say anything he continued silkily, 'So, if you aren't, as you claim, working for Roy Jarvis any more, then who are you working for?'

His question caught Suzy off guard, and she had to wrench her thoughts away from the pain his insult had caused her in order to answer it.

'I'm not working for anyone at the moment. I haven't got another job yet...at least...' She paused, her eyes darkening as his question reactivated her own anxiety about her future. After the contempt he had already shown her there was no way she was going to tell him that in order to make ends meet she had taken a job in a local supermarket.

Suddenly she had had enough.

'Why are you questioning me like this?' she demanded wearily. 'Just because you're here, guarding some government bigwig, that doesn't give you the right to...to treat me as some kind of...of criminal. What is it? Why are you looking at me like that?' she demanded nervously, fear trickling through her veins as she sensed that somehow something had changed, that the anger she had sensed in him before had been replaced by a steely determination.

'How do you know who is staying at the villa?' Luke questioned quietly.

For a moment Suzy was too bemused to answer him. Was it *that* that was responsible for the intimidating change in him?

'I heard someone talking about it,' she told him honestly. 'I thought he was supposed to be here on holiday, but of course now that I've seen you, and those men who were leaving, I realise...'

Her voice trailed away, when she saw his expression, and Luke prompted her softly.

'Yes? What is it exactly that you now realise? Something you know your boss Jarvis would be very interested in? Something that you just can't wait to report to him?'

Suzy stared at him aghast.

'No! No—nothing like that. He isn't my boss anymore,' she denied. 'I've already told you that.'

Something about the way he was watching her made her feel very afraid.

'So I was right.'

Suzy could feel her heart bumping heavily against her ribs as the deceptively soft words penetrated her awareness.

'You realise, of course, what this means?'

Suzy stared at him uncomprehendingly. He had lost her completely now, she acknowledged, and she fought to drag her unwilling mind away from her worry about the physical effect Lucas Soames was having on her emotions to what he was saying to her.

'What *what* means?' she asked.

Lucas's mouth thinned. He had no time for games, no matter how much Suzy Roberts might enjoy her play-acting. One minute the *ingénue*, another the *femme fatale*. A tiny muscle twitched in his jaw as he tensed his body against memories he didn't want to have. Memories of the feel of Suzy's body against his own, the taste of her mouth, the scent of her skin...

Savagely he turned away from her. This—she—was a complication he just did not need. It was bad enough that Jarvis had sent anyone here at all—but that it should be her!

Angrily, he examined the facts—and his options! Yes, they both knew why Suzy was here, but just how much did she know? How much information did she actually have?

He had destroyed the photographs she had taken of the African President's private guards, but he could not eradicate that information from her memory. And he certainly could not allow her to pass it on to anyone else—and most especially not to Roy Jarvis, to publish in his wretched magazine!

There was only one thing he could do now, little as he relished the prospect!

Luke had had his fill of reporters, both male and female! He had seen at first hand the damage, the devastation their single-minded determination could cause. He had seen fighting men's lives risked and innocent civilians' lives lost for the sake of a 'hot' story. And he had seen... His mouth twisted, his expression hardening even further.

He'd seen children under school age, half starved, fighting for water and food...whilst excited reporters tried to film their pitiable situation. And worse! Much, much worse! He moved, and the scar low on his belly pulled against the wound it covered.

He had learned over the years to mistrust the media at large.

And Ms Suzy Roberts was not going to be an exception to his rule that all media personnel were to be treated as guilty and kept under strict surveillance!

Luke's gaze narrowed.

Despite the fact that he was trained to keep his body still for hours on end, he suddenly felt he needed to move, step back a little from Suzy, and he grimly suppressed the unwanted knowledge that her proximity was affecting him.

'You realise, of course, that I can't let you tell anyone what you've seen?' Luke informed her.

A cold thrill of horror ran through her.

'But I'm not going to tell anyone,' she protested.

'I suppose the best and easiest thing to do would be for me to confiscate your passport and then have you thrown in jail,' Luke said calmly.

'What?' Suzy's face paled. 'No—you can't do that…' She could hardly believe what she was hearing, but one look at Lucas Soames's face assured her that he was deadly serious.

'Oh, I think you'll find that I can,' Luke assured her. 'But, knowing what you are capable of doing in order to get what you want, I think the best place for you right now is where I can make sure you aren't able to make any kind of contact with Roy Jarvis.'

'What—what are you going to do?' Suzy asked anxiously,

'I'm going to take you back to the villa with me—as my partner.'

CHAPTER THREE

'*WHAT?*'

Suzy was totally lost for words as she struggled to comprehend what he had said. His partner! But that meant… Fear and then longing shot through her like a firework showering her insides and touching every single nerve-ending she possessed. Partners…lovers… soul mates! No. She just wasn't strong enough to withstand this kind of torture!

'No—no! You can't do that. I won't!' she protested shakily.

He had already released her wrist, and as she spoke she was backing away from him, adrenalin pulsing through her veins. She had to get away! She had to!

As soon as she was out of his arm's reach she turned and started to run, driven by her instinct to flee, to protect herself, to hide herself from the danger she knew lay waiting for her!

Intent on her escape, she did not even think about sticking to the path which led back to the resort, instead plunging headlong straight down the steep hillside, sending up a shower of dry earth and small stones as she did so.

Luke watched her, knowing how easily he could catch her, his grim look turning to a frown as he saw the obstacle ahead of her—a large boulder, right in her path. He waited for her to change direction to avoid it, knowing that if she didn't—if she ran right into it—which she *was* going to do!

He caught her with a couple of yards to spare, knocking the breath out of her body as she fell towards the ground. But somehow, to Suzy's astonishment, before she hit the ground their positions were reversed, and it was Lucas Soames who was lying on the hard earth, with her held fast on top of him. His arms were fastened around her like iron bands, one gripping her body the other cradling her head.

Winded and frightened, Suzy tried to free herself—only to find that she could hardly move.

'Let go of me!' she demanded, struggling frantically.

'Stop that, you little fool, otherwise we'll both be—' Lucas began, and then stopped as one of Suzy's flailing hands caught the side of his mouth.

Against instinct, certainly against training, and surely against wanting, he opened his mouth and caught hold of the two offending fingers.

Heat and shock poured through Suzy's body.

Lucas Soames had her fingers in his mouth and he was…

She completely forgot what had been happening, and her own desperate attempt to break free of his imprisonment of her. Her body, her mind, her heart—all flooded with pure undistilled pleasure as his tongue slowly caressed her flesh.

The warm, wet slide of his tongue against her fingers caused images of shocking and unfamiliar sensuality to burst into her head. She wanted to replace her fingers with her mouth, her tongue. She wanted… Suzy could feel the dangerous familiarity of the ache inside her, in her breasts and low down in her body.

Desperate to protect herself, she wrenched her fingers away.

Deprived of the feel of her soft, sweet flesh against his tongue, Luke reacted immediately. The hand at the back of her head forced her towards him, and his mouth covered hers in devastatingly sensual punishment.

Suzy tried to resist but it was too late. Her lips were betraying her, softening beneath those of her captor!

And it was no wonder Lucas Soames was taking their reaction as an indication that she was inviting him to investigate their closed line, to torment it with the firm flick of his tongue. He probed the effectiveness of her defence and discovered that it was all too easily penetrated.

Held fast on top of him, his hands controlling her ability to move, there was nothing Suzy could do other than submit.

Submit? This was submission? This eager opening of her lips? This hungry greeting of his tongue with her own? This feeling that was spiking through her, impaling her on a rack of tormented feverish longing and need, whilst her hands gripped his shoulders and she forgot every single word of the promises she had made to herself. She was responding to him! Allowing herself to be deceived that the fierce, demanding pressure of his mouth on hers meant something! That the feeling possessing her was also possessing him. That they were…soul mates?

She gave a small gasp.

Luke wrenched his mouth from Suzy's, his fingers

biting into her soft flesh as he tried to find a logical explanation for what he had done.

And for what he was feeling!

He could feel his muscles straining as he willed his aroused body into submission. What the hell was happening to him? Physically he might be able to contain what he was feeling—the urgency of his arousal, the savage need he had to hold her and possess her—but it was what was going on inside his head, not his body, that was causing him the most concern. He had never mixed his professional life and his private life. And he had certainly never needed anyone with the intensity with which he had just been driven to possess Suzy Roberts's mouth!

Angrily he fought to ignore both the ache the loss of contact with Suzy's body was causing him and the inner voice that was urging him to continue, to possess the soft warmth of her breasts with his hands, to stroke and explore their feminine softness until he could feel the tight buds of her nipples rising to his touch…

Furious with himself, Luke checked his erotic thoughts.

'Let go of you?' he challenged Suzy, as if the kiss had never happened, angling their bodies so that she could see the rocks below them. 'Take a look! You were heading right for them, and if I hadn't stopped you right now you would be down there.'

Lifting her head cautiously, Suzy looked down the hillside, her stomach lurching as the saw the jagged rock less than a yard away from them.

'I wasn't anywhere near it,' she lied.

But she was shuddering, and for some reason she

was closing her eyes and turning her face into his shoulder.

Immediately Luke stopped her, his fingers digging into her arms as he held her away, a look of tightly reined anger compressing his mouth.

'If I'd any sense I should have let you go ahead,' she heard him muttering. 'It would have saved me a hell of a lot of trouble.'

He loathed and despised her that much?

'Then why didn't you? I can assure you that as far as I am concerned it would have been preferable to what I've just been subjected to!'

Luke had an almost violent need to take her back in his arms and prove to her that she was lying, but instead he derided, 'If that's your way of trying to persuade me you're someone who'd choose death before dishonour, you are wasting your time!'

It wasn't him who was causing her such pain, it was her own anger, Suzy told herself fiercely.

She couldn't bring herself to look down at those rocks again, and she couldn't escape from the knowledge that if he hadn't actually saved her life then he had certainly saved her from hurting herself very badly.

No, she couldn't escape from that knowledge, and it seemed that she couldn't escape from him either. Right now, whilst the solid protection of his hard body beneath her own and the equally hard feel of his arms around her body might be protecting her physically, emotionally this kind of intimacy with him was not doing her any favours at all.

Emotionally? What was she thinking? Suzy knew perfectly well what she was thinking, even if she did not want to acknowledge it. With just one searing kiss Lucas Soames had shown her that, far from being over what she had fought so hard to convince herself had been a moment of uncharacteristic silliness the first time she had seen him, she was if anything even more vulnerable to him now.

But not for much longer, Suzy promised herself determinedly.

She made a small movement, impatient to be free of him, and then froze with disbelief at the speed with which her flesh reacted to her careless action.

Her face was burning with mortified embarrassment, and she prayed that Lucas Soames could not feel, as she could, the sudden sensual tensing and swelling of her breasts. Her nipples were tightening and thrusting against her top, as though eager for his attention, whilst her stomach clenched and a slow ache possessed the lower part of her body. The urge to put her hand over her sex to quell its silent demand was so strong that it was just as well that his hold of her prevented her from doing so.

Prevented her from doing that, yes, but it didn't prevent her from reacting to the intimate pressure of his body against hers, and the soft mound covering her sex began to swell wantonly, a totally unfamiliar desire to grind her hips against him pulsing through her with increasingly demanding intensity.

Engrossed in her own dismay, she heard Lucas saying harshly, 'Unfortunately for me, on this occasion at least, I prefer to protect human life rather than to destroy it.'

'Protect human life?' Suzy demanded scornfully, secretly relieved to be able to focus on something other than her unwanted reaction to him. 'You were a soldier! Soldiers don't protect lives,' she told him with hostility. 'They—'

She wasn't allowed to get any further. His hold on her tightened. She could see the anger darkening his eyes as he looked at her, and her heart jolted painfully against her ribs.

'I suppose I should have expected that kind of ill-informed and gratuitously offensive remark from someone like you,' he said with scathing contempt. 'In the modern Army our purpose is to do the job we have to do with as little loss of human life as possible!'

His reaction had been immediate and savage—and surely out of proportion to what she had said, Suzy reflected inwardly, refusing to allow herself to be intimidated by it. He might generally prefer to save lives, but in her case she suspected he would have been more than ready to make an exception, if instinct and training had not been so ingrained in him!

Women reporters! Lucas felt the sour taste of old bitterness clogging his throat. And yet despite everything he was still holding on to her. He was holding on to her because he wasn't going to risk so much as letting her move a foot from his side, Luke assured himself acidly.

Even so...

'Time to go,' he announced, moving so swiftly that Suzy could barely catch her breath.

One moment she was lying on top of him on the ground, the next somehow she was standing up on her own, with Lucas next to her.

'Go?' she questioned warily 'You're going to let me go?'

That surely wasn't disappointment that was dampening down her relief, was it?

'I give you my word that I won't say anything about the villa to anyone,' she began to assure him earnestly.

'Your word?' Lucas rapped out contemptuously. 'We both know that your word is as worthless and overused—as…as you are yourself!'

The pain was everywhere. Inside her head, inside her heart, inside her body. With every breath she took she was breathing in its poison, its rank bitterness contaminating her.

Worthless…overused… Immediately Suzy wanted to hit back at him, to hurt him as deeply as he had hurt her, to mark him in a way that would leave him wounded for life, as she knew she herself would be.

Some women might shrug it off and even laugh at such a branding, but she was not one of them.

Overused. That was what he thought of her. She felt sick inside with emotional agony.

Something had changed. Some subtle shifting had occurred that had wrongfooted him, Luke's instincts told him. But he couldn't fathom what it was.

Suzy was staring fixedly past him, her body immobile. Was it her silence that was triggering the sixth sense that told him he had overlooked something? Had he expected her to argue with him, try to win him round, convince him that he was wrong and that she was to be trusted?

Frowning, he looked away, and so didn't see the

single tear that welled in each of Suzy's eyes, to hang glistening on her eyelashes before rolling down her face.

His words had hurt more than if he had physically attacked her—more than if he had turned and walked away from her—more than if he had simply left her to die in a crushed heap of flesh and bones against the jagged rocks from which he had saved her. One day she would be grateful for them, she promised herself. One day she would look back on this and know that what he had said to her had destroyed every minute seed of feeling she might have had for him with the force of a nuclear attack.

One day. But not this day. This day she felt as though she wanted to crawl into a hole and hide herself away, somewhere private and dark, where she and the pain would be alone to confront one another.

CHAPTER FOUR

Suzy could feel her legs trembling as she took a step away from Lucas Soames, her gaze fixed on the path ahead.

Did she really think he was just going to let her walk away? Luke could not credit her woeful lack of reality. He had grabbed her before she had taken more than a few paces, jerking her back towards him.

Suzy only had time to recognise that despite his violent gesture he did not actually hurt her before she was clamped to his side.

'You'd better get one thing clear,' Luke told her curtly. 'From now on where I go, you go. And you can take your choice whether it is by my side, two steps ahead of me or two steps behind. But two steps is going to be as far away as I let you get.'

'You can't do that. You can't make me!' Suzy protested shakily, real fear in her eyes as she looked at him.

'I can and will do anything and everything I deem necessary in order to protect the interests I am here to protect,' Lucas told her uncompromisingly. 'Now,' he demanded, 'where are you staying?'

Mutinously Suzy refused to answer him, compressing her lips and looking away from him. Out of the corner of her eye she saw him shrug.

'Very well then, we'll go straight to the villa. If you

choose to spend the next few weeks with only the clothes you are now wearing, then you may do so!'

Unable to stop herself, Suzy turned towards him.

'The next few weeks?' she protested in despair. 'I can't—I...'

'The name of your hotel?' Luke repeated.

Her lips numb, Suzy told him. Luke watched her in silence.

'Right, we'll go there now and get your stuff.' He glanced at his watch. 'It will soon be dinner time, and that will be a perfect opportunity for me to introduce you. Which reminds me—you had better get used to calling me Luke.'

'Luke?' Suzy checked him, confused. 'But I thought your name was Lucas?'

'Officially, it is,' he agreed coolly. 'Lucas is an old family name, from my father's family, but my mother always called me Luke.' His expression shadowed a little, and against her will Suzy felt an emotional tug on her heartstrings. 'My friends call me Luke, and as my partner so must you.'

'As your partner...' Suzy began shakily. Her heart was thumping, and not solely because of the speed with which Luke was forcing her to walk down the hill alongside him.

'Partner as in living together. Partner as in lovers!' Luke answered calmly.

Lovers? Suzy heart jerked frantically. She couldn't. She wouldn't!

'I... Will I have my own room?' Suzy could hear the wobble in her voice.

Luke stood still and looked at her. What kind of

game was she trying to play now? The Little Miss
Innocent nervous act certainly didn't fool him, and he
was surprised that she should try it.

'Of course you will have your own room,' he said
silkily.

Suzy began to exhale in a rush.

'However, it will also be my room,' Luke informed
her grimly. 'And let me warn you right now that I am
a very light sleeper, and trained to wake at the slightest
sound. If there's one thing I hate it's having my sleep
disturbed, so if you were rash enough to try to leave
the room during the night I warn you that I am not
likely to react with either charity or gentleness. Do I
make myself understood?'

Suzy lingered mentally over a handful of biting re-
torts before reluctantly abandoning in favour of safety
and silence.

'And whilst we are on the subject I might as well
point out to you that there are guards posted at every
exit from the villa and my men patrol the grounds.

Trying not to look afraid, Suzy demanded, 'Won't it
look odd for me to suddenly turn up at the villa? I
mean, you're here on business, and you don't strike me
as the kind of man who would allow his partner to just
appear and expect…'

He was watching her with a narrow-eyed intensity
that unnerved her.

'We had a quarrel about how much time we have to
spend apart before I left London,' Luke told her
smoothly. 'You've realised how idiotic you were being
and you've come here to apologise to me.'

'I was being idiotic?' Suzy stopped him wrathfully,

her fear forgotten as she leapt to the defence of her sex. 'And now I'm apologising...?'

'Since I'm here on holiday with an old friend and his children—' Luke ignored her outburst '—what could be more natural than that you should join us?'

'You're here on holiday?' Suzy shook her head challengingly. 'I saw with my own eyes those men and that car and—'

'*You* may have seen them,' Luke said with cold menace, 'but I intend to make sure you do not get the opportunity to say so—to anyone. And most especially not to Roy Jarvis!'

'Why won't you accept that I do not work for the magazine any more?' Suzy demanded in frustration. 'And as for the men I saw—' She gave a dismissive shrug. 'I just saw them, that's all.'

'You just saw them? I saw you photographing them,' Luke reminded her damningly.

'Because I thought it would make a good photograph to show my friends. They run a holiday company,' Suzie told him in frustration. 'Look, I can give you their name and phone number and you can ring them and—'

'Credit me with some intelligence.' Luke stopped her dryly. 'Of course Jarvis will have set up an alibi for you!'

'No. You can ring them now. Look, I've got my mobile,' Suzy insisted, putting her hand in her pocket to retrieve it.

Instantly Luke's hand clamped over her own. 'I'll take that, thank you,' he announced, removing her hand from her pocket and then sliding his own into it to remove the phone.

The sensation of his hand pressing against her hip-bone made her whole body burn. Warily, Suzy held her breath, exhaling with relief when Luke removed his hand, along with her phone.

But, to her shock, once he had transferred her mobile into his own possession he reached out and took hold of her hand as they approached the resort.

To anyone else they would look like a couple enjoying the warmth of the Italian sunshine, Suzy recognised. But of course they were no such thing. Experimentally she tried to remove her hand, wincing as she felt the crushing pressure of Luke's imprisoning response.

'Where is your hotel?' Luke asked.

He might be addressing her, but his gaze was measuring everything and everyone around them, Suzy saw as she glanced up at him. He was scanning the happy crowd of holidaymakers surrounding them.

Even in casual holiday clothes there was still an aura of command and authority about him. Suzy could see the way women's heads turned towards him, their glances lingering on him.

Had they really been a couple… A quiver of emotion ran through her.

'Where's your hotel?' Luke repeated, shooting her a cold, impatient look.

Suzy wondered wrathfully how she could allow herself to be vulnerable to a man like this. A man who could not recognise the truth when it and she were standing here beside him!

'It's here,' Suzy told him reluctantly, nodding in the direction of the drive which led up to the discreetly elegant boutique hotel where she was staying.

'You're staying here?'

She could see Luke frowning as though he was surprised.

'Where did you think I'd be staying?' Suzy taunted as walked through the entrance, their progress noted by the sharp-eyed doorman who seemed instinctively to know who was resident at the hotel without having to check. 'Somewhere brash and flashy?'

'Well, that would certainly be more in keeping with your boss's tastes,' Luke agreed coolly.

They had reached the hotel now. Originally a private villa, it had only recently been converted and extended into its present form. A cool tiled hallway led into the reception area and the clerk on duty smiled at Suzy in recognition, reaching for her room key before she had to ask.

'I'll take that,' Luke announced, ignoring the clerk's uncertain look.

'Ms Roberts will be checking out as of now,' he informed him. 'Where's your passport?' he asked Suzy, turning to look at her.

If the clerk had thought originally that she was taking Luke back to her room so that they could make love, and Suzy suspected he must have done, he obviously did not think so now. Suzy saw his manner towards Luke change from uncertainty to respect.

But then there was quite definitely something about Luke that set him apart from other men, Suzy acknowledged grudgingly, angrily aware of his presence behind her as she walked to her room.

Her room—the room originally to have been provided for her friends—was elegant and extremely luxurious, with French doors which led out onto a private balcony large enough for her to have had a tea party on, had she so wished.

'Expensive,' was Luke's cynical comment as he followed her inside, and then locked the door and leaned against it, pocketing the old-fashioned key. If there had been an ounce of truth in her story that she was unemployed she could never have afforded to stay in a place like this, he acknowledged.

'But then I'm sure your boss has his own way of making sure he gets value for money.'

Angry heat burned Suzy's face as she started to open the wardrobe doors. Her whole body trembled in reaction to his taunt that she would have sex with a man she loathed! Unable to stop herself, she turned to confront Luke, pride and anger burning red flags in her small face.

'I know what you're trying to insinuate, but you couldn't be more wrong. You know nothing about me, and yet you think—'

'On the contrary. I know a good deal about you.' Luke stopped her smoothly. 'Everyone who attended the Prince's reception was vetted, including you.'

Vetted, yes, but he did not have an in-depth report on her, Luke acknowledged, and made a mental note to inform his staff in London that he required one—if only for formality's sake.

The intensity of her own emotions was exhausting

her, and she just did not have the energy to argue with him any more, Suzy decided wearily.

'How long do you intend to keep me here in Italy?' she demanded as she opened her case and started to fold her clothes neatly.

'For as long as it takes,' Luke answered her laconically, his eyes narrowing as he focused on the clothes she was packing.

Neat round-necked tee shirts, modest pairs of walking shorts, a couple of long dresses—simple, anonymous clothes of a type he would have expected a conventional, rather cautious young woman to favour, hardly in keeping with the woman he knew her to be.

She had planned for her current role quite well, he acknowledged reluctantly as he watched the way she folded every garment before packing it.

Warily Suzy gave a glance in Luke's direction. He was still leaning against the bedroom door, arms folded, eyelids dropping over his eyes so that she couldn't be sure whether he was watching her or not.

She had packed virtually everything now, except her underwear, and for some ridiculous reason she discovered that she was reluctant to do so with him watching her.

She stole another glance at Luke.

'Finished?'

'Er, no…'

'Perhaps I'd better help you, then.'

Suzy's mouth opened and closed again as he levered his shoulders off the door and came towards her. Automatically she fell back, putting a protective hand on the drawer which contained her underwear.

She was trying to hide something from him, Luke recognised, his gaze narrowing on the betraying movement of her hand. What was it she had in the drawer that she didn't want him to see? He intended to find out.

'Have you got anything in the bathroom?' he asked casually. 'Toilet bag? Make-up?'

Unwittingly Suzy took the bait he had offered her. 'Yes...'

'You'd better go and get them, then, hadn't you?' Luke told her impatiently, glancing at his watch and informing her, 'You've got two minutes. After that, anything you haven't packed will have to be left behind.'

Automatically Suzy hurried to the bathroom.

The minute she was out of sight, Luke pulled open the drawer she had been guarding.

Neat piles of clean white underwear greeted his searching gaze.

Quickly and expertly he searched through it, frowning as his senses unwantedly relayed to him the cool, soft feel of the white fabric and its innocent virginal message.

Innocent? Virginal? Suzy Roberts?

She had researched her role well, he reflected, his frown deepening as he recognised that a part of him was reacting to the intimacy of what he was doing in a way that was both unprofessional and totally unfamiliar.

In his hand he held the semi-sheer white lace-trimmed bra he had just removed to check that the underwiring was just that.

He remembered with what ease and lack of any kind of sexual interest or arousal he had removed the TV news reporter's openly sexual underwear from the 'washing line' she had managed to delude one of the raw recruits into erecting for her. It seemed incomprehensible to him that he should be feeling such a fierce surge of sexual reaction now!

The sensation of his body beginning to strain against the constriction of his clothes had him ceasing his search to question what on earth his body thought it was doing.

Suzy, her toiletries packed, emerged from the bathroom and froze at the sight of Luke standing in front of the chest, one of her bras in his hand.

'What are you doing? How dare you touch my…my clothes?'

Like a small whirlwind, Suzy dropped her toiletries bag on the bed and snatched her bra from Luke's grasp, bundling it and as much of the other contents of the drawer as she could manage into her open case.

He had sent her into the bathroom deliberately so that he could go through her things! What in hell's name was happening to him? Luke wondered in disbelief as her angry, almost anguished movements caused an unexpected and fierce resurgence of the erection he thought he had tamed.

Furious with himself for his physical response to her, he told her sharply, 'Forget the shocked virgin act—it doesn't work. It stopped working for any woman over eighteen years ago, and when it comes to a woman like you…'

What would he do if she turned round now and told

him just how wrong he was? Suzy wondered bitterly as her hands trembled over her final packing. But of course she already knew, didn't she? He simply would not believe her. He would not accept that her experience was limited to one fumbling incident whilst at university, in which she and her partner had both lost their virginity. Their relationship had ended with no regrets on either part when she had decided to give up her studies to nurse her mother...

'Time's up,' Luke announced tersely.

Another minute in this room, with its huge bed and her scent lying on the warm afternoon air, and he was not sure...

He was not sure what? Luke questioned himself brutally.

His body gave him an answer his professionalism wanted to deny.

He wasn't sure he wouldn't be able to stop himself from spreading her on that bed and...

Ignoring the savage ache in his groin, Luke searched the room silently, checking every drawer and cupboard and even looking under the bed and on top of the wardrobe before reaching for Suzy's suitcase.

CHAPTER FIVE

'COME on—and remember I shall be watching your every step and your every word. One move out of line and you'll be in an Italian prison faster than you can take another breath,' Luke warned Suzy as they stood in the late-afternoon sunshine of the villa's impressive forecourt, with the villa itself behind them and Suzy's case at Luke's feet. Any chance she might have had of escaping disappeared, as their taxi drove away.

'You will never be able to get away with this,' Suzy warned him angrily. 'Someone is bound to suspect...'

'If by "someone" you mean Sir Peter Verey, then I'm afraid you're going to be disappointed. He's far too busy trying to cope with his children,' Luke told her grimly.

'What do you mean "cope with his children"?' Suzy demanded.

Luke's comment had all the hallmarks of the kind of old-fashioned attitude towards parenting which she personally deplored.

'Why shouldn't he look after them? If his wife—'

Luke looked at her, well aware of her antagonism.

'Their mother is actually his ex-wife. She left him for someone much richer! And as for looking after his children... They are probably more capable of looking after him than the other way around,' Luke announced dryly. 'Peter is the product of a typical upper-class upbringing and totally incapable of any kind of hands-on parenting.'

Luke's grim words evoked Suzy's immediate sympathy on behalf of the two children. She too had had a parent—her mother, in her case—who had not been able to provide her with strong and loving parenting.

Suzy's eyes darkened as she became lost in her thoughts. Her mother had never really got over being widowed, and even before her health had begun to fail Suzy had found herself as a very young girl taking on the role of 'mothering' her own mother.

Her sympathies aroused on behalf of the children, she demanded, 'Why are they here, then? Or can I guess?' she asked angrily. 'I suppose you organised it for some machiavellian reason of your own. Have you no feelings? Don't you realise how much harm it could do them, to be here under such circumstances? Doesn't their mother—'

Luke listened to her passionate outburst in silence. What would she say if he were to tell her that he himself had been orphaned at a young age? Would that fiercely passionate championship he could see in her eyes for Peter Verey's children be there for the child he had been?

'Children are so vulnerable,' Suzy railed furiously. 'Surely their mother...'

Children are so vulnerable. Luke looked away from her, momentarily forgetting who she was. There was a bitter taste in his mouth and his gaze was clouded by painful memories.

Some children—as he had good cause to know—were more vulnerable than others. Abruptly inside his head images he didn't want to relive were starting to form. He banished them. They belonged to the past, and right now he needed to concentrate on the present.

'Their mother is more interested in scoring points against their father than concerning herself about the children they created together. She has a new partner now, who has no intention of playing happy families with them, so the children have become both a means of remaining a thorn in her ex-husband's side, and a punishment, because she now sees them as a burden she is forced to bear. She's put them both into boarding school, and it seems that the summer holidays and the departure of the girl she employed to take charge of them means their presence is a nuisance. Hence her decision to send them to their father. Conveniently, the day she informed Sir Peter he had to take charge of them was also the day she left on an extended holiday with her second husband.'

As she saw the anger in Luke's eyes Suzy immediately jumped to the wrong conclusion. It was obvious that he too considered the poor children to be an unwanted nuisance, she decided angrily—an inconvenience to mar his plans, just like her!

'Of course you don't want them here any more than their father,' she accused him.

'I don't want them here,' Luke agreed grimly.

He didn't want any child ever again to be anywhere it might be in danger, no matter how small that risk might be.

If he closed his eyes now Luke knew he would see the most terrible images of carnage and destruction etched in fire and blood. Images he would never be able to forget.

The situation here was dangerously volatile. The African President had a reputation for seeing threats round every corner and reacting punishingly to them. Violence was a way of life to him, and to his followers.

A simple mission, MI5 had called it. But how could it possibly be simple with a woman like Suzy Roberts and two innocent children involved?

'Come on,' Luke commanded, picking up Suzy's case. 'And remember, take one step just one centimetre over the line and you'll be locked up in jail before you can take another.'

He meant it Suzy recognised apprehensively, and she fought not to back away from him and let him know how much he was intimidating her.

'We're lovers, remember?' Luke warned her, closing the gap between them.

Ignoring the lynx-eyed look he was giving her, Suzy took a deep breath. Lovers! Panic shot through her as she recognised that her instinctive response to the thought was not one of abhorrence and rejection. Why wasn't it? She wasn't still holding onto that idiotic thing about them being soul mates, was she?

Lovers! Inside her head images were forming. Dangerous, wanton and tormenting images that made her body ache and burn.

Beneath her thin top Suzy could feel her nipples stiffening and peaking. Her heart thudding erratically, she turned away from him to look up at the villa. It was awesomely elegant and magnificent.

'Built by an Italian prince for his favourite mistress

and the children she had by him,' Lucas informed her. 'The frescoes around the hall and staircase include images of both her and their sons. Come on.'

The visually gentle clasp of his hand around hers was in reality anything but, Suzy recognised and she flinched beneath his tight grip.

'My things—' she began, but Luke shook his head.

'I'll get someone to come out for them.'

The supposed butler who opened the door to them exchanged a look with Luke which made her suspect that the man was more than just a servant. One of Luke's men? Suzy suspected so, but before she could voice her suspicions one of the doors off the hallway opened and a young boy of around six came running out, hotly pursued by a pre-teenage girl who was protesting crossly,

'That's mine, Charlie, give it back to me now.'

'Children! Oh—Luke.'

This must be the children's father, Suzy guessed, and she waited to be introduced to her unsuspecting host.

He was tall and good-looking, with crinkly blue eyes and a nice smile, but Suzy still recognised that of the two of them it was obvious that Luke was the one in charge.

'Peter, I am delighted to tell you that you have an additional guest,' Luke announced. 'My partner, Suzy Roberts. Darling, this is Sir Peter Verey,'

'Luke, I applaud your taste.' Peter Verey smiled warmly, his words for Luke but his admiring gaze fixed very firmly on Suzy.

There was something almost endearing about Peter Verey, Suzy decided as she tried rebelliously to move away from Luke, but then tensed as his fingers closed around her wrist in steely warning.

'I'm going to take Suzy up to my room. It's almost dinnertime…'

Suzy opened her mouth to say something, but Luke took immediate action to forestall her by the simple expedient of silencing her protest with the pressure of his mouth on her own.

Caught like a rabbit in a car's headlights, she stared up into his eyes and saw the warning glinting there. But the warning certainly didn't match the soft, sensual pressure of his mouth as it moved on hers, Suzy recognised as her heart thumped painfully. He was holding her, kissing her as though…

A huge lump formed in her throat and she had to close her eyes against the sharp pain that speared her heart. As she did so she felt him lifting his mouth from hers.

They were alone in the vast hallway, Sir Peter having discreetly disappeared.

'This way,' Luke announced curtly.

He had released her wrist and Suzy noticed that he made no attempt to re-imprison her. In fact as she walked numbly towards the stairs he seemed to deliberately hang back a little from her. The lump in her throat turned to icy panic as she realised how bereft her body felt at its lack of contact with him.

He was a monster. She ought to hate and loathe him. She *did* hate and loathe him. It was just her body that was vulnerable to him. That was all.

Stopping mid-step, she turned on the stair and looked at Luke. He was two stairs below her and their eyes were on the same level. As she looked into his her heart gave a funny little kick-beat before flinging itself at the wall of her chest.

'Do we really have to share a room?' she asked, anxiety thickening her voice to a husky whisper.

Something in the soft timbre of her voice was touching a nerve he didn't want to have touched, Luke recognised angrily—arousing a reaction he didn't want to have aroused. What the devil was the matter with him?

'Yes, because that will ensure that I can keep a very close eye on you, and it will reinforce the necessary fiction I've had to create that we are lovers,' Luke said to her prosaically, adding scathingly, 'I should have thought you could have worked that out for yourself. I assure you there's no other reason for it.'

Mutely Suzy looked at him, then turned away and began to climb the remaining stairs.

What was it about those eyes that made him want to take hold of her?

Infuriated by the effect Suzy was having on him, Luke followed her up the stairs.

'This way.' Tensing beneath Luke's brief touch on her bare arm, Suzy willed herself not to betray how emotionally vulnerable he was making her feel.

He had come to a halt outside a door which he unlocked and pushed open.

Warily Suzy stepped inside, her eyes widening as she took in the magnificence of her surroundings.

What she was standing in wasn't just a room but a suite. Almost an apartment, she decided, and she gazed around in awe, recognising wryly that her own small flat would have fitted easily into the elegant and spaciously proportioned sitting room in which she was now standing. Through the three tall windows she could see the grounds of the villa, but it wasn't the view from the windows that caught and held her attention. As she stared through the double doors which opened into what was obviously the bedroom Suzy felt her throat constrict.

Because she could see that the bedroom did in fact possess only one bed. A very large bed, admittedly, but still only one.

'I am not sleeping in that bed with you,' she announced flatly.

She looked and sounded shocked and outraged, Luke recognised. Pink flags of apparent distress were flying in her cheeks and her eyes were glittering with emotion. Even her body language, her tightly balled fists and tensely held body, was perfect for the part she had chosen to play.

She was good, he told himself angrily. She was very, very good. But he wasn't fooled!

'Well, you certainly won't be doing anything other than sleeping!' he told her emphatically. 'So you can disabuse yourself of any ideas you might be entertaining of favouring me with your sexual expertise. Because I'm not in the market for it.'

Somewhere inside her a small, sensible voice was trying to make itself heard, to tell her that she ought to be relieved by his words and the message of safety they held for her. But it was being drowned out by the outraged protests of her emotions, Suzy knew, and she recoiled from the rejection in Luke's words.

'I am not going to sleep with you!'

Could he hear the panic in her voice? Suzy no longer cared. All she cared about was saving herself from the humiliation of having to share a bed with a man she already knew had the most dangerous effect on her body—especially when he had made it so clear how he felt about her. She could not, *would* not share Luke's bed!

Was it because she was afraid that if she did she might somehow forget herself and…?

And what? Suzy derided herself mirthlessly. Seduce him? Her? Seduce a man like Luke?

'I'll sleep in the sitting room on one of the sofas,' she announced shakily.

'No!' Luke checked her immediately.

The cool word offered no hope of a compromise.

Uncertainly Suzy looked at him.

'Didn't you listen to what I told you?' he asked softly. 'I am not going to let you out of my sight! Night and day, wherever I go, you come with me. Besides, we are supposed to be lovers. I don't want the maids gossiping that we aren't sleeping together. Of course, if you prefer to spend the next few weeks in prison…' he offered cordially.

There was a cold look in his eyes that told her he wasn't joking. Wildly Suzy contemplated telling him that she *would* prefer the option of prison. Surely anything was better than having to share his bed! Than lying there beside him, terrified that she might somehow be overwhelmed by temptation and reach out to him and be rejected.

'The bathroom's through here,' she heard Luke informing her, quite obviously waiting for her to follow him.

A small spurt of rebellion surged through her. Suzy stayed where she was.

Luke paused and turned to look at her. 'Are you waiting for me to come and get you?' he asked softly.

Silently they looked at one another.

Something unseen and dangerous sizzled in the air between them. Suzy might not be able to see it, but she could certainly feel it. Inside she was trembling, teetering on a tightrope of hyped-up sexual excitement and overstretched emotions.

If she stayed here what would Luke do? Just the thought of his hands on her body in any kind of way sent a high-voltage shock of sensual longing jolting through her.

What was happening to her?

Gritting her teeth, she took a step towards him. Anything, even giving in to him now, was a million times better than putting herself in a position where she might humiliate herself by letting Luke see...

See what? What was there to see? she asked herself with angry defiance. But of course she knew!

How on earth could she be unlucky enough to have the kind of emotional and sexual feelings she did towards a man like Luke? And why, knowing what he thought of her, hadn't she been able to destroy them?

And, as if that wasn't enough for her to have to cope with, why had fate deemed it necessary to condemn her to this current situation, where she would be exposed day and night to Luke's proximity? Day and night!

Luke frowned as he watched the expressions chase one another over Suzy's face. That look of agonised despair he had just seen darken her eyes had surely been pure theatre!

Numbly Suzy followed Luke into the bathroom, then stopped dead to stare in disbelief and bemusement around the room.

'The current owner renovated the whole place, with particular attention to the bathrooms,' she heard Luke explaining calmly while she stood and stared, then turned and closed her eyes, and then opened them again.

The bathroom was like something out of a private fantasy!

The bath was huge, round and half-sunk into the floor. It was dark green marble with marble steps leading down to it and gold dolphin-head taps attached.

As though that were not enough five columns surrounded it, supporting a cupola-type canopy the centre of which was painted with...Suzy blinked, and then blinked again at the scenes of extremely explicit sensuality above her head. And not just above her head, she realised, but all along the wall frieze as well! Luscious-breasted women, each with her godlike Adonis entwined in a variety of intimate sexual embraces! Huge mirrors covered one of the walls, and on another she could see handbasins...

'I...' she began falteringly, shaking her head when her voice failed her and her gaze was drawn back to the frieze!

Hastily she refocused it on the bathtub, and then

wished she had not as, out of nowhere, the most intimate and erotic images presented themselves to her.

Luke sleekly wet and naked... Luke bending over her as one Adonis on the frieze was bending over his lover...

A dizzying surge of sensual heat gripped her body. Fiercely she tried to repel it.

Luke himself, who had previously derided and then ignored the flamboyantly sensual décor of the bathroom, had a sudden and unwanted image of Suzy lying in the ornate tub, her naked body gleaming with pearly iridescence. Would the tangle of curls between her thighs be the same unique shade of gold as her hair? And when he lifted her out of the water and laid her down, so that he could caress the taut peaks of her breasts with his fingers, before he touched her more intimately, would those curls cling lovingly to his fingers as he parted the folded lips of her sex?

Furious with himself, Luke turned away from Suzy to stop her from seeing the effect his thoughts were having on him. His erection was straining against his clothes and throbbing almost painfully. The physical rebelliousness of his body was a hazard he had not accounted for, never having had to deal with it before, and mentally Luke cursed that unexpected kiss Suzy had given him the first time they had met.

Then she had caught him off guard, and somehow superimposed on his body and his arousal mechanism an imprinted response to her which right now he seemed powerless to destroy!

'The shower is over there,' he told Suzy curtly,

breaking off as they both heard a discreet knock on the outside door to the suite. 'That will be your stuff.'

Glad of a reason to escape from the overwhelming sensuality of the bathroom, Suzy hurried back into the suite, Luke at her heels. A young Italian was standing beside the door with Suzy's case. As Suzy thanked him he gave her an intense and admiring look.

'I'll take that,' Luke announced tersely, somehow managing to insert himself between Suzy and the young man as he dismissed him. 'You've got half an hour before dinner,' he told Suzy as he closed the door, shutting her inside the suite, on her own with him. 'I've only used part of the wardrobe, so you'll have plenty of space for your stuff.'

Her stuff? It was just as well that the exclusivity of her hotel meant that she had brought a couple of outfits with her more formal than she would normally have packed for a holiday, Suzy acknowledged.

'You can use the shower first if you like.'

'Yes, thanks—I will,' she told him woodenly, unzipping her case and trying to be discreet as she extracted clean underwear. But it was next to impossible when Luke was standing right next to her.

'If you need anything pressing now's the time to say,' he told her, ignoring her discomfort.

'Well, what kind of thing should I wear? I mean, how formal…?' she began uncertainly. Something told her that Sir Peter Verey was not someone who sat down to dinner wearing a pair of jeans!

'Will these be okay?' she asked reluctantly, removing a pair of linen trousers from her case. She hated to have to ask him for anything, even a small piece of advice, but she knew that she had no choice.

'They won't need pressing,' she told him, and he nodded his head.

Quickly hanging them up, she found her toilet bag and headed for the bathroom. As she did so she thought she heard Luke call something after her, but she refused to turn back to find out what it was. Another criticism of her, no doubt, she decided, and she closed the bathroom door with a satisfying bang.

Fortunately the shower was modern and plain, and no way in danger of inclining her toward wanton thoughts concerning her jailer!

Determinedly Suzy pushed away her dangerous fantasies and turned on the shower, carefully adjusting the heat and letting the water run for a few seconds before testing it to make sure the temperature was right.

Quickly stripping off her clothes, she stepped into it, enjoying the warm cascade of water over her skin. The warmth of the water was just perfect.

'Aaagrh!' Suzy screamed as suddenly icy cold water pelted her unprepared skin. Frozen, she reached for the towel she had hung over the shower door, but felt it slip from her grasp. It only took her seconds to escape from the shower's icy blast, but by the time she had she was shivering with cold and shock.

'I tried to warn you about the water but you didn't bother to listen.'

Soaking wet, shivering and totally naked, she stared in affronted outrage at Luke, who was standing in the doorway, having heard her scream and guessed its cause.

CHAPTER SIX

'HERE.' In two quick strides Luke was beside her, having grabbed hold of a towel.

'No, don't—I can manage.' She began to protest, but the words became a muddled muffle as he wrapped her unceremoniously in the towel and started to rub her dry so fiercely that her skin began to glow.

His actions were spare, rigorous and practical, and there was no reason at all why they should remind her of the loving care of her mother when she was a little girl, but they did. And then she turned her head and stiffened as she saw the way he was looking at her. He had stopped towelling her, and what she could see in his eyes was making her heart turn over and her resistance melt.

Frantically she forced herself to remember who he was and what he had done! Glaring at him, she turned away and headed for the bedroom, only to give a gasp of shock as she tripped on the hem of her towel.

The speed with which Luke moved was very impressive. One minute he was standing beside her, the next he was catching her in his arms and swinging her up off the floor, so that instead of taking a nasty tumble she was held securely against his warm chest.

Initially she struggled to break free, then suddenly the whole world stopped turning and her heartbeat was suspended with it.

'Luke…'

She had barely whispered his name, but he must have heard her because she could feel him registering it. His body tensed, as though there was something in her one little word that he needed every bit of his formidable artillery of weaponry to repel.

'I just don't need this,' Suzy heard him mutter savagely, but then his hand was pushing through her hair, securing her head at just the right angle for his mouth to home in on hers, to take it and make her want to return the passion she could feel in his kiss. It was the same passion that was running through her like liquid fire and honey. Any thought of resisting him or of denying herself the pleasure her body craved was forgotten!

She lifted up her arms and put them round him. This time it was *her* tongue-tip that probed the line of *his* lips, but it was Luke who drew it deep inside the dark, warm sensuality of his mouth, coaxing it, encouraging it, and then fiercely mating with it. Her heart was bouncing around inside her chest like a yo-yo. She could hardly breathe—and not just because of the way Luke was kissing her.

Like a snake sloughing off an unwanted skin, she wriggled her body until the towel dropped off, her action driven by instinct and not any deliberate thought. She was incapable of that! Incapable of anything other than responding to the subtle pressure of Luke's hard hand holding her head, Luke's equally hard mouth on hers.

His hands were on her naked back, splaying out against her skin, sliding downwards to her waist and then her buttocks, cupping their rounded softness and then pulling her fiercely into his own body, his own arousal. Helpless to stop herself, Suzy ground her hips against him.

What he was doing was crazy, Luke warned himself. He must be out of his mind for even thinking about contemplating what he was contemplating. If he had any sense he would back off right now and—

He felt Suzy's body move against his own, heard the soft, hot sound of excitement she made against his skin and his aroused body refused to obey his demands. He lifted his hand to cover her naked breast, feeling the taut nub push eagerly against his palm.

Suddenly Suzy realised what she was doing. With a small moan of anguish she pushed at Luke's chest.

Immediately he set her free. His face was hard with anger and her own face felt tight with shock and misery.

Unsteadily Suzy retrieved her towel, dreading what Luke might be going to say. Had he guessed what he had done to her? How he had made her feel? How he had made her want him?

To her relief he strode towards the bathroom without saying anything, leaving her alone to dress.

In the bathroom Luke fought furiously to sandbag his feelings. How could he have allowed himself to react to her like that—to respond to her like that? He tried to pinpoint the second things had got out of control, and the reason, rerunning the whole thing through his head in order to reexamine it and sort out some kind of damage limitation plan. But to his disbelief he realised that remembering how Suzy had looked standing there naked was already arousing him again.

Turning on the shower, Luke stepped under its icy blast, savagely angry with himself and equally angry with Suzy. Did she really think he had been deceived by the role she was trying to play, or by the white-faced look of despair he had seen in her eyes as she tore herself out of his arms?

As she tore herself out of his arms. The icy jets of water needled onto Luke's skin unnoticed as he stood still.

Suzy had been the one to end their intimacy, not him, and if she had not done so by now she would be lying beneath his body.

Cursing himself Luke tried to ignore the images his mind was relaying to him. He was a man who intended to live his life to a specific moral code; she was a woman who didn't have a moral bone in her body! An impossible coupling! And he intended to ensure that it remained impossible!

'Ready?'

Numbly Suzy nodded her head, not trusting herself to speak.

She was wearing a simple linen top with shoestring straps with her trousers, and Luke frowned as he looked at her, recognising how effective the outfit was at making her appear fragile and somehow vulnerable.

As he opened the suite door for her Suzy snatched a brief look at Luke, helplessly aware that the sight of him, in a pair of immaculate dark-coloured trousers and an equally immaculate soft white shirt, was doing things to her she had no wish whatsoever to acknowledge.

As they descended the impressive staircase together, Suzy was acutely conscious of him at her side. When they reached the hallway he touched her bare arm lightly, and immediately she flinched.

'We're a couple, remember?' Luke warned her in a low, cold voice.

As he reached past her to push open the door Suzy caught the clean male smell of his skin, and immediately a quiver of response ran down her spine. She felt an overwhelming urge to turn round and bury her face in his throat, just breathe in the smell of him until she was drunk on it.

'In here!'

The door opened and Suzy stepped through it, Luke behind her. The two children she had seen earlier were seated on a windowseat, their heads bent over a computer game. Suzy felt an unexpected tug of emotion as she saw that, despite their clean clothes, they somehow had a heart-rending air of neglect about them.

Was it because of her own childhood she was so immediately and instinctively aware that these children lacked a mother's loving input into their lives? Suzy wondered ruefully as she watched them.

Sir Peter was picking up the drink which had just been poured for him by the smartly dressed waiter. As he saw them he put it down.

'There you are! Suzy, my dear, what will you have to drink, Luke, are you going to break your normal abstinence tonight?'

For all that he was their host, Suzy could see that

Sir Peter was actually a little in awe of Luke, and she watched the interaction between the two men curiously as Luke announced that he would simply have a tonic.

'And Suzy?' Sir Peter pressed, giving her another warm smile.

'Tonic for me too,' she echoed.

'I'm afraid we have to let the children have dinner with us,' Sir Peter apologised to Suzy as the young Italian waiter handed her her drink. 'It really is a nuisance having them here, but I'm afraid I wasn't given the opportunity to refuse.'

A heavy sigh accompanied the frowning look Sir Peter gave his children, and Suzy's sympathy for them increased.

'Perhaps I should go and introduce myself to them,' she suggested gently, leaving Luke standing with Sir Peter whilst she made her way over to the windowseat.

As Suzy walked away Luke discovered that his gaze was focused on the gentle sway of her hips and the rounded curves of her bottom.

'Lovely girl,' he heard Peter saying appreciatively at his side. 'I envy you, old chap.'

Luke saw that the other man's gaze was lingering on Suzy's curvy posterior as well.

For no reason he could think of Luke moved to block his view.

'I wish we could hear definitely that our chap is going to come through…' Peter was complaining, and automatically Luke turned his attention to what he was saying.

'Hello, I'm Suzy.' Suzy introduced herself to the children with a smile.

'You're Lucas's girlfriend, aren't you?' the little boy demanded, adding importantly, 'Maria told us. She's one of the maids.'

Luke's girlfriend! Something turned over inside Suzy's chest, and an odd and unwanted feeling of loss and pain ached inside her.

'Charlie, you shouldn't gossip with the servants. Mummy wouldn't like it,' the little girl announced primly, and Suzy could see the mixture of anxiety and protectiveness in her eyes as she looked at her younger brother.

'You can't tell me what to do, Lucy,' He retaliated immediately. 'Does being Luke's girlfriend mean that you are going to get married?' he asked Suzy.

Married! To Luke!

A feeling of fierce intensity shot through her.

'Charlie, it's rude to ask personal questions,' Lucy told him imperiously.

'Our mother and father were married,' Charlie told her, ignoring his sister, 'but they aren't any more. Our mother is married to someone else, and he doesn't like us, does he, Lucy?'

'Charlie, you aren't supposed to say things like that,' Lucy hissed, red-faced.

'Why not? I heard Mummy saying it to Aunt Catherine.'

Poor children, Suzy thought sadly. Charlie was still too young to be aware of what he was saying, but Lucy was old enough to be embarrassed and upset by her younger brother's revelations. Suzy could see that, so she gently distracted them, asking, 'What was that game I saw you playing?'

Her simple ploy had the desired effect. Immediately Charlie began to enthuse about the game and his skill with it.

As she listened to him Suzy turned to look at Lucy. The little girl gave her a hesitant smile. The pristinely laundered dress she was wearing, whilst unmistakably expensive, was too short and too tight, Suzy recognised, and she wondered absently if she had perhaps chosen to wear it because it was an old favourite.

Still listening to Peter complaining about the way the visiting Head of State kept changing the carefully made arrangements, Luke looked towards the window.

The children were now seated either side of Suzy, apparently hanging onto her every word—nestling against her, almost.

For some absurd reason the sight of the three of them together aroused an emotion inside him he wasn't prepared to name, and it was with relief that he heard the sound of the dinner gong.

'Suzy, my dear, you don't know what a pleasure it is for me to have the company of such a very attractive and charming young woman,' Sir Peter announced flatteringly once they were all seated around the magnificent antique table. 'And I'm sure the children agree with me—don't you, children?'

Obediently Charlie and Lucy nodded their heads.

'Luke, you are an extremely fortunate man. I just hope, Suzy, that we will be able to persuade you to spend some time with us as well as with Luke. The children would certainly welcome your company, I know.'

Suzy hid a smile as she realised what Sir Peter was trying to do. He obviously saw in her arrival an opportunity to persuade her into helping out with his children. And to be honest, she acknowledged, she would be perfectly happy to do so. It would give her something to occupy her time during her enforced imprisonment.

With that in mind, she smiled compliantly at her host.

'You must take Suzy for a walk through the gardens after dinner, Luke,' Sir Peter announced amiably, after giving Suzy a warmly approving smile. 'The grounds to the villa are very beautiful. There's a lake—'

'And a grotto,' Charlie broke in eagerly. 'I want to explore it.'

Immediately his father gave him a stern look. 'Charlie, I've already told you that you are not to go near the grotto. It's unsafe and too dangerous, and that's why a metal gate has been placed across it—it's too dangerous for anyone to enter!' Turning to Suzy, he told her, 'There is supposed to be some sort of tunnel and an underground chamber beneath the grotto, which was built originally as a folly.'

Suzy shivered as she listened to him. She had always had a fear of such places, and certainly did not share Charlie's enthusiasm.

'But you must show Suzy the sunken garden, Luke. It's a very romantic walk, Suzy,' he added warmly, 'and if Luke hadn't bagged you first, I can assure you I would have enjoyed showing it to you myself.'

Sir Peter was flirting with her!

Hastily Suzy took a sip of her wine, and then choked a little as she realised how strong it was.

The food was delicious, but she seemed to have lost her usual appetite, Suzy acknowledged as her churning stomach prevented her from eating more than a few mouthfuls of her meal.

Was it because every minute that passed meant that it was getting closer to the time when she would have to go back upstairs with Luke to that suite? Their suite. Their bed.

A tense shudder ripped through her and she reached for her wine again, hoping to distract herself.

The children were looking tired and had started bickering. It was far too late for them to be eating, in Suzy's opinion, and the food was surely too rich for young digestion.

'Charlie, that's enough!'

Peter was giving his son an angry look, but Suzy could see that the little boy's behaviour was caused more by tiredness than wilfulness.

'Finish your dinner,' Sir Peter instructed.

'I don't want it. I don't like it.' Charlie resisted stubbornly.

'Charles!'

'I think the children are tired,' Suzy intervened gently. 'It is rather late. I don't know what time they normally go to bed…'

'Of course. You are quite right! It *is* late!' Sir Peter agreed immediately. 'I'd better send for one of the maids to take them upstairs and put them to bed,' he added, signalling to the hovering waiter.

Within minutes a plump, elderly woman appeared, and their father instructed the children to go with her.

A small frown creased Suzy's forehead as both children followed the maid without receiving a goodnight kiss from their father.

Half an hour later, their own meal over, Suzy was beginning to feel tired herself—and to regret the two glasses of red wine she had drunk!

Coffee was to be served in the same salon where they had had their pre-dinner cocktails, and once they had made their way there Sir Peter settled himself on one of the damask sofas. Patting the space beside himself, he invited, 'Come and sit here, next to me, Suzy, and tell me all about yourself.'

Hesitantly Suzy began to walk towards him, only to come to an unsteady stop as Luke stepped in front of her.

'If you don't mind, Peter, I think I'd like to have her to myself for a while,' he announced smoothly, taking hold of Suzy's arm as he did so.

Just the feel of his fingers on her bare arm was enough to make her quiver from head to foot, Suzy recognised dizzily.

'Of course, of course. Don't blame you, old chap,' Sir Peter responded heartily.

Before she could say or do anything Suzy discovered that she was being almost force-marched in the direction of the salon door. She could almost feel the blast of heat from Luke's anger as he opened the door and propelled her out into the hallway, up the stairs and into their suite.

As soon as he had closed the door behind them he

rounded on her, demanding savagely, 'What the devil do you think you are playing at? Or do I need to ask? It's the same old trick, isn't it? I warned you—'

'I'm not playing at anything!' Suzy denied fiercely.

'Liar! You've seen that Peter is susceptible to you, so you're doing everything you can to encourage him...giving him limpid-eyed looks, pretending to be concerned about his children—'

'I *am* concerned about them!' Suzy stopped him. 'And as for me encouraging him—I was doing no such thing! You're behaving like a jealous lover!' she threw furiously at him. 'Accusing me of things I haven't done, and have no intention of doing!'

A jealous lover! Luke stared at her.

Suzy gasped as she was dragged into Luke's arms. She tried to protest. And she tried to resist. But the wine had obviously weakened her resistance. Of its own accord her hand clutched at the sleeve of his shirt and her body leaned into his. Greedily her senses absorbed the feel of him. Tough, male, strong... She looked at his mouth. She looked into his eyes. And then she looked at his mouth again. She could feel the sound he was making in his throat vibrate through his body in a feral growl of warning male arousal.

He was lowering his head and she wanted to reach up and hold it, so that he couldn't escape, so that his mouth had to cover her own...

And it did! How long had she yearned for this? Suzy wondered dizzily as her lips clung to his. Surrounded by the sensual soft dark of the Italian night, she gave in to her own need. She was in his arms and then in his hands—quite literally, she realised in soaring shocked pleasure as they moved over her, shaping her, learning her…

Into the darkness of their room she moaned her un-inhibited delight. She could feel her breasts swelling into his hands whilst her stomach tightened with ex-pectation. She lifted her arms to wrap them around him, her fingers sliding into the softness of his hair. His mouth tasted erotically of wine and man, and she wanted to feed on it until all her senses were sated with the pleasure of him. The straps of her top had slipped down her arms and were digging into her flesh, and she wanted to beg Luke to remove it from her body, right here and right now.

Helplessly Luke gave in to the need he had felt the first time she had kissed him. Then he had denied it, buried it, but somehow it had survived, tormenting him in his dreams. Luke felt his body shudder as his hunger for her ripped through his defences. Now he was be-yond reason, beyond sanity, beyond anything and ev-erything but wanting her. He was, Luke recognised dis-tantly, completely out of control. And she was the one who had done this to him, who had driven him, aroused him, made him so insane with need for her. That eager female sound she had just made had logged straight into his body and switched on every damn thing, send-ing him completely crazy. He lifted his hand to push Suzy's auburn hair off her creamy neck and shoulder, leaving them exposed to the exploration of his hungry mouth. A tiny pulse jumped and skittered beneath his kiss and he paused to touch it with his tongue.

She was openly trembling with longing, Suzy rec-ognised as her head fell back to allow Luke even more access to the curve of her throat. Behind her she had the hardness of the heavy wooden door, and in front of her she had the hardness that was Luke. A deep shudder tormented her as he started to explore the delicate whorls of her ear, his thumb on the pulse at the base of her throat.

Someone was tugging frantically at the straps of her top trying to remove it. How could Luke be doing that and touching her as well?

It wasn't Luke who was tearing off her clothes and exhaling in a rush of fierce pleasure as they fell to the ground, Suzy realised. It was her.

Luke had felt her clothes slither to the floor as his eyes adjusted to the velvet darkness, and now he could see the pale outline of her body. Her almost naked body.

He had known that she wasn't wearing a bra—had known it and registered Peter's equal awareness of that fact—but that knowledge and the knowledge he had now, of the soft, pure nakedness of her torso, with the outline of her breasts sketched in blurred charcoal light, were a world apart.

Almost as though it was happening in slow motion Suzy watched as Luke turned his head and looked down at her body. His hand came out and slid beneath one breast, gently supporting it.

If she was any more perfect she wouldn't be human, Luke thought as he felt the delicious weight of Suzy's breast on his palm. His thumb searched for her nipple.

She gave a sharp, electrified moan and her whole body stiffened in response to his touch.

She was a conniving, manipulative wanton who had

never had a genuine emotion or reaction in her life, Luke told himself savagely. But his body was beyond listening. His hand was working urgently on her breast, preparing it for the hungry possession of his mouth. Every sweet moan she made was causing the sensation in the pit of his belly to screw down harder. If he didn't have the taste of her in his mouth soon he was going to...

His free hand slid down her body and encountered the lacy edge of her underwear. He hooked one finger under what he thought was elastic and then realised that it was a ribbon bow. A bow he could untie with his fingers, or...Luke had a sudden mental picture of himself laying her on the bed, tugging the bows loose with his teeth. He wanted to eat her like a fresh peach, filling his mouth with her taste until the juice of her ran from his fingers and his lips.

His erection was straining against his clothes, and he could tell from the small urgent sounds Suzy was making that she was equally aroused.

They were partners, after all, he reminded himself with inner black humour. Partners on opposite sides of a very sharp divide, he acknowledged, and reality suddenly kicked in.

Suzy tensed as she felt Luke's hand start to leave her breast. Something had happened. Something had made him draw back from her, and she didn't want that something. She wanted *him*.

Suzy's sexual experience was relatively limited. And yet she discovered that her body knew far more than she had given it credit for. It knew, for instance, that if she reached out and touched Luke the way she was doing, just the merest brush of her fingertips, slowly, oh so slowly against that tight bulge she could feel beneath his clothing, that instead of pushing her away he would draw her to him again.

He shouldn't be doing this. Oh, he should not be doing this, Luke warned himself. But that provocative touch that Suzy was subjecting him to, just the slightest brush of delicate fingertips against his erection, was more than he could stand.

He wanted her right now.

He didn't just want to taste her, he wanted to take her and fill her and spill himself inside her.

Taking hold of her hands, Luke pinned them above her head, his body leaning into hers.

Her eyes had adjusted to the dark now, and Suzy could see his expression quite clearly. A fast, furious surge of shocked excitement raced through her. He had lost control now. She could see it in his eyes, feel it in the way he was grinding his body into hers—and she loved it…

As Luke felt Suzy's hips lift and writhe tormentingly against him he knew that there was no going back.

There was nothing he wanted more than to take her right here, against the damned door, as primitively as though every layer of civilisation had been stripped from them both. He wanted to hook his fingers in those ridiculous bows and leave himself free to give her every pleasure. He wanted to lift her up against him and have her wrap her legs around him whilst he buried himself so deep inside her that no other man would ever pleasure her as much.

Her fingers touched him again, and this time she was tracing his erection, gauging it—measuring it?

Suzy's chest tightened as her uncertain touch revealed to her just how much of a man Luke was! She could feel Luke lifting her up against him. Shocked pleasure surged through her on a riptide. He was going to make love to her here against the door!

She weighed next to nothing, Luke acknowledged as he lifted Suzy off the floor. The lacy thong she was wearing left the rounded contours of her bottom free to his touch. He could see the bright, aroused glitter of her eyes and he could feel the exhalation of her breath. His tongue touched her lips and then pierced her mouth. She tasted soft and sweet, warm and welcoming.

'Open your legs,' he commanded her.

Hot, urgent, immediate sex—that was what he wanted with her.

His hand was on his zip before he recognised that he wanted far more than that.

CHAPTER SEVEN

'WHAT are you doing?' Suzy protested as Luke suddenly swung her up into his arms. Had he changed his mind? Wasn't he going to make love to her after all? 'Why—?'

'Why?' He stopped her as he laid her on the bed. 'Because where we were would have been fine for a quickie,' he told her rawly. 'But right now I need to have much more than just that. Much, much more!' he said thickly, and brushed his lips against her half-parted mouth, then touched them to each nipple in turn before returning to her mouth to kiss her with deep ferocity.

Whilst he stripped off his clothes he told her what he wanted to do with her, how he wanted to touch her and how he wanted her to touch him. By the time he was fully nude Suzy was ready to explode. The heat in her lower body was unbearable, and so was the pressure.

Impulsively she reached down to remove her ribbon-tied thong.

'No!'

His hand was over hers, but instead of unfastening the bow he started to kiss her again. Her mouth, her shoulder, her breast, laving the tight peak until she was thrashing around beneath him. And then the other breast, taking his time whilst she cried out, her hands on his shoulders, her nails digging into his skin.

But that was nothing to what she felt when his mouth moved lower, his lips caressing her stomach and then his tongue rimming her navel, tracing the lacy edge of her thong from one bow to the other and then back again. She could feel his hands sliding beneath her, lifting her, and she writhed in urgent need. She felt his breath against her skin and watched in a sensual daze of arousal as he tugged at the bow with his teeth. When it came free he pressed his lips to her naked skin and his hand to her naked body, discovering, exploring, parting the swollen folds of flesh to expose her sex to his touch and his taste.

Suzy heard the sounds of pleasure flooding the room and knew they must be her own, but she had no awareness of having made them. She had no awareness of anything at all other than the touch of Luke's fingers and the lave of his tongue.

She felt the tightening warning of her body, but it was impossible for her to hold back her orgasm. As she cried out her pleasure she felt Luke's mouth taking it from her into his own keeping.

She was still trembling with its aftershock seconds later, when he moved up the bed to hold her, wrapping her tightly in his arms, his breath warm against the top of her head.

Was it because it had been such a long time since he had done this that her reaction had affected him so much? Luke questioned himself. Had he somehow forgotten just how intense the pleasure of pleasuring a woman was for him? Had he somehow managed to overlook the way it made him feel? Because he was damn sure that no one had given him this feeling before. Exhilarated, Suzy clung to Luke. His naked flesh felt smooth and warm beneath her fingertips. Idly she traced the line of his collarbone, and then pressed a small kiss to it for no other reason than that she wanted to. She ran her finger around the aureole of his nipple, dark and flat, unlike the rosy fullness of her own. The nipple itself was different too. She teased it languidly and then burrowed her face against his chest, relishing the scent and taste of him.

'If you keep doing that...' Luke warned her rawly.

'You'll do what?' Suzy challenged him deliberately.

'This,' he responded promptly, rolling her over and then beneath him.

Eagerly Suzy opened her legs and wrapped them round him, welcoming him into her soft warmth. Desire ran through her with liquid heat, but more than that, as her hips lifted and writhed and her body welcomed him with fierce female longing, Suzy recognised that it wasn't just her body that could feel him, that wanted him. It was her heart and her mind as well! And that meant—

But, no, she did not want to think about what that meant right now. In fact she did not want to think at all. She simply wanted to know. To experience. To feel. To be here in this place at this time with this man, and to hold on to what they were sharing for ever.

A sensation of exquisite urgency was filling her, taking her with him through time and space. Each thrust of his powerful body within her own brought them closer, physically and emotionally.

The increasingly fast movement of his thrusts was

pushing her up the bed, and Suzy had to reach out to grab hold of the bedpost behind her.

In that same moment she heard his harsh cry, and felt again that same rainbow explosion within herself as she reached her climax, and it showered her whole body with quick silver darts of pleasure.

Soul mates. Meant to be together.

The words, the knowledge floated through her like precious stars set in a perfect sky.

As they lay in a damp and relaxed tumble of arms and legs, Suzy's head on his chest, his arms wrapped hard around her, Luke marvelled again at the intensity of his own pleasure. He had been so overwhelmed by his need for her that he hadn't even had time to think about any practicalities.

In his youth, when he had been as keen on exploring sex as any other teenager, he had practised safe sex—primarily because he had had no wish to become a father before he was ready. Over the last few years his career had meant that sex, safe or otherwise, simply wasn't on his personal agenda. But he had taken Suzy to bed without even taking the most rudimentary health precautions. She would be protected against pregnancy, of course, but it was a bit late now to demand a full report on her sexual health and history!

Moonlight streamed in through the window, leaving a silver trail on Luke's naked body. Suzy traced it with one loving finger, frowning as she suddenly found the hard ridge of a scar. Leaning up, she looked down at it, her heart twisting as she saw its raw newness. Overwhelmed by her feelings for him, she bent her head and tenderly placed her lips against the puckered ridge of flesh.

Immediately Luke tensed, wrenching himself away from her.

'What is it?' Suzy asked him in concern. 'Did I hurt you?'

When he shook his head she asked softly. 'How did it happen, Luke?' She couldn't bear to think of him being in danger, being hurt.

Pushing her away, Luke said harshly, 'If you must know it was caused by a woman just like you!'

He could see the shock in her face, but he ignored it.

'She may not have fired the bullet that caused it, but she was still responsible.'

A dark, frightening anger filled his expression, banishing the intimacy they had shared. Bitterly Luke contemplated what he had done. How could he not have controlled himself? Stopped himself? How could she have made him feel like that? How could she have made him want like that, when she was everything he did *not* want in a woman? Anger and self-disgust left a sour taste in his mouth.

'Luke?' Suzy whispered hesitantly.

Why wasn't he saying anything to her? Why was he turning away from her instead of holding her as she longed for him to do?

He had to make it plain to her that what had just happened between them hadn't left him vulnerable or open to any kind of persuasion, Luke told himself. He could still feel the soft warmth of her lips against his scar. Anger burned through him. A gunshot wound was nothing compared with what he could see inside his head. He saw the smouldering rubble of what had once been a home, the body of the pretty young woman who had lived in it lying on the ground like that of a broken doll, murdered, and all because some damn female journalist had ignored his explicit instructions so that she could get her human interest story...

'Don't make the mistake of thinking that the fact that we've had sex changes anything,' he told Suzy brutally. 'It doesn't! After all, we both know that sex is the currency you favour. On this occasion it didn't work!'

A cold feeling of sickness was crawling through her. Shock, anguish, despair—she could feel them all.

Luke was making it humiliatingly plain that he had simply used her for sex. How could she have been so stupid as to allow herself to think— To think what? That because for her sexual intimacy was inextricably linked to emotional intimacy Luke would think the same thing? That because she could not stop herself from feeling the way she did about him he shared those feelings? Was she totally crazy? Hadn't he just made it brutally plain to her that he did not?

Silently Suzy turned away from him, whilst pain raked her with burning claws.

CHAPTER EIGHT

'I'M BORED!'

Charlie's petulant comment was a welcome interruption to Suzy's agonised inner examination of what had happened with Luke last night.

She and the children had breakfasted alone, Lucy informing her with a world-weary sigh that, 'Daddy and Luke are talking business and we aren't allowed to interrupt them.'

Was it business that had been responsible for Luke's absence from both the bed they had shared last night and the suite when she had woken up this morning? Suzy didn't really care! She was glad he seemed to have forgotten his threat to stay with her day and night, and was just relieved that she hadn't had to go through the embarrassment and humiliation of seeing him.

In fact she wished passionately that she might never have to see him again! How could he have used her so cold-bloodedly—and more importantly, how could she have let him?

'It's a beautiful day,' she responded to Charlie's statement of his boredom. 'Why don't you go for a swim?'

She had seen the swimming pool from her vantage point on the hillside above the villa, and had admired the elegance of its tranquil setting.

'We can't go swimming,' Charlie told her crossly.

Suzy frowned, wondering if perhaps their father had put a ban on them swimming without adult supervision. But before she could say anything Lucy told her unhappily, 'We can't swim because Mummy sent us with the wrong clothes. She forgot about packing our swimming things.'

Forgot? Suzy felt a sharp stab of anger against the children's mother as she looked at Lucy's downbent head, and wondered cynically if it *was* just that the children's swimming things had been forgotten or if she had deliberately sent them away with the wrong clothes in order to make life difficult for their father.

'Well, perhaps you could ask Daddy to buy some new things for you?' she suggested practically. The resort had any number of shops selling clothes and, whilst they might be expensive, Sir Peter Verey did not strike her as a man who had to watch his budget!

A maid came in to clear away the breakfast things, and through the open door Suzy could see a powerfully built man standing in the hallway.

One of Luke's men? Although there was no obvious evidence of the villa being heavily guarded, Suzy suspected that if she tried to make any attempt to leave she would find that she wasn't allowed to get very far.

Idly she wondered just what it was that demanded Luke's presence here. Certainly the soldiers she had seen departing must have something to do with it. It must be politically delicate rather than dangerous, she suspected, otherwise the children wouldn't be here. Sir Peter might not be a particularly hands-on father, but surely he wouldn't risk exposing his children to danger?

'It's no use us asking Daddy to take us shopping. He'll just say that he's too busy.' Lucy informed Suzy, her words breaking into her thoughts.

The weary resignation in her voice made Suzy's heart ache for her. It told of a small lifetime of being told that her parents were 'too busy'.

'But Suzy could take us! Lucy, let's go and ask Daddy if she can!' Charlie suggested excitedly, getting off his chair.

'If she can what?'

Suzy spun round as Sir Peter and Luke came into the room.

'Daddy, Mummy forgot to pack our swimsuits and our shorts and things,' Lucy answered her father, a little reluctantly.

She obviously felt that what she was saying was a betrayal of her mother, Suzy recognised.

'Yes, and we want Suzy to take us out and buy some new ones,' Charlie added importantly.

Suzy could feel both Sir Peter and Luke looking at her. The relaxed approval in Sir Peter's eyes certainly wasn't mirrored in Luke's.

Suzy's heart gave a painful jerk. The sight of him was releasing the despair and anguish she had been fighting to ignore. Self-contempt and misery crawled through her veins like poison. And yet, as she dragged her gaze from Luke's face, Suzy acknowledged that it wasn't the anger she should be feeling that was making her tremble inwardly, but a destructive and humiliating ache of longing!

She was distantly aware of Sir Peter exclaiming enthusiastically, 'What an excellent idea! My dear, you are a godsend!'

'Peter, I don't think—' Luke began, an ominous expression in his eyes as he cast Suzy a freezing look of contempt.

'Luke, I know you want her all to yourself, and I can't blame you.' Sir Peter smiled. 'But we mustn't disappoint the children!'

Luke had intended to spend the morning catching up on some paperwork and trying to see if there wasn't some way that President Njambla could be pinned down to a definite date in order that he could wind up the whole exercise with as much speed as possible. He told himself he should have guessed that Suzy would try to pull this kind of trick.

He had already given orders that no one was to be allowed to leave the villa without his permission, and thanks to the high wall that surrounded the property it was impossible to leave other than via one of the discreetly guarded gates.

The staff all lived in, and had been thoroughly vetted, and it should have been an easy task to ensure that Suzy did not have any outside contact with anyone. He had taken possession of her mobile phone and her passport.

Taken possession! Luke wished his brain had not supplied him with those two particular words. Last night he had physically taken possession of Suzy herself, but only because his desire for her had taken possession of him!

'Indeed we mustn't,' Luke answered Sir Peter

grimly. 'I'll organise a car. Are you ready to leave now?' he asked Suzy curtly.

'Well, I need to go upstairs and get my bag,' Suzy responded shakily as she tried to withstand the look he was giving her.

'I'll come with you,' Luke announced, leaving her with no option other than to walk towards the door, uncomfortably aware as she did so that he was following her.

Halfway up the stairs she asked herself bitterly why, after what he had done to her and what he had said to her, the reaction of her body to the knowledge that he was so close behind her now was one of longing and not rejection.

Quickening her step, she headed for their suite. But as she reached for the door handle Luke was there before her. Suzy flinched as she felt the brief brush of hard fingertips against her wrist.

'Quite a clever move,' Luke said conversationally as he closed the door, imprisoning her with him in the room's heavy silence. 'I had forgotten that female reporters are different from the rest of their sex and do not possess any scruples where children are concerned.'

There was a look in his eyes that confused Suzy—a mixture of biting contempt and savage anger laced with pain, as though somehow his words had a personal meaning for him.

'I am not using the children!' Suzy denied heatedly. 'It was their idea to approach their father. And besides, I could hardly manufacture the fact that their mother has been spiteful enough to send them here without proper holiday clothes. The dress Lucy was wearing last night looked so uncomfortable. Poor little scraps— I feel so sorry for them,' Suzy told him emotionally.

Luke could feel himself tensing as he listened to her. Why, when he knew she was acting, was he allowing himself to react to her faked emotions, allowing her to needle her way under his professional skin, letting her touch personal nerve-endings he had no damned business allowing her to touch?

'And as for using them! You're a fine one to talk about that!' she accused him angrily. 'You're keeping me imprisoned here because whatever it is that is going on might potentially be dangerous—and yet you are using the children as camouflage!'

'The children's presence here is directly against my wishes,' Luke told her shortly, looking away from her.

'So you mean that there is actually someone who can't be bullied, threatened and coerced into doing what you want?' Suzy couldn't resist demanding.

Immediately Luke turned round, subjecting her to a narrow-eyed gaze that made her want to shiver, as though her flesh had been touched by a blast of cold air.

'Coerced?' Luke challenged her. 'If by that you are trying to imply that last night I coerced you…you certainly didn't give me the impression that you didn't want what was happening. In fact—'

'I don't want to talk about last night,' Suzy interrupted him wildly. 'I don't.'

Was that because she didn't want to have the pathetic remnants of the fantasies and daydreams she was holding onto wrenched from her? Why not? What was the point in stubbornly clinging to them? They were worthless...meaningless...like the physical act she had shared with Luke!

'Save the emotional histrionics for Peter,' Luke told her contemptuously. 'He's becoming besotted enough with you to believe them!'

His words made Suzy frown. Certainly Peter was enjoying pretending to flirt with her, but a pretence at flirtation was all it was. If Suzy could see that she wondered why Luke, who was surely trained to observe and analyse people's behaviour and reactions, could not.

'The children will be waiting,' she told him stiffly. 'I'll just get my bag.'

Before she could move, Luke said, 'Stay here. I'll get it.'

His unexpected chivalrous gesture caught her off guard, but nowhere near so much as his casual question as he picked up a briefcase and opened it.

'Are you all right for money?'

'Yes. I've got enough of my own.' Suzy stopped him quickly.

His concern for her after his earlier comments was like balm on a painful wound, and she watched silently as he closed his case and then crossed the room to pick up her small handbag. It looked tiny grasped in his large hand as he brought it to her.

'And just remember,' he warned her grimly, 'I'm going to be right beside you. If you were thinking—'

'You mean that you're coming with us?'

Luke's hand was pressing against her wrist and Suzy

could barely think for the effect his touch was having on her body.

'Why not? You're my partner, after all, and according to Peter I can't bear to let you out of my sight,' he told her derisively.

He certainly wasn't exhibiting any concern for her now, Suzy recognised. He was standing so close that she felt as though she could hardly breathe.

Automatically Suzy stepped back. Her mind and body were tearing her apart with the ferocity of the conflicting messages they were sending her. She wanted to go somewhere quiet and dark and stay there until she felt able to cope. Instead she was going to have to go to the resort, with Luke at her side and a smile pinned to her face.

Impulsively she turned to Luke, driven to get him to believe her and to set her free, but the words died unspoken as she saw the look on his face.

Well, if he could feel contemptuous about her then somehow she would learn to feel the same way about him, she told herself fiercely, and walked towards the door.

As he watched her Luke too was prey to conflicting emotions. He had absolutely no doubt that his suspicions concerning her were correct. And, that being the case, it was essential that he prevented her from having any kind of contact with anyone she might pass information on to. In that sense, in the professional sense, she was his enemy.

But his anger and bitterness towards her because of what she was—they were not professionally objective feelings, in any way, shape or form. They were personal. And on that personal level those feelings were unacceptable, Luke told himself grimly. Unacceptable and potentially prejudicial to his ability to do his job.

When fighting men became battle-weary they ceased to be effective. That was one of the reasons why he had left the Army. Because he had begun to feel he had fought too many wars and seen too much death. Was he now experiencing a similar syndrome within his current work? Was Suzy Roberts getting to him because for some reason he was no longer an effective operative? Or was he no longer an effective operative because Suzy Roberts was getting to him?

It wasn't going to be the latter. No way would he allow himself that weakness! To lose it over a woman like her? To want her, ache for her; hunger for her to the point where those feelings dominated every other aspect of his life?

No way!

Her subtle manipulation of the children this morning proved that he was right to be suspicious of her. So why, knowing all of that, when she had looked at him earlier with that faked pain in her eyes, had he been driven to take her in his arms and—?

And what? And nothing, Luke told himself savagely. Absolutely nothing!

'Luke, there's a parking space.' Suzy called as she looked out of the window of the large four-wheel drive vehicle in which Luke had driven them down to the resort.

'I've seen it,' was Luke's clipped response, and he neatly reversed the large vehicle into the small space.

Her eyes shadowed, Suzy turned her face away from him, angry with herself for letting such a small and unimportant rejection of help bring betraying tears to her eyes. She turned to get out of the Jeep.

'Wait there,' Luke told her imperiously, sliding out of his own seat.

Was he afraid that she might jump out and try to run away? Suzy wondered scathingly as she watched him come round to her own door and open it. Immediately she made to scramble out, but as she did so Luke took hold of her, lifting her bodily out of the car and placing her gently on the ground.

Raw pain scalded Suzy's throat, making it impossible for her to speak as she stood stiffly in his hold.

To anyone looking at them his gesture would have seemed one of loving consideration. But he did not love her. He loathed and despised her!

The pain in her throat had reached her chest. She could feel Luke looking at her, but she refused to return his gaze. She did have some pride, and there was no way she was going to let him see the anguish she knew must be in her eyes.

With a small twist of her body she pulled away from him in mute rejection, and then tensed as she felt him tighten his grip on her, constraining her. Now she *did* look at him, resentment emanating from every pore of her body as she resisted his hold.

What the hell was that damned perfume Suzy was wearing? Luke wondered savagely as the air around filled with the scent of her. It conjured up for him mental images his senses had retained: her body, silky smooth beneath his hands, fire and passion beneath his touch as she moved against him, with him...

A thousand brilliant images flooded his senses as the warm morning air wafted her scent around him. It might be morning outside his body, but inside it, inside his head, it was night, with its soft, sensual darkness, its dangerous memories...

Against his will Luke felt his gaze sliding slowly from her eyes to her mouth, to absorb in greedy silence its shape and beauty. His mouth already knew its texture, her texture, but those memories were not enough. Suddenly he wanted to know it again. To trace its tender outline, to stroke its soft warmth, to probe the sweet resistance it offered him and capture its innermost sweetness.

Suzy felt as though she was about to collapse. Luke was looking at her mouth and his look was scorching her, making her want to lift her face to him and plead for his kiss. Frantically she dragged her hot gaze away from his face and looked at the car.

The children! To her shame, she realised that she had actually forgotten about them!

Her small frantic movement brought Luke back to reality. Releasing her, he turned towards the car and went to help the children out.

CHAPTER NINE

'LUKE nearly kissed you then,' Lucy confided inno-cently to Suzy as she fell into step beside her, whilst her brother, boy-like, immediately stationed himself at Luke's side.

Kissed her? What for? Punishment? A gesture of his contempt? Suzy wondered sadly as the four of them made their way from the car park to the town's quaintly narrow and very steep streets.

'I think there's a children's shop not far from here,' Suzy announced, indicating the small square they were just entering.

Before they had left Sir Peter had handed her a very large sum of euros, telling her to get whatever she thought the children might need. And Suzy intended to do just that! It appalled her that their mother should be so selfish as to send them on holiday without the necessary clothes purely to spite her ex-husband, without giving a thought to how the children themselves might feel.

However, she was by nature thrifty—she had had to be, she acknowledged wryly. So she would get the best she could for the money.

Several cafés fronted onto the ancient cobbled square, their canvas sun umbrellas adding a bright splash of colour to the greyness of the weathered stone.

'It's just down here,' Suzy told Luke, indicating the narrow alleyway in front of them.

The children's clothes shop was three doors down, and Suzy could see Lucy's eyes light up as they walked inside. Within seconds the little girl was standing in silence, absorbed in the racks of clothes. Silent maybe, but her expression said it all, Suzy reflected as she watched the pleasure and excitement illuminating her face.

'Tell me what you think you would like, Lucy,' she suggested. 'And then we can have a look.'

She could feel Luke standing behind her, and in any other circumstances she would have suggested that he take Charlie to the other side of the shop and pick out some clothes for him. But she was too conscious of Luke's biting statement that he was going to remain glued to her side to do so.

Instead she waited patiently whilst Lucy went slowly through the rack, stopping every now and then to look enquiringly at Suzy.

'You need a couple of swimsuits and some shorts, Lucy,' Suzy said gently. 'Some tee shirts, and perhaps a dress?'

A tender smile curled her mouth as she saw that Lucy was hovering over a trendy pre-teen outfit of which wasn't really suitable for holidaywear, but Suzy could see its appeal for her.

Watching the interplay between child and woman, Luke reminded himself angrily that Suzy was a skilled actress.

More than an hour after they had entered the shop both children were kitted out, and Lucy's face was glowing with delight because Suzy had ruefully agreed that she could have the outfit she had set her heart on.

'Can we have an ice cream now?' Charlie asked as soon as they reached the square.

'It's almost lunchtime,' Luke told him, but instead of insisting that they needed to return to the villa to Suzy's surprise he suggested that they find a table at one of the cafés and have an early lunch there.

'Yes!' Charlie exclaimed excitedly.

Five minutes later they were sitting at a table, menus in their hands.

'Suzy, do you think I could wear my new trousers for dinner tonight?' Lucy asked earnestly, after the waiter had taken their order.

Suzy couldn't help it. Over Lucy's head her gaze met Luke's, her eyes brimming with tender amusement.

'I don't see why not—so long as your father doesn't mind,' she agreed.

Completely happy, Lucy leaned her head against Suzy and stroked her bare arm with loving fingers.

Her small, innocent gesture and the message of trust it carried made Luke feel as though a giant clamp was tightening around his heart.

How could one woman be two such very different people?

Different? What the hell was he thinking? She was only one person—a devious, manipulative, despicable person, incapable of any kind of genuine emotion.

The waiter brought their food, and Suzy was just beginning to eat hers when she happened to glance across the square.

Shock froze her into immobility as she saw the man standing only yards away and immediately recognised him. Jerry Needham! He was one of the reporters from the magazine; one of the men who had made her life such a misery when she had worked there.

What was he doing here? Taking a holiday? Or something more sinister—like trying to find out what was going on at the villa? Her heart was jerking around inside her chest as though someone had it on a string. What if he saw her and came over? Introduced himself? Luke would immediately suspect the worst.

Her appetite had completely deserted her, but then she saw Jerry was walking away from them and disappearing into the crowd on the other side of the square. Suzy tried to relax, but her insides were a tight ball of anxiety and apprehension. She had never liked Jerry—he was loud-mouthed, boorish and vulgar, and the sexual innuendo of the comments he had made to her had filled her with nausea. But she knew that he was an exceptionally shrewd reporter.

To her relief she heard Luke asking the children, 'Finished, you two?' He signalled for the waiter and asked Suzy, 'If you're ready to go...?'

Suzy was on her feet before he had finished speaking, but they had no sooner walked back into the crowded square when Charlie suddenly piped up urgently. 'I need the bathroom!'

An innocent enough request, but it was one that caused the two adults who heard it to tense in silent dismay.

One look at Charlie's screwed-up and anxious face

told Suzy that there was no way the little boy
could wait.

'There must have been lavatories back at the café,'
she told Luke. 'You'll have to take him back there.
Lucy and I will wait here.'

Luke looked down at Charlie and inwardly cursed.
The square was busy and Charlie was only young—
there was no way he could let him go alone. It was
obvious that he would have to take him to the lavatory.
Which meant that he would have to leave Suzy here
unguarded.

'Why don't you take Lucy?' he suggested, as Charlie
tugged anxiously on his arm.

'I don't want to go.' Lucy forestalled his attempt to
at least keep some check on Suzy.

'We'll wait here for you,' Suzy told him, quickly
checking the crowd to make sure there was no sign of
the reporter.

Luke hurried Charlie through the crowd. He could
not blame the little boy for what had happened, and
neither could he accuse Suzy of having engineered the
situation.

How much longer were Luke and Charlie going to be?
Suzy wondered anxiously, willing them to return so
that they could leave.

'Lucy, where are you going?' she protested as Lucy
suddenly started to hurry towards one of the stalls.

'It's all right, I just want to look at something,' Lucy
called back to her.

Suzy suddenly froze as the crowd parted and a couple of yards behind her she saw Jerry—looking right back at her.

She turned away, hoping to disappear into the throng of sightseers, but he was too quick for her, and she tensed as she felt his hand on her arm.

'Suzy! Suzy Roberts! What a coincidence!'

The oily, speculative look he was giving her made Suzy feel sick as it brought back unwanted memories.

'What are you doing here?' he demanded, still watching her with a look in his eyes which Suzy did not like.

'I'm on holiday with my partner,' Suzy lied uncomfortably, adding quickly, 'I must go. He'll be wondering where I am—we got separated by the crowd.' Turning away from him, she went to where Lucy was standing, looking at a stall selling handmade jewellery.

'Why didn't you stay where I left you?'

Suzy could hear the censorious note in Luke's voice. Had he seen Jerry? She looked round anxiously, but the reporter was nowhere to be seen.

'I wanted to look at one of the stalls,' Lucy answered sunnily. 'Are we going back to the villa now?'

'Yes, we are,' Luke agreed.

Suzy shivered as she saw him looking searchingly at her. Surely if he had seen Jerry with her he would have said something, only too delighted to have his suspicions of her confirmed? But it was not so much her fear that Luke might have seen Jerry with her that was making her feel so anxious, Suzy acknowledged as Luke guided them through the crowd, it was her concern about the reporter's presence here in the resort, so close to the villa.

The owner of the magazine did have excellent sources of sensitive information, although who they were Suzy had never known. It was not entirely beyond the bounds of possibility that Roy Jarvis could have sent Jerry to Italy to check up on what was happening at the villa.

And, that being the case, didn't she, as an honest citizen, have a moral obligation to tell Luke that she had seen him?

From his vantage point several yards away Jerry watched Luke and Suzy making their way through the crowd with the two children.

He had recognised Luke, of course, and unless he was mistaken—and he was sure that he was not—those two kids with them were the Verey kids, who were staying with their father.

Jerry had only arrived at the resort the previous day, sent there to check out a tip-off about Sir Peter Verey's real reason for being in Italy. Now he had the happy feeling that things were very definitely going his way!

Suzy Roberts and Lucas Soames. Well, well, what a piece of luck!

Suzy was still struggling with her moral dilemma when they got back to the villa.

Jerry might just be at the resort on holiday, or even following some other story involving the celebrities who stayed there, she tried to tell herself. But her conscience refused to be convinced.

CHAPTER TEN

'LUKE, can I have a word?'

Luke frowned as the operative he had put in charge of the perimeter security at the villa approached him.

It was twenty-four hours since he had driven Suzy and the children back from the resort—twenty-four hours, far too many of which he had spent fighting against his own emotions instead of concentrating on his professional business, which was why he had this morning finally instructed one of his London operatives to supply him with a full and detailed report on Suzy. He was sure the information in the report would back up his professional distrust of her and help him to banish these unwanted emotions she was causing him! The more information he had about her, the better.

Last night after dinner he had escorted Suzy to their suite and pretended to busy himself with some work whilst she prepared for bed. Only when he had been sure she was soundly asleep had he gone to bed himself, and even then he had not been able to relax.

In her sleep she had turned over to lie facing him, and he had wanted...

Luke did not want to think about what he had wanted to do.

Unable to trust himself not to give in to the temptation she represented, he had got up and spent the rest of the night sleeping uncomfortably in a chair.

He had got up and dressed before she had woken, though, determined not to allow her to suspect how vulnerable he had become to her. He had even caught himself thinking that if things could be different, if they could somehow find a way... To what? he had challenged himself. To forget what she was and what she did? Impossible! Furiously angry with himself, he wished he had never set eyes on her.

She was with the Verey children now, sunbathing beside the pool. The swimsuit she had been wearing when he had walked past earlier had made him remember what it had felt like to hold her naked body.

Hell, but he would be glad when all this was over.

'Yes, Phillips, what is it?' he asked his operative.

'The guards have reported that a chap's been hanging around the gates, asking questions about Ms Roberts.'

Luke's eyes narrowed. 'What chap?' he demanded grimly.

Hugh Phillips was young and keen, and quickly told Luke what he knew.

'He said he was just a friend, and refused to give any name, but according to the guards he was asking rather too many questions—and not just about Ms Roberts.'

Luke felt his stomach churn with anger—and something else! What the hell was he feeling like *that* for? He ought to be feeling vindicated, because he had been right to suspect Suzy, instead of savagely angry.

'Well, if he's so keen to see Ms Roberts, then perhaps he should be allowed to do so, Hugh. Tell the guards to allow him to persuade them to let him in.

Don't make it too easy for him, though. I don't want him getting suspicious. We need to know who he is and what he's up to. Keep him away from the house. You can let Ms Roberts meet him in the surrounds.'

Luke could see that Hugh Phillips was battling not to show any reaction to the mention of Suzy's name. Like everyone else, Hugh believed that Suzy was Luke's own partner.

'Have you got all that?' he checked coolly.

'Yes,' Hugh answered woodenly.

'Good—and remember, the minute he comes back I want to know!'

Once Hugh had gone Luke went to stand in front of the window of the small room he used as his office.

He had received unofficial confirmation this morning that the African President was finally satisfied with the security arrangements and was prepared to set a firm date for the meeting.

With that in view, and his suspicions regarding Suzy confirmed, he should be feeling pleased. Instead of which he felt strangely disappointed. Suzy must somehow have made contact with her 'friend' when he had had to take Charlie to the lavatory, and that was surely a predictable move on her part, so why was he feeling as though what she had done was some kind of personal betrayal? What the hell was happening to him? He was thinking—feeling—more like a betrayed lover than a man with no emotional involvement with her.

And as for the man who had come asking for her! Her 'friend'… Luke's muscles clenched against the pain of the surge of jealousy and male anger that pounded through him. He had to be someone from the magazine—not Roy Jarvis, of course. Another reporter, perhaps.

They would soon know, Luke promised himself, and when Suzy did meet up with him he would need to know what was being said.

He unlocked one of the drawers in his desk and searched through until he had found what he wanted. The minute recording device lying on the palm of his hand was so sophisticated that it was almost impossible to believe that so much technology could be packed into such a small thing. Designed to be slipped underneath a watch, it could record and transmit conversations with remarkable clarity. It could also reveal the location of the wearer to within a metre.

Slipping it on his own watch, Luke locked the drawer and left the room...

'Look, Suzy, watch me dive!' Charlie shouted as he jumped into the swimming pool, sending up a splash of water.

'That isn't a dive,' Lucy told him scornfully when he got out. 'You just jumped in.'

'Yes, it was. It was a dive,' Charlie argued.

'No, it wasn't—was it, Suzy?' Lucy appealed.

'Yes, it was,' Charlie continued to insist.

Ruefully Suzy got up and went over to them. She had a bit of a headache—a legacy from not being able to sleep properly last night, she suspected.

She had gone to bed before Luke, all too relieved to be able to shower and quickly jump into bed whilst he was still in the suite's sitting room. But, much as she had longed to fall asleep before he joined her in the large bed, her guilty conscience had refused to let her.

Eventually she had dropped off, only to wake up to discover that she had turned over and was now lying facing Luke, one hand outstretched, as though she was trying to reach out to him in her sleep. Afraid of waking him up if she moved, she had lain there motionless, worrying about Jerry and what he was doing so close to the villa.

She had still been awake when Luke had suddenly slid out of the bed to pad naked into the suite's sitting room.

The large bed had felt empty and lonely without him, and she had found herself moving over to where he had been lying so that she could breathe in the scent of him from the warm sheets and pillows.

He had been up and dressed when she had woken this morning, and she had been under no illusion as to why he had waited in the sitting room for her whilst she showered and dressed.

In grim silence he had accompanied her downstairs for breakfast, and then later out here, to the swimming pool.

And she still hadn't told him about Jerry! Because there hadn't been any opportunity to do so, she tried to reassure herself.

'Luke's here.'

Lucy's pleased announcement broke into her thoughts and brought a swift surge of colour to her skin.

Hoping that he wouldn't see it, and guess at its cause, Suzy pretended not to have heard Lucy's state-

ment and kept her head down, moving only when
Charlie suddenly jumped into the pool and she was
showered with water.

'See—that isn't a dive, it's a jump,' Lucy pronounced as Suzy shook the water off her face and stood
up. 'Tell him, Luke,' she begged. 'Tell him that he
can't dive.'

Smiling at the little girl, Luke surveyed the protected
area around the pool. Suzy had left her wrap by her
lounger, and when Luke turned his head to look at her
an intensely strong physical reaction kicked at her
stomach. She could feel her nipples peaking and thrusting provocatively against the fabric of her swimsuit,
and she knew from the downward sweep of Luke's
eyelashes that he was looking at their wanton flaunting.

She took a deep breath and fought off the desire to
wrap her arms tightly around her body.

Luke cursed himself under his breath as he fought
to drag his gaze away from Suzy's body. Already the
evidence of her swollen nipples was affecting him—
arousing him. All it would take was one step forward
and then he could tug those thin swimsuit straps down
her shoulders and expose the full creaminess of her
breasts to his hands and his lips. He could take each
of those nipples into his mouth in turn and show them
what they were inciting when they tormented his senses
until his self-control was at breaking point.

'Luke, Luke—tell her that I can dive.'

Charlie's high-pitched voice broke through the
heated pressure of his thoughts, and quickly he turned
away from Suzy. Her watch was lying on a small table,

along with her sunglasses and some suntan cream. Luke walked towards it.

'Watch this, then!'

There was the sound of a noisy splash, followed almost immediately by an angry scream. Suzy swung round to see Lucy standing beside the pool, dripping wet from Charlie's 'dive'.

His small task completed, Luke strolled over to help calm the commotion.

From now on, until he removed the small device, every sound Suzy made, even down to her heartbeat, would be transmitted to the receiver locked in his desk. There wouldn't be a single word she spoke, a single breath she took whilst she was with her 'friend' that he would not know about!

As she towelled Charlie dry Suzy looked over his head to where Luke was standing. She could tell him now, her conscience prodded her. All she needed to do was open her mouth and just say the words.

But what if he doesn't believe me? What if he thinks that I'm lying, that I'm part of whatever it is that's going on?

What if he did? her conscience demanded sternly. Were her own personal feelings really more important than something that was obviously very serious?

Suzy took a deep breath.

'Luke?'

She stopped speaking when his mobile started to ring, and watched in heavy-hearted disappointment as he answered it and began to walk away.

She could always tell him later, she comforted herself as she reached for her wrap and informed the children it was time to go inside. Perhaps this evening, whilst they were alone and getting ready for dinner.

Her heart did a back somersault that caused just as much devastation inside her chest as Charlie's 'dives' had done around the pool!

'He's back—refuses to give any name, but he's biting on the bait we've floated. He's offered the two guards a fistful of euros to let him in. The guards are making sure he has to work hard to persuade them, and I've told them to say they'll let him in through that side gate in the perimeter wall.'

'The one closest to the lake and the grotto?' Luke questioned sharply.

'Yes, that's the one—is that okay?'

'Yes, that's fine. What's he going to do when he gets in, though? I don't want him wandering freely anywhere.'

'That's okay. Nico is going to ask him if he wants a message sent to Ms Roberts, arranging to meet her.'

'Okay, let me know when he's taken the bait, Hugh.'

Suzy had just showered and changed when she heard a knock on the door of the suite.

Going to open it, she was surprised to see a young Italian standing there.

'I have a message for you, miss,' he announced, before Suzy could speak. 'There is a man—a friend of yours. He wishes you to meet him beside the grotto.'

Suzy stared at him, her heart hammering with apprehension.

'What man? Who is this man?' she began to demand, but the Italian was already walking quickly away from her.

It was Jerry—it had to be. Although how on earth he had got into the grounds and past Luke's guards Suzy could not imagine.

Anxiously she rushed down the stairs and out into the garden, glancing at her watch as she did so. The lake and the grotto were quite a long walk away from the villa, and she kept looking anxiously around herself as she hurried towards them.

She skirted the lake using the footpath, hurrying past the sign that warned against anyone entering the grotto because it was unsafe. A padlocked iron gate guarded the entrance, and Suzy frowned to see that there was a key in the lock. She must mention it at the villa, just in case the children should stray down this way!

Once she reached the other side of the grotto she paused, looking around uncertainly and then tensing when Jerry suddenly stepped out of the shadow of the trees and shrubs where he had been waiting for her.

'Jerry! What are you doing? How did you get in here?' she demanded apprehensively.

'Never mind that.' He stopped her curtly. 'I want to know what's going on here. Come on, Suzy, spill the beans. What a piece of luck, finding you here. We got a tip-off that there was something important going on.'

'There's nothing going on,' Suzy lied determinedly. Jerry's comments had confirmed her worst fears. She was certainly not going to tell him anything! But perhaps if she found out what Jerry was up to the information might actually be useful to Luke—as well as help to prove her own innocence.

'Oh, come off it! If that's true what's Soames doing here? And how did you get hooked up with him anyway?'

'We're here on holiday, that's all—and as to how Luke and I met, that's not really any of your business,' Suzy told him coolly.

In his office Luke frowned as he listened in on their conversation. Had Suzy somehow realised that they were on to her?

'"Luke and I"?' Jerry mimicked sneeringly. 'Typical that you'd go for someone like Soames—he's as bloody moralistic as you are! Met those kids of his yet, have you?'

Suzy's heart somersaulted. Kids? Luke had children? And children meant a mother, a woman he loved. No, that couldn't be true.

'Just as well he's wealthy. I've heard that their medical bills will run into thousands. Risking his own life to save some refugee brats! I'd have left 'em, myself. Got shot for his pains, didn't he?'

Refugee brats? As she rcoiled from Jerry's unpleasantness Suzy felt the tight band of pain around her heart slacken a little. There was no woman Luke loved enough to give her his children. But this was no time to think about her own feelings.

'You've got to leave, Jerry,' she insisted shakily. 'There's nothing happening here of any interest to you or the magazine.'

'You're lying,' Jerry accused her, putting his face so close to Suzy's that she stepped back. 'The boss has had a tip-off. That's why I'm here. Knew I'd got lucky when I saw you with the Verey kids.'

'They're here on holiday with their father.'

'They may be on holiday, but Verey's here for something more than that—and that's why Soames is here as well. They've got guards on the gate, for goodness' sake.'

'The owner of the villa employs the guards,' Suzy fibbed inventively. 'And, as I have just told you, Luke and I are here on holiday. Sir Peter is a friend of Luke's and he invited us to stay.'

'Sleeping with Soames, are you?'

Luke heard the small indrawn breath Suzy took before she told him firmly, 'Yes, of course I am.'

'Well, that's turn-up, isn't it? Little Miss Don't-Touch-Me-I'm-Only-Just-This-Side-of-Being-a-Virgin crawling into bed with Soames. The boss wasn't too pleased with you for leaving like that, you know. He'd got a pretty heavy bet set up that he'd be the one to teach you a thing or two about sex.'

Jerry was leering at her and Suzy had to fight down her furious disgust.

'Good, is he? Soames? I reckon you owe the boss one for depriving him of his pleasure. Come on, Suzy, tell me what's going on—for old times' sake.'

Suzy had had enough.

'For old times' sake?' she snapped, her eyes flashing with fury. 'You and the rest of those disgusting men at the magazine made my life a misery. And if you think for one moment that if there was anything to tell—which there isn't—I would betray national secrets to someone like you... Well, if you want my advice, Jerry, you should leave here right now—before—'

'Before what?' Jerry stopped her, an ugly look on

his face. 'Before you go running to Luke to give the game away?'

A chilly little breeze seemed to have sprung up, and Suzy shivered. Suddenly she felt not just cold but frightened as well.

'Jerry, I don't know what you want,' she began, but Jerry stopped her.

'You know damned well what I want,' he told her viciously. 'I want to know what's going on here, and one way or another I intend to find out.'

As he spoke he reached out and grabbed Suzy's arm, looking past her at the grotto.

'Jerry—what are you doing? Jerry, let me go!' Suzy started to protest, trying to resist as he dragged her towards the grotto and unlocked the iron gate.

'Let's see if you feel a bit more like talking after a few hours in here,' he told Suzy, panting heavily as he released her and gave her a savage push.

Suzy cried out as she lost her balance.

'Jerry, it isn't safe in here,' she protested anxiously as she struggled to get to her feet. But Jerry wasn't listening to her. Instead he was locking her inside the grotto and walking away with the key.

Luke cursed as he got to his feet, rapping out a message to Hugh Phillips to apprehend Jerry. Giving a cursory glance through the office window, he started to hurry out of the villa.

He had been wrong about Suzy! Utterly and completely wrong. And beneath his surprise at the discovery, and his concern for the danger she was in, he could feel a swift, deep tide of joy running through him.

Locked in the grotto, Suzy tried not to give in to her

fear. Someone was bound to come past and rescue her, surely? One of the gardeners, or one of Luke's men.

She tensed as she heard a low, threatening rumble. Stones and debris were falling all around her. Panicking, she ran to the back of the grotto, to avoid being hit by the growing avalanche of boulders, and then gave a terrified scream as the ground suddenly gave way beneath her.

She was falling down some kind of tunnel, Suzy recognised, with twigs and soil raining down all around her in the darkness. And then suddenly her fall came to an end, and the air jolted out of her lungs as she hit the cold dampness of a hard earth floor.

Somewhere in the distance she could still hear rumbling, but as she strained her ears to listen to it abruptly it ceased and there was silence.

Silence and darkness.

Her body hurt, but her fear was much greater than her physical pain. She was trapped somewhere underground beneath the grotto. Dust filled the air above and around her, making her cough and gag. How long would it be before someone found her—if they found her at all?

CHAPTER ELEVEN

LUKE had once run for his school—and, alerted by the sound of falling rocks, he reached the grotto just as it started to collapse in on itself. White-faced he looked at the pile of rubble beneath which Suzy was now buried.

Whilst his mind was coolly and mechanically planning what had to be done his heart was racing, thudding, swelling with emotions he couldn't afford to allow to torment him.

'Get on to the emergency services!' he shouted over his shoulder to Hugh, who had followed him. 'And then get the men down here!'

Suzy! Anguish, guilt, despair—he could feel all of them. Why had he waited so long? Why hadn't he come for her the moment he had realised she had not lied to him? Why had he allowed her to be placed in danger in the first place?

Suzy, Suzy, Suzy. He could feel her name ringing inside his head, inside his heart.

The guards had arrived and quickly he began to instruct them, telling them what to do as he began to move heavy boulders.

As he worked, grimly Luke tried to blot out images of another place and another time. Another pile of debris oozing dust and silence. That one under the heat of the sun, with the taste of smoke and anger in his mouth, the shocked wailing of the bereaved rising from the throats of women as he had looked in bitter fury at the house so unnecessarily destroyed, people killed and maimed by their own. A young woman dead, her children buried beneath the rubble of their home.

'Luke, if they are in there they'll be dead,' one of his comrades had muttered to him, but Luke had ignored him.

They had found the baby first, perfectly still, and then the older child. Luke knew he hadn't been the only one who had wept.

Those images were inside his head now, those images and those desperate feelings. He had hurt then, for those children, but if he had feared for them then that was nothing to what he was feeling right now.

And, what was more, Luke knew that it would not have made one iota of difference to him right now if Suzy *had* been colluding with the magazine, if she *had* been about to betray a hundred security secrets—he loved her, and his love for her was the strongest and most powerful emotion he had ever felt. It was so strong, in fact, that he had been afraid of it—afraid of acknowledging its power over him, afraid of admitting it to himself.

Suzy! He had loved her, he suspected, from the minute he had felt the brush of her soft lips against his own.

'Luke! Take it easy!'

It was only when he felt Hugh's restraining hand on his arm that he realised that he was tearing at the fallen boulders, his throat blocked with the pain of crying her name.

* * *

They worked late into the evening, under searchlights which had been rigged up and with the teams of experts Luke had called in.

Several times Luke was told to take a break and allow others to continue with the task that their expertise equipped them for, but he refused to listen. What he wouldn't give for a team of trained sappers here right now, he thought bitterly, as he watched the painfully slow progress, grim-faced.

If Suzy died it would be his fault. He would have killed her, killed the woman he loved, the woman he should have cherished and protected above everyone and anyone else, even above and beyond his duty. That was how he felt about her. How he would always feel about her. Admitting his love for her had been like taking a bung out of a dyke. The pressure of his denied feelings was pouring through him, drowning out everything else.

Why hadn't he listened to his emotions? Why had he persisted in disbelieving her and them?

He knew the answer to that, Luke acknowledged, his gaze never wavering from the harsh beam of light directed on to the fallen rocks. He had been afraid of admitting the truth.

He had decided a long time ago not to marry. He had seen too many Army marriages fall apart under the strain it imposed on them and he had thought he could prevent himself from falling in love, from wanting to spend the rest of his life with that one special person. Until Suzy had come into his life.

Into his life! And out of it?

The harsh lights bleached the colour from his face, leaving it leached of blood, his eyes two dark, burning sockets of pain fixed on the spot beneath which Suzy lay.

For Suzy, trapped inside her small cave, time blurred.

She was a child again, trying to comfort her crying mother, telling her everything would be all right—only her mother wasn't there, and she was the one who was crying.

Images and memories came and went, sweeping over her in waves of semi-consciousness. Curled up in a foetal position, she relived the happiest of her memories and experiences. And thought of Luke, whose name, whose taste would surely be on her lips as she took her last breath...

Luke stood grim-lipped in front of the Italian in charge of the rescue operation.

'I do not care how well trained your men are,' he told him curtly. 'I go in first. And now.'

It was nearly midnight, and the rescue team had managed to tunnel down to where Suzy was trapped—thanks, in the main, to Luke's experience and leadership. The watch Suzy was wearing had registered the fact that she was still breathing, and the bugging device had also helped them pinpoint her location. They had discovered that Suzy had fallen down some kind of tunnel or shaft, and now lay in a small space below it.

'It is still too risky for anyone to go in!' the Italian protested, trying to sound authoritative but failing when confronted by Luke's implacable will and air of command. He tried to persist. 'It will be several more hours before we can send someone in to bring out the young lady.'

'I'm going in now,' Luke told him bluntly.

'The tunnel is not yet secure. It could collapse and bury you both,' he warned, but Luke wasn't listening to him. He had already gathered together everything he might need, including medical equipment, food and water.

As the leader of the rescuers had said, the newly dug tunnel still wasn't safe. Its roof needed strengthening before they could risk bringing Suzy out. But it was strong enough to allow Luke to go to her, and that was exactly what he intended to do. No matter what the risk to himself. He had to be with her!

Moving carefully, Luke crawled slowly through the tunnel. He had never liked tunnelling, it made him feel slightly claustrophobic and all too aware of his own vulnerability, but right now he wouldn't have cared how long the tunnel was just so long as it took him to Suzy.

The brightness of the torch Luke was carrying woke Suzy from the exhausted doze she had fallen into.

Confused, and half in shock, she thought for a moment that she was hallucinating when she saw Luke crawling into the small space illuminated by the torch.

'Luke!' Her voice shook, and so did her body. 'Luke!' she repeated. 'How...? What...?'

Her words were smothered against his chest as he took her in his arms and held her there—held her as though he was never going to let her go, Suzy thought.

She made a sound. Something between a laugh and a whimper, shivering as she clung to the warmth of his body.

'It's so cold in here, and so dark. I thought...' She fell silent, unable to tell him that she had feared she would die here, in this small dark space beneath the ground. 'Are we going to get out now?' she asked him looking towards the tunnel.

'Soon,' Luke answered, giving their surroundings one searching inspection and then switching off the torch—partially to save its light for when they needed it, but also to save Suzy the reality of seeing how dangerous their prison was.

The feel of her in his arms was making his heart thud heavily with emotion. He was with her. He was holding her safe, as he should have held her all along. His hand cupped her face and stroked her hair whilst his other arm held her close to his body.

Half dazed, Suzy decided that she must be imagining the soft brush of Luke's lips against her hair, that it was a fantasy she was allowing herself to drift into.

Even so, she reached out a dusty hand to touch him. Something about the darkness and their intimacy was allowing her to drop the barriers she had put up against him to protect herself.

'I'm so glad you're here. I was afraid I was going to die here.'

Something about the quality of his silence made her tremble.

'We are going to get out of here, aren't we, Luke?' They must be—otherwise he wouldn't be here with her, risking his own life.

There was just the merest pause, the merest missed rhythm in his heartbeat before he told her calmly, 'Yes, of course we are. But we could be here for a while yet.'

'A while?' Suzy's own heart started to thump. 'But if it isn't safe what—? Why—?' Her mouth had gone dry.

'I owe you an apology, Suzy,' Luke told her lightly. 'And now that I've got you to myself, I have got the perfect opportunity to deliver it.'

He was trying to make light of the situation, Suzy recognised, her heart flooding with bittersweet emotion.

There was so much Luke wanted to say to her, but he was fully aware that up above them every sound from their chamber was being monitored via Suzy's watch—hardly an asset when one wanted to whisper words of love and regret.

As he touched her wrist Suzy opened her mouth to ask what he was doing, but Luke silenced her, placing his finger against her lips as he removed the small device and muffled it.

'What—?' Suzy demanded when he'd finished.

'It's what's commonly referred to as a "bug",' Luke told her wryly.

'You *bugged* me?'

The pain in her voice tore at his heart.

'I had no choice,' he told her quietly. He gave a small sigh. 'I do owe you an apology, Suzy—we both know that.'

'You were just doing your job.'

Her defence of him made him wonder grimly how

he could ever have thought of doubting her. Her honesty was so patently obvious.

'How long are we going to be down here, Luke?'

'I don't know,' he admitted honestly. 'Are you feeling okay? I've brought some water, and they will be putting an airline through the tunnel.'

'An airline?' Suzy's body trembled. 'You mean in case the tunnel collapses again?'

That was exactly what Luke did mean, and he cursed himself inwardly for adding to her distress.

'It's just a precaution,' he tried to reassure her.

Suzy felt faint and sick. Even with Luke so close to her, holding her, she still felt afraid, her thoughts going round and round.

'We could die in here,' she said in a small panicky voice.

'Don't think about it,' Luke advised her firmly.

'Talk to me, Luke,' Suzy begged him, desperate to have her mind taken off their danger.

'What do you want me to talk to you about?' Luke responded.

'Tell me about the children you rescued,' she replied.

Half of her still didn't dare to believe that he was actually here with her, that she wasn't alone any more. She needed to hear his voice to keep her fears at bay.

Sensing what she was feeling, Luke hesitated and then settled her more comfortably against his body, frowning a little as he realised how cold she was.

The children! Those were the very last memories he wanted to resurrect right now, but how could he deny Suzy anything?

'What do you want to know about them?' he asked quietly.

'Everything,' Suzy answered. 'But first tell me—are they all right now?'

'They're recovering,' Luke told her slowly, 'and with time, and proper medical care, hopefully they will be able to return and live reasonably normal lives. Raschid, the little boy, lost an arm.'

He felt Suzy's tension and cursed himself beneath his breath for having told her.

'Halek, the little girl—the baby—is fine,' he added.

'And their parents—their mother?' Suzy asked tentatively, not really sure why she felt so impelled to ask that particular question.

Was she reading his mind? Luke wondered helplessly.

'Both dead.'

'Tell me what happened,' Suzy whispered.

She could feel the rise and fall of Luke's chest as he breathed in and then exhaled slowly.

'The children's mother was helping us with information. Her husband, their father, had been killed trying to resist the tyranny they were facing. She wanted to avenge his death by helping us to set her people free. It was a dangerous situation for her, and important that we kept her identity hidden, that no one gave away the fact that she was helping us.'

'But someone did,' Suzy hazarded, lifting her head from its resting place against Luke's shoulder to try to peer up into his face.

'Yes,' he agreed heavily. 'Someone did.'

She could feel his remembered anger in the increased thud of his heartbeat, and suddenly out of nowhere she knew!

'Was it—was she a reporter?' she guessed intuitively.

She was still looking up at him; he could tell by her her gentle breaths as they fell on his face.

'Yes, she was,' he confirmed. 'Somehow or other she'd heard about Maram and decided to she wanted to interview her for a human interest story. Of course I informed her that she was going to do no such thing, and I pointed out to her the danger she would be putting Maram in. She ignored my warning, though, and managed to find a young rookie soldier foolish enough to be seduced by her—and I mean literally—into giving her Maram's name. Two days after she interviewed her Maram was murdered, and that was when I found out what Sarah had done.'

'Perhaps she didn't realise the danger she was exposing her to,' Suzy suggested huskily.

'Oh, she realised all right,' Luke told Suzy harshly. 'I had told her myself. But she just didn't care. Nothing mattered more to her than getting her story—not even another woman's life. She even had the gall to try to photograph Maram's children as they were being lifted out of the rubble of their home—the rubble that still contained their mother's body!'

'Jerry said that you have taken financial responsibility for the children,' Suzy murmured.

'They needed medical attention they couldn't get in their own country, and they could only be brought to the UK for treatment if someone agreed to sponsor them. It was the least I could do, seeing as I was responsible for the death of their mother.'

'No! It wasn't your fault,' Suzy protested immediately.

'I was the Commanding Officer, and I'd had enough experience of the determination of reporters to get their story to realise that this particular reporter wasn't going to put another woman's life before her own career,' Luke responded grimly.

'And is that why you hate women reporters?' Suzy asked him quietly. 'Because of what she did?'

'Well, let's just say that she reinforced everything I'd already experienced and felt about them as a breed,' Luke acknowledged. 'One woman murdered, two children nearly killed, three of my men shot and a gunshot wound myself didn't exactly endear her type to me!'

'You were shot?' Suzy exclaimed anxiously, before putting two and two together and asking softly, 'That scar—is that—?'

'Yes,' Luke told her tersely, anticipating her question, before continuing. 'Fortunately the children are survivors—and once they are medically fit to do so they will be returning to their own country to live with their mother's sister, who will love them as her own. Why are you crying?' he asked Suzy gently.

'I'm not,' Suzy fibbed.

But she was, and her tears were tears of sadness for the children and tears of joy for herself, because she was so proud of the man she loved.

The man she loved! Suddenly Suzy wanted to tell him how she felt, how much she loved him. How she had believed the first time she had seen him that fate had brought them together and that he was her one true love, her soul mate. It didn't matter any more that he didn't share her feelings, or that he didn't love her back. She wasn't going to die without saying the words that were locked up inside her heart.

'Luke,' she began shakily, 'if we don't get out of here I—'

'We *will* get out,' Luke began, and then stopped speaking as a sudden rumbling above them had them both looking upwards. 'Don't worry,' he reassured her. 'It just means that they're closer to getting us out, that's all.'

Suzy stared into the darkness, wishing she could see his face and his eyes so that she might have some clue as to what expression they were holding and if he really believed what he was saying or was merely trying to comfort her.

'Suzy—'

The raw urgency of the way Luke was saying her name had Suzy turning to him.

'This is all my fault,' he told her grimly. 'If I hadn't been so determined not to believe you—'

Suzy felt the pad of his thumb brush against her lips.

'I'm sorry, Suzy,' she heard him whisper. 'Oh, God, I am so sorry. I'd give anything, do anything, to get you out of here safely.'

Suzy could feel the warmth of his breath against her mouth, and suddenly, sweetly, she recognised that he was going to kiss her. She was lifting her face towards him when they both heard the sound of activity in the tunnel.

A shower of debris fell down from the ceiling above

them, and immediately Luke moved to cover Suzy's body with his own.

'Luke, what's happening?' she demanded, terrified.

'It's all right,' Luke reassured her, holding her tightly. 'Everything's going to be all right. We'll soon be out of here.'

Just hearing his voice made her feel better, Suzy acknowledged as she leaned into him, soaking up the comfort of his presence and his warmth whilst his hand shielded her head from the stones rattling down around them.

Suzy was still wrapped in Luke's arms ten minutes later when their rescuers arrived.

'Take Suzy first,' Luke instructed them. But when they came to lift her away from him she could hardly bear to let go!

CHAPTER TWELVE

'LUKE?'

The moment he heard the small, anxious cry Luke was awake, throwing off the duvet he had covered himself with and padding across the suite to where Suzy was lying frozen with terror in the middle of the large bed.

It was three days since they had been rescued from the grotto, and every night Suzy had had the same nightmare. Every night Luke had gone to her to take her in his arms, to comfort her and reassure her that she was safe. And once he had done that he had gone back to his makeshift bed on one of the sofas.

It was Suzy who had been insistent that there was no point in declaring now that they were not partners—not with the African President's visit so imminent.

'You've got enough to worry about without having to explain who I really am,' she had told Luke when he had told her that although he would prefer it if she didn't leave the villa until after the meeting, he would, if she wanted, make it clear to Sir Peter that they were not partners and ensure that she was provided with her own room.

In the event it was perhaps just as well that they were still sharing the suite. Her nightmare had woken her every night, leaving her shivering with cold and fear, only able to go back to sleep once he was holding her safely in his arms.

'They'll stop soon,' Suzy had told him last night, her teeth chattering as she clung to him.

Luke hadn't said anything. Locked away in his desk drawer was the report he had commissioned on her. And the information it contained had increased his guilt and his shame. She was innocent of everything he had accused her of. She had not lied to him. She had told him the truth and he had refused to believe her. He had treated her with contempt and cruelty. Luke knew he would never forgive himself. When he had read about her life as a child, with her mother, Luke had felt the acid burn of tears stinging his eyes, and his anger against himself had trebled. His anger, but not his love. His love, he recognised now, had been born fully formed and complete the moment he had set eyes on her!

His love. Broodingly, Luke went towards the bed, lithe and silent as a panther as he moved through the darkness. His love was a burden he would never lay on Suzy's shoulders. His report had told him what kind of person she was: the kind of person who put others before herself, the kind of person who gave up her own future to look after the mother who had never cared enough to love and protect her as she deserved. One day Suzy would meet someone for whom she felt as he felt about her. Someone she could love as he loved her!

A savage pain tore through him. He had reached the bed and he sat down on it. Because of Suzy's night-mares he had taken to wearing a pair of boxers to bed, but he still had to turn sideways so that she wouldn't see the telltale outline of his erection.

'It's all right Suzy, I'm here,' he told her gently.

'Oh, Luke hold me, please!' Suzy begged him.

Her nightmare terrified her. In it she was trapped underground on her own. She could hear Luke talking to her, but he wasn't there with her, and she was afraid. Afraid that she would die without seeing or touching him again.

Physically she had not suffered any harm from her incarceration in the vault beneath the grotto, but emotionally and mentally it was taking her longer than she had expected to recover.

Reluctantly Luke took hold of her, tensing as she burrowed closer to him. His body registered the fact that she wasn't wearing anything other than a pair of silky briefs.

Here in Luke's arms was the only place she felt safe, Suzy acknowledged as the nightmare receded and the warmth of his body comforted her. Comforted her and then aroused her, she admitted shakily, as the familiar feelings of longing and love filled her.

Unable to stop herself she leaned forward and brushed her lips against his shoulder, and then his throat, her tongue-tip investigating the taut flesh over his Adam's apple.

Luke felt as though he had been speared by a firebolt His erection was no longer a mere outline beneath his boxers, but a hard and obvious straining of flesh, aching to be touched and tasted as she was touching and tasting his throat.

'Luke, please kiss me,' Suzy whispered against his lips.

'Suzy...'

'Please,' she begged.

'Suzy, this isn't—'

'I love you, Luke,' Suzy burst out, unable to keep her feelings to herself any longer. 'I love you and I want you. You saved my life, and in some ancient cultures when a person saves another person's life it means that that person belongs to them for ever. And I want to belong you, Luke—even if it is just for tonight.' She was speaking so quickly her words were falling over one another. She had had it all worked out, what she would say to him, but suddenly, halfway through her planned speech, her courage began to desert her. 'You are my soul mate, Luke,' she whispered.

Everything she was saying was true, but once she would never, ever have said such words—because her pride would not have allowed her to do so! Her brush with death had changed her, Suzy recognised. She was no longer afraid of being laughed at or rejected. She wanted—she needed Luke to know how she felt.

Luke tried to control what he was feeling. She didn't mean it! She might think she meant it, but she didn't. It was the trauma of what she had experienced that was making Suzy feel that she loved him. That and her belief that he had saved her life. After all, she hadn't loved him before, had she? Once she was over her trauma she would realise that she didn't love him at all.

Just because he loved her it didn't mean that he could take advantage of what she was offering right now.

'Luke…'

Her pleading whisper burned into him like fire. Her hand was touching his belly, tracing the curve of his scar. Luke felt as though he was about to explode with need and hunger.

'Luke…'

Her breath whispered past his mouth and Luke knew that he was lost. Hungrily he possessed the softness of her lips, savouring them, parting them, thrusting his tongue with hard demand into the sweetness of her mouth.

Without him knowing how it had happened his hand found her breast and cupped it, moulding it, teasing the peak to rise up into his palm as he stroked and tugged its tautness.

He wanted her.

He loved her!

Abruptly Luke reined in his feelings. He loved her and he had to protect her from her traumatised belief that she loved him.

The small whimper of distress she made as he firmly put her from him tore at his heart as nothing ever would tear at it again.

'Luke…' Suzy protested achingly. 'Please stay with me, Luke. Please…'

But he had already gone, firmly closing the door between the bedroom and the sitting room and leaving her on her own.

Suzy gave a small start, unable to believe she had slept for so long. She had originally come up to the bedroom halfway through the afternoon, intending to catch up on the sleep she had lost the previous night, lying awake and longing for Luke.

Luke! She wasn't sorry that she had told him how she felt about him. She was glad! She was proud of her love, and proud of loving him. Her brush with death had altered her attitude a great deal, she acknowledged, but it did not seem to have altered Luke's attitude towards her.

He might not love her, but he wanted her, Suzy told herself. Last night he had wanted her—even if he *had* left her.

Getting out of the bed, she went into the bathroom. She still hadn't got used to the sensuality of the room, or the open sexuality of its erotic décor. She hadn't used the huge bath as yet—which was more of a sunken pool than a mere bath—but suddenly she was tempted to try it.

Returning to the bedroom, Suzy picked up the ice bucket and the complimentary book of matches from the pretty desk. Back in the bathroom, she pushed the door closed, put down the ice bucket and then carefully lit the candles that surrounded the bath. Even their shadows seemed to cast intimate and erotic dancing images around the room, and a sensual shudder ran through her. This was dangerous. She knew it was dangerous. But still she filled the bath. The water gushing from the dolphin jets glittered against the mosaic tiles.

The circular pool was so deep that she had to walk down into it. Like a Jacuzzi, it had a ledge to sit on, and was easily large enough to accommodate two people. Two people? Her and Luke? Suzy scooped up a handful of blue-green bath crystals from the jar beside her. As she dropped them into the water it turned a deep cloudy aquamarine before slowly clearing to the colour of the purest sea water. Self indulgently she lay back in it, floating in sumptuous, languid pleasure.

Worriedly Luke opened the bedroom door. It had been Lucy who had told him that Suzy had felt tired after lunch and had gone to lie down. A doctor had checked her over after her ordeal, and had pronounced her fine, but what if he was wrong—what if he had missed something?

And where was Suzy now? Not in either the suite's sitting room or the bed. Had she got up and gone back outside to join the children by the swimming pool?

It had been a long day—he had been cooped up in his office all morning, rearranging security for the President Njambla's visit because he had not been happy with it after all. He felt hot and tired and in need of a shower.

Unfastening his shirt, he removed it. In the mirror he could just see the tip of the small, still livid scar that disappeared below the belt of his chinos. The scar Suzy had touched and kissed.

Luke dropped the shirt and rubbed his hand across his forehead and then his eyes. He had to put Suzy first, not himself! But he couldn't stop thinking about how she had touched him last night in bed, how she had told him that she loved him! Irritated with himself, he stripped off the rest of his clothes. Somehow Suzy had got under his skin in a way that no other woman ever had—under his skin and into his heart. Just thinking about her brought a familiar ache to his body—a fiercely elemental and dangerous ache!

He opened the bathroom door and strode in. And stopped. And stared. He cursed under his breath, because his body was way ahead of him, in reacting to what he could see, and there wasn't a damn thing he could do about it other than make a grab for a towel.

What the hell was Suzy doing anyway? Just lying there, so that from where he was standing he could see quite plainly every silk-skinned inch of her. She hadn't seen him yet, though. She was facing away from him, and the steam from the water had made her hair curl wildly.

The scent of the candles she had lit filled his nostrils. Heat, need, hunger poured through him in an unstoppable torrent, filling every nerve-ending.

The towel slid from his fingers as he advanced towards the tub.

The candlelight seemed to highlight the sexuality of the wall frieze, and Suzy stared at it, lost in her own private Luke-filled fantasy. If Luke was with her now... A liquid ache of longing curled up through her body. And then she blinked as suddenly she saw that he was actually standing in front of her.

Pleasure touched her every nerve. She gave him a blissful, adoring smile and murmured his name on a happy sigh before asking curiously, 'Is that really physically possible?'

As Luke looked up and saw what she was studying a hard burn of colour ran up under his skin. That round-eyed look of innocence she was giving him was destroying him—and his self-control! He looked at the frieze again, and then back at her, where she lay floating in the bath, surrounded by the candles. His gut twisted as he saw the wet tangle of curls between her thighs and the dark peaks of her nipples.

Ignoring her, he headed for the shower.

Suzy could hear its noisy water running and her face burned as she wondered what on earth had possessed her to make such an idiotic remark.

Luke turned off the shower. It had been a wasted exercise, since it had cooled neither his emotions nor his arousal. Padding naked back to the tub, he demanded grimly, 'Do you want me to tell you if it's possible—or do you want me to show you?'

'Luke!' Suzy turned over too quickly and choked on a mouthful of water as Luke stepped down into the tub beside her.

He was crazy for doing this. Luke knew that. And even more crazy about the woman who was staring at him, her huge eyes already darkened with smoky, sensual arousal and excitement.

'Which one do you want to try first?' Suzy heard Luke whisper in her ear as he nibbled deliciously on the lobe and stroked a wet fingertip along her collarbone, and down to the valley between her breasts, and then along the upper curve, seeking out the wet thrust of her nipple where it surged above the water in excited eagerness for his touch.

'Mmm… Well?' Luke was demanding.

She gave a shocked gasp, her thoughts scattering like raindrops as Luke sank beneath the water, only the top of his head visible, his hair seal-dark and wet. His

mouth was cool and firm as he took captive the nipple
he had previously claimed, and the sensation of her
body floating in the water, Luke's head between her
breasts, his mouth on her nipple, his hand moving determinedly between her thighs was too much for Suzy's
self-control.

The water in the tub might be cooling, but the wetness inside her certainly wasn't. She could feel its heat
spreading through her as Luke's fingers found her—
found her and touched her, stroked her, opened her...

She was beyond reason, beyond reality—beyond
anything but this. The stroke of his hand, the suckle of
his mouth, the soft rhythmic sensation of the water...

She could feel the surge of her orgasm beginning to
mount, as unstemmable as the tide itself, and, as though
Luke could feel it too, he picked her up and carried her
towards the steps.

The thud of his own arousal beat through his body
and echoed in his ears. This wasn't need, and it wasn't
desire. It went way, way above and beyond that, and
it had taken him to a place where he was a stranger, a
humble acolyte, only just beginning to learn the true
meaning of the new world he had entered.

As he carried her up the steps to the floor, Suzy
could see their reflections in the mirror. Water ran from
their bodies and her nipples, swollen from his caresses,
peaked dark and hard in the candlelit room.

'Which position do you want to try first?' he asked
again.

Luke had placed her on a pile of soft towels and was
leaning over her. Excitement, shock and disbelief ran
through her veins like liquid fire. Her body ached

heavily with unsatisfied need, and Suzy knew she didn't care how he completed their union just so long as he did. She was in physical pain with her desire to have him inside her, her emotions and her body coiled to breaking point.

'This one?' His voice was a dark, tormenting whisper against the back of her neck as he moved her.

Shudders ran through her body as his hands stroked the skin of her bowed back. In the mirror she could see him leaning over her, his erection straining from the silky mat of hair surrounding its base.

'Is this what you want?' he whispered dangerously.

His hands were on her hips, and as she tilted her head back to look above the mirror and over their reflections she could see the position he was mimicking on the wall above them.

Violent shudders convulsed her.

'Or would you prefer this one?'

Suzy had to grit her teeth to prevent herself from crying out for him to stop tormenting her as he moved her again. Her body seemed to have no means of moving by itself. It had become completely obedient to his touch, whilst deep inside her the tension continued to grow so that she felt as though at any second it would spill from her and flood through her.

Her gaze embraced his erection with a molten look of longing and hunger. She reached out and touched him, hot flesh beneath her shaking fingertips, stretched over him, the foreskin pushed back to expose the rounded tip, dark and rosy. She rimmed her fingertip around it feeling his whole body jerk.

Luke could feel himself starting to shudder as his

control collapsed in on itself. Her touch was destroying everything he had put up against her. He had become a mindless physical instrument, reliant on her touch, dependent on her response.

He could feel the onset of his orgasm. From a distance he could hear her moaning his name, pleading with him to fill her with his body.

They were still lying on the towels together, and Luke was holding her, lifting her, entering her only just in time. On a surging explosion of relief and release his one powerful thrust carried them to completion on fierce, unending surges of pleasure that racked them again and again whilst he spilled hotly into the waiting, wanting heat of her body.

They were only just in time for dinner. Suzy was pale and lost in her own private bliss-filled world. Her mouth was swollen, but nowhere near as swollen as her breasts and nipples, which she had thankfully been able to conceal beneath her clothes. Her eyes looked slumberous, and somehow sensuously knowing.

As they reached the drawing room door she drew back a little unsteadily to look up at Luke, her gaze filled with so much emotion it hurt Luke to look back at her.

It wasn't real, he told himself grimly. She just *thought* she loved him. He had had no right to do what he had just done, and one day she was going hate him for it!

As he already hated himself!

He could feel Suzy quivering at his side. He looked at her again. Her face was pale, her eyes luminous, her mouth… Luke could feel his own pupils dilating in response to the message of those swollen lips. Inside his head he could see, feel, taste the more intimate flesh their swollen softness mimicked.

To his disbelief, Luke realised he had an erection.

'You go in,' he told Suzy curtly. 'I've got something I need to do.'

Oblivious to the real meaning of his words, Suzy tried to calm herself as he walked away from her, leaving her to enter the room alone.

Immediately Lucy and Charlie bounded over to her side. They were lovely children, she acknowledged tenderly, and they deserved to have a woman in their lives who truly loved them.

As he stood in his office and willed his erection to subside Luke knew that he could not allow the situation to continue. For Suzy's sake. If he allowed her to stay on at the villa now he knew he didn't have a hope of keeping out of her bed…their bed.

Right now she believed she loved him, but Luke knew that she did not. He had to send her away!

CHAPTER THIRTEEN

SUZY stared out of the salon window. She felt heavy-eyed from another night of too much thinking. And she had no idea where Luke had spent the night—it certainly hadn't been with her, in the suite!

The salon door opened and she spun round quickly, but it was Lucy.

'Are you waiting for Luke?' she asked Suzy. 'He's with Daddy. I wish you were going to be with us always, Suzy,' Lucy burst out, and then blushed. 'Some of the girls at school have got stepmothers and they say that they don't like them, but I think it would be cool if we had one—especially if she was like you.'

Suzy couldn't stop herself from giving the girl a fierce hug. She was still holding her when the door opened and Luke walked in. He had been avoiding her since they had made love in the bathroom, and Suzy knew it was only Lucy's presence that prevented her from begging him to tell her why.

'I wish that you were my stepmother, Suzy,' Lucy said passionately, hugging her tightly.

Luke frowned when he heard Lucy's outburst. It was no secret to him that Peter Verey was attracted to Suzy—what sane man would not be? He had had to fight off his own jealousy every evening since Suzy had been at the villa as he'd watched the other man flirting with her, but now it was surging almost out of control, forcing him to turn on his heel and stride out of the room.

Suzy watched him go, confusion filling her. What had caused him to suddenly walk away.

'So, it looks as though the President isn't going to show, then?' Sir Peter questioned.

'I'm afraid that it does look very much like that,' Luke agreed grimly as they stood together in his office. 'We've spoken to his people, and reiterated to them just how important this discussion is, but apparently he feels that he would be too exposed if he comes to Europe.' Luke's mouth compressed. 'He's playing with us, of course. We all know that. But there's nothing we can do other than wait. There's a rumour that he needs to be at home at the moment to quell some potential unrest. If that's true it could be several months before he's ready to set up fresh talks.'

'It looks like we've dragged you out here for nothing, Luke,' Sir Peter apologised.

Luke remained silent. After Sir Peter had left, he typed out a report and made several telephone calls. He had e-mails to answer and a variety of other correspondence to deal with…

It was late afternoon before Luke saw Suzy again. She was playing with the children, oblivious to the fact that he was watching her with a hungry lover's gaze. Right now he wanted nothing more than to take her in his arms and take her to bed, make her tell him how much she loved him.

But he wasn't going to it. No he was going to send her away.

Suzy looked up as she saw Luke approaching them Her skin was glazed with perspiration and her hair was sticking in exercise-dampened curls to her neck and face. She had enjoyed herself with the children, but Luke had never been out of her thoughts. Automatically she went towards him, and then stopped as he stepped back from her.

'You shouldn't be out here overdoing things.' His voice was clipped, and Suzy stifled her dangerous need to believe that he was speaking so because he cared.

'I'm fully recovered now,' she told him valiantly.

'Good, I'm glad to hear it.' He paused and looked at her, and something went still and cold inside Suzy's heart. 'Sir Peter's meeting with President Njambla has been cancelled,' Luke went on, in the clipped voice. 'I've booked you on to a flight for London mid-morning tomorrow.'

'What? No—Luke…' Suzy started to protest, but he was already walking away from her, leaving her white faced and desolate as she struggled to contain her pain.

She was still aching with misery a couple of hours later, when she went back to the suite to pack her clothes and have a shower.

For some reason she couldn't explain, even to herself, she did something she had never done the whole time she had been staying at the villa—and that was to turn the key in the outer door to the suite, locking herself inside and Luke outside! Out of temptation's way!

Her packing finished, she went to shower, determinedly refusing to look at the tub as she walked past it on her way back to the bedroom, before tiredly wrapping herself in a towel and crawling onto the bed.

Luke frowned as he turned the handle of the suite and realised the door was locked.

Wryly he wondered if Suzy had the least idea of what his Army training had equipped him for, and several seconds later he opened the door with silent ease.

She was lying on the bed, curled up on her side with her back towards him, quite obviously asleep.

Stripping off, he headed for the shower. He had a busy night ahead of him, sorting out the chaos caused by the African President's machinations, and he had come up to the room to grab a power-nap first.

Half an hour later he was to all intents and purposes still fast asleep on the sofa in the sitting room when he heard it. The smallest of muffled sounds. But he was awake immediately and on his feet in one smooth, predatory move.

Suzy was still asleep—but no longer peacefully. Her hands were clenched and she was moving frantically in panic. She gave a small, shrill whimper of terror. She was having her nightmare again!

Luke reached out and touched her bare shoulder.

Immediately she screamed, and then woke up. She sat up, shivering as she wrapped her arms around her knees, oblivious to her own nudity.

'Luke!' Suzy's eyes rounded, her gaze flickering towards the door to the sitting room. 'How…? What are you doing in here?' she demanded.

'It's our room,' Like reminded her calmly.

'Our room?' Suzy looked bravely at him. 'But you don't want me here.'

She was starting to tremble, and Luke had to grit his teeth to stop himself from reaching out and taking her in his arms.

'Why don't you try and go back to sleep?' he suggested.

It would certainly suit him if she did, and it would suit him even more if she covered herself up. Right now just the knowledge that he had only to turn his head and he would be able to see the silky curve of her naked shoulder, the small hollow at the base of her throat which he had already explored so thoroughly, was driving him crazy.

'No!'

The vehemence of her denial made him freeze.

'No. I can't go back to sleep. I'm afraid that I'll start dreaming again about the grotto,' she whispered.

Like her, Luke must have showered, she recognised, because he was wearing a towel wrapped around his hips so low that she could see the beginnings of his scar. Automatically she reached out and touched it with her fingers, and then with her lips. He stood at the side of the bed as immobile as a statue.

What was she doing? Was she going crazy? Suzy didn't know and she didn't care. She was high on the scent and the taste of Luke, drugged by her own need for him.

Luke tried to resist, to remind himself that it was for her own sake that he was sending her away, but his body overruled him. One minute he was telling himself he wouldn't touch her, the next she was in his arms and he was kissing her as though he was starving for the taste and feel of her!

Kissing her was like tasting a freshly picked peach—each taste made him eager for another, and then another, so that he could posses her unique sweet juiciness for ever...

Suzy pulled away from Luke's kiss to press her lips to his throat, and then his chest, stroking her fingertips through the soft warmth of his body hair as just for this moment she allowed herself to pretend that Luke was really hers, that she had rights of territorial possession over his body—it was hers to do with as she wished, to enjoy as she wanted, to touch, explore and know in a hundred different ways, so that she could store that knowledge for her future enjoyment.

Her tongue-tip rimmed his navel and felt the fierce clench of his muscles. She lifted her head and looked sideways at the purple scar, and she reached out to touch it again, liquid emotion shining in her eyes. A badge of courage and more importantly—to her, at least—a badge of love for his fellow human beings.

She bent her head, her lips poised to breathe a tender kiss against it. But Luke's harsh objection savaged the silence, and suddenly she was rolled underneath him, pinned there by the hard weight of his body whilst he stilled her soft sounds of pleasure with the savage heat of his mouth.

She shouldn't be doing this, Suzy knew. Luke did not love her as she did him. But how could she stop? How could she resist the need that was filling her, overruling reason and pride? She loved him! She wanted him! And right now nothing else mattered other than that he was holding her.

As his hands sculpted Suzy's body Luke told himself that it was for the last time. He cupped her breasts, savouring the malleability of them. He wanted to kiss them, lick them, pleasure them until she arched under him and writhed against him in hungry need. He wanted...

'No!'

Abruptly he released Suzy and stood up, his back to her as he stared out of the window.

Suzy waited, whilst her heart jerked in pain, and then, when he didn't move, she picked up her towel, wrapped it around herself and walked silently into the bathroom so that she could cry her eyes out under cover of the noise of the running shower.

Oh, why hadn't she stopped him before he had rejected her?

Outside in the bedroom Luke touched the scar on his side. She had touched it, kissed it, looked at him with luminous loving eyes.

She *didn't* love him, he reminded himself. She just thought she did. She just believed she did because she thought he had saved her life! If she did love him she would have known it before that time in the grotto, just as he had known he loved her.

But love could grow, Luke told himself fiercely. And if Suzy believed that she loved him then who was to say that she might not in time—?

No, Luke told himself savagely. No. He would not

do that to her. He would not lock her into a relationship that denied her the right to love freely. He could not.

He could not bear to let her go—but he had to for her own sake!

The first thing Suzy saw when she woke up was the small package on the bedside table. Picking it up, she opened it. Inside was her passport and her flight ticket, plus a generous amount of euros.

Tears filled her eyes as she carefully removed the money and put it down on the bedside table.

She had breakfast in her room—though there was no need for her to feel so anxious, she assured herself miserably. Luke wasn't likely to come in and say goodbye, so there was no risk of her flinging herself into his arms and telling him how much she loved him, begging him to give her a chance.

A chance? Did she really think there was one after the way he had rejected her last night—even though his body had wanted her? That could only mean that he didn't love her. She knew that!

There was nothing for her to linger for. She had already said her goodbyes to the children, and to Sir Peter, and given him her thanks for their hospitality.

'Will you come and see us at school?' Lucy had begged Suzy, tears in her eyes as she hugged her fiercely.

'Of course I will,' Suzy had assured her.

Poor little scraps! They had so much in material terms, and yet so very little in all the ways that mattered.

She stayed upstairs until she saw the taxi arriving from her bedroom window, and then she went down, carrying her small case with her.

The children were waiting to wave her off, wearing the clothes they had bought together. Suzy had to blink away tears as she hugged them and promised again to keep in touch.

Unable to stop herself, she looked towards the closed door to Luke's office, willing him to come out. But to what purpose? The only thing she really wanted him to say was, Please don't go! followed by, I love you! And she was not likely to hear him say those words, was she? Forcing a wan smile, Suzy gave the children one last kiss and then walked out to her taxi.

Standing in front of the window of his small office, Luke watched her. He had been deliberately avoiding her—why make problems for himself? Why put himself in a situation he already knew he couldn't fully control? She was opening the taxi door. By the time he took one deep breath and counted to ten she would be gone.

One deep breath...

He flung open the door to his office and raced towards the front door. He had almost reached it when Sir Peter suddenly emerged from his own office and called out urgently to him, 'Luke—quick! I need you. The Prime Minister's on the phone, Njambla's people have been back in touch. The meeting's on again.'

For a second Luke was tempted to ignore him—breaking one of his own unbreakable rules—but he could hear the taxi door closing, and his conscience was telling him that he had to let her go. His face stripped of expression, he turned away from the front door and walked towards Sir Peter.

CHAPTER FOURTEEN

SUZY had read the breaking story about a certain African President's meeting in Italy over her breakfast, not long after her departure from the villa—the same morning, in fact, as the post had brought her another letter advising her that regretfully its senders could not offer her a job with them.

Following her return home, she had written to every library and organisation she could think of, determined to pursue her dream of finding work as a trainee archivist. But it was a narrow field, with very few vacancies.

'You mustn't give up,' Kate had told her firmly.

'I don't want to,' Suzy had admitted. 'But it's not an easy market to break into, and at my age—'

'Your age?' Kate had shaken her head chidingly. 'For heaven's sake, Suzy, you aren't old!'

'I'm not twenty-one, and just down from university,' Suzy had reminded her ruefully. 'Potential employers want to know what I've been doing for the last few years, and why I didn't finish my degree first time round.'

'What? You were nursing your mother,' Kate had defended indignantly.

'And then there's the fact that I left the magazine— and I don't have any references from them.'

'They were subjecting you to sexual harassment,'

Kate had argued, but Suzy had been able to see from her friend's expression that Kate knew that things did not look good for her.

'Still, there is somewhere I can get a job,' Suzy had told Kate cheerfully.

'Yes—with us,' Kate had replied promptly.

Even though she was grateful to her friend, Suzy had shaken her head. 'No, Kate. You know that I won't take charity,' she had told her gently. 'I was referring to the supermarket—I've worked there before.'

'Suzy, you don't need to do that!' Kate had protested. 'You know we'd love to have you working for us.'

'Kate, you told me yourself only last week that you were struggling to find enough work for the part-time girl you've already got,' Suzy reminded her. 'No. The supermarket will be fine!' she had told her, and she had meant it.

She felt very guilty about the fact that she had said nothing to Kate about either Luke or her time at the villa. But somehow she had just not been able to bring herself to do so...

'I hate this job. I've only been working here a week and it feels like for ever. And as for that supervisor— she's more like a prison warden!'

Suzy smiled sympathetically at the pouting teenage girl sitting grumpily at the till next to her own.

'It's okay once you get used to it,' she assured her, whilst privately acknowledging that she could understand her dislike of their supervisor, whom Suzy thought was a bit of a bully.

The supervisor apart, though, Suzy quite enjoyed working on the supermarket checkout— After nearly three months she actually had her own regular customers, who favoured her till—old ladies, in the main, who were lonely and appreciated the fact that Suzy did not rush them and had time to listen to them.

The bullying supervisor didn't approve. She constantly hectored Suzy about the time she spent listening, complaining that Suzy wasn't pulling her weight because she wasn't dealing with as many customers as some of the other girls. She had urged Suzy to discourage them.

'But they're lonely,' Suzy had protested.

'So what? We aren't here to provide them with someone to talk to!' the supervisor had told Suzy angrily. 'And it's not as though they spend very much. Just a few bits and pieces, that's all.'

'They like coming in because they can go to the coffee shop,' Suzy had responded. But her defence of her elderly customers had only infuriated the supervisor all the more.

'Yes, and they'll go in there and sit all day if they can, just drinking one cup of tea!' she had snorted grimly.

Suzy tried not to think about her supervisor. She needed this job because she needed the money. They had had a good summer, so at least she hadn't had to spend money keeping the flat heated. Every penny counted now—she had even thought of applying to the council for an allotment. Fresh air and fresh food would be good for her—

She checked her thoughts and she looked down at

the small bulge of her stomach. To say that it had been a shock to discover that she was pregnant was more than an understatement!

Of course the discovery of her pregnancy had meant that she'd had to come clean to Kate about Luke, and although she had been surprised, her friend was being wonderfully supportive.

Luke's baby!

A soft absorbed look filled Suzy's eyes followed by a flash of fiery maternal protectiveness. Unlike her own mother, she was not going to bring her baby up in an atmosphere of misery and complaint. But if her baby was a girl, Suzy had decided she would warn her against falling for a man like her father!

Her doctor had assured her that everything was fine and normal—single motherhood didn't raise any eyebrows or comments any more—and now that she had got used to the fact that she was pregnant Suzy was thrilled and excited. But not as thrilled and excited as she would have been if she had been sharing things with Luke—a Luke who loved her...

Now she was entering fantasyland, she derided herself. And what was more she was demeaning herself by even thinking about wanting to have him love her.

There was a lot of commotion and noise coming from the supervisor's office, which was behind her and several yards away, and in front of her at the checkout a young mother with a screaming toddler was struggling to unload her trolley.

Suzy smiled sympathetically, unable to stop herself from mentally fast-forwarding to the arrival of her baby. Money would be very tight, but she was determined that somehow she would manage.

There was still a lot of noise coming from behind her. She could hear the supervisor's voice raised in protest, and she could hear a man. A man? That was *Luke's* voice—she was sure of it.

Luke had had enough.

The last fourteen weeks had been the longest of his life. First he had told himself that he was a man of honour, and that as such he was honour-bound to leave Suzy to make a life for herself without him. Then he had told himself that it was only natural that he should check up on her to make sure she was okay after what she had been through.

Then he had admitted that if he *did* check up on her he was going find it damned hard to walk away—especially if she was still under the delusion that she loved him. And then finally he had admitted that there was no way he could live without her and that he had to see her again!

He had finished the contract he'd been working on, handed over his active role in their shared business to his partner, and announced that from now on he was going to be running the small estate he had inherited.

A hiccup in the children's recovery and their return to their homeland had added to the delay, making it fourteen weeks instead of the fourteen days he would have preferred before he was finally free to seek Suzy out.

When he had called round at her flat the woman who had the apartment below hers had informed him that she was at work. It had taken him an hour and a good deal of patience and flattery before she had finally given him the information that Suzy was working in a supermarket.

He had wasted another hour driving through the traffic to find it, and now this shrill-voiced woman was telling him that it was impossible for her to take Suzy off the till she was operating, and that if he wanted to see her he would have to wait until her shift was over.

Luke wasn't prepared to wait a single minute longer—not after having waited nearly four months—and so, ignoring the supervisor, he strode towards Suzy.

'Luke!' Suzy wasn't even aware that she had spoken his name, never mind stood up, to stare in disbelief as Luke strode towards her.

Then he stopped, his gaze going from her face to her body. He couldn't possibly tell, Suzy assured herself frantically. She was barely showing. Her bump was still relatively small. Even so her hand crept protectively towards it as she tried to cover it from him.

Shock and awe! Where had he heard those words before? Luke wondered, dazed. Certainly not in connection with what he was feeling right now. Suzy was pregnant! Suzy was having his baby!

Whilst the young mother watched in fascinated interest, Luke shifted his gaze from Suzy's stomach to her face.

'Go and get your things,' he commanded brusquely.

'My things?' Suzy gulped. 'What? I—'

'We're leaving—and now!' Luke told her fiercely.

Suzy told herself that she should refuse to have anything to do with him, but instead she heard herself protesting shakily, 'Luke, I can't just leave. I'm working. There's no reason—'

'There's every reason,' Luke corrected her savagely.

And before Suzy could stop him he had reached for her and placed his hand where hers had been, flat and hard against her belly, where his child was growing.

'There's this, for starters,' he told her thickly. 'My child. And if that isn't enough…'

Suddenly Suzy was conscious of the silence surrounding them. The curious looks of the customers and the angry face of her supervisor.

'If you leave this till now you will be in breach of your employment terms and your job could be at risk,' the supervisor was intoning.

'She'll be handing in her notice anyway,' Luke answered coldly.

Handing in her notice? Suzy glared at him.

'You can't say that!' she hissed, as Luke put his hand beneath her elbow and almost frogmarched her away from the till. 'I need this job, Luke.'

'What you need and what I need are not my prime concerns right now,' Luke told her flatly. 'Our child's needs are.'

He shouldn't be feeling like this, Luke told himself. He shouldn't be feeling triumphant, exuberant, delighted that the child Suzy was carrying—his child— meant that he had a logical and undeniable reason for forcing his way into her life. But he was!

Our child! Suzy could have wept.

Outside in the car park he bundled her into a large four-wheel drive vehicle and then got in himself. It was nearly four months since she had seen him. And he hadn't even looked at her properly, never mind attempted to touch her…kiss her…

'I've just got back from seeing the children,' Luke said to her. 'They're well enough to receive treatment from a hospital in their own country now, and their aunt has officially taken charge of them.'

'Oh, Luke, that's such good news,' Suzy responded in delight.

'Yes, it is,' he agreed quietly. 'Suzy, why didn't you let me know about the baby?'

'Let you know?' she stared at him. 'I…'

How could she tell him that she hadn't wanted him to feel responsible, that she hadn't wanted him to feel that she had deliberately allowed herself to become pregnant in order to trap him. He already knew how much she loved him, and she imagined that in a man's eyes a woman who became pregnant with his child after he had rejected her had to be doing so in order to force his hand.

She didn't feel she could tell him any of that, so instead, she simply said huskily, 'I…I just didn't think that it was necessary.'

Luke felt the pain of her words explode inside him.

'I heard from Peter the other day. He mentioned that you've kept in touch with the children,' he announced abruptly.

'Yes…yes, I have,' Suzy agreed. 'I feel so sorry for them. They need a woman in their lives who loves them. A stepmother, perhaps.'

As she spoke Suzy was thinking of the young woman Lucy had written to her about—the daughter of some older friends of Peter's who had taken quite an interest in Lucy and Charlie.

'Thinking of applying for the job yourself, are you?' Luke demanded harshly.

Suzy stared at him, his words coming as a shock after her own private thoughts.

'How could I?' She asked. 'I'm pregnant with your child.'

Her answer wasn't the one Luke wanted to hear. What he wanted was to hear her telling him, as she had done before, in that soft, loving voice of hers, that she loved him and only him and that she would always do so!

'Why are you working in that supermarket?' he asked curtly.

'Because it was the only place I could get a job!' Suzy returned tartly. 'Now that I'm going to have a child to support—' She stopped and bit her lip. The last thing she wanted was for him to think she was trying to get money out of him.

'*You* are going to have a child to support?' Luke demanded as he turned the car in the direction of the motorway. 'This child is our child, Suzy, and I consider that I have as much responsibility for supporting him or her as you do—if not more.'

'Luke, where are you taking me?' Suzy asked, as she silently digested his statement.

Things were happening too fast. She was still in a state of shock. In fact she was still expecting to wake up and open her eyes and find that she had been dreaming!

'Home,' Luke replied, further astounding her.

They were heading towards the country, leaving the city behind.

'Home?' Suzy queried uncertainly. 'But...'

'Where else would I be taking you?' Luke asked. 'After all, it's where you and our child now belong!'

'I have my own home,' Suzy protested sharply. 'I have my flat.'

'You can't bring up a child up there,' Luke told her flatly. 'And you certainly will not be bringing up *my* child there.'

Suzy drew in a sharp breath of indignation. 'There is nothing wrong with my flat,' she told him. 'You have no right to do this, Luke.'

'You are carrying my baby,' Luke said harshly. 'How much more right than that do I need?'

'Maybe I am—but that doesn't mean that you can just walk into my life and...take over...or kidnap me!' Suzy wasn't far from tears of emotional reaction.

'No? I beg to differ. You see, the way I look at it, Suzy, you gave me some damn important rights when you gave yourself to me—when I gave you my child.'

Shocked into silence, Suzy leaned back in her seat and closed her eyes. She just could not believe that any of this was happening—that Luke had conducted this swift and effective campaign of repossession which had brought her totally into his power.

As she tried to fight the wave of tiredness that suddenly gripped her Luke turned off the motorway.

'It isn't very far now,' he told her. 'The estate is just the other side of the village. You'll be able to see the church spire first.'

Estate...village...church spire. Suzy's head was thumping with a reactionary headache.

They were right in the heart of the English countryside at its quaint best. Autumn might be just around the corner, but the trees were still in full summer dress—the hedges heavy with leaf, fields of crops waiting to be harvested stretching away from the road.

Suzy saw a sign, Flintock-upon-Adder, and then they were driving through a picturesque village. Its houses clustered around an immaculate green, with weeping willows dipping into the waters of a sedate river and then the road curved past a small Norman church to run alongside a stone wall. Beyond it Suzy could see a small park, and then she caught her breath at the beauty of the Queen Anne house she could just glimpse through the trees.

Luke was turning in to a tree-lined drive and the house lay in front of them.

As he brought the car to a halt outside it Suzy turned and told him determinedly, 'Luke, I want you to take me back to my own flat.'

'Not yet,' Luke refused calmly. 'Not until we've had time to talk. Come on—I'll take you in and introduce you to Mrs Mattock. She's the housekeeper—I inherited her along with the house.'

'You inherited this house?'

'Yes, from my father. It's been in the family ever since it was first built.'

Mrs Mattock was calm and welcoming, apparently not in the least bit fazed that Luke had returned with an unexpected guest.

Although she was both pleasant and discreet, Suzy

suspected that the housekeeper was well aware of her pregnancy as she escorted her upstairs to a pretty guest bedroom. It was decorated in a simple and traditional style, complete with its own bathroom so that Suzy could, as the housekeeper put it, 'freshen up'.

'Mr Luke said that I was to serve tea in the library, miss,' she informed Suzy before turning to leave. 'It's the third door on your left off the hallway. A lovely room it is too. It was the old master's favourite. He would have been right pleased that Mr Luke had taken it over, that he would!'

From the window of the guest room Suzy could see the house's lovely English country garden, and the church just visible through the greenery of ancient trees.

In the bathroom, with its plain white sanitaryware, she found immaculate white guest towels and a tablet of what looked like handmade soap. Against her will she found herself thinking what a wonderful home this house would be for a family.

A wonderful home, maybe, but never *her* home—nor her child's, she reminded herself sharply as she left the room and headed for the stairs, breathing in the soft scent of lavender and beeswax from the well-polished furniture.

Dutifully following Mrs Mattock's instructions, she resisted doing more than just peeping inside the half-open door of what was a lovely sunny south-facing sitting room, and headed instead for the door to the library.

Outside the room she paused, reluctant to go in. But determinedly she took a deep breath, and then reached for the door handle and turned it. As she opened the door and walked in, Suzy acknowledged that the very masculine panelled room, with its impressive partners' desk, suited Luke. She could see that he felt very much at home in this lovely house. But then why shouldn't he?

'Suzy.' As he came towards her she backed away from him. 'Mrs. Mattock is going to bring us some tea,' Luke said.

'Yes. She told me,' Suzy answered curtly, wondering what on earth they were doing, exchanging such stilted small talk when they had far more important matters to discuss—like Luke's high-handed virtual abduction of her!

'Luke, you shouldn't have done this,' she said angrily. 'You have no right to—'

'To what? To be concerned about the welfare of my child and his or her mother?'

Suzy had to blink frantically to banish her threatening tears. Hormonal emotions, she told herself crossly.

'This baby I am having wasn't planned, Luke—we both know that,' she reminded him. 'He or she was…was an accident. I don't consider myself to have any claim on you—and anyway, you don't…'

'I don't what?'' Luke probed, when Suzy fell silent without finishing her sentence.

'Suzy took a deep breath. 'You don't love me!' There—she had said it! 'You don't love me. You don't even like me very much.'

'I don't love you?' Luke gave a harsh laugh.

'And why on earth did you come to the supermarket in the first place?' Suzy persisted, ignoring him.

Luke had had enough! It was hell on earth for him, having her standing there in front of him when what he wanted more than anything else was to have her in his arms—her *and* their child!

'Why did I come to the supermarket? Why do you think I came?'

Suzy's heart was beating crazily now, with a mixture of dangerous emotions.

'I don't know,' she admitted, wetting her lips nervously with the tip of her tongue. She had been so caught up in Luke's reaction to the discovery that she was pregnant that she hadn't been able to think past it and question why he had come looking for her in the first place.

'In Italy you told me that you loved me,' Luke said curtly, half turning away from her as he stood staring out of the library window.

Suzy could really feel her heart thumping now. Yes, she had told Luke that she loved him and he had shown her in no uncertain terms that he did not want that love. She had more than her own feelings to consider now. She had her child's to think of as well! No way was her child going to suffer the same unhappy childhood she had known! For her baby's sake she needed to be strong.

'I did say that, yes,' she acknowledged a little unsteadily. 'But I realise now that I—'

Idiotically she discovered that something inside her just would not let her say the words *I don't love you!*

'That you made a mistake.' Luke finished her sentence for her flatly, causing relief to surge through her as he inadvertently rescued her.

'I...'

Suzy had to bite on her lip to hold back the pain seizing her as she tried to deny her love. Something inside her was telling her that to deny her feelings was as great a betrayal of her child as humiliating herself by loving a man who did not want her.

'You didn't have to come to the supermarket to find that out, Luke,' she said instead. 'Surely the fact that I haven't made any attempt to contact you must have reassured you that I—'

'Reassured me!' The violence in Luke's voice as he swung round to confront her silenced her. 'Reassured me?' he repeated savagely. 'What the hell are you talking about, Suzy?' He broke off abruptly as there was a discreet rap on the door and Mrs Mattock came in wheeling an immaculately set tea trolley, complete with a heavy silver teapot.

'Will Ms Roberts be staying the night, Mr Luke?' she asked politely.

'Yes!'

'No!'

Locked in mutual anger, Suzy and Luke glared at one another as the housekeeper discreetly departed.

'Would you like me to pour the tea?'

As Luke nodded tersely Suzy had to quash a hysterical sound of mingled pain and disbelief. Here they were, in the middle of a situation so tense and painful that she felt faint from the stress of it, and she was pouring tea—like someone out of a Victorian novel!

But automatically she went to pick up the heavy teapot.

'Of course I realised that your belief that you loved me sprang from the trauma you'd undergone,' she could hear Luke saying tightly behind her. 'I may have realised I loved you before that event, but—'

The teapot wobbled in Suzy's hand as shock weakened her muscles. There was tea in the cup, in the saucer, and on the immaculately starched traycloth.

'Suzy!'

Luke grabbed the heavy silver teapot with one hand and put a steadying arm around her.

'What did you just say?' she demanded weakly. She was shaking so much she could hardly stand, and it was heaven to lean into Luke's warm strength. 'Are you trying to say that you fell in love with me before I got trapped in the grotto?' she asked dizzily.

'Yes. Not that I wanted to admit it. I was still labouring under a misapprehension about you then, and whilst a part of me wanted to be proved right about you, a much larger part of me most certainly did not.'

Suzy was having to struggle to assimilate what he was saying. Luke loved her? Luke had loved her even when he had thought he ought to hate her? Joy was beginning to well up inside her, flooding through her veins.

'Are you feeling all right?' Luke was fussing, manlike. 'Why don't you come and sit down?'

'No,' Suzy told him fiercely. 'No. I'm not going anywhere, and most especially not out of your arms, Luke, until you tell me exactly when you knew you loved me!'

'Exactly when?' Luke looked down into her unguarded face, and what he could see there made his heart start to sing.

'Probably the first time you kissed me,' he admitted ruefully. 'And certainly by the time you ran away from me on that hilltop and I realised that if I didn't do something you were going to hurt yourself.'

A pink blush stained Suzy's face as she remembered how he had held her, her body spread on top of his.

'When I told you I loved you, you rejected me, though,' she pointed out quietly. She could feel his chest rising and then falling with the intensity of his sigh.

'I had to, Suzy. It's well known that the kind of trauma you went through can make a person feel the strongest kind of emotion towards the people they shared it with. I knew I loved you, but I didn't want to trap you into a relationship when I was afraid that your love might not be the real thing.'

'Oh, Luke I fell in love with you the moment I set eyes on you,' Suzy told him softly. 'I looked at you and it was just as though... I looked at you and I knew you were my soul mate,' she told him huskily.

For a moment she thought he wasn't going to make any response, but then he put down the teapot and turned her gently in his arms. Placing one hand on her belly, he whispered softly, 'Sorry baby, but I think you'd better close your eyes whilst I kiss your mother!'

And then he lifted both hands to Suzy's face and, cupping it, began to kiss her with a slow, gentle passion that grew and built until they were so closely entwined that even their heartbeats matched.

'I can't begin to tell you how long these last fourteen weeks have felt,' Luke whispered achingly to her. 'First the meeting with Njambla, and then I had to persuade my partner to take over my active role in the business. Then there were problems with the children, and all the time I kept warning myself that by the time I did get to see you, you would have realised that you didn't love me after all. You don't know how many times I cursed myself for not keeping you with me when I had the chance, for not taking the love you were offering me. And then when I saw you today and I realised you were pregnant...'

She could see the pain in his eyes, as well as the love.

'I didn't want you to feel you owed me anything,' she told him quietly. 'I didn't want anything from you, Luke, that you couldn't give with love.'

'Are you sure you're feeling okay?'

'I'm fine,' Suzy reassured Luke as he led her out of the church and into the late autumn sunshine to the joyful sound of wedding bells ringing.

Her elegant cream silk dress discreetly concealed the curve of her belly, and under the benign gaze of their wedding guests Luke leaned down to kiss her.

'Who would have thought that first kiss you stole from me would lead to this?' he murmured teasingly in her ear.

Suzy laughed in real amusement. 'I may have stolen it,' she reminded him, 'but you returned it—and with interest.'

Luke laughed back, placing his hand on the curve of her belly as he did so.

A hovering photographer snapped the pose, and then the one following it, when Luke drew Suzy firmly into his arms and kissed her tenderly and thoroughly.

EPILOGUE

'LUCY looks very serious and important.' Luke smiled at Suzy as they watched Lucy, Charlie and Sir Peter, along with Anne, the young woman he had asked if he could bring with him to baby Robert's christening, getting out of their car.

'Well, being Robert's godmother is a very serious and important role for her,' Suzy told him with a smile.

Lucy had been thrilled when Suzy had asked her if she would like to be one of Robert's godmothers, along with Kate.

'Oh, Suzy, do you mean it?' she had asked, her face pink with excitement.

Suzy smiled now at the memory, shifting Robert's sturdy six-month weight in her arms as she looked at Luke.

They had had Sir Peter, Lucy and Charlie to stay with them over Christmas, and Suzy had heard a great deal then from Lucy about Anne, the young family friend who was now Sir Peter's fiancée.

'I know Lucy is perhaps a little young, but it means so much to her, Luke. She told me that she is hoping that when her father remarries there will be babies.'

Robert's two godfathers were friends of Luke's from his Army days and, like Sir Peter and his family, they had been regular visitors over the months since Luke and Suzy's marriage.

Knowing the sad story of how Luke had lost his parents, and how lonely he had felt, had increased Suzy's determination to provide their own children with the kind of warm, happy family environment neither she nor Luke had known.

When Luke had taken her hand, white-faced and worried after Robert's birth, anxious for her, having witnessed her labour, Suzy had smiled up at him and warned teasingly, 'You're going to have to get used to this, Luke, because this baby is not going to be lonely, like we were.'

A small smile touched Suzy's mouth as she remembered this and then looked down at Robert.

Some might consider it too soon, but she suspected that she was already pregnant with their second child, and had told Luke so only this morning.

'What? Already?'

'What do you mean, already?' she had teased. 'It only takes one successful attempt, as we both know.'

Luke had smiled, giving her a deeply sensual look that had made her both laugh and colour up a bit. 'Of course, if you would like to be sure...' he had said as he advanced towards her.

'Luke!' Suzy had protested as he had removed the bathrobe she had been wearing and taken her in his arms. 'Luke, we've got guests,' she had reminded him mock primly. 'And they will be waiting for their breakfast.'

'Let them wait,' he had murmured, finding the exact

spot at the side of her neck where the touch of his lips always reduced her to hungry need.

'It's Robert's christening today,' she had added, several seconds later, but without any real urgency in her voice.

'Mmm...so it is,' he had replied.

If any of their guests had found it odd that they should arrive at the breakfast table rather later than planned none of them had been impolite enough to say so, but Suzy thought she had caught Sir Peter Verey's fiancée, Anne, focusing on her thoughtfully.

She liked Anne, and thought she would make Sir Peter a good wife and the children an excellent stepmother. Already she was building rapport with them, and it made Suzy smile to hear how many times Lucy mentioned her name when she was talking to her.

The sun was shining and their guests were now filing into the old church.

Robert woke up and looked around with interest.

He was very much his father's son, Suzy reflected—and not just in the way he looked. He had Luke's sometimes imperious and questioning manner, even at six months old.

As they followed their guests into the church Luke took Robert from her, cradling him expertly. And as she watched them Suzy saw father and son exchange a knowing male-to-male look.

Her heart flooded with emotion and instinctively she moved closer to Luke. She was so happy, so blessed, so loved.

Luke was her other half and she his. Deep down

inside herself Suzy knew that they had been fated to meet. Fated to meet one another and fated to love one another.

They were soul mates.

In Luke's arms Robert smiled up at his father, and Suzy touched her stomach gently.

A CONVENIENT
HUSBAND

by

Kim Lawrence

Kim Lawrence lives on a farm in rural Anglesey. She runs two miles daily and finds this an excellent opportunity to unwind and seek inspiration for her writing! It also helps her keep up with her husband, two active sons, and the various stray animals which have adopted them. Always a fanatical consumer of fiction, she is now equally enthusiastic about writing. She loves a happy ending!

Don't miss Kim Lawrence's exciting new novel *The Demetrios Bridal Bargain*, out in December 2007 from Mills & Boon® Modern™.

CHAPTER ONE

'TOMORROW…? So soon…?'

Tess Trelawny closed her eyes tight in denial and willed herself to wake up from this nightmare. Minor—no, *major* flaw in this plan: she already was awake, awake and shaking as if she had a fever. Along with the deluge of adrenalin, blind, gut-twisting panic raced through her body. The leaden hand she lifted to her throbbing head was trembling and icily cold.

Chloe chose not to respond to the pulsating note of entreaty in her aunt's voice. She often ignored things which made her feel uncomfortable; besides, there was no reason for her to feel guilty. If Tess got awkward, Ian would back her up. Tess would listen to him; everyone did. He was the smartest person she'd ever met…and he was hers… A dreamily content smile curved her collagen-enhanced, red-painted lips…

'Ian is just *dying* to meet dear little Benjy.' Her lips tightened in exasperation as the pedicurist began to paint her toenails. 'Hold on a sec, Aunty Tess…'

The prefix invariably made Tess feel as if a generation separated her from her elder sister's only child, not a mere seven years. Now was no exception.

'This *stupid* girl is using the wrong colour.'

Tess could hear the muffled sounds over the phone as Chloe paused long enough to sharply inform the unfortunate young woman attending her that she had no intention of being seen with a shade that was so sadly dated.

'I was wondering,' Chloe continued once she'd satisfied herself the right shade was being applied to her toes. 'Has he got more hair these days?'

5

The question bewildered Tess. 'Why do you ask?'

'Well, you keep saying it's going to grow!' Chloe responded in an ill-used tone that implied Tess had been heartlessly leading her on. 'I mean, those little wispy bits are not very attractive, are they?' she elaborated sulkily. 'And they look gingery.' Her worried tone implied there were few things in life worse than a red-headed child.

Tess closed her eyes and took a deep breath…sometimes she felt the unworthy desire to shake her beautiful niece until her white even teeth rattled.

'Yes, Chloe,' she replied woodenly. 'Ben does have some hair now, and you'll be pleased to hear it's a gorgeous strawberry blonde.'

'You mean sandy…?'

'No, I mean strawberry blonde.'

'That's excellent,' came the relieved reply. 'And, Aunty Tess, for God's sake dress him in something half decent. How about that nice little outfit I sent from Milan…?'

Chloe's fleeting visits had always been infrequent, but during the last few months her acting career had taken off with several small but well received film roles, and the visits had become almost non-existent.

Tess was guiltily aware that she should have remonstrated with the younger girl, but the truth was life was easier without the stress and disruption of Chloe's visits. The problem was her niece resented not being the centre of attention and she didn't like to share that attention with anyone—not even a baby.

'He grew out of it.'

'Oh, pity…at least make sure he's not covered in jam or anything!' Chloe found it hard to accept that spotless, freshly scrubbed and sweet smelling wasn't the normal state of babies. 'I want him to make a good impression on Ian.'

If she were here right now, so help me, I'd strangle her! Tess's voice shook with suppressed outrage as she responded. 'This isn't an audition, Chloe.'

'No, this is the start of the rest of my life!' came back the dramatic, throbbing response. To Tess's uncharitable ears it sounded as though she were practising a line from her latest part. Abruptly Chloe's tone changed. 'Must dash, Aunty Tess...I've got a yoga class in half an hour, and I really can't miss it. You should try it yourself—I've really attained an inner harmony you wouldn't believe. See you soon!' The phone line went dead.

Tess didn't think she'd ever feel harmony, inner or otherwise, again as she responded urgently to the stomach-churning nausea and dashed up the narrow flight of stairs two at a time to reach the bathroom. When her stomach was quite empty she splashed her face with cold water. The face that looked back at her from the mirror was waxily pale, dominated by a pair of wide green eyes. The desperation and panic she felt was clearly reflected in those haunted emerald depths, and, even though speaking to Chloe always made her feel middle-aged, the person staring back at her looked a lot younger than her *nearly* thirty years.

Her feet automatically took her to the half-open door of the smaller of the two bedrooms in the cottage. Quietly she went inside. The curtains were drawn against the afternoon sunlight. She went to stand silently by the cot in which a small figure was taking his afternoon nap. He was dressed in dungarees—he was sound asleep.

The figure's ruffled blonde hair lay in spiky tufts over his little head. His face was rosily tinged and his long eyelashes lay dark against the full curve of his infant cheek.

Tess closed her eyes and a single tear slid down her cheek. Not so very long ago if anyone had told the dedicated career girl she had been that it was possible to love anyone so much it hurt—with the possible exception of George Clooney—she'd have laughed. But she did; she loved this little boy with all her heart and soul. Part of her wanted to bundle him up and run away somewhere safe, somewhere Chloe would never find them.

The sleeping figure opened his eyes, saw Tess and, with a sleepy smile, closed them again. Tess held the noisy sobs in check until she had stumbled out of the room.

The village was in total darkness as Rafe Farrar drove towards the stone manor house tucked behind its high walls on the outskirts of this picturesque little hamlet. A hamlet that was just far enough away from the popular stretch of coast to avoid exploitation and remain relatively unspoilt and sleepy.

He'd spent what most people would consider his idyllic childhood here. Since the death of his elder brother, Alec, and their father's enforced retreat to the Riviera, the only permanent occupant of the Farrar family home was his grandfather, an elderly but far from frail individual who was not adapting well to his belated retirement from the world of international banking. His relationship with his grandfather being what it was, Rafe could be sure of a *tepid* welcome from the old man, who didn't consider the black sheep of the family warranted breaking out the fatted calf for.

When he'd made the arrangements for this duty visit he hadn't planned on making the journey alone; a third party to act as buffer zone was always helpful when he and the old man came face to face. In this instance he'd been hoping to introduce the third party as his future wife. This had always been a situation with explosive possibilities, especially when his grandparent had learnt this future bride would have to rid herself of a husband before she made her second trip to the altar. At least he didn't have that problem now.

Thinking about the reason for his solitary state—for an individual not given to brooding or self-pity, he was catching on fast—kept the mobile curve of Rafe's sensual lips in a firm thin line. He was normally a scrupulously careful driver, but his dark embittered gaze did not on this occasion flicker towards the speedometer as his big powerful motor sped grimly through the narrow silent main street.

'Hell!' His language went rapidly downhill from this point as, with a display of reflexes that bordered on the supernatural, he only hit the dog that had darted out in front of him a glancing blow.

Still cursing, he leapt from the car, performing this simple task with the athletic fluidity that typified all his movements. He noticed immediately that his front headlight had not escaped as lightly as the animal. He kicked aside the broken glass that surrounded the tree he'd collided with. His unbroken headlight picked up the mongrel that lay trembling on the grass verge.

'All right, boy,' he crooned in a firm but soothing voice. With the careless confidence of someone who had never experienced a moment's nervousness with any animal—and this one was big and powerful—Rafe's capable hands moved gently over the animal's spare frame. The dog endured his examination passively. Rafe was no expert but it seemed likely to him that the animal was suffering from shock rather than anything more immediately life-threatening.

'Looks like this was your lucky night, mate.' Rafe scratched the dog, who gazed up at him with slavish adoration, beneath one ear. 'That makes one of us,' he added bitterly. He didn't need to look at the tag on the mutt's collar to work out where this jaywalker originated from.

This wasn't the sort of animal most people would consider worth a broken headlight. This was the sort of animal that looked mean, the sort of animal that was left behind at the animal shelter when all the more appealing ones had been selected. His off-white tatty coat didn't gleam, it was covered in an interlaced network of old scars; then there was the mega-bad case of canine halitosis. Given all this, there was only one person this animal *could* belong to. Even when they'd been kids she'd always managed to pick up every waif and stray within a ten-mile radius!

Trying not to think about what was happening to his pale leather upholstery, Rafe laid the old dog out on the back seat. Climbing back into the car, he headed in the direction of the picture-postcard cottage Tess Trelawny had inherited from her grandmother, old Agnes Trelawny, four years back.

Even if the lights hadn't been unexpectedly on in the cottage Rafe would have had no qualms about waking Tess up. Actually he welcomed the fact he had a legitimate reason to yell at someone—tonight he *really* wanted to yell! And with Tess he didn't have to fret about delicate female sensitivities; she was as tough as old boots and well able to give as good as she got. The more he thought about it, the happier he felt about his enforced detour.

Arms full of damp, smelly dog, he gave the kitchen door a belligerent kick. It opened of its own accord with a horror-movie series of loud creaks.

'Your door needs oiling,' he announced, stepping over the well-lit threshold.

It wasn't just the bright light that made him blink and recoil in shock, it was the disordered state of the room. For some reason the entire contents of the kitchen cupboards seemed to be stacked in haphazard piles all around the room.

'My God!' he ejaculated. 'Has there been a break-in?' He voiced the first most likely possibility that came to mind.

The shortish, slim figure, dressed incongruously in a cotton jersey nightshirt and yellow rubber gloves—a fashion statement this ensemble was not—ignored this question completely.

Tess rose in some agitation from her crouched position in front of one of the empty kitchen cupboards and rushed forward.

'Baggins!' she shrieked huskily. 'What have you done to him?' she demanded indignantly of Rafe.

'Why didn't you lock the door?' he enquired with a censorious frown. 'I could have been anyone!'

Tess spared her caller a brief unfriendly glare before her attention returned to the dog. 'But you turned out to be you. *Aren't I the lucky one?*' she drawled.

'Quit that!' he rapped out sternly as she tried to forcibly transfer the animal from his arms to her skinny ones. 'He's too heavy for you. Besides, the miserable, misbegotten hound is quite capable of walking under his own steam.'

To demonstrate this he placed the animal on the floor. 'I just didn't want to risk him sloping off again and killing some poor unsuspecting motorist.' He pointedly snapped shut the door behind him.

'Oh!' Tess's anxiety retreated slightly as Baggins began to behave like the puppy he no longer was. 'I fixed the fence, only he's started burrowing under it. You hit him with that flashy car of yours, I suppose?' Her full lips pursed in disapproval.

'Barely.' He noticed that Tess's narrow feet were bare too. Like the rest of her they were small, and though she was skinny it wasn't a matchstick, angular sort of skinniness, more a pleasing, rounded, supple svelteness...*all over*.

Rafe was unprepared for the mental postscript, only once the thought was out there it seemed natural to speculate on what was underneath the skimpy shirt thing. He cleared his throat and managed to drag his wayward thoughts to a slightly less tacky level—it wasn't thinking about sex that bothered him, it was thinking about sex and Tess simultaneously!

'Spare me chapter and verse on your lightning reflexes...*please*.'

Rafe, who was working up a cold sweat getting other reflexes under control, smiled grimly, displaying a set of perfect white teeth. 'Your gratitude for my sacrifice is duly noted.'

'What sacrifice?'

'One smashed headlight, and, yes, thanks for your concern, I did escape uninjured.' Testosterone surge firmly in check, Rafe found to his intense relief he could look her in the eye and see Tess, his friend, not Tess, a woman. It was a well-known fact that rejection could make a man act and think weird.

'I can see that for myself.'

'Why am I getting the distinct impression you'd have preferred it if I was sporting the odd broken bone or three?' he mused wryly. 'If this is the sort of welcome your guests usually receive, I'm surprised you get any.'

'I might be happier if I didn't,' she snarled.

'Thinking of becoming a recluse, are we?'

'You may be lord of the manor and the product of generations of in-breeding, but isn't the royal *we* a bit over the top, even for you?'

'I wasn't actually referring to myself.' He flexed his shoulders and rotated his head slowly to ease the tension in his neck. 'But what's a bit of poetic licence between friends?' Another shrug. 'And that was a *great* line.'

This drew a rueful laugh from Tess. 'It was, wasn't it?'

'Before you fling any more stones, try and remember, angel, that beneath this strong, manly *inbred* exterior there lurks a sensitive soul.' He took Tess's hand and planted it with a slap against his chest. 'See, I'm flesh and blood.'

Tess couldn't feel any evidence of a soul, but she could feel his body heat and the slow, steady beat of his heart. She stared at her own fingers splayed out against his shirt for what seemed like a long time; it was a strangely enervating experience to stand there like that. The distant buzzing in her head got closer. Feeling slightly dizzy, even a little confused, she lifted her eyes to his face...it swam dizzily out of focus.

Rafe looked down into her wide-spaced jewel-bright eyes and he hastily removed his fingers from around her wrist. Her hand fell bonelessly to her side.

He cleared his throat. 'And, incidentally, you may not be aware of the difference, but there is a big one between class and flash.'

'Toys for boys.' I really should have eaten something, she decided, lifting a worried hand to her gently spinning head.

'Insult my car, insult me.'

She gave a relieved sigh and grinned; she was no longer seeing him through soft focus. 'I'd prefer to insult you.'

'I thought you were.'

Tess gave a concessionary shrug—he was actually taking her nastiness pretty well, which made her feel even more guilty than she already did. She knew perfectly well that it was Chloe she wanted to yell at…only she wasn't here and Rafe was… Just as well he had a broad back—very broad, as it happened, she mused, her eyes sliding briefly to the impressive muscular solidity of his powerful shoulders. Her empty stomach squirmed uncomfortably.

'Well, Baggins doesn't seem to be holding a grudge,' she admitted. The undiscriminating animal's juvenile performance was obviously for Rafe's benefit, not her own. 'You naughty, naughty boy,' she clucked lovingly.

Rafe didn't make the mistake of thinking her affectionate scolding was meant for him. 'You always did have a novel approach to discipline, Tess,' he observed drily.

Tess sniffed. 'I'm glad *I'm* not a blustering bully,' she retaliated. 'I saw you being incredibly horrid to that poor man last night.'

'I thought you didn't have a telly. Not in keeping with your green, eco-friendly, lentil-eating, brown-rice lifestyle…?'

His amused scorn really got under her skin. How dared he look down his autocratic nose at her? It obviously hadn't occurred to him that she might actually miss the odd trip to a concert or the theatre that had once been an important part of her life.

'*Gran* didn't have a telly, I have a small portable, and just because I grow vegetables I resent the implication I've turned into one,' she told him tartly. 'Besides, you've room to talk. At least when I do things it's out of personal conviction.' Or in this case a desire to cut down on the grocery bill—fresh organic vegetables cost the earth to buy!

'Meaning I don't…?'

'Well, you didn't show much interest in saving the planet before *Nicola*.' Nicola, the environmental activist, had been one of Rafe's first serious girlfriends. Along with strong convictions Nicola had possessed—in common with all the girlfriends who had followed her—endless legs, a great body and long, flowing blonde hair. 'You haven't forgotten her, have you?'

Nicola had been a long time ago and in point of fact his recall was a little hazy.

'A man doesn't forget a girl like Nicola.' He gave a lecherous grin just in case she'd missed the point—Tess hadn't. 'That girl had boundless enthusiasm.'

Not to mention a D cup had she chosen to wear a bra, Tess recalled cynically. 'Some might call it fanaticism.'

She was distracted from her theme when at that moment Baggins' tail caught a pile of plates and sent the top one spinning towards the floor. Rafe neatly caught it just before impact.

'This dog's a liability,' he grunted.

'Insult me, insult my dog,' she responded, mimicking his earlier retort. 'Perhaps,' she fretted anxiously, 'I should call the vet just to be absolutely sure…?' She ran an exploratory hand over the dog's back.

'If he was a horse he'd be dog meat.'

'Not if he was my horse.'

'You sentimental old thing, you.'

'That's rich coming from someone who has his first childhood pony munching happily away in the lap of luxury.'

'Reasonable comfort,' he modified. There was a twinkle in Rafe's eyes as he acknowledged her pot-shot with a rueful grin. 'If you're really worried about the mutt, I'm sure the worthy Andrew would be happy to make a house call.'

Rafe wasn't up to speed with the status of their romance,

but it was well known locally that the middle-aged veterinarian had been sniffing after Tess since he'd bought into the local practice. Even though his acquaintance with that individual had been brief, Rafe didn't doubt that his estimation of the man as dull, pompous and self-righteous was essentially correct.

Tess flushed at the snide comment and her spine grew defensively rigid. 'Didn't you know, Andrew sold the practice? He's moved up north.' She knew what Rafe, like everyone else, thought. If he *dared* offer her any false sympathy…

Why did everyone automatically assume that because she was single, female and just about on the right side of thirty she had to be gagging for the romantic attentions of any half-decent male in the vicinity? Admittedly, half-decent males were thin on the ground, and Andrew had been pleasant company, but even though the only thing they'd shared had been the odd meal the entire neighbourhood, if sly comments and knowing looks were anything to go by, had assumed Tess had been sharing a lot more with him.

Rafe's upper lip curled. 'I always thought he was slimy,' he drawled insultingly.

'If it's any comfort, he didn't like you much either.'

Rafe patted the fawning animal. 'He's new…?'

'So are most things since you last honoured us with your presence.'

'You're still the same.'

Tess wasn't flattered; she didn't think she was meant to be. 'He's pretty second-hand, actually. He was Mr Pettifer's dog—you remember him…?'

Rafe nodded, dimly recalling a frail octogenarian.

'Nobody wanted him.'

'What a surprise!' He couldn't imagine there were many households that would be likely to welcome this ugly brute.

Exasperated, Tess pushed the heavy fringe of chestnut hair, which was overdue a trim, impatiently from her eyes and focused on Rafe's sternly handsome face.

'He's got a lovely nature.'

'And bad breath.'

'Well, Ben loves him.' From the way she said it he could tell that, as far as she was concerned, there was no greater recommendation.

She might be wrong—she didn't see Rafe much these days—but there seemed to be something a bit different about him tonight. She couldn't quite put her finger on it...

'Have you been drinking?' she speculated out loud.

'Not yet,' he told her with a jarring, reckless kind of laugh. 'Just the thing!' he announced, swooping on a dusty bottle from the wine rack. His dark eyes scanned the label. 'Elderberry, my favourite. Corkscrew...?' he added imperiously, holding out his hand expectantly.

Gran's elderberry! She now knew for sure that something was up! In other circumstances it might have nagged him to tell her what it was. Only at that moment she didn't much care what was bothering him, she just wanted him out of her hair so she could think...not that that had got her anywhere so far, she was reluctantly forced to acknowledge.

'*You're* not proposing to expose your discerning taste buds to gran's home-made wine?' she mocked.

'Not alone.'

'A tempting invitation, but it's three o'clock in the morning,' she reminded him, automatically consulting her bare wrist to confirm this statement and realising she wasn't wearing her wrist-watch. Come to think of it, she wasn't wearing much, she acknowledged uncomfortably, pulling fretfully at the hem of her washed-out cotton nightshirt.

She had a distinct recollection of waving her arms around wildly, revealing in the process God knew what! Still, it was only Rafe and it wasn't likely he'd turn a hair if he'd walked in to find her stark naked!

Three a.m. or not, Rafe, of course, was looking as tiresomely perfect as ever. It went without saying that his outfit was tasteful and expensive. It consisted of dark olive trousers and a lightweight knitted polo shirt—not that the details really mattered, not when you were at least six feet four, possessed an athletic, broad-shouldered, skinny-hipped, long-legged body, and went around projecting the sort of brooding sensuality that made females more than willing to overlook the fact you had a face that wasn't strictly pretty. Strong, attractive and interesting, yes…pretty…no.

'I know what time it is, I was kind of wondering about you…' His gaze moved rather pointedly over the disarray in the room. 'Do you often get the urge to spring-clean in the wee small hours, Tess?'

'I couldn't sleep,' she explained defensively, peeling off the yellow rubber gloves and throwing them on the draining-board.

She didn't much care if Rafe thought her eccentric, bordering on loopy; she didn't much care what Rafe thought at all these days. In her opinion success had not changed Rafe for the better. He'd been a nice, if irritating kid when he'd been two years younger than her.

She supposed he still must be two years younger, time being what it was, only the intervening years seemed to have swallowed up the two-year gap and had deprived her of the comfortable feeling of superiority that a few extra months gave you as a child.

Superiority wasn't something people around Rafe were likely to feel, she mused. He was one of those rare people folk automatically turned to for leadership—not that she classed herself as one of those mesmerised sheep who hung on his every word.

Still, although she often teased him about his old family name, he wasn't like the rest of the Farrars who were a snooty lot, firmly rooted in the dark ages. Traditionally— they were *big* on tradition—the younger son entered the military and the elder worked his way up through the echelons of the merchant bank which had been founded by some long-dead Farrar.

His elder brother Alec had obligingly entered the bank, even though as far as Tess could see the only interest he'd had in money had been spending it. She didn't suppose that his family had been particularly surprised when Rafe hadn't meekly co-operated with their plans for him. Since he'd been expelled from the prestigious boarding-school that generations of Farrars had attended they'd expected the worst of him and he'd usually fulfilled their expectations.

He hadn't even obliged them and turned into a worthless bum as had been confidently predicted. He'd worked his way up, quite rapidly as it happened, on the payroll of a national daily. He'd made a favourable impression there, but it was working as the anchor of a prestigious current affairs programme that had really made his name.

The job was tailor-made for Rafe. He wasn't aggressive or hostile; he didn't need to be. Rafe had the rare ability of being able to charm honest answers from the wiliest of politicians. He made it look so easy that not everyone appreciated the skill of his technique, or realised how much grinding background research he did to back up those deceptively casual questions.

Such was his reputation that people in public life were virtually queuing up to be interviewed by him, all no doubt convinced that they were too sharp to be lulled into a false sense of security. Without decrying his undoubted abilities, Tess cynically suspected that being incredibly photogenic had something to do with him achieving an almost cult-like status overnight.

'I think better when I keep busy,' she explained glibly. Tonight, it would seem, was the exception to that rule. Fresh panic clawed deep in her belly as she realised afresh that there was no magical solution to her dilemma.

Rafe's narrowed gaze objectively noted the blotchy puffiness under her wide-spaced green eyes. She had that pale, almost translucent type of skin that tended to reflect her every mood, not to mention every tear! He recalled how impossibly fragile her wrist had felt when he'd caught hold of her hand.

'I promise I won't tell you things will get better—they probably won't.'

Tell me something I didn't already know! 'You always were a little ray of sunshine, but the depressive traits are new.'

'I'm a realist, angel. Life sucks…' He pulled the cork on the bottle and glugged an ample amount into a stray mug.

'I'm so glad you stopped by, I feel better already.' Absent-mindedly she accepted the mug he handed her. 'This is actually rather nice,' she announced with some surprise, before taking another, less tentative sip of her grandmother's famous wine—famous at least within the narrow precincts of this parish and then for its potency rather than its delicate bouquet.

Rafe shuddered as he followed suit and decided not to disillusion her. 'What's happened to you that's so bad?' he enquired carelessly, refilling his mug.

'Still the same!' It gave her a feeling of perverse pleasure to see her sharp, sarcastic tone ignite a spark of irritation in his dark eyes. 'You always did have to go one better than everyone else, didn't you? You even have to be miserable on a grand scale!' There was a warm glow in the pit of Tess's empty stomach; she hadn't been able to eat a thing since that awful phone call from Chloe.

'Meaning…?'

'Meaning my simple life can't possibly be expected to reach the supreme highs and hopeless depths of yours.'

Rafe's dark brows rose to his equally dark hairline. 'You got all that from a simple, *what's up*?'

'You asked, but you weren't really interested!' she accused, waving her mug in front of him for a refill. 'But then why should you be?'

'I thought we were friends, Tess.'

'We were friends when we were ten and eight respectively,' she corrected, injecting sharp scorn into her observation. 'Actually, I didn't think you went in much for slumming these days, Rafe.'

There was just enough truth in her words to make him feel uncomfortable and just enough unfairness to make him feel resentful. Before she'd had the baby and left behind her city lifestyle they'd got together pretty frequently. Things being the way they were, he wasn't likely to visit home often and after the first few refusals he'd stopped inviting Tess up to town.

'You moved away too,' he reminded her.

'I came back.' And that was the crux of the matter. When she'd been a driven, goal-orientated career woman they'd still had common ground, but that common ground had vanished when her life had become baby-orientated. *She* felt her life was pretty fulfilling, but she wasn't so naive as to expect others, including Rafe, to share her interest in Ben's teething problems!

It was on the tip of Rafe's tongue to ungallantly remind her that decision hadn't been initiated entirely by a nostalgia for the rural idyll of their childhood. He restrained himself and instead poked a finger against his own substantial chest.

'What do you call this, a hologram?'

'I call it visiting royalty.' She performed a low mocking bow, blissfully unaware that the gaping neck of her loose nightshirt gave him an excellent view of her cleavage and more than a hint of rosy nipples.

'Got the latest girlfriend in tow again? Going to impress her with the family crypt or maybe the family ghost?'

Her soft, teasing chuckle suddenly emerged as she misread the reason for the dark tell-tale stain across the angle of his high cheekbones.

'Or is that the problem—she *isn't* here? A frustrated libido would explain why you stalked in here with a chip a mile wide on your shoulder. Smouldering like something out of a Greek tragedy…I'm right, aren't I? The girlfriend couldn't or *wouldn't* come…?' she speculated shrewdly.

At least theorising insensitively about someone else's problems stopped her thinking—if only in the short term—about her own!

Now he had a pretty good idea what was under the shirt thing it was even less easy to stop thinking about it. 'Is it that obvious I've been flung aside?' he bit back.

'Like an old sock?' she chipped in helpfully.

There didn't seem much point indulging Rafe's inclinations towards drama; she'd had enough of that with Chloe. He thought *his* life was a mess, he should try wearing her shoes—not that they'd fit, she conceded, comparing his large, expensively shod feet with her own size fours.

It was hard to feel sympathetic when the worst thing likely to happen to Rafe Farrar was a bad haircut! She gave his thick, healthily shining dark hair an extra-resentful glare.

'It didn't take a psychic to see you came here spoiling for a fight!'

Despite his growing anger, Rafe couldn't help but laugh at the irony of her accusation. 'I knocked on the right door, then, didn't I?'

'You didn't knock, you just barged in…' Quite as abruptly as it had arisen, the aggression drained from Tess. Feeling weak, she gave a deep, shuddering sigh. 'Maybe I just got tired of being patronised…? Has someone *really* given you the push?' Her wondering smile was wry. It hardly seemed credible.

'You find that possibility amusing?'

She found the possibility incredible. 'You must admit that it does have a certain novelty value. Look on the bright side…'

'I can't guarantee I won't throttle you if you go into a Pollyanna routine,' he warned darkly.

'I'm trembling.'

Rafe's jaw tightened as he encountered the sparkling

mockery in her eyes. He found himself grimly contemplating how hard it would be to make her tremble for real…and he wasn't thinking of scare tactics! What he was thinking of scared him a little, though. If he was going to vent his frustration on anyone, it couldn't be Tess!

'It might actually do you some good,' she mused thoughtfully. 'You're way overdue a dose of humility,' she explained frankly.

Looking at him properly for the first time, Tess saw that he actually did look pretty haggard in a handsome, vital sort of way. She couldn't recall ever seeing that hard light in his eyes before. The price of partying at all the right night spots?

'Then I'll give you a real laugh, shall I?' he flung the words angrily at her. 'The woman I wanted to spend the rest of my life with—have children with—has decided not to leave her husband!'

Tess's startled gasp was audible in the short, tense silence that followed his words.

'Does that have the required degree of character-enhancing humility to suit you?'

CHAPTER TWO

'You were going out with a *married* woman?' Tess didn't know what made her feel most uncomfortable: the part that Rafe had been messing with a married woman, or the part that said he'd been contemplating wedding bells and babies. 'You want to have *babies*…?'

Rafe, regretting his unusual episode of soul-baring the instant the self-pitying words emerged from his lips, dragged an angry hand through his hair as Tess, after visibly recoiling from him as though he had a particularly nasty disease, started staring at him with the expression she obviously reserved for moral degenerates. He resisted the impulse to unkindly point out she was no saint herself!

'I don't think I've got the hips for it.' He didn't understand why this sarcastic response should make her flinch. 'And just for the record I didn't know she was married until it was too late.' He didn't know why the hell he was explaining himself to her.

'Too late for what?'

Rafe scowled at her dogged persistence. 'Too late not to fall in love!' he bellowed.

He saw her soft wide lips quiver and a misty expression drift over her almost pretty features. Oh, God, not sympathy…*please*…he thought with a nauseated grimace.

'What are you doing?'

'I need to sit down, and from the look of you so do you.'

Tess looked askance at the guiding hand on her arm but decided not to object; she found that she did need to sit down too. She made no immediate connection between the half-empty mug of wine still clutched in her hand and the shaky quality of her knees.

23

Rafe was relieved to find that Tess's spring-cleaning efforts hadn't extended as far as the small oak-beamed sitting room. He pushed a sleeping cat off the overstuffed chintzy sofa and sat down with a grunt. The grunt became a pained yelp as he quickly leapt up. A quick search behind the cushion recovered the item responsible for his bruised dignity.

He held aloft the culprit, a battered-looking three-wheeled tractor.

'I searched everywhere for that earlier,' Tess choked thickly, taking the toy from his unresisting fingers and nursing it against her chest.

'Are you *crying*...?' Rafe wondered suspiciously. He didn't associate feminine tears or even more obviously feminine bosoms, of which he'd had that unexpected eyeful, with Tess, and he was getting both tonight. It intensified that vague feeling of discomfort.

Tess sharply turned her slender back on him and stowed the toy away in an overflowing, brightly painted toy chest tucked in the corner of the room. Scrubbing her knuckles across her damp cheeks, she turned back.

'What if I am?' she growled mutinously.

A nasty thought occurred to Rafe. 'Ben is all right, isn't he?' he asked sharply. A picture of a dribbly baby came into his head and he felt an unexpected twinge of affection. 'I mean, he's not ill or anything...?'

It occurred to him, as it perhaps should have done sooner if he was the friend he claimed to be, that it must be hard bringing up a baby alone. He couldn't be a babe in arms any longer, he must be—what? One...more, even...?

'Ben's fine...asleep upstairs.' The tears were starting to flow again and there was zilch she could do about it, so Tess abandoned her attempt at pretence of being normal or in control—of her tears ducts, her life...anything!

'Something's wrong, though.'

'You don't usually state the obvious,' she croaked.

Rafe gave an indulgent sigh. 'You'd better tell me.'

'Why bother?' she asked with a wild little laugh. 'You can't do anything!'

'Oh, ye of little faith.'

'Nobody can,' she insisted bleakly. The alcohol had broken down all the defensive walls she'd built up with a resounding bang. Without lifting her head to look at him, she laid it against the wide expanse of chest that was suddenly conveniently close to hand. Eyes tight closed, hardly aware of what she was doing, she brought her fist down once, twice, three times hard against his shoulder.

At some deep subconscious level that dealt with things beyond her immediate misery her brain was storing irrelevant information like the level of hard toughness in his body and the nice, musky, warm scent that rose from his skin.

'I can't bear to lose him. I just can't bear it, Rafe!' she sobbed in a tortured whisper.

Her distress made him feel helpless. Helpless and a rat! Tess was putting herself quite literally in his hands, displaying a trust and confidence she had every right to expect if he was any sort of friend. It made the response of his body to the soft, fragrant female frame plastered against it all the more of a betrayal!

'Lose who? Your vet...?' he prompted. He took her by the shoulders and gave her an urgent little shake.

'You can't lose what you never had and furthermore don't want! Don't you ever listen?' she demanded hotly.

'Then who or what have you lost?'

'Lost my inhibitions—it must be the wine.'

'Stop laughing.'

Fine! If he preferred tears, he could have them! 'Lose Ben!'

'You're not going to lose Ben,' he soothed confidently.

Rafe always did think he knew everything—well, not this time! Angrily she lifted her head; tears sparkled on the ends of her spiky dark eyelashes.

'I am. Chloe wants him!' she wailed.

Rafe looked at her blankly. She wasn't making sense at all...maybe she had an even lower tolerance for alcohol than he'd thought.

'I know Chloe gets what she wants,' he observed drily, 'but on this occasion I don't think you're obliged to say yes. You really shouldn't drink, Tess...'

'You don't understand!'

Rafe shook his head and didn't dispute her claim as haunted, anguish-filled emerald eyes fixed once more on his face.

'I'm not Ben's mother, Chloe is...' Sobbing pitifully, she collapsed once more against Rafe's chest, leaving him to digest the incredible information she'd just hit him with.

If it was true, and he couldn't for the life of him think why she'd lie about something like that, it was a hell of a lot to take in.

When Tess had taken leave of absence from her job as a high-powered commodities trader, he'd been as shocked as her other friends when she'd returned afterwards complete with a baby. Compared to that, the shock had been relatively mild when she'd walked away from the job she'd loved after a brief, unsuccessful attempt to combine motherhood with a demanding career and moved into the cottage she'd inherited from her grandmother.

Now she was saying she wasn't Ben's mother! She wasn't anyone's mother!

It was a good ten minutes before Tess was capable of continuing their discussion. Looking at her stubborn, closed-in expression as she sat with primly folded arms in the old rocking-chair, Rafe could see that talking to him was the last thing she wanted to do.

'Why?'

'Morgan and Edward were out of the country, some jungle or other,' Tess recalled dully, speaking of her elder sister and brother-in-law who were both brilliant, but unworldly palaeontologists of international renown. They might be the first people everybody thought of consulting when a prehistoric skull was unearthed, but when it came to a pregnant daughter they wouldn't have been high on anybody's list.

'Besides which they would have been worse than useless even if they had been around.'

Tess chose to ignore this accurate summing-up. 'Chloe was five months gone before she realised and absolutely distraught when she was told it was too late to...' Tess paused and looked self-consciously uncomfortable.

'She wanted to be rid of it.' Rafe shrugged. 'That figures. She always was a selfish, spoilt brat.'

Honesty prevented Tess disputing this cruel assessment. Her elder sister and her husband always had either indulged or ignored their only child, and the product of this upbringing had turned into a stunningly beautiful but extremely self-absorbed young woman.

'A *scared* spoilt brat back then,' Tess snapped sharply. 'She didn't want anyone to know about it; she made me promise. So I took her away.'

'Isn't that a bit...I don't know, Victorian melodrama...?'

'You've not the faintest idea of how weird she was acting.' Tess had been genuinely worried that Chloe might have done something drastic. 'I thought a change of scene, away from people that knew her, might help. I imagined,' she recalled, 'that after the birth she'd...'

'Be overcome by maternal instincts.' Rafe gave a scornful snort.

'People are,' Tess retorted indignantly.

'A classic case of optimism overcoming what's right under your nose. Chloe was never going to give up partying to stay at home and baby-sit. I can't believe you were that stupid.'

'Why?' she asked, roused to anger by his superior, condescending attitude. It was easy for him to condemn—he hadn't been there; he couldn't possibly understand what it had been like. 'You don't usually have any problem believing I'm an idiot!' She shook her head miserably.

'I don't know why I'm even telling you all this. It won't make any difference. The fact is, Chloe is his mother and if she wants him there's nothing, short of skipping the country, that I can do about it! I wish now I'd adopted him legally myself when she suggested it,' she ended on a bleak note of self-condemnation.

'Don't worry,' she added, slanting him a small, bitter smile. 'I haven't got the cash to skip the country.'

That was another thing that had been nagging away at him. Tess had lived a starkly simple life since she'd moved here, she owned this place outright, had no debts that he was aware of, and she must have made a tidy pile during her brief but successful career. Yet this place needed a lick of paint. In fact it needed a lot of things—not big things, but… And when had she stopped running a car? He couldn't remember; it hadn't seemed important at the time. But covering the primaries in the States had been? In light of Tess's distress there was a big question mark hanging over his priorities.

'I could lend it to you.'

Just as well he didn't know how tempting she found his offer, even though she knew it was meant as a joke. '"Neither a borrower nor a lender be,"' she quoted sadly.

'I can't believe you've fooled everyone all this time.' Rafe was looking at her as though he were seeing her for the first time. It had taken him long enough to get his head around the idea that she was a mother—now he'd have to unlearn something that had been surprisingly hard for him to accept in the first place.

'It wasn't intentional, it just sort of happened,' she replied, knowing her explanation sounded lame.

'You didn't just sort of *happen* to give up a great job you loved. You didn't just sort of *happen* to spend over a year of your life bringing up someone else's child.'

'I forgot that sometimes,' she admitted. 'That he wasn't really mine,' she explained self-consciously. 'And I know what I did must seem a bit surreal to you now, but it was never meant to be a permanent solution. Chloe didn't want Ben, she wanted to give him up, have him adopted. It seemed so awfully final. You hear about women who have given up their babies suffering, never coming to terms with the regret.

'I didn't want that to be Chloe ten years down the line. I thought it was only a matter of time before she realised, and then I suppose as time went on I lost sight of the fact I was just a stopgap.' With a choked sound she buried her face in her shaking hands. 'I was right, wasn't I? She has realised that she wants him. Only it's been so long I...'

'God, Tess!' Rafe thundered, banging his fist angrily down on a blameless bureau. A dozen images he didn't even know he'd retained of Tess with the baby drifted through his mind—she loved that kid and he loved her. Mother or no mother, they should be together. 'She can't just take him away from you!'

Tess's lips, almost bloodless in her pale face, quivered. The eyes that met his were tragic. 'Yes, Rafe, yes, she can.'

'Don't give me all that martyr stuff, Tess. You don't actually believe it's in Ben's best interests to live with Chloe, do you?' he grated incredulously. 'You know Chloe—the novelty will wear off within a couple of months and where will that leave Ben?' he intoned heavily as her eyes slid miserably away from his. 'So stop crying and decide how you're going to stop her.'

The callous implication that she was behaving like a wimp really stung. 'What do you think I've been doing? Whichever way you look at it, Chloe is his mother!' she reminded him shrilly. 'I'm just a distant relation.'

'You're the only mother Ben has ever known.'

Tess choked back a sob and turned her ashen face away from him. 'I've been so selfish keeping him. I should have encouraged Chloe to take an active part in…' The horror in her voice deepened as she wailed. 'He won't know what's happening…God, what have I done…?'

Rafe dropped down on his knees beside her chair and took her chin firmly in his hand. 'You loved him,' he rebuked her quietly. 'There's one person you haven't mentioned…'

Tess looked at him blankly.

'What about the father?'

Tess's slender back stiffened defensively. 'What about him?'

'Doesn't he have some influence? I take it she does know who…'

'Of course she does.'

'He's been providing financial support?'

'He's not around.'

'You could contact him and ask—'

'He's dead,' she interrupted harshly. 'He died before Ben was born. Chloe is getting married, that's why she feels that now is the time to have Ben live with her.'

'Who's the lucky man?'

'Ian Osborne.'

Rafe's brow wrinkled. 'That name seems familiar.'

'Ian Osborne the actor…?'

Rafe shook his head.

'He's got his own series…'

Rafe nodded. 'The medical soap.'

'Drama,' Tess corrected automatically.

'A canny career move on Chloe's part rather than true love, I take it.'

'Actually, she's besotted,' Tess told him gloomily. From their telephone conversation she had the impression that Ian Osborne had a lot to do with Chloe's change of heart. 'You're such a cynic, Rafe.'

'Better than being a victim.'

His casual contempt really hurt. 'I am not—!'

He was pleased to see the spark of anger in her eyes;

anger was way better than that awful dull, despairing blankness.

'Whatever,' he drawled. 'You could convince this Osborne guy he doesn't want a kid around.' With a thoughtful expression he drew a hand slowly through his thick hair.

Tess stared at him. Only Rafe could come up with an idea like that and make it sound reasonable. 'I don't think I want to know what machiavellian schemes are running around in your warped little mind. I need to do what is best for Ben,' she responded firmly, trying to sound braver than she felt. 'I need to do what I should have been doing all along, I need to prepare Ben to go live with his mother.'

If it was going to happen she'd have to put her feelings on the back burner and make this transition as painless as possible. And if Chloe and this Ian person made him unhappy she'd make them wish they'd never been born!

'You can't prepare someone to lose the only mother they've ever known!' His hooded eyes were veiled as she stiffly turned away from him. 'What we need is inspiration. In the meantime, will you settle for coffee?'

'I don't want coffee.'

'You need it; you're drunk.'

She opened her mouth to deny this when it occurred to her he was probably right. If she weren't drunk they wouldn't be having this conversation. If she weren't drunk his shirt wouldn't still be damp from her copious tears.

'Don't move, I'll make it.'

Tess, who hadn't been going to offer, retained her seat. If she hadn't felt so dog-tired she might have asked Rafe since when he'd made her problem his crusade. She already knew, of course, even if he didn't recognise the reason himself at least consciously. The parallels might be tenuous, but she could see exactly why he was so fired up.

Rafe had doted on his own mother; he still did. The reasons that had made her run away, leaving her two young sons behind, had been wide and varied depending on who you listened to in the small community—everyone had their own pet theory.

To say Rafe's relationship with his stepmother had been bad would have been like saying he was *quite* tall and *fairly* good-looking. A child of seven or eight didn't have the weapons required to prevent a clever, manipulative woman from alienating him from his father. These days Rafe wasn't short of weapons, or overburdened with moral qualms about using them. In short, Rafe could be pretty ruthless. Maybe that was what the situation called for...? She firmly pushed aside the tempting idea of letting Rafe have free rein.

A few minutes later Rafe returned carrying two mugs of strong black coffee. 'Do you take sugar? I couldn't remember...'

The small figure on the rocker stirred restlessly in her sleep, but didn't waken.

CHAPTER THREE

GROANING, Tess subsided weakly back against the pillow. Her head felt as though it might well explode.

'That wine should carry a warning.' The not unsympathetic response to her visible discomfort came from a point not too far from her left ear.

If her head hadn't felt so fragile she'd have nodded in rueful agreement. 'If I go so far as to look at that stuff again...' With a disorientated gasp she opened her heavy eyelids with a snap—actually, in her head it sounded like a loud, painful clang.

Dark eyes smiled solicitously back at her. Her disorientation deepened and the clanging got infinitely worse.

'You're in my bed.'

Tess tried to sound as though finding an extraordinarily attractive man in her bed was an everyday occurrence. She failed miserably to achieve the right degree of insouciance.

Her manic thoughts continued to race around in unhelpful circles without delivering a single clue to explain away this bizarre situation.

'On your bed,' Rafe corrected pedantically as he curved an arm comfortably under his neck and rolled onto one side.

Did that make a difference? She hoped it did! A quick glance beneath the cosy duvet confirmed she was still wearing the least glamorous night apparel in her admittedly largely unglamorous wardrobe. Tess felt anything but cosy at that moment but she did clutch eagerly at this small crumb of comfort. And Rafe was fully clothed; that had to be a good sign...didn't it?

A sign of what? a drily satirical voice in her head enquired. It wasn't as if Rafe had ever displayed anything remotely resembling interest in her body. Why would he, when he had an obvious weakness for the tall, statuesque type? His married lover was probably another in the long line of blonde confident goddesses.

When she looked at the situation sensibly Tess was forced to concede that it bordered on the bizzarely improbable that he'd been overcome by lust! A fact which ought to have cheered her up, but since when did being forced to face the fact you didn't have any sex appeal cheer up any girl?

Hell! I just wish I could remember so I know what I need to forget!

Unfortunately her amnesia only covered the problem of how, when and with whom—cancel the with whom, that was fairly obvious—she had gone to bed. The other awful events of the previous day were not at all fuzzy. Chloe and her betrothed were coming to take Ben to the zoo. Even Chloe had recognized—after a little judicious nudging—that she couldn't remove her baby son without a little preparatory work.

Discovering she'd done something she would definitely regret with *Rafe* of all people might confirm her irresistibility, but it would also round off the worst day of her life *perfectly*! No, I couldn't have…could I…? She surreptitiously searched his handsome face for some clue and discovered only a moderate degree of amusement, which could mean just about anything.

'It isn't the first time I've shared your bed, Tess—not by a long chalk, if you recall.'

Tess was surprised at the reference. Her tense expression softened. She did recall; she recalled hugging his skinny juvenile body to her own and as often as not falling to sleep with his dark head cradled against her flat chest.

The poignant image unexpectedly brought a lump to her throat. She'd never had a friendship as close as the one she'd once shared with a much younger, more vulnerable Rafe. It wasn't reasonable to expect that degree of intimacy to extend into adulthood, but it was depressing to realise how far apart they'd grown recently. If something was that good it was worth making a bit of effort to preserve it. Their friendship might not have thrived on neglect, but at least it hadn't withered and died.

She let out a tiny sigh and allowed herself to feel hopeful. If this time had been as innocent as those far-off occasions he was referring to, she had nothing to worry about. She'd have felt even more relieved if Rafe didn't have the sort of voice that could make something as innocent as a nursery rhyme sound suggestive.

'Is the old walnut tree still outside the bedroom window?'

These days women usually opened the door for him...except for Claudine... His eyes grew chilly as he recalled that significant door that had been closed firmly in his face. Pity it hadn't closed before he'd made a total fool of himself!

'No, it was diseased, we had to have it chopped down,' Tess told him in a brisk tone that didn't even hint at how upset she'd been by this necessity.

'Time gets to us all,' he sighed mournfully.

Her eyes made a swift, resentful journey over his large, virile person. *Sure*, he looked really decrepit! To add insult to injury, she suspected that even in this sizzlingly spectacular condition he was some way off his prime just yet.

'It doesn't seem right,' he continued. 'A Walnut Cottage without a walnut tree.'

The same thought had occurred to her but she didn't let on. 'You're not going all nostalgic on me, are you? If it makes you feel any better,' she conceded, 'I planted several seedlings after they cut the old one down. And in the interests of accuracy I ought to point out that this was Gran's room back then; so was the bed.'

The one he had shared with her had been a narrow metal-framed affair that would probably collapse under him these days, she thought, letting her eyes roam over his lengthy, muscular frame.

Who'd have thought that skinny kid would turn into something as perfectly developed as this awesome specimen? Aware that her breath was coming faster as her eyes lingered, she took a deep breath and passed the tip of her tongue over her dry lips. When she swallowed, her throat was equally dry and aching as if she wanted to cry—only she didn't.

It was all right to notice that a man oozed sexual magnetism; it was quite another to let the fact turn you ga-ga. Rafe had enough people raving on about his physical perfection without her joining the fan club! She looked up anxiously to see if he'd noticed her drooling display and saw his eyes weren't on her face at all.

'A lot of things have changed since then.' His deep voice was warmly appreciative as he continued to stare at the up-tilted outline of her small breasts.

He lifted his head and his eyes were slumberously sexy. Her breasts responded as though he'd touched the soft mounds of quivering flesh with his warm mouth. The startling image banished all rational thoughts from her head for one long, steamy moment. Nostrils flared, cheeks burning, she fought her way back to sanity.

'Some things don't change—things like your complete disregard for other people's feelings.' It was a whopping big lie, so to justify it she began to feverishly search her memory for some example to prove her point. Triumphantly she discovered one. 'Your family must have worried like crazy about you when you went missing all those times…?' Looking at it now through adult eyes, she saw aspects to Rafe's frequent nocturnal wanderings that her childish eyes had never seen.

'If concern is expressed by the vigour of the punishment, they were *deeply* concerned.' Something in his cynical voice made her search his stony face.

The memory of the bruises she'd once seen on his back when they had all gone swimming popped into her head. Suddenly all those times he'd refused to take off his heavy, long-sleeved sweater on a hot summer day made horrible sense. Everything clicked into place and she felt sick.

Tess forgot her throbbing head; she jerked herself upright.

Outrage glowed in her eyes. 'He hit you!' She thought of Guy Farrar with his mean little mouth and big meaty fists and her skin crawled. 'You never said!' she began angrily.

Nobody, not her dimly remembered parents or dear gran Aggie had ever laid a finger on her. Her chest felt tight and her eyes stung. She knew now what should have been obvious to her ages ago: their efforts to force Rafe to fit the mould of a perfect Farrar had gone beyond the verbal chastisements she'd heard often enough for herself...they'd tried to beat him into submission!

'Leave it, Tess,' Rafe said curtly.

'But—!'

'You're hyperventilating,' he told her, studying with clinical interest the agitated rise and fall of her small but shapely breasts. So, he'd noticed she had breasts! It was no big deal. However, noticing was one thing, staring was another. He firmly averted his eyes.

Tess wasn't about to apologise for her emotional response; she couldn't understand his lack of it! 'I'm not!' she denied breathlessly. 'Doesn't it make you mad?' she persisted incredulously.

For a long time it had, but Rafe had no intention of explaining how much effort and determination it had taken him to finally shelve the resentment that had simmered for years.

Her firm jaw tightened and her smouldering eyes narrowed. 'I'd like to—!' she began hotly.

Rafe took hold of her hands and, inserting his thumbs inside her clenched fingers, slowly unfurled her white-knuckled fists. 'I can see what you'd like to do...' he remonstrated softly.

Rafe frequently thanked his lucky stars that his only personal legacy from a father who'd automatically raised his fist on the frequent occasions when his troublesome younger son had annoyed him was a deep revulsion for violence and individuals who used it to control those who were weaker and more vulnerable. He was well aware that all too often the pattern repeated itself in each successive generation.

There had only been the one occasion when he'd used his physical strength to punish someone else—actually there had been three of them, sixth formers who had been making the life of another fourth former a living hell.

It was a sad fact of life, he reflected, but some kids had victim written all over them, and bullies of all ages could smell fear. You only had to be a little bit different—different but desperate to be the same as everyone else.

Rafe had walked into the common room one day to find them holding the kid up against a wall taking it in turns to punch him. He'd literally seen red; a red haze had actually danced before his eyes. That day he'd rid himself of several devils, and got expelled.

The touch of his thumb against the skin of her palm made Tess grow very still. The odd shivery sensation deep inside brought a troubled frown to her smooth wide brow as, warily, her eyes encountered his rather dark, rather luscious velvety orbs.

She hadn't been prepared to discover this sort of intensity in the searching quality of his dark glance. Quite suddenly the quality of the tension that gripped her altered. If anything, this fresh, tingling jolt of sexual awareness was even more intense than before. It left her incapable of doing anything but staring dry-throated and breathless back at him.

'I know you're aching to ask...'

Tess ignored the melting sensation low in her belly. It was perfectly understandable—Rafe's low drawl was pitched at an intimate, toe-curling level guaranteed to bemuse, bewilder and befuddle just about any female with a hormone to call her own. Tess's hormones, after years of wilful neglect, were staging an ill-timed comeback. She was aching all right, in ways she didn't want to think about; it was all extremely embarrassing.

'But, no, I didn't accept your drunken invitation. However, I couldn't leave you asleep in that chair so I carried you up to bed.'

'I didn't invite you into my bed!' Fists clenched, she robustly rejected his gentle taunt.

Stomach lurching horridly, she glanced uncomfortably at the solidity of his biceps. It wasn't difficult to see how he'd carried her up the stairs. It was so easy, in fact, that a ridiculously romanticised version of this event was playing in her head at that very second. The only thing that was difficult to see was how she'd forgotten it…

'No,' he agreed with a grin that was slightly strained around the edges. The frequent occasions in the night when she'd cuddled up to him couldn't legitimately be called invitations—they could be called extremely…provoking, however, and they had been a reminder that, though his heart might be broken, his more basic bodily functions were still in full working order!

The enigmatic quirk of his sensual lips sent her tummy muscles into a fresh series of uncomfortable fluttery acrobatics. Tess ruthlessly gathered her straying wits and recognised that this was only half an explanation. Rafe had carried her up, but that didn't mean he'd had to stay—in fact if he'd been a gentleman the idea would have occurred to him!

'And you were overcome by exhaustion…?' she suggested tartly.

'I guess I was,' he conceded, not responding to the challenge in her eyes.

Tess permitted herself a little snort of disbelief. He didn't look exhausted; in fact, she decided crankily, it ought to be illegal for anyone to exude that sort of vitality this early in the morning.

'Trust *you* to turn out to be a morning person,' she grumbled.

'Not exclusively,' Rafe corrected her solemnly.

Tess's puzzled frown encountered the sensual, amused gleam in his eyes; a few seconds later heat washed over her as the meaning of his smutty innuendo hit home.

'You always did have an overdeveloped opinion of your own abilities.' She aimed for amused but tolerant and almost made it.

Rafe heard the *almost* and grinned as he defended himself. 'I've had some very positive feedback,' he reflected innocently.

Tess could imagine but she tried not to. 'I don't require references, glowing or otherwise. What time is it?'

He told her and with a yelp she leapt out of bed. 'Chloe and her boyfriend are coming this morning.'

'What are you going to do—roll out the red carpet?' he drawled.

His critical tone really got under Tess's skin. He made it sound as though she had a choice. 'I know what I'm not going to *do* and that is resort to covert dirty tricks and manipulation.'

'Have it your own way.'

She shot him a sweetly malicious smile. 'I will,' she assured him calmly.

'I don't understand it,' she continued fretfully as she pulled a motley assortment of garments from deep drawers in the heavy old mahogany chest. 'Ben *always* wakes up before seven.' She'd found that having a baby made her alarm clock redundant.

Rafe's hand shot out and he caught the latest garment she'd carelessly flung over her shoulder in the general direction of the bed. It turned out to be a flimsy bra. A passing glance told him his educated guess had been bang on size-wise.

There had been a plus side to his sleepless speculation: he hadn't thought too much about Claudine. An arrested expression crossed his face when he realised how *little* he'd been thinking about her.

'Ben did look in earlier.'

'*He what…?*' she snapped, stomping towards the bed, hands on her hips.

'I suppose he decided there wasn't much room this morning,' Rafe speculated, gazing at the narrow stretch of tumbled bed she'd just vacated. On impulse he reached out and felt the warmth that still lingered from her body on the cotton bed linen. 'He tootled off. I did go check on him—he seemed happy playing with his toys so I left him to it.'

She gazed at him incredulously. 'Didn't it occur to you he must have climbed over the bars of his cot?' She'd known for some weeks that the cot's days were numbered. Ben had been eyeing up the bars lately with a very determined eye, and she'd already foiled a couple of abortive escape attempts.

'And that is…?'

His laid-back approach was intensely irritating. 'Dangerous!' she snapped.

'Well, he looked fine to me.'

'I can't believe you just let him wander around unsupervised! He could have fallen down the stairs!' she cried out, her voice rising sharply in alarm.

'Calm down, there's a gate thing over the top of the stairs. I should know—I nearly killed myself trying to step over it while I was carrying you last night.'

Tess gave a sigh of relief. That was Ben's physical well-being sorted. There were other traumas. 'He must have seen me in bed with you!' she wailed.

'What has got your knickers in a twist—the fact Ben saw

you in bed with someone, or the fact that he saw you in bed with *me*?'

Tess recognised immediately that there was some merit in what he said, only she'd have died before she admitted it to him or herself.

'Like I said,' Rafe continued, a shade of impatience creeping into his languid tone, 'I hardly think the sight will have seriously corrupted his morals.'

'That's not the point, you should have woken me. Routine is very important for children.'

'Remember to tell Chloe that, won't you?' Tess flinched and looked so stricken that he instantly regretted his cheap wisecrack. 'I would have woken you if he'd seemed distressed. What are you going to do about Chloe?' he asked her gently.

He swung his long legs over the side of the bed and stretched. The light material of his shirt stretched taut across his broad chest and Tess looked hastily away.

'What can I do?' She did her best to resist the tide of helplessness that washed over her. 'I'm going to remind Chloe that this thing has to be done slowly, sensitively, with as little disruption as possible. In fact, at Ben's pace. It's not like I won't still be seeing him...' There was a tell-tale little tremor in her voice as she lifted her chin defiantly. 'He'll visit, I'll visit...I'll be his favourite aunt...' It wouldn't get her very far if she let herself wallow in self-pity; being an aunt would have to be enough.

'And you think she'll agree to the cautious approach...?'

Rafe watched as Tess's delicate heart-shaped little face screwed up into a mask of iron determination.

'She'll agree, all right,' she intoned grimly. Stern-faced, she picked up the bundle of clothes she'd selected *en masse* from the bed. 'I take it you can find your own way out.' Distractions she didn't need and Rafe could now be safely categorised under that heading.

'Shower...?'

Tess gave a snort of exasperation. It was a mistake to try the pathetic Spaniel look when you resembled more closely a sleekly muscled Doberman.

'I suppose so,' she conceded ungraciously. Halfway to the door she paused and turned back. 'I don't need to say that I'd prefer it if you didn't mention to everyone just yet about…about what I said…Ben not being mine. I got a bit silly…' Not to mention deeply embarrassing. She winced inwardly as she recalled sobbing pathetically on his chest.

Another memory attached itself to the coat-tails of this recollection: the masculine scent of warm skin was so real it unnerved her totally. 'T-To be honest, Chloe's phone call out of the blue…it was all a bit of a sh-shock,' she stammered.

A nerve in Rafe's lean jaw clenched and his nostrils flared. So much for supposed friendship! This little display of trust was just charming!

'You mean I can't run around the village with my loudspeaker…?' Rafe knew a lot of people, but he was pretty selective about the people he called friends, he always had been, and he trusted that select band implicitly. It didn't seem too much to expect them to return that trust.

Tess sighed. Perhaps he did have a right to act a bit miffed—she probably could have made her request a bit more tactfully. But the fact was she had more to worry about just now than Rafe's feelings.

'All right, all right…there's no need to get all huffy, I was just checking.'

'It may have escaped your notice, but you're not the only one that feels a little emotionally exposed after last night. Perhaps I should be asking you to sign the Official Secret Act, too.'

'Oh, I forgot about that,' she lied fluently. She wasn't quite sure why the idea of being the recipient of further confidences concerning Rafe's love life should make her want to run and hide. It had been easy to mock and be mildly contemptuous, even laugh in her more tolerant moments, about Rafe's numerous, shallow affairs. She couldn't see the funny side for some reason of Rafe in love, Rafe talking marriage...

'You make it sound so easy.' The flicker of torment in his dark eyes made her look quickly away. 'Forgetting...'

Tess decided at that moment she *definitely* didn't want to know anything more about the woman who had discovered Rafe's heart only to comprehensively break it.

'I didn't mean to be insensitive, but...' An intriguing thought occurred to her and she made a tentative effort to explore the idea further. 'Didn't you want to be alone last night? Is that why you didn't leave?'

'Regressing to behaviour patterns laid down in child-hood?' He rubbed a hand thoughtfully over the short dark growth over his jaw. Tess had never been kissed by a man who was other than smoothly shaven; she found herself idly wondering... 'Sanctuary? I wondered about that myself...'

Tess, her cheeks a little flushed, brought her own line of *wondering* to an abrupt halt.

'Wouldn't it be something if I headed for your bed every time I needed a bit of TLC?' he mused, lifting his dark eyes to her face thoughtfully.

The thud of her heart sounded odd and echoey in her ears. 'Very funny!' she responded hoarsely.

'Yeah, hilarious,' he confirmed without a trace of humour.

When Rafe emerged from his shower Tess was in the kitchen having produced breakfast for Ben, who as usual was in no hurry to finish it. There was as much porridge on the floor as was in his stomach. She had stopped trying to tempt the baby to another mouthful and had returned to her frenzied task of refilling the cupboards when Rafe strolled in.

'Morning, mate.' Rafe, who could deal with the wiliest of politicians, felt distinctly unsure of how you were meant to speak to a one-year-old. He winked at the solemn-faced youngster.

Ben responded with a grin that suggested he wasn't quite as angelic as he looked. 'Seed man!' he cried, poking his chubby finger in Rafe's direction.

'Saw, Ben,' Tess responded automatically. At least Ben's limited vocabulary meant she was spared any embarrassing elaboration on this theme.

'Seed,' the toddler responded immediately. Eyes bright, he waited expectantly for Tess to praise him.

'Well done, darling.' When she looked away she saw Rafe was watching her with a curiously intense expression on his lean hungry features, which faded as he turned to the baby.

'I don't expect you remember me, but my name's Rafe. Or should that be *Uncle* Rafe?' he enquired, turning his attention once more to Tess. 'Can he talk?'

'After a fashion, but you might need the aid of an interpreter,' she admitted. 'You and Ben can decide between you what he calls you. My money's on complete nuisance...' she added softly.

'I heard that.'

'You were meant to.' She reached up on tiptoe to replace a casserole dish in a high cupboard.

Rafe found himself unexpectedly noticing the way stretching pulled her already neat, high behind extremely taut. Despite the fact that her clothes could have been designed specifically to conceal the fact, it was hard to miss the fact she had a good—no, better than good body. Dark brows almost meeting above the bridge of his masterful nose, Rafe reached over her head and took the item from her extended hand.

'Do you know that most accidents occur in the home?'

'Don't take that hectoring, lecturing tone with me!' Angrily Tess spun around to find he was almost close enough to fall over. Not content with wondering whether he'd catch her if she did fall, her wayward brain began to theorise about how it might feel.

A tiny sound of denial slipped past her frozen vocal chords. She was close to tipping over into outright panic as, arms extended protectively in front of her, she backed hastily up until the small of her back made contact with the wooden worktop.

The atmosphere was suddenly so charged with sexual tension that she could hardly breathe. He feels it too, she thought, staring in a bemused fashion into his dark, dilated eyes.

'Brekkie!' a small voice piped up severely.

The adults, both recalling with a guilty start that they weren't alone, looked in the direction of the small speaker. Simultaneously they both decided to ignore what had just happened.

'Good idea, Ben. Is this seat taken?' Rafe asked, noisily dragging out a kitchen chair with a stagey flourish and, straddling it, he rested his hands lightly on the back.

'Is Tess always so grumpy in the morning?' Now wouldn't you like to know? a sly voice in his head drawled knowingly.

With a confused frown, Tess watched his smile fade.

'Powige,' the child announced mournfully, dipping his hand into the goo left in his dish.

'He likes to feed himself.'

'He looks as if he likes to bathe in the stuff. Nasty porridge. Mush...*ugh*!' Rafe's theatrical shudder drew a giggle from the child.

Tess could see the beginnings of male conspiracy here. 'Last week it was his favourite.'

'Mush, mush, mush, *mush*!' Ben, his grubby face animated, shrieked loudly.

'All right, I get the message.' Tess sighed. She knew from experience that was going to be the favourite word for the foreseeable future. It could be worse, she reflected philosophically, and it had been when Ben had overheard the colourful expletives employed by the electrician who had fixed their security light. The entire mother and baby group now thought she swore like a trooper at home.

Mind you, that notoriety would be nothing compared with what was heading her way once the true identity of Ben's mother was public knowledge! Some people already knew, of course: their GP, the kindergarten head at the school she'd already put Ben's name down for.

'I like bacon and eggs.'

'No...no!' Ben bounced in his seat as he enthusiastically concurred.

'No means yes,' she felt obliged to explain. 'Actually, no means a lot of other things too. Mostly finding out what he wants is a matter of elimination.'

'In this case I feel sure that it means he wants bacon and eggs.'

'He won't eat it,' she predicted.

'I will.'

'You,' she announced in exasperation, 'are nothing but a troublemaker! Anyhow, I haven't got any,' she lied.

'Ah...shopping day.'

As if he knew about such things!

'And I'm sure you're a whiz with the supermarket trolley.' She permitted herself a loud snort packed with scornful scepticism.

'I was merely about to mention that you might like to add razor blades to that shopping list,' Rafe announced, ignoring her sarcastic interjection. 'Do you know that dinky little razor of yours is blunt?'

Bubbling with indignation, Tess watched him rub a hand over the intact dark stubble that adorned his square chin.

'It wasn't...and the reason it's *dinky* is because it wasn't designed to remove a dirty great beard.'

Ignoring the fact the dark growth gave him a dangerous, dissipated but not unattractive air—in fact some women might actually go for that moody menace look in a big way. Some women—the ones lost to all sense of decency—might even wonder what that dark growth would feel like when applied to sensitive areas...a breast, for example...even...?

Two bright spots of guilty colour apeared on the smooth curve of her cheeks. She glared with exaggerated distaste at the shadow on his jawline.

'I could have told you that if you had bothered to ask before you went poking around in my private things.'

'You want to watch this possessive streak...it's not attractive. I mention this only to be helpful.'

'In this mood,' she told him frankly, 'you're about as helpful as a hole in the head!'

'You're cranky because you're busy, stressed and ever so slightly hung-over.'

'And whose fault is that? I don't drink alone...' Which meant, as she rarely had adult company, she didn't drink full stop, which no doubt explained her rapid descent into her inconveniently garrulous state of the previous night...

'Admirable, I'm sure. There are some things I never do alone either.'

Nothing, she decided, could be more deceptive than the open, innocent look on his face. She thought it wise to rise above responding to the wicked earthy innuendo.

'But drinking,' he confessed cheerfully, 'is not one of them. I'll make us some breakfast, shall I?'

'I'm not hungry and I don't recall offering you any breakfast.' Her cheeks refused to cool as quickly as she'd like.

'I assumed that was a mere oversight.'

'No, a rude and calculated rejection.' Which he seemed to be coping with irritatingly well.

'You ought to eat.'

He subjected her small person to a critical examination. His expression suggested he hadn't found much to approve of. 'You're too thin.'

'Luckily for me beauty is in the eye of the beholder!'

Wanted, one short-sighted, sensitive hunk. A tall order by any standards!

'This could eventually work in your favour. I mean, a lot of guys could be put off by the notion of taking on a ready-made family.'

'I suppose you would know all about being shallow and selfish. Actually, I can do without men like that!' she told him with confident contempt. 'In fact, I can do without men full stop.'

With a mouth like that he somehow doubted it. Rafe had a sudden strong impulse to test his theory about generously passionate lips. You can't blame it on the booze now, mate!

'Is that what put your vet off?'

When it came to insensitivity, Rafe was right up there with the all-time greats.

'For the last time, he wasn't my vet, and, no, actually, it was something *quite* different.' He hadn't believed her when she'd said she *really* didn't want to marry him so she'd had to resort to the truth—he hadn't been able to get away fast enough then.

'Found out about your snoring, did he…?'

Something flickered in her eyes before her glance slid unobtrusively away from his. A speculative frown tugged gently at the taut, unlined skin across his broad brow.

How would Rafe react if she told him? Embarrassed, pitying…? Taking a deep breath, Tess lifted her chin and, pushing aside the intrusive shaft of self-pity, pinned a stoical expression on her face. Major shock, hold the front page…life isn't fair! She'd had plenty of time to get used to the idea, but sometimes, as now, it still caught her on the raw.

'I don't snore.'

One dark brow shot up. 'Want to bet?' he drawled. From where he was sitting he opened the fridge door with the toe of his shoe. 'Well, what do you know?' he drawled, turning a cheerful face to Ben. 'Bacon and, unless my eyes deceive me, eggs too. Free range, I hope…' He turned to Ben. 'Tess must have forgotten.'

'The only thing I'd forgotten,' she announced, gaining very little satisfaction from viciously slamming a cupboard door, 'is how infuriating and thick-skinned you are!'

'But you miss me when I'm not around…right…?'

She didn't pause to think about the possible consequences of replying honestly. 'Weird as it might seem,' she agreed tartly, 'I do.'

Rafe turned to look at her in time to see a shocked expression appear on her face. He found he could readily identify with the emotion.

'Which just goes to show how starved for adult company I must be.' Her attempt at making a joke of it didn't quite come off. I always did have lousy timing, she reflected grimly…

'I miss you too, Tess.' Wary green eyes clashed and locked with thoughtful brown.

'You miss someone to boss around,' she accused gruffly when the silence started to get hard to ignore.

'There aren't many people in the world you can be yourself with, warts and all.'

'You mean you've got a licence to be unconscionably rude and generally awful with me!'

'Here's to bad manners!' Rafe agreed, appropriating Ben's juice beaker to toast her with.

Tess tried to look severe, she tried not to smile back, but his good humour was contagious.

Rafe and Ben were halfway through the meal she'd grudgingly prepared—Rafe had even gone so far as to feed Ben several spoonfuls of his mushed-up version—when Tess saw the big shiny car draw up. 'Oh, no!' she wailed, throwing her hands up. 'They're here! It's too early.' Frankly, ten years hence would still be too early. 'What'll I do…?'

Rafe watched her agitated routine with a bland expression

and a quizzically raised brow. 'Slam the door in their faces…?'

'If you can't say something constructive,' she hissed, rounding on him, 'don't say anything! The place looks a mess.'

Rafe didn't see the relevance of this inaccurate comment, but he knew women seemed to set great store by a dust-free environment. 'It doesn't, but you do,' he announced with casual brutality.

Tess caught her breath. There was such a thing as stretching friendship too far and Rafe was getting perilously close!

'Here, let me.' She eyed him suspiciously as he levered his rangy athletic frame up from the chair. 'For starters, you can take this thing off.' Tess was startled into immobility as he calmly began to unbutton her long baggy cardigan. He slid it off her shoulders with a flourish.

He did it very slickly, but then he had probably had a lot of experience removing items of female clothing… Perhaps she should have forced herself to eat breakfast; she did feel distinctly queasy.

'Well, what did you expect?' she snapped tartly as he continued to look with obvious discontent at the simple slit-necked black tee shirt she wore underneath. She failed completely to appreciate how well it displayed her taut, firm figure and neat waist. 'Besides, I fail to see what difference the way I look makes to anything.'

'Don't be naive, Tess.' Rafe lifted a distracted hand and, with a brooding expression, rubbed it back and forth over his unshaven chin. 'Would you have turned up in your scruffy jeans for a big meeting when you were working in the City? No, you wanted to make the right impression and feel in control. Now is no different. I'm not saying clothes maketh the woman, but I am saying—and so will you, if you're strictly honest—that the right outfit doesn't do any harm. People like Chloe judge folk by the way they dress, the car they drive…'

'I don't drive any more.'

'I haven't forgotten that.'

Maybe his thoughtful expression wasn't significant. Maybe it was her guilty conscience making her see things that weren't there.

'If you look good you'll be sending a subliminal message to Chloe.'

'Saying what?'

'I'm in control…you can't push me around.'

'I can't make breakfast wearing stilettos and a sharp suit. I dress like every other mum…' she explained obstinately.

Rafe saw the precise moment when the meaning of what she'd said hit her. For a split second the depth of her anguish was there for him to see. He'd like to throttle Chloe and her celebrity boyfriend!

Biting viciously down on her trembling lower lip, Tess steeled herself to meet the pity in his eyes. 'Only, of course, I'm not.' She spoke with quiet composure.

'Tess…' Frustration was building steadily inside him. Why the hell didn't she let him hug her instead of sprouting as many prickles as a porcupine?

Tess shook her head in silent rejection of his empathy. If he was nice to her now she'd make a total fool of herself.

'Anyhow, this conversation is academic—it's too late now for a make-over,' she babbled nervously. 'You can't make a silk purse out of…leave my hair alone!' she cried, batting away his intrusive hand.

His objective achieved, Rafe thrust the scrunchy thing he'd slid from her thick hair into his pocket, and gave her an unrepentant grin. 'Good,' he said, regarding his handi-work. 'But this…' with his other hand he began to tease out the ruthlessly restrained locks into a mass of gleaming soft waves '…is better…much better.'

'Now look what you've done!' Tess fumed, belatedly pulling away. She couldn't understand why she'd just stood there and let him. It wasn't as if she'd *enjoyed* the soft touch of his fingertips against her scalp. The drugged lethargy that had stolen over her couldn't possibly be classified along with pleasure.

'*I am.*' There was unnecessary force in his voice. There was also a weird expression on his face—it was the sort of expression that made Tess's heart thud and her throat close up.

'It's all mussed up.' She lifted a fretful hand to her head. 'I must look messy.'

'Want to muss mine?' he offered, raising a hand to his glossy raven head.

Hot desire smothered her like a heavy blanket. She couldn't breathe, she couldn't think—she could imagine, though. Her fingertips actually tingled as she imagined sinking them deep into that luscious dark mass to trace the outline of his skull.

Emerald eyes wide and shocked, she shook her head dumbly.

Rafe shrugged. 'Fair enough. Don't forget I offered, though.'

'I won't.'

'I think you should definitely aim for sexy, not neat.' His eyes were on the glossy waving chestnut strands that fell just below her shoulders. 'Competition will distract Chloe.'

That was uncalled for and a little bit cruel. 'Very funny!' she snapped. The day she could offer Chloe competition was never likely to dawn and they both knew it.

'If Chloe went out without her make-up and designer clothes nobody would give her a second glance.'

It occurred to Tess as he took hold of her chin and tilted her face first one way and then the other, subjecting her clear-cut profile to a comprehensive appraisal, that she really ought to complain about this sort of high-handed treatment.

'You've got the most incredible skin.' He made it sound like an accusation. 'All over,' he added hoarsely.

Tess stiffened and tugged her chin free. 'How would you

know?' Galloping alarm deepened the green of her eyes by several shades.

Rafe shrugged. 'I did put you to bed, and you weren't wearing anything under that...' he searched for an accurate description of her nightwear '...thing.'

'What a complete sleaze you are!' She choked, going hot and sweaty all over.

'My hand quite unintentionally—yes, *unintentionally*,' he repeated firmly in response to her hoarse derisive hoot, 'came into contact with your behind—*so hang me*! I could have dropped you—would you have preferred that? I'll remember the next time.'

'There won't be a next time.' Tess's breathing was laboured and noisy. She couldn't wipe away the image in her head of his fingers moving over... Self-derision swelled in her tight chest. *Has it come to the point when sexual thrills are so sparse in my life that I'm reduced to wishing I'd been conscious while I was being accidentally groped?*

'I had no idea you were such a prude.'

If he had been privy to some of the fantasies swirling around in her head, he'd know how wildly inappropriate that description was! 'Don't you dare take that patronising tone with me, Rafe Farrar!'

'And considering you were the one squirming and strangling me... Talk about overreaction.' He began to talk fast to cover up the fact that he'd just revealed how memorable her sleepy embrace was turning out to be. 'What did you think I'd done? I like a bit of response from the women I sleep with,' he teased.

'*Ben!*' Tess protested, her eyes belatedly going to the child who was happily immersing a toy car in the congealing remains of his cooked breakfast.

'Is not interested in what we're saying, and if I lower my voice much more I'll be whispering. I'll tell you something for nothing...'

Tess planted her hands on her slim hips and tossed her head. 'Since when was anything you said worth more?'

'You know,' he observed, eyeing her through narrowed, unfriendly eyes, 'you never used to be such an uptight bundle of repressions. Sex with me last night would have done you more good than half a bottle of vintage elderberry wine! For that matter,' he added grimly, 'it would have done me more good too.' If she tried to deny it he could always provide the proof...somehow he didn't think he'd find the task too tedious.

Total mind-blowing shock swept over Tess. She focused hard on the shock and outrage and turned a deaf ear to the pulsing excitement that all but deafened her.

'Have sex...with you!' she yelped, abandoning the hushed undertone they'd automatically adopted during their heated interchange in favour of strangled squeak.

'You make it sound as if the thought had never occurred to you!'

'It hasn't!' she responded, horrified.

'Like hell!' he thundered scornfully. 'You know perfectly well we've both been tiptoeing around it all morning.'

It was at this point Tess stopped pretending there was anything controlled about her panic. 'And I suppose you're going to tell me now what a great lover you are,' she sneered.

His eyes narrowed as he sucked in his breath sharply. 'Modesty forbids,' he drawled, 'but I can guarantee you wouldn't be this uptight this morning if we had had sex last night, and I might have actually got some sleep!'

'You think it would have been that boring...' She nodded and gave a twisted smile. 'You're probably right. I may have been happy playing the surrogate sister for you when we were kids but I'm not about to play the surrogate lover now!'

The idea of him closing his eyes and pretending she was the woman he loved filled her with an intense repugnance.

'I'm sure there are less…less *drastic* cures for insomnia,' she choked.

'A pill isn't going to solve my problem. Or yours.'

'And…' she cast a worried look in Ben's direction and lowered her voice to a hushed whisper '…sex is…?'

'No,' he conceded through gritted teeth, 'but it might make us both forget for a little while.'

The bleakness in his deep voice penetrated her anger and inconveniently touched her soft heart. She'd been too wrapped up in her own problems to think much about his.

'Is it really that bad for you, Rafe?' she asked sadly. Without being aware of what she was doing, she reached out and touched his face.

Eyes dark as night moved from the compassion shining in her eyes to her slim arm. His own hand came up to cover hers where it lay. She felt the controlled strength in the grip of his long fingers and shivered.

'Bad enough for me to think about sleeping with you, Tess?' He gave a harsh laugh. 'You really do take this modesty thing way too far. You're a lovely woman.'

'Not beautiful?' She didn't lay awake at night contemplating cosmetic surgery to correct her deficiencies, but right now making a joke about it was surprisingly hard.

'Beauty fades. You've got good bones,' he announced firmly.

'How poetic!'

'One of these days you're going to make one wisecrack too many,' he predicted darkly. 'As I was saying, when a man's in bed with an attractive woman his mind naturally turns to…' At least that was the way he'd eventually justified his fantasies during the long, *long* night.

'The gutter?' Maybe she was just starved for admiration of the male variety. It might explain the way her senses leapt in response to his casual announcement. After all, she knew it was just talk. If there had been any spark between them she'd have noticed years ago…it wasn't as if they hadn't had plenty of opportunities to have sex over the years if they'd wanted. They just hadn't wanted to.

'Is it so bad, Tess, to want to give and receive a little comfort?' The cynicism she hated was absent from his voice as his eyes slowly searched her face.

Put it like that and I sound churlish if I disagree. My God, but this man had a great way with words. It wasn't just what he said, it was the way he did it. Those eyes, that charisma— was it any wonder her brain had stopped functioning?

'No...yes...You're confusing me...' she protested weakly.

'The more I think about it, the more I think that closing the bedroom door and saying to hell with the world would be the best thing for us both!' He sank his fingers into the rich softness of her hair and brought his face down to hers. 'Who would we be hurting?' he growled.

Tess was sure there were several good answers to that husky, intimate question, but at that moment she couldn't bring one to mind.

'Right now you're hurting me.' She twisted her confined head a little to show him how. An ambiguous mixture of fear and excitement ripped through her as his fingers slid under the heavy weight of her hair down to the back of her neck.

The touch was like neat electricity; it blitzed along her nerve-endings. Eyes half closed, breath coming fast and shallow, Tess moved her head from side to side, not actually to resist the fresh constraint, more to appreciate the texture of his fingertips against her skin. Did it make her a sad, undersexed excuse for a woman that this was the single most sensual incident in her life?

Rafe felt the voluptuous shudder of pleasure that quivered through her slight frame and his eyes darkened. 'I knew you'd agree.' The intensity of his own relief took him by surprise. It was almost as great as the anticipation that sharpened every sense in his body.

Roused by the 'I told you so' note in his voice, Tess opened her mouth to put him right. She would have, too, in no uncertain terms if he hadn't at that same moment covered it with his.

Her eyes widened in shock and refocused on his face so close to her own. At this distance she could have appreciated how fine-textured his olive-toned skin actually was if she'd been in a fit state to think about such matters. It was the expression in his spectacular eyes, which like her own were open, that obliterated every other thought. She gave a deep sigh as her eyelids drooped over her burning eyes. The flood of pleasure was so intense, she moaned low in her throat, the sound merging with the masculine groan that vibrated deep in Rafe's chest.

Tess's hands clutched at empty space, and curled into tight balls to stop herself grabbing at him and hauling him on top of her... Yes, she realised as he lifted his head, that was *exactly* what she wanted to do.

Eyes spitting green flames, she wiped the back of her hand firmly across her mouth. It didn't stop her tasting him but she wasn't about to tell him that.

'You kissed me.'

'I'd have been disappointed if you hadn't noticed. What's the verdict?'

'The verdict is you're off your head if you think I'd agree to have sex with you!' She decided last minute to rephrase the *why would I do that*? She'd be deep in trouble if he took it into his head to show her why! 'If you can't read my body language, read my lips.' She pointed to her mouth and very slowly mouthed, 'Last night was the last time you'll be sharing my bed!'

CHAPTER FOUR

'THAT'S the sort of statement that is destined to come back and haunt you,' Rafe remonstrated, testing the springy resilience of the pouting curve of her lower lip with the tip of his thumb.

It was stupid to just stand there and let him take liberties, but for some reason Tess found she couldn't move. She was intensely conscious of the heavy aching feeling low in her belly.

'Just think how silly you're going to feel, angel, when I remind you of that the next time we're in bed together.'

Joke or no joke, his arrogance took her breath away. It did other things too, things like making her breasts tingle and swell against the thin top she wore. Graphic images crowded into her head, several involving sweaty bodies entwined. Her body temperature soared.

Tess caught her breath sharply and willed her weak limbs not to tremble. Angrily she wrenched her eyes away from the hypnotic warmth of his. She'd never expected to see the famed Farrar charisma this close up and she didn't imagine for one moment that it was accidental.

Even if he wasn't accustomed to rejection, it wasn't fair of him to use Tess to massage his damaged ego! Resentment mingled with a nerve-stretching excitement that made her head spin.

Serve him right if I bit him, she decided with uncharacteristic venom as her eyes continued to be mesmerised by the hand which probed the soft moisture of her inner lip.

She'd never before appreciated just how beautiful his elegant hands were, strong with the most lovely long, tapering fingers. Disturbingly, as her violent feeling evaporated, she

59

was left with a compulsion to extend her tongue and run
it… A tiny fearful moan escaped her parted lips… Cut this
out, Tess! Right now.

She jerked her head away to dislodge his hand. His fingers
trailed along the skin of her neck before they fell away completely. Tess gave a sigh of relief.

'One rejection and you've got to prove you've still got
what it takes…?' she taunted hoarsely.

'And have I?'

She couldn't think of an honest reply that wouldn't seriously incriminate her.

The sound of distant voices became clearer. 'Here, have
your keys! I'm sure I don't *want* to drive your beloved car
again. It's not my fault the lane is so narrow. Aunty Tess!'

Tess fought her way through the fog of sexual arousal. It
was like swimming against a particularly strong tide and
several unfriendly currents.

Chloe! How the hell did I forget about her…? The answer
was standing, all six feet four of him, beside her looking
quite unfazed by the entrance of her two visitors.

'Trouble in Paradise?' Rafe wasn't looking at her guests
when he spoke. Tess tore her eyes away from his mocking
face and turned to face the music and her niece. Incredulity
and shock warred for supremacy on her lovely young face
as Chloe looked from her aunt to Rafe and back again. She
didn't seem to like what she was seeing or thinking. Her
full lips trembled.

Surely fuller than the last time Tess had seen them; the
fleeting thought was replaced by far more urgent matters.
Had Chloe seen and understood what was going on? Perhaps
I should get her to explain it to me. Tess pushed aside this
whimsical thought.

'Is that your car out there?' The surprisingly boyish face
of Chloe's companion bore an apologetic grimace.

Rafe looked from the keys the older man was pocketing
to Chloe. 'How bad is it?' he enquired stoically.

'Pooh! It's only a scratch!' Chloe protested dismissively.

Whatever Chloe had seen or understood about the scene she'd walked in on, it had made her look as sick as the proverbial parrot. Chloe might be in love with the handsome man beside her, who was, Tess noted worriedly, *much* older than he appeared on the small screen, but she obviously hadn't reached the point in her life where she could laugh at her teenage crush on Rafe.

A laugh—surely hysteria, for there was nothing *remotely* funny about this situation—was ruthlessly bitten back. Tess closed her eyes for a brief moment and forced her stiff lips into a welcoming smile.

'Chloe, how lovely to see you.' The patent insincerity jarred on her ears. 'And you must be Ian.'

It was at this point it struck home that during their altercation Rafe had taken hold of her wrist, which he now twisted neatly behind her back before plastering himself in a very misleading manner to her side.

Normally Tess wouldn't have thought twice about the casually affectionate body contact. Only normally Rafe hadn't just… What the hell had he just done—made a pass…? She didn't know and, she told herself firmly, she didn't much care. It was perfectly understandable for her to feel ultra-conscious and uncomfortable about the hardness of the muscular thigh that was tightly pressed against her. Struggling would make this all look worse than it already did.

The smile she received from the older man in return for her cautious one was warm and open. She'd expected to automatically feel antagonistic, only she didn't. She'd expected to get slick and instead she got sincere—it was pretty disorientating. Rafe had to take his share of the blame for her disorientation; the faint scent that rose from his body made her sensitive nostrils flare. It was so…so *male*.

'Ben, look who's here, it's Mummy.' Tess didn't see the startled expression on Rafe's face when she made the introductions.

The rigid smile was still fixed on her lips as she shot him a seething glare. It was hard to see the expression in his eyes from under the decadent sweep of his dark lashes. Her glance slid downwards to his mouth...don't think kissing...don't think kissing... Just what was he playing at now?

Ben didn't appear overly impressed by all the 'darlings', 'dear little Benjys' and 'isn't he sweet?' and even less impressed by the burning kisses pressed to his small grubby face. Tess dreaded what he might do any moment—when it came to tactlessness eighteen-month-olds were in class of their own. Ben might be limited verbally, but he had effective ways of making his likes and dislikes known!

Chloe smiled expectantly at Ben, who was not looking happy. Tess started to gush, she knew it, she could hear herself, but for the life of her she couldn't stop.

'He was so excited when I told him about your visit, he couldn't go to sleep last night. To make matters worse he was awake very early this morning. He's exhausted, but will he admit it? You know how it is with kids.' That's the problem, idiot, she reminded herself: Chloe doesn't begin to know how it is with kids, and certainly not this particular kid.

Would she know you had to look inside his wardrobe to check for aliens before he could go to sleep? Would she know he came out in a rash if he ate cheese, or that he threw up if he got too excited? The resentful pain inside was almost impossible to contain.

'It always makes him a little bit cranky if his routine is disrupted.'

'Are you calling me a disruption?' Rafe drawled.

Now that he mentioned it. Actually, Tess didn't mind the interruption, without which she might still be burbling on this time next week!

'She's called me worse,' he confided to his attentive audience.

'We wondered who belonged to the car outside.'

If Chloe's sharp blue gaze had missed a single detail of the tall, spectacular man's appearance the first time she'd subjected him to a slow head-to-toe scrutiny, she would have surely discovered it on the repeat performance.

Tess found herself feeling uncomfortable on Ian's behalf. A quick glance in his direction revealed he wasn't looking at Chloe, but at herself. She smiled tentatively back, relieved he was taking his fiancée's admiration of a much younger man so well.

'You look marvellous.'

Tess considered this observation a little unnecessary after all that drooling.

'Whatever brings you here of all places?' Chloe persisted, placing her hands on his shoulders and kissing the air artistically either side of his face.

Perhaps, Tess brooded, the stubble put her off. It wouldn't me… Rafe's eyes met hers over Chloe's head and she blushed, as any girl would caught looking at a man as if he were a piece of cream cake she couldn't wait to jam into her mouth.

'I always was eccentric.' Chloe didn't pick up on the irony in his voice—he hadn't expected her to—but rather to his surprise there was no answering gleam of humour in Tess's eyes either when he sought her gaze. 'It is my home, Chloe.'

'Oh, I expect you've come to see your grandfather.' Chloe looked happier now she'd come up with a reasonable explanation for finding him in her aunt's company. 'He's not dead, is he?' she enquired, with a worried afterthought. 'Silly me, of course he isn't. I mean, he's famous, isn't he? It would have been on the news.'

Rafe struggled to keep his face straight.

'I did come to see Grandfather,' he agreed. 'I arrived last night, actually, only I haven't made it out there yet.' He solicitously pounded Tess on the back as she began to choke.

Tess, her eyes still watering, watched the smile fade from Chloe's lips. She shot Tess a poisonous look before linking her arm through her partner's and pulling him forward. 'This is Ian!' she announced with a verbal flourish.

Shall I curtsy or just applaud? Tess wondered. It was obvious to her now why Ian hadn't been troubled by Chloe's interest in Rafe; the girl quite obviously worshipped him! Being worshipped must give a person a nice feeling of security, she mused wistfully.

'No need for introductions, Chloe, I know who Ian is. I never miss an episode.'

It was impossible to tell from the older man's polite expression if he believed Rafe's outright and not very convincing lie, and from the slight wince Tess detected as they exchanged a manly handshake she suspected it might have been firmer than was strictly required on Rafe's side. The urge to kick him intensified. What made him think she needed him to fight her battles for her?

Ian, who had up to this point reserved his attention for Tess, turned to the young woman who proudly wore his ring upon her finger. 'You didn't tell me you knew Rafe Farrar, darling. I'm surprised we've never met before, Rafe.'

'Yes, it's amazing,' Tess agreed, casting a malicious glance towards Rafe. 'Considering how Rafe hovers diligently around on the *lovey* fringes hoping someone will mistake him for someone *really* famous and take his photo.'

Tess was immediately mortified that she'd allowed Rafe to provoke her into this display of shrewish bad manners.

Ian's understanding expression reminded Tess that everything she knew about this man had been gleaned second-hand from Chloe. Given this fact, something might well have got lost in the translation! Tess had taken it for granted Chloe's love interest had an outsized ego and she'd hoped he had a mouse-sized intellect to match! Now it looked as if she was wrong on both counts.

'I hope Ben isn't too tired after his early start to come out with us for the day. We've got a picnic…'

'I ordered it from Fortnum's,' Chloe explained. Did she expect an eighteen-month-old to be impressed? Tess wondered.

'He loves the animals. Don't you, Ben…?' If the high-class hamper didn't include crisps and his favourite tuna-paste sandwiches Tess could foresee some toddler-sized tantrums on the horizon. If I was a nice person I'd warn them, she thought guiltily. Admit it, Tess, you're hoping exposure to a couple of Ben's best tantrums will make Chloe think twice about the joys of motherhood.

'He likes snakes best,' she elaborated. 'Hsss!' She demonstrated her best snake noise and Chloe looked at her as if she'd gone mad.

'Hssss, hssss,' Ben responded, displaying an immediate grasp of the situation.

'Then we'll definitely find some snakes for him.' Ian laughed.

Chloe looked almost comically horrified by her fiancé's easygoing response. Tess was glad about this for Ben's sake, of course she was, but at the same time she couldn't help thinking that the fact that he seemed a nice guy who didn't think kids came from another planet was not going to help her own case.

With Ian to support Chloe, the scene in which a tearfully grateful Chloe said, 'Ben belongs with you, Tess,' was growing fuzzier by the second.

'Don't you like nice furry things like…like…?' Chloe persisted hopefully.

'Rabbits?' Rafe put in helpfully. This was better than TV. If he hadn't been aware of how much Tess was suffering he'd have settled back to enjoy the entertainment.

Chloe smiled gratefully at him. 'Yes, bunnies. Do you like sweet little bunnies, Benjy?'

'Hsss.' Ben chortled happily.

'Would everyone like coffee?' Tess leapt in to fill the silence that followed and took the opportunity to remove herself as far from Rafe as possible.

'Very kind, but we ought to be off. We'll have him back in time for tea.'

'Ess,' Ben appealed, holding out his arms to Tess.

Tess ached to pick him up. 'Not today, Ben.'

'Some other time, perhaps,' Ian agreed. 'It's been nice to meet you, Tess. I hope you won't mind if I don't call you aunt.'

'Almost anything else would be preferable,' Tess admitted bluntly.

'You're not at all what I was expecting...' A faint twitch of Ian's photogenic lips accompanied this last wry comment.

Despite the bleakness that had settled around her heart, Tess responded with wry humour. 'Let me guess—a shawl, slippers and rheumatism?'

'Well, not Titian hair and great bones, at any rate.' He studied her face with the objective eye of a connoisseur.

The *objectivity* didn't fool Rafe for one second!

'The camera would just love that face, it's so expressive.' Rafe rolled his eyes.

Tess, who was trying hard not to be expressive, looked uncomfortable.

'Have you ever done any acting or—?'

Tess, aware that her niece was looking ready to pull out the said Titian hair follicle by follicle, cut him off hastily. 'I don't have my Equity card, and isn't there a bit more to being an actor than a pretty face?'

'Tess, you really haven't watched my programme, have you?' he chided her with attractive self-derision. 'Still, at least nobody has ever accused me of being highbrow and élitist.'

Tess found it hard not to laugh as she listened to this sly jibe. Ian might not be accusing Rafe directly, but he didn't really have to—a high-profile victim of Rafe's lethal interviewing techniques had recently made both accusations loudly on national television.

'Well, shouldn't you do something with his face and hands before we take him?' Chloe, toe tapping impatiently, looked pointedly at Ben's grubby hands.

'You're right, Chloe.' Tess subdued her natural instincts to respond to the child's need and held her ground. If Chloe wanted to be a mum, fine, she could be a mum and all that entailed. The sooner she learnt there was more to the job than supplying presents and picnic hampers, the better. 'You know where the bathroom is, there's a pile of fresh nappies in the wicker basket, and I left a change of clothes out in his bedroom.'

'Nappies?' Chloe echoed, looking pale.

If Ian was worrying about sticky baby fingers on his upholstery, he didn't show it. Tess wished she could figure out what the expression on his face meant as he watched Chloe, wearing her plucky but ill-used heroine face, leave the room with her son.

'I think I'd better give her a hand,' he said, excusing himself after a moment with an attractive smile.

He might not be as tall or as young as he appeared on the screen, but he was a million times warmer and more human.

'He's nice, isn't he?' As stepfather material went, they probably didn't get much better, Tess admitted gloomily to herself. The male influence was something she had never been able to supply in Ben's life and, things being the way they were, probably never would.

'Nice!' Rafe's tongue curled around the word with scathing distaste.

His vicious tone startled Tess, who twirled around to face him.

'Do you mean you actually swallowed all that Titian hair, great bones, I'll get you a screen test guff?' His laughter was nothing short of insulting. 'Besides,' he added in a disgruntled tone, 'you don't have *Titian* hair.' His brooding glance strayed and paused on the top of her shining head. 'It's chestnut.'

'Just like your dumpy old pony eating her head off in your grandfather's stables,' she suggested with a spurt of childish petulance. Titian might not be strictly accurate, but it had a much more glamorous sound to it than chestnut

'Much glossier, actually.' Rafe had the strongest urge to let the glossy strands run through his fingers. He actually started to reach out before it occurred to him that this might not be the moment for spontaneous tactile gestures. 'Talk about laying it on with a trowel! I didn't think you were that simple, Tess! The man's a complete con artist.'

'Meaning he's automatically insincere if he thinks I'm good to look at.' A dangerous note crept into her voice as she lifted her arms from her sides and subjected her jeans-clad figure to a tight-lipped critical scrutiny. 'You're just mad because he got your measure at first glance.'

'I *mean*,' Rafe corrected impatiently, 'that the man knows you could make things difficult for them. He's trying to keep you sweet. No, cancel that, he's *succeeding* in keeping you sweet, though if he carries on being so full-on playing up to you,' he predicted with grim satisfaction, 'he's going to have trouble on his hands with Chloe. She looked fairly green, and I can't say I blame her!'

'You don't blame her!' Tess echoed incredulously. 'I don't believe you, I really don't. Ian is right, you have become an intellectual snob,' she breathed wrathfully, shaking her head slowly from side to side. 'Unusual it may be, but I'm not so *desperate* yet that I turn into some sort of compliant puppet when a man says something flattering to me. I was simply making an objective observation.'

'Objective, *sure*!'

'Well, a damned sight more objective than you're being. What are you frowning like that for?' she snapped.

'I was trying to figure out how come you called Chloe *Mummy* in front of Ben?'

'Because she is!' Tess wondered if he was being dense just to annoy her. 'That's no secret.'

'Pardon me, but I thought it was?' Rafe began with a frown. 'You mean he…Ben…knows?' he puzzled.

'Of course he knows. Well,' she modified, 'he knows, but he only understands as much as any one-year-old can under the circumstances. I may wish I was Ben's mother but I know I'm not,' she told him fiercely. 'And I'm neither stupid or selfish enough to lie to him. People assume I'm Ben's mum and I don't go out of my way to explain the relationship, but if they ask me…'

'You mean if *I'd* asked…?'

'I'd have told you, sure I would. Only you didn't ask. In fact, you didn't say much at all, the way I recall it.' It was the one time she could recall when Rafe had genuinely been at a loss for words.

'Well, what did you expect?' he exploded.

Tess pressed an urgent finger to her lips and glanced furtively up the stairs. 'Will you keep your voice down?' she hissed nervously.

'If you want to whisper in your own house that's up to you, but I'm damned if I will!'

'That would only make any sort of sense if this was your house and, even though you treat it as if it is, it isn't! Which makes that an extremely silly thing to say.'

'Your house, my house!' He clicked his fingers dismissively. 'The point is you hadn't even told me you were pregnant! That tends to make a bloke who was supposedly your best friend feel excluded.'

Tess's lips twitched. 'I probably didn't tell you because I wasn't pregnant,' she reminded him. 'It's not my fault that you turned out to be judgemental and narrow-minded,' she announced with sweet malice.

The breath hissed out from between his clamped teeth. 'I like that!' He didn't sound or look as if he liked anything she was saying. 'I tried to be supportive, it was you who gave me the cold shoulder. You used that patronising little smile to make me feel male and useless, then for good measure retreated behind that bottle of formula!' he accused.

'You *are* male and useless.'

'You've not got that bottle of formula to hide behind.'

Tess's chin went up. 'Is that a threat?' She was horrified to hear that give-away catch in her husky voice. It was the sort of catch that turned a question into an invitation. There was no escaping the fact that *breathless* was entirely the wrong message to be sending!

'It's a simple observation.'

Tess didn't find anything simple about the dangerous gleam in his dark eyes. 'Well, you can keep your observations to yourself,' she blustered. 'And that goes for your hands too,' she added for good measure. 'I don't know what you were playing at...'

'You know, I always wondered why you didn't breast-feed.' His eyes rested thoughtfully on the area involved. It took all of her will-power not to cover herself with her hands. She didn't dare look down; it was bad enough just *feeling* what effect his scrutiny was having.

She forced herself to breathe. 'Well, now you know.'

'Now I know.'

Tess silently prayed his knowledge didn't extend to the state of her rioting hormones.

'Chloe's wondering whether we're sleeping together.'

His expression suggested this was a good thing and she should congratulate him... She should probably strangle him. A fleeting glance at the strong brown column of his neck made her wonder what it would feel like to run her fingers... Her homicidal urges were replaced by other far more disturbing urges.

'*I wonder why?*' Tess drawled hoarsely.

'I think it's probably better for you to worry about what I'm going to do or say than worry about losing Ben. When you saw their car pull up you looked frantic.'

The provocation of his cool words made Tess abandon her discreet whisper. 'Your groping might have been purely altruistic, but it felt like groping to me!' she yelled.

'I didn't say that. The distraction part was good but I groped you...I prefer fondled,' he mused. 'It has a much nicer sound to it. I fondled you because I can't do what I actually want to.' The mocking smile faded totally from his face. 'Aren't you going to ask me what that is?'

'No...no!' she denied, shaking her head vigorously from side to side. 'Now will you just shut up?' she snapped, hearing the clatter of feet on the staircase. 'They're coming.'

This time he would be coming home, she thought as she watched Ben being strapped into the car; the next time she could be waving farewell for good. Contemplating this event was so painful that Tess made her excuses and dashed back into the house before the car had drawn away. She'd only just reached the kitchen when Chloe's breathless return to the kitchen ruined her bitter introspection.

'I forgot my bag...see,' Chloe explained, producing a decorative sugar-pink number that wasn't big enough to hold a comb.

Her next words were so calculated to injure—and injure they did—that Tess no longer had any doubts that the bag had been deliberately left behind.

'I'm not heartless. I know how you must feel losing Benjy. But I'm his mother.' She sighed. 'One day when you have a child of your own...' Her hand went to her mouth. 'Sorry, Tess, I forgot—you can't, can you?'

'No, I can't.'

Something that might have been remorse flickered in Chloe's blue eyes before she remembered how Tess had shamelessly monopolised the male attention.

'Does Rafe know?'

'Know what?'

'That you can't have a baby of your own.'

'There's no reason he should know,' Tess replied, wondering when Chloe would decide she'd sunk her knife in deep enough.

'Then you're not sleeping with him…?'

Tess didn't feel inclined to make Chloe feel any happier so she avoided giving a direct answer. 'I don't give my medical history to all my lovers,' she replied, fighting hard to retain her fragile composure.

'A word to the wise, Tess. I thought Rafe looked a bit embarrassed when you were throwing yourself at him earlier. I'm only telling you this—'

'I know,' Tess interrupted drily. 'Out of the goodness of your heart. Your concern is noted, but actually, Chloe, I'm not sure the situation has been invented which could embarrass Rafe.' Irritate, annoy and aggravate, yes; embarrass, no!

'You know me so well.' Despite the laconic drawl, Rafe was showing classic signs of annoyance at that moment.

'Rafe!' The voice at her shoulder made Chloe spin around. Her much practised flirtatious smile faded as she absorbed the furious contempt in his eyes. 'I didn't see you there.'

'I know, and just for the record, Chloe, your aunt isn't a kiss-and-tell sort of lady.' Rafe didn't spare her more than a few seconds before he turned his attention to Tess, but the contact had been long enough for Chloe to feel as bad about herself as she ever had allowed herself to.

'I'll be off, then,' Chloe said weakly.

'Might be a good idea,' Tess agreed without looking at her niece.

'Is it true?' Rafe stepped over the threshold and closed the door firmly behind him.

Tess's unrealistic hope that he hadn't been standing there long enough to hear what Chloe had said vanished.

'I thought you'd gone.' She picked up a plate from the table and promptly dropped it on the floor where it smashed into a thousand pieces. 'Look what you made me do…' Her voice quivered.

'I asked you a question.'

'I chose not to answer it,' she responded flippantly.

'Will you stop doing that? You're going to cut yourself.' He came up behind her and, arms around her narrow ribcage, hauled her to her feet. He brushed the tiny fragments of powdery china off her knees before straightening up himself. Placing his fingers beneath her chin, he searched with grim eyes the flushed face she turned reluctantly up to him.

'I wish you wouldn't tower over me.'

'Blame my genes and a well-balanced diet.'

'Let go of me,' she whispered shakily.

'You can't have children…?'

Tess closed her eyes. 'That's right, I'm sterile.'

Or as good as damn it, anyhow! Improbable, but not impossible was the way the doctor who had patiently explained about her condition had put it. He'd gone on to speak at length about IVF and associated treatments, but Tess, who irrationally had felt as if her very femininity had been cast into doubt by the news, hadn't actually taken in much of what he'd said.

She supposed that it was something she'd just taken for granted…the fact that one day she'd meet someone and they'd have children. She had never actually thought about it and if anyone had asked her she wouldn't have claimed to be a particularly maternal person. It was only when she'd realised this was never going to happen that she'd known how strong the desire to one day be a mother was.

'You didn't tell me.'

This resentful observation wrenched a bitter laugh from her. 'It isn't the sort of thing that crops up in conversation very often! By the way, when my appendix burst that time it seems it left me a bit tied up, quite literally.'

Rafe winced. He couldn't begin to imagine what this sort

of thing meant to a woman. 'How long have you known about it?'

'About five years.'

The sound of his startled inhalation was audible. 'So long...?' he wondered.

'And, no matter what Chloe implied, it wouldn't make any difference if I could have a hundred children of my own—no child could replace Ben!' She glared at him obstinately, daring him to think otherwise.

He swore. 'I know that, Tess.'

She glared but his dark eyes were kind and caring. Tess felt her antagonism slide away, leaving a raw sadness in its place.

'I know you know,' she mumbled indistinctly as with a sigh she finally allowed herself to relax into the embrace and succour his waiting arms offered.

'You should have told me.'

'I wish I had,' she mumbled honestly. Deep down she supposed she'd been afraid that Rafe would look at her differently when he knew.

She didn't weep, she just held onto him as though her life depended on it. In his turn Rafe stroked her hair, caressed the curve of her spine. It wasn't the soft, silly things he said that comforted her so much as the reassuring sound of his deep voice.

'Thanks.' Feeling suddenly intensely shy, Tess experienced an urgent desire to be released from the strong arms that held her. Rafe seemed to have no trouble interpreting the sudden rigidity in her slender body.

Standing back on her own two feet, she smoothed her hair and avoided his compassionate eyes.

'You know, maybe it would be better if Chloe does have Ben to live with her and Ian,' she announced, trying to look at the problem objectively. 'I've never been able to offer Ben a father. A boy needs a man in his life...role model...that sort of thing...'

'You'll marry one day and someone who'd be a better role model than that creep Chloe's got herself involved with.'

Given Rafe's antagonism to Ian, Tess decided to leave the *creep* issue well alone. She shook her head firmly. 'No, I'll never get married.'

'You say that now, but when you meet someone…'

It made Tess angry that he was just telling her what he thought she wanted to hear—a pretty pointless exercise when they both knew the reality was that no man would want her once he knew the truth.

'I said *never*.' Her expression hardened. 'Marriage is all about providing a loving, secure environment for children. That's why a man gets married.'

'That's why women get married,' he corrected. 'They're the practical ones. A man gets married for other reasons.'

'You really don't have to try and make me feel better, Rafe. I've had a lot of time to get used to the idea and I'm quite realistic about it.'

'That must account for the saintly aura,' he snapped. 'Who made you the expert on what men want?'

His anger continued to confuse her. 'Well, I'm not, but—'

'But nothing! I can see that you've written yourself this naff script that says you've got to be brave and stoical, and quite frankly it makes me want to wring your stupid neck.'

'I'd noticed,' she responded faintly.

'Being a man.'

'I'd noticed that too.' On reflection this was a subject it might be better not to pursue.

'I feel,' he continued, in no mood to be sidetracked by her interruptions, 'that I'm *slightly* better qualified to comment on the subject than you. We get some bad press but most men are thinking about love when they get married, Tess, not good child-bearing hips…' His eyes slid of their own volition to a point below Tess's tiny waist. He cleared his throat; it wasn't the child-bearing qualities or lack of them that made it hard for him to look away.

'You're talking about sex. A man doesn't have to get married to have sex, Rafe. But then I'm not telling you something you didn't already know, am I?'

'There's a difference between sex and love, one which even we *shallow* men can recognise.'

Tess blinked at the angry intensity of his words. Oh, God, she'd forgotten; he'd loved and lost! It was small wonder that under the circumstances he felt passionate about the subject.

'Is that why you wanted to get married, Rafe?'

With a frown he brushed aside her slightly wistful question. 'We're not discussing me.'

'That fact seems rather unfair considering we're having an open day on my most intimate feelings,' she grumbled.

'One day I'm sure you'll find the man who wants you for you, not for what you can provide him with.'

'A nice thought...'

'You don't believe me, do you?'

She folded her arms across her chest and gave him a clear-eyed direct look. 'Frankly, no. When I told Andrew, he was off as fast as his four-by-four would take him.' She didn't add that that had been the desired outcome.

'You told the vet?' For some reason the fact that Tess had shared her secret with another man—especially *that* one—while he had been kept in the dark incensed Rafe.

'Well, he did propose to me.'

'Damn cheek!' Rafe muttered. 'All that goes to prove is what a prize pillock he is.'

This was going a bit far, considering Rafe had never spoken to Andrew above twice as far as she knew.

'What is it with you, Rafe?' she puzzled. 'Do you take a dislike to any man I like on principle? I thought women were meant to be the irrational ones.'

'Irrational! Me?' Rafe looked predictably amazed at the idea.

'First Andrew and now Ian. The poor man hasn't done anything but be pleasant.'

'The *poor* man is the pathetic type who at the first sign of a receding hairline and expanding waistline—'

'I didn't see either on Ian,' she couldn't resist interjecting.

'He spends a sack full of money to make sure you don't.'

'God, but you've got a cruel tongue.'

'Stock in trade, angel,' he admitted unrepentantly. 'Your Ian has nabbed himself the first nubile young beauty who is stupid, or infatuated enough—in Chloe's case both—to make himself an object of universal envy. His mates will pat him on the back and call him a hell of a bloke! It's classic.'

'It's a generalization, is what it is,' she retorted scornfully.

He tried another tack. 'Are you trying to tell me that you approve of an age gap that dramatic, Tess?'

'I can see it might be problematic,' Tess conceded, 'but it shouldn't matter when two people are in love.'

'I always knew you were a closet romantic under all that pragmatism.' Mockery glittered savagely in his dark eyes. 'At this point I'm resisting my natural inclination to quote Ben...' She looked back at him blankly. *'Mush?'* he reminded her.

'I don't blame you for being bitter...' She cleared her throat, skating delicately around his masculine sensitivity. 'It's only natural that you feel a little bit cynical at the moment.'

'I'm cynical for a living,' he snarled.

'There's no need to sound so proud of it,' she remonstrated tartly.

'I take it you fall into the love-conquers-all camp...with one significant exception.'

Confusion flickered across her face. 'What exception?'

'Yourself.'

The colour that had only recently returned to her cheeks rapidly receded. 'That's different.'

'Odd,' he drawled. 'I rather thought it would be.'

'And I wouldn't know, would I, never having been in love?'

He looked thunderstruck by her angry assertion. *'Never!'*

If he knew some of the other things she'd never done, he'd *really* stare! 'I've no desire to discuss my love life with you. Who asked for your opinion about anything anyhow?' Her face stiff with defensive disdain, she tossed her head, sending the warm rich strands of hair whipping across her face. 'For that matter, who asked you to stay?'

'Perhaps I find your *warmth* slightly less chilly than the reception I'll no doubt receive at home.'

His ironic twisted smile aggravated the hell out of her. It wouldn't have taken much effort to pretend the pleasure of her company had anything to do with it, but why be kind when you could be sarcastic? Wasn't that just Rafe all over?

'I don't know why you insist on fighting with your grandfather. He's an old man...'

Rafe's lips twitched. 'I'll tell him you said so. The news of his decrepitude should go down nearly as well as the knowledge his death should make it onto the six o'clock news. I thought maybe you could do with a friend around.' His broad shoulders lifted dismissively. 'It would seem I was wrong. I'll make myself scarce.' He bent to pick up the jacket he'd discarded over the back of a chair the previous evening.

CHAPTER FIVE

'YOU'RE going…?' Perversely the thought filled Tess with dismay. Why the panic? It's not as if I'm not used to being alone.

'Wasn't that the idea?'

'Yes…no…'

Rafe's dark brows drew into a quizzical line. 'Are you making me a better offer?' He'd intended the question to be ironic, then he saw the expression on her face and he grew very still.

Tess's eyes widened. Am I…? The muscles of her pale smooth throat worked as her lips moved silently. Why not? some inner reckless voice challenged. It's what you want isn't it…? It's what you haven't stopped thinking about.

'Well, Tess…?' he prompted with husky impatience.

'I don't think I want to be alone. I'll just be sitting here…thinking…' She swallowed. 'I want what's best for Ben, but I don't want to lose him.' She fought back a sob and caught the pink flesh of her lower lip between her teeth. 'Do you think I'm very selfish?' Her wide green eyes fixed on his face.

Rafe swallowed hard. 'No more than the rest of us. I'll stay if you want, Tess,' he agreed hoarsely and was rewarded with a watery smile. 'But you've got to promise me one thing.'

'What?'

'Don't look at me like that!' he pleaded throatily.

'I don't understand…'

'Men have hormones, Tess, and I'm no exception. Do you hear what I'm saying?'

She heard, all right. She raised her hand and touched the

side of his face. It wasn't an innocent action and she felt a
surge of satisfaction when Rafe jerked away.

'I've got hormones too,' she whispered softly. 'And I've
been thinking about what you said before…' It wasn't until
the confession emerged that she realised just how much
she'd been thinking about it.

'I say a lot of things,' he reflected grimly. 'Some more
worth listening to than others.'

Was this his way of saying he hadn't really meant
it…he'd just been talking big, safe in the knowledge that
she'd never call his bluff? Only a total idiot could fail to
recognise that this situation had a potential for humiliation
on a big scale, and Tess was no idiot. But she found she'd
gone too far to back down now. Besides, a compulsion she
didn't recognise was driving her onwards.

'I want to…' Tess swallowed to relieve the aching constriction in her throat. Her eyes shone with unshed tears as
she willed herself not to flinch from Rafe's gaze. 'I want to
forget…I want to feel…' The words sounded so breathily
needy that for a moment she couldn't believe they'd
emerged from her own mouth.

He still hadn't said anything, which was definitely not a
good sign. She wasn't sure whether it was obstinacy or lu-
nacy that made her stumble on regardless.

'Don't look at me like that. You're the one who planted
the idea in my head!' she shouted resentfully. '*You* said we
wouldn't be hurting anyone. *You* said there was nothing
wrong in giving and receiving a little comfort…' She tried
not to think about how flawed she'd found his logic at the
time.

Rafe didn't need reminding of what he'd said any more
than he needed telling he couldn't go through with it if he
had any shred of decency left.

'I could do with a little comfort right now.' Actually, she
reflected, what I actually need is a great dollop of the stuff.

It was the harsh sound of Rafe's sharp inhalation that

finally brought her reckless babble to an abrupt halt. The enormity of what she'd done hit her with the force of a runaway truck.

She didn't—she *couldn't* look at him as she stumbled towards the door. 'Please, forget I said any of that, it was stupid, I didn't mean…' If only that were true, she would feel less cringeingly humiliated.

'Tess!'

She flinched away from the touch of his hand on her shoulders; the contact was like a jolt of neat electricity running through her body.

'Don't think I took any of that stuff you said this morning seriously.'

He couldn't let her walk away looking like that; perhaps she'd feel better if he confessed he didn't feel so crash-hot happy himself!

Rafe rapidly discovered that making Tess stop still long enough to listen to him—to look at him, even—wasn't as simple a task as he'd bargained for. She struggled against the light restraint as if her life depended on it. Rafe could hardly credit that anyone who appeared as physically delicate as Tess could be so strong. He was afraid she'd hurt herself, or him—the Marquess of Queensberry would have been shocked out of his wig by her tactics—before she exhausted herself.

'You've got a kick like a mule!' He winced as her foot made contact for the second time with his shin. 'You'll give up before I do…' he promised.

Tess gave up so abruptly she almost slithered out of his arms onto the floor. It took a couple of seconds for enough strength to return to her legs to enable them to take her weight and when it did she had only one thought in her head…*escape*!

Rafe's hands closed around her wrists as she began to back impetuously away from him. He could feel the resistance was purely superficial; her heart was no longer in it.

He let her struggle weakly for a moment before jerking her towards him.

'I'm sorry you don't believe I meant what I said,' he grated, speaking from between clenched teeth, 'because I meant every word of it. There's nothing I'd like better than to take you to bed, but you're...'

Was this patent untruth supposed to make her feel better? 'I'm what, Rafe?' She stood passively and turned a seething, resentful gaze upon him. 'Too thin, too ugly, too *easy...*?'

'A man doesn't take advantage when someone is hurting as much as you are. I mean, under normal circumstances would you want to sleep with me? Let alone ask—' He stopped abruptly.

'Don't be squeamish, Rafe, spit it out!' she recommended bitterly. 'We both know I asked you to take me to bed. Why,' she pondered aloud, 'I decide to change the habit of a lifetime and be spontaneous now, I've not the faintest idea.'

'Emotional trauma will do that to a person.'

'Let's leave my emotional trauma out of this for a second, shall we? I'm curious—what man doesn't take advantage? *You?*' Her voice rose to an incredulous squeak. 'You were perfectly willing to take advantage this morning,' she jeered.

A dull colour ran up under his tan. 'I wasn't thinking. I'd be using you!'

Thinking wasn't all it was cracked up to be. If he hadn't started now we'd be... It brought a hectic flush to her cheeks to think about where they'd be if she'd had her wanton way.

'Maybe I want to be used!'

'You don't mean that, Tess.'

'I hate it when you tell me what I mean!'

'I was being selfish, and right now,' he announced explosively, 'at this precise second I have an overwhelming urge to be *extremely* selfish.' The hunger in his restless glance was immensely soothing to Tess's bruised self-esteem—and injurious to her pulse-rate.

That *extremely* sounded very promising and there was no

mistaking the sincerity in his loaded announcement. Relief washed over her. It was slightly less humiliating if the person you'd thrown yourself at found you moderately attractive.

'You do...?' The line between her shapely eyebrows deepened suspiciously.

'Give a man a break, Tess. I'm trying to do the decent thing here, and...' his impressive chest heaved deeply '...if you must know, it's painful!'

'Good!' She meant it, and it showed.

A sliver of amusement slid across his sternly handsome face. 'I'm really glad my agony gives you pleasure. Seriously, Tess...'

'I never stopped being serious.'

'Sex is no cure-all when life stinks.'

She choked quietly on her disbelief. Talk about moving the goalposts! 'You've changed your tune.' For that matter, so have I!

'We're not talking about me, we're talking about you. You're not the type that goes in for casual sex,' he announced firmly.

He thought he would have noticed if Tess had had a string of lovers. Of course, there must have been some, but she'd been pretty discreet. The thought of these anonymous individuals didn't improve his humour.

Does he think I don't already know that? Knowing it hadn't stopped her throwing herself at him like some sex-starved bimbo.

'But you are?'

'No, of course not,' he denied with irritated impatience. 'I'm strictly into monogamy.'

'*Serial* monogamy.'

'If you like,' he conceded testily. 'I'm trying to explain that I can separate my emotions from—'

'Sex!' she supplied shrilly. 'Neat trick, Rafe,' she admired.

The nerve in his clenched jaw started jumping again. 'You only *think* you want to go to bed with me.'

'Now the man knows what I'm thinking! Is there no end to his talents?' she marvelled.

'I'm not going to be responsible for—'

'For what, exactly?' she interrupted hotly. 'This is sex we're talking here, not a lifelong commitment. You think you'd spoil me for other men? You think sleeping with you would be so great I'd fall instantly and inconveniently in love with you? My God, but you really do rate yourself highly these days.'

His sternly reproachful look silenced her scornful laughter. It made her feel mean and petty. What he said next intensified the feeling.

'We're mates…?'

Tess found herself nodding mutely in reply to the probing look in his dark eyes.

'I wouldn't want anything to spoil that, Tess. Not my libido or your loneliness…'

'How do you know I'm lonely?' Lonely had such a pathetic, loserish ring to it. Such an *accurate* ring to it, she acknowledged reluctantly. Without Ben her life was empty. She found herself wondering uncomfortably whether there wasn't some element missing even with Ben. 'As a matter of fact, I'm celibate out of choice, not necessity!'

Rafe thought he probably hid his surprise at this unsolicited piece of information quite well; he didn't have as much success keeping a lid on his raging curiosity.

'How long…?' The pink tinge of her skin became a deeper red as she glared back at him. He held up a pacifying hand. 'None of my business.'

'Too right it isn't,' she growled belligerently.

'I know Chloe's decision has turned your life upside down until you don't know day from night…'

Thoughtfully Tess nodded her head.

'Or friend from lover.'

He was talking sense, of course, but that didn't stop her stomach doing a double flip when she looked at his mouth. It was totally irrational, but she'd never craved anything in her life as much as she craved the touch of Rafe's lips against hers, the touch of his hands on her overheated skin. Hell-fire, girl, it's your overheated imagination you need to worry about!

'And Claudine has done much the same thing to me.'

Tess pushed aside the embarrassing problem of her sensual preoccupation. 'Claudine is the one...?'

His nostrils flared. 'Yes, she's the one.'

A sharp, sobering stab of jealousy lanced through her. 'I'm sorry, Rafe.' Her small hand closed over his forearm. Some friend I am. The warmth in her voice was to compensate for her shameful gut response. Tess's indignation rose. What a bitch this woman must be! Just because Rafe came across as pretty invulnerable, there was no need to play fast and loose with his emotions.

'I thought you prescribed a dose of humility.' He looked from the sincerity of her upturned face to the small hand on his sleeve.

'I'm a sanctimonious cow sometimes.'

Amused affection deepened the creases around his eyes. 'I don't think there's anything remotely bovine about you, Tess. Possibly something slightly feline,' he suggested, his mind flickering back to the way she'd wound herself around him as he'd carried her upstairs the previous night. She certainly had the suppleness of a cat and the green eyes. The smile faded from his own eyes.

Tess had always thought it a cruel twist of fate that a man could have ludicrously long, luscious eyelashes she would have given her eye-teeth for. Now she found herself wondering why she'd never noticed before how expressive those lash-shielded eyes were.

'You can tell me about it if you like,' she offered bravely.

Wasn't that what friends were for…listening? It was just tough that the subject happened to make her skin crawl.

'Who needs sex when you have good old-fashioned friendship?' Rafe wondered harshly. The skin was stretched tightly over the sharp planes and intriguing angles of his strong face. Tess watched dry-mouthed as his breathing perceptively quickened.

'Exactly. We won't even mention sex again,' she agreed miserably.

Her sensible smile faded and died as his hooded eyes continued to rest unblinkingly on her pale face. 'Forbidden subject…?'

Tess nodded. She couldn't take her eyes from the erratic pulse that beat beside his mouth. The silence stretched on and on almost to breaking-point.

'Tess…?' A fine sheen of moisture glistened on the bronzed skin of his face.

She could hardly make out the faraway sound of his curiously strained voice over the slow but thunderous pounding of her own heart.

'Yes, Rafe?'

'It's not important.' His eyes closed and his head went back, displaying the strong line of his throat. After a long tension-soaked moment he lifted it; his eyes were blazing with reckless purpose.

'Yes!' he yelled. 'Yes, it damn well is important! For pity's sake, woman! Kiss me!' he groaned thickly, lunging towards her.

With a small cry of relief Tess closed her arms tightly about his neck as he swung her up off the ground. She could feel the febrile tremors that ran through his lean body.

'Tess…Tess…Tess…' He interspersed the fevered kisses he rained over her face with husky repetitions of her name. 'I know this is slightly crazy, but, God help me,' he breathed against her ear, 'I've got to do this or I'll…'

She didn't want his apologies, she wanted his kisses. 'Me too,' she confessed ecstatically.

To the casual observer, the inarticulate but encouraging noises that emerged from her aching throat might have sounded like whimpers, but Rafe didn't seem to have any trouble interpreting them. He tightened his grip on Tess's pliant frame, drawing it closer to his body, which betrayed even more overtly than his lips did the driving urgency that held him in its grip.

The flurry of shock at discovering just how urgent Rafe was feeling dissipated as a flood of wild, sensual need washed over her. Tess's lips moved inexpertly but with boundless enthusiasm over the hard, clean-cut contours of his olive-skinned face, taking delight in the faintly salty taste of his flesh until their lips finally collided. The collision came not a moment too soon for her needs.

His teeth tugged at the soft, tender skin of her pink parted lips before, with a deep groan, his tongue plunged inside, plundering the moist, receptive warmth of her mouth. The shock of the contact slid so swiftly through her body, the fallout hit her toes even before she started kissing him back with a hunger and urgency that matched his.

Lips still attached to hers, Rafe cleared the table with a single sweeping gesture just before he sat her down on the hard surface.

'We'll still be friends…'

Tess curled her legs around his slim hips and continued to press her lips to the smooth, strong column of his neck while nodding her enthusiastic agreement to his defiant observation.

'That goes without saying.' She lifted her head and found his eyes had a hot, unfocused expression. On seeing that dark, dangerous look she felt a delicious shiver of anticipation join the tiny rivulets of sweat running down her quivering spine.

She let out an ecstatic cry and her body arched when his

hand brushed against the engorged peak of one aching breast.

'Hush,' he soothed thickly as she bit her lip. 'You're so wonderfully sensitive,' he marvelled, his eyes on the point where her nipples protruded through the cotton covering of her dark top. As her lips began to move Rafe bent his head to catch her faint words.

'If we were strangers I couldn't want you to do this.'

She insinuated her hand through the gap where two buttons on his shirt had parted company. Tess felt his powerful stomach muscles contract helplessly as she spread her fingers wide over his amazingly satiny skin. Rafe held her eyes as he hooked a finger under the top button of his shirt and pulled it down impatiently. Several buttons flung across the room as the fabric gaped open.

The breath caught in Tess's throat as her hot, slumberous gaze moved hungrily over his incredibly hard body. His skin glistened under its fine covering of sweat. There wasn't an ounce of surplus flesh to conceal the perfect muscle definition of his broad chest with its light sprinkling of dark hair and washboard-flat belly. Intermittent quivers ran visibly through his body, making the muscles just below the surface ripple. He was quite, *quite* perfect, she thought gloatingly.

'You're right, we don't need the dinner dates and the awkward pauses. We don't need to waste time on all those tedious preliminaries.' If she didn't agree he was in deep trouble! 'We already know everything there is to know about each other,' he panted, tugging her black tee shirt free of the waistband of her jeans and pushing his hands under the thin cotton. Her warm skin felt unbelievably smooth under his hands.

Tess's heavy eyelids lifted to reveal a sultry stare. 'Not quite *everything*, but hopefully we will before much longer.' Her wicked throaty chuckle delighted him before it was lost inside the warmth of his mouth.

The big, strong hand that touched the side of her face wasn't quite steady. 'It's a natural progression.'

Was he trying to convince himself? She didn't waste more than a second on that thought because she was just as eager as he was to skip the preliminaries and satisfy the primal urgency that seemed to have taken her over. She obligingly lifted her bottom to enable him to slide her jeans over her hips and down her legs. The truth be told, at that moment Tess would have agreed if he'd announced he were actually the true King of England.

'It feels natural,' she confided throatily as he stopped kissing her long enough to pull her top over her head.

Rafe was struck by the truth in her pleasing observation, but he was in too much of a hurry to slow down and tell her so. He didn't bother unclipping her bra, just pushed down the lacy fabric that concealed her breasts from his hungry view.

A greedy, guttural sound emerged from low in his throat as her engorged breasts sprang free from their confinement. The feral sound made all the fine hairs over her body stand on end. Her quivering thighs opened to accommodate the knee he placed on the edge of the table. The friction as his knee nudged the highly sensitised area between her legs made her gasp; it was a raw, fractured sound.

Either the faint noise had been abnormally amplified or his senses were highly attuned to her because Tess found his eyes immediately sought hers.

'Sorry, I was clumsy.' He made a minor adjustment that relieved the pressure.

'You're anything but clumsy,' she breathed appreciatively. 'And that's not flattery,' she added forcefully, 'it's fact!' she explained with fervour.

'I stand corrected.' He reached down and his fingers slowly slid under the lacy edge of her pants to touch the ultra-sensitive skin of her inner thigh. 'Did I hurt you here…?' He pushed the fabric aside and let his fingers touch the sweet, damp heat. His delicate, teasing touch pushed Tess to the very limit of pleasure and beyond; every muscle in her abdomen contracted in unison, she simply melted.

'So slick, so hot... You want this...you want me...?'

'That has to be the most ridiculous thing you've ever asked me!' she told him hoarsely.

He responded with a look so primitive and predatory that a low keening cry was wrenched from deep inside her.

'I...you, *please*, Rafe!' she panted.

Rafe didn't seem to have any trouble deciphering her inarticulate plea. For a moment he watched her pale body writhe sinuously beneath him. Then, with one foot still on the floor, his body curved fully over hers and he pushed her slowly backwards until she lay there with her hair spread out around her delicately flushed face.

His eyes moved hungrily over the slender contours of her almost naked body. Perversely the tiny scraps of lace stretched across her lower body and beneath her breasts made her appear more naked, more *his*.

He fought with the last dregs of his control to subdue the primitive desire to possess that stretched every nerve and sinew in his body to breaking-point. Slow and gentle had its place, but that place wasn't here and now. On the other hand he didn't want to spoil things by rushing her.

He watched with covetous, burning eyes the rise and fall of her deliciously rounded pink-tipped breasts. Slowly he touched the side of one quivering mound before his mouth moved hungrily to the rosy swollen peak.

The sight of his dark head against the pale skin of her breasts was the most erotic thing Tess had ever seen. She cried out as his tongue lashed and his lips expertly teased.

She lay there in a delicious sensual haze until the pleasure centres of her brain finally overloaded. She simply couldn't take any more of this! Frantically she clutched awkwardly at the smooth golden skin that covered his broad back. Her nails left raised red grooves as they slid down the powerful curve before coming to rest on the taut firmness of his behind.

'If you don't do something I'll die!' She genuinely believed what she said and it showed.

'You won't be alone,' he rumbled.

Tess was vaguely conscious of him adjusting his clothing before he slid his hands under her buttocks. She heard the sound of tearing fabric an instant before he settled between her legs; she felt the hard tip of his arousal against her belly. The stark reality of what she was about to do hit her then; what surprised her most was that it didn't scare her.

Fingernails inscribing small half-moons in the delicate flesh of her palms, she lifted her arms up over her head. 'I want to see...' There was stark appeal in the feverish eyes she lifted to his face. Intent on increasing the intimate contact, she shifted and rotated her hips restlessly beneath his.

Rafe covered her hands with his and pinioned them either side of her head. 'You want to see what...?'

'You.'

It was the most incredible thing to see him slide slowly into her, until to all intents and appearances they were one. It was even more incredible, not to mention indescribably pleasurable, that her body could accommodate him. She was sobbing from the wonder of it when she raised her eyes to his. If it never got any better than this, it was still the most marvellous she'd ever felt in her life.

'Is this the sort of something you had in mind?'

She shook her head—the words hadn't been invented that could accurately describe anything this mind-blowingly erotic! Besides, she didn't trust herself to open her mouth because she was experiencing an almost incapacitating desire to say she loved him.

'And this sort of something...?'

He began to move. Tess closed her eyes tightly as things began to get very much better indeed! She was never quite sure, but she thought she might have screamed something to that effect just before his slow thrusts—it seemed impossible that such a big man could move with such incredible controlled precision—became more vigorous. *Much* more vigorous.

Then there were no thoughts at all, just the fierce, primitive rhythm that swept her along until a shattering climax ripped through her. Barely seconds later she heard Rafe cry out and felt his release pulse deep within.

Now she was here she could understand why they'd both been in such a hurry to reach the journey's end.

CHAPTER SIX

'WHAT are you doing?' Tess protested as Rafe bundled her and as many stray items of clothing as came within his grasp up into his arms.

She'd been quite content—well, a bit more than content, actually—to lie there beneath his heavy, sweat-slick body and enjoy the extraordinary intimacy of the quiet following the storm.

And what a storm! Tess had never imagined she would find herself in a situation, or with a man, who could make her forget her natural inhibitions and behave with such wonderful, wanton abandon.

Control had never been something Tess had had to work hard at; she had buckets of the stuff. How could surrender be fulfilling erotically or otherwise? From her comfortable position of smug security she had never been able to understand how women of her acquaintance—women who in every other way were strong and confident—could allow and actively *desire* to surrender that control to a man. Now she knew…*boy, oh, boy, did she know*!

The memory of the driving, all-consuming need to be possessed still had an almost surreal quality to it. There was nothing surreal, however, about the warm ache of fulfilment that was snugly curled up low in her belly. The total belief that Rafe had been just as much a helpless victim of his desires as she had been of hers made her feel neither victim or defeated; in fact she'd never dreamt that this sort of fulfilment existed!

She was vaguely aware that she ought to feel embarrassed. Maybe I will, she mused, when I'm able to think about what happened with cold, clinical objectivity. Tess had never felt quite this far away from clinical objectivity in her life! Mellow didn't begin to describe the warm, satisfied glow that engulfed her. She'd never considered herself the uptight sort, but this was a new experience for her…and not the first of the day, she mused, a small smile tugging at the corners of her generous mouth.

'To bed.'

There was no sexual significance to his prosaic reply, but heat flooded her body. As foolish as it obviously was, she couldn't deny that the sound of his deep voice seemed to be enough to send a shudder of desire all the way down to her curling toes.

'Isn't that a bit like shutting the stable door after the horse has bolted?' She swallowed to lubricate the dryness of her throat, watching Rafe move to lock the door.

'Do you fancy any Tom, Dick or Harry walking in to find you stretched out on the kitchen table?' he enquired.

Tess felt the first stirrings of unease threaten to spoil her laid-back mood. And small wonder, she reflected. He'd managed to conjure up a painfully stark image.

'What a tasteless comment,' she complained.

'Crude but accurate.'

There was no arguing with that even though she'd have liked to.

Rafe used her silence to elaborate on his theme—quite unnecessarily, as far as she was concerned. 'Can you imagine how swiftly that story would spread around the village?'

Tess grimaced; she could. 'I'd have to move house.' She wasn't entirely joking.

'That might not be such a bad idea,' he observed cryptically just before he dumped her on the bed.

Tess lay there in an unselfconscious tangle of pale naked limbs puzzling over what he'd said. 'What do you mean?' she began.

It was the expression on Rafe's lean face as he looked down at her that made her lose the thread. It also made her intensely conscious of every inch of naked flesh she was casually flaunting.

Of course he was staring; she was female and naked. Given the opportunity, wouldn't most men stare at a naked woman? *Any* naked woman—*any* being the significant word here. Testosterone would win over manners every time.

'I wish you wouldn't look at me like that,' she fretted with a disapproving frown.

'Like what?' he asked, without shifting the focus of his attention.

'Like you're salivating.'

A laugh was wrenched from him. 'Not visibly, I hope?'

'You doing anything that wasn't aesthetically pleasing…I don't think so!' He had to be the most naturally elegant creature she'd ever laid eyes on, she decided. Furthermore his grace was totally unstudied, an intrinsic part of him. No wonder she often felt challenged in the grace department in his company. 'I'm sure you look pretty damned great with egg on your face.'

Even though her spiky observation sounded more like a criticism than a compliment, her eyes were eating up every detail of his appearance. Tiny insignificant things delighted and fascinated her, like the oval-shaped mole just above his right nipple, and the way…dear God, Tess, anyone would think you were in love or something! Her eyes widened in acute anxiety. No, I can't be, not now…not with Rafe!

'You're very kind, but all the same that's a situation I prefer to avoid… Just to be on the safe side, you understand.'

Tess didn't respond to the whimsy.

'Are you all right?' Rafe frowned. The colour had fled so dramatically from her face that he thought for an uncomfortable couple of seconds she was going to pass out. Women didn't normally look as though they were about to throw up after he'd made love to them.

'I'm fine…absolutely fine!' Her voice cracked comically on the last syllable.

Her squeaking response didn't make Rafe smile; his angular jaw set stubbornly. He refused point-blank to believe that she was regretting what had happened. He wouldn't damn well let her!

'You have to expect a bit of drooling, Tess, when you're flaunting your beautiful body like this.' His fierce grin showed signs of strain just before Tess, unable to stand the exposure any longer, slid awkwardly under the covers, her cheeks burning.

A classic case of too little too late, she thought, feeling ridiculously gauche. It's not as if there is much he hasn't already seen, and even less he hasn't touched.

'That wasn't a complaint. However,' Rafe conceded with a regretful sigh, 'it will make it easier to talk, and we do need to talk.'

Easier for whom? she wondered. Rafe might have pulled on his trousers, though he hadn't stopped to fasten his belt, but he wasn't wearing his shirt. A face full of perfect pectorals made it hard for a girl to concentrate. Lust she could cope with, she told herself briskly—it was the other *L* word that made her jumpy.

'Talk…about what?' Not the start of a deep and meaningful relationship—that went without saying. She ignored the first stirrings of dissatisfaction in her breast. He was probably worried she'd start getting emotional and clingy, so now probably wasn't the moment to tell him.

'You don't have to worry, Rafe, I know it didn't mean anything.' She managed a creditably light-hearted smile. He looked unaccountably annoyed, which seemed pretty unreasonable even by his standards.

'I can see the attractions of your strategy,' he reflected thoughtfully.

Talk of *strategy* came as a surprise to Tess, who was

having trouble with the simplest of mental processes. 'What strategy?' she puzzled.

'If you think someone's about to kick you where it hurts, get the boot in first.'

To listen to him talk anyone would think she'd wounded him. She brushed aside that ludicrous piece of wishful thinking. 'Since when did you get so sensitive? I'm sorry if you think I was being too blunt, but it's a bit late in the day for us to start pretending.'

'That would be foolish,' he agreed gravely.

Tess bit her lip. He was literally oozing polite disbelief. 'I'm trying to keep this as painless as possible,' she reproached. 'There's bound to be a bit of…awkwardness involved when you sleep with someone you've been friends with. I'm only trying to make this easier for you. I'm sure you've got too much on your plate to want any added *complications*—I know I have.'

Right now she needed to devote all her energy to the Ben dilemma. There had never been a less appropriate time to pursue her own selfish pleasures. 'At least we don't have to worry about unwanted pregnancies.' Smiling about this was one of the hardest things she'd ever done. And what did she get for her efforts…? He didn't even look relieved.

'Actually, I've no interest in debating how empty and meaningless you found our love-making.'

'Don't put words into my mouth!' she protested.

'Now there's a sentiment I can identify with,' Rafe came back grimly. He fixed her with a stern, unblinking stare and wasted no more time before introducing the subject that had been and still was uppermost in his mind. 'The celibacy thing…just what sort of time scale are we talking here?' he enquired with deceptive casualness.

Nothing could have sounded more offhand than her response…possibly too offhand, she worried. 'A while…' She threaded the fringe of the brightly coloured throw around her finger before arranging it in an artistically pleasing pattern against the white sheet.

'A *long* while…? Will you stop doing that?' he rapped abruptly, snatching the material from her restless fingers and seating himself on the side of the bed.

'It might be,' she conceded defiantly.

He watched the flicker of emotion run across her deeply expressive face and cursed. It didn't seem possible, but deep down he'd known that against all the odds he was right! Worse still, part of him—the politically incorrect, Neanderthal part—had felt a primitive gloating delight at the notion of being the first.

'There's no need to swear!'

Rafe thought there was every need. 'A long time as in never?' He hit his forehead with his hand before dragging it through his thick mop of glossy dark hair. The expression on her face had said it all!

'And if it is?' she challenged, lifting her hot-cheeked face to his. 'So what? There's certainly no need to hold an inquest.'

'We'll have to agree to differ on that one.'

'So what's new?' she flung at him carelessly. 'Since when have we ever agreed on anything?' He was the most unreasonable person she knew. Being friends is hard enough— whatever made me think that being lovers would work out any better? That argument lost its validity when she reluctantly acknowledged that *thinking* hadn't had a whole lot to do with it at the time! Now, if you were talking blind lust, compulsion, frenzied urgency…

Rafe's chiselled nostrils flared as his sensual lips thinned. 'I can't believe you gave away something you obviously valued so highly so casually!'

Was Rafe of all people lecturing her on morals?

'It wasn't casual!' she yelled, coming up onto her knees and drawing the sheet with her up to her chin.

The wariness in his sharp glance made her realise how easily what she had said could be misinterpreted…or not…?

'I didn't mean *casual* exactly,' she contradicted swiftly. 'I meant this was different…obviously.'

'Obviously?' he enquired unsmilingly.

'It had been a very stressful twenty-four hours for us both.' She gave an exasperated sigh as a stony-faced Rafe failed to display any appreciation of the point she was trying to make. 'A series of freak circumstances.'

'Not to mention insatiable lust.'

'All right!' she exclaimed. 'Insatiable lust. There! Does that make you feel any better?' He'd made her feel better—a *lot* better, and now he was spoiling it with this interrogation. 'It's not like I was waiting for Mr Right or anything,' she assured him scornfully.

'Well, you wouldn't be, would you?' he bit back.

'Am I supposed to know what the hell you're getting at?'

'I'm saying the victim look does nothing for you,' he announced brutally.

'I don't think of myself like that!' Tess exclaimed, genuinely horrified that anyone could think she cultivated a martyred attitude.

'*No?*' Rafe's dark brows arched sceptically. 'You talk like you're some sort of cripple…not quite a *whole* woman.'

His accusation stung. 'I'm just being realistic. I'm sorry if it makes you feel uncomfortable.'

'Realistic!' Rafe found himself responding furiously. 'Self-pitying, more like, but don't expect me to make any concessions for your *disability*! Thousands of people live perfectly productive, happy lives with *real* disabilities. You can't have a baby—'

'*So what!*' she jumped in. How could a man, especially one as selfish and insensitive as Rafe, begin to understand? 'Is that what you're saying?'

'I'm saying that it's tough and unfair, but then that's life. The fact you can't have babies is part of what you are, like the colour of your eyes, it's not *who* you are.' His voice had become surprisingly gentle and Tess felt her throat grow tight with emotion. 'There's always adoption...?' Two slashes of colour stained the sharp angle of his cheekbones as he watched her blink back the tears that sparkled in those vulnerable green depths. 'Anyhow, you certainly felt all woman to me.' His abrupt tone suggested she'd done this just to aggravate him.

'I did?' Hell, why don't you just start purring, Tess? she asked herself bitterly. He's just virtually designated you an emotional disaster area and all you can think about is some throw-away remark that he probably only added to make you feel better!

She hardened her heart and her expression before she looked directly at him. 'Pardon me,' she said coldly, 'if I don't take advice from a man who thinks it's a good idea to fall in love with a married woman!' Remorse washed over her the instant the words were out of her mouth.

Eyes coldly angry, he grinned humourlessly back at her, displaying a set of perfect, even whiter than white teeth. 'You do go for the jugular, don't you, angel?'

'I'm sorr—'

'Don't apologise, you're right. I think the children tipped the balance in the end.' If she was going to look at him as though he was a moral degenerate, he might as well give her the opportunity to look all the way down her cute nose—yes, it is, isn't it? he realized, looking at her small tip-tilted appendage with a surge of affection tinged with definite lust.

That had always been the way of it with Tess. One minute you wanted to strangle her—his eyes darkened as they automatically flickered to the smooth, pale length of her slender throat—the next you wanted... Rafe stiffened. Actually, until very recently he'd never wanted to do *that* before.

'She has children...?' Tess gasped, looking shocked enough to fulfil even his cynical expectations.

'Two. But aren't we straying off the subject? Now, let me think…what was it? I know, virginity.'

'I wish you'd leave it alone,' she breathed wearily. 'The fact is, I'm not terribly highly sexed.'

There wasn't even a trace of irony in her grave explanation. Rafe threw back his head and laughed. There was still mirth in his eyes when he'd managed to compose himself; the slashing white grin disappeared in deference to her icy disapproval.

'You're a tonic, Tess.'

'I'm so glad I've managed to brighten your day,' she responded frigidly.

Not to mention complicate my life, he amended silently. He had a gut certainty—Rafe relied heavily on gut certainty—that there were ramifications to this he hadn't even thought of yet!

'It's not like I've been deliberately holding onto it or anything. Actually,' she continued, 'I was in a fairly serious relationship and was on the point of…giving it away, as you so tastefully phrase it,' she snapped, 'when the doctor told me about…that I couldn't…you know… I told Tom. It wasn't as if we were going to get married or anything, but I thought he had the right to know.' A faraway look entered her wide-spaced eyes as she recalled the events of five years earlier.

'And *Tom* did what?' Rafe asked in that deceptively languid tone.

'He said he was sorry, but…'

'The creep dumped you!' Rafe ground out savagely.

Tess shrugged. 'Illness really freaked him out. I know I wasn't ill, precisely, but he—'

'Now I know where you got all these bloody stupid ideas from.'

'Don't be silly, Rafe. I'm not denying I was hurt at the time, but it doesn't matter now. He did me a favour really—'

'You mean he jumped off the nearest high building?' Rafe

smiled in what Tess considered a sinister, scary way as he contemplated this scenario.

Rafe could make sinister look not only scary, but *sexy* too... Tess instinctively knew it would be a bad idea to follow that thought to its conclusion, especially when all she had to do was reach out to touch acres of golden firm flesh...

She jammed quivering fingertips under her knee and ran her tongue over the outline of her dry lips. 'I mean,' she explained brusquely, 'that it made me see how pointless it would be to get seriously involved with anyone when there could be no future. I thought about casual sex,' she confessed.

'Don't we all?' he came back flippantly. Didn't casual imply a fun, relaxed, no headaches, no emotional trauma situation? The throb in his temples kicked up another notch as she began to idly chew a stray strand of rich reddish-tinged hair.

Once she'd even gone so far as to go clubbing with a friend whose idea of a good night out was to pick up an able and willing male—*any* able and willing male! It had taken Tess about half an hour to realise that it wasn't the route for her to go. She could think of better ways to prove she was as liberated as a man!

'Only I haven't got the stomach for it.'

'Until now.'

'That was different.' She gritted her teeth and wished he'd stop being so tiresome about the entire business.

'So you keep saying. Why? That's what I want to know.'

Don't we all? 'I suppose you think I should have told you? The fact is, I didn't even think about it...actually, I wasn't thinking at all,' she amended wryly, recalling with a deep blush the frantic urgency that had gripped her. 'Except about...you know...' She looked self-consciously away.

'I know, all right,' he conceded drily. A man who had slept with a vulnerable virgin ought to feel like a first-class heel—Rafe had—but that feeling was fading fast as his sexual interest was being stirred…actually, *stirred* was a pretty anaemic description of the prowling hunger that was beginning to twist his guts into tortuous knots. He suddenly had a strong mental picture of some other faceless male taking over where he'd left off and the muscles in his belly cramped hard in fierce rejection. It wasn't in his nature to leave anything half finished.

'It honestly wasn't an issue for me. I don't feel defiled or anything daft like that.' With a laugh designed to illustrate how lacking she was in neuroses, Tess firmly rejected this idea. 'If you must know I feel liberated…empowered, even!' she elaborated, resorting to a humorously extravagant gesture. The gesture fell flat on its face at approximately the same moment the sheet slid down to her waist. She didn't feel particularly empowered as she scrabbled to pull it up again. 'I should have done it years ago,' she gritted with determined and audibly forced humour.

Rafe was watching her with that dark, brooding, enigmatic expression of his.

'All you had to do was ask.'

Tess's laughter was genuine this time, if tinged with bitterness. 'What a whoppa!' she gasped. 'You've never fancied me even slightly.' Which was probably the only reason their friendship had survived past puberty! 'See,' she jeered, wagging her finger at him. 'You can't deny it!'

He caught her finger and, holding her eyes with his own, raised it to his lips. He kissed the tip softly before he drew it slowly into his mouth. He sucked.

All her stomach muscles, including the deep neglected ones, contracted in unison. Tess's eyes darkened dramatically as she gave a deep, voluptuous sigh.

'I keep telling you some things change.'

Not the sexiness of his voice…that was one of life's eternal features. 'Not *that* much,' she croaked in a dazed, resentful whisper as she snatched her damp finger away. She suspected he was making fun of her.

'Then why,' he enquired with unforgivable insight, 'are you trembling?'

'I'm not saying you're not attractive—especially,' she added drily, 'when you try so hard.' Why, she wondered a little hazily, was he trying at all?

'If you think that was trying, angel…'

'All right, all right,' she responded, anxious to avoid any and all demonstrations of Rafe's seductive powers. 'Let's take your stud status as read, shall we?' she offered sweetly.

'Cow!' he countered affectionately.

'When I needed someone, you were there.' And even if she had been the type to waste her tears over spilt milk, Tess knew she would never regret it. 'But now is different.'

'Now you know what you're doing,' he suggested quietly.

'Exactly.' She couldn't help but feel slightly regretful that she was in full possession of her senses.

'I'm going to remind you that you said that,' he responded cryptically. 'The next time we make love,' he added, not at all cryptically, in response to her puzzled expression.

'You're not suggesting we…we do this sort of thing on a…a…'

'Regular basis?' The metal bed-frame shuddered as he disposed his long, lean frame comfortably beside her. 'I can't think of any sensible reason not to.'

'I can. I can think of several hundred!'

'I said a *sensible* reason. We both have needs which are not being fulfilled anywhere else at the moment.'

'As propositions go, that has all the old-fashioned charm of a demographic survey! I'm damned if I'm going to make myself available for you when you just happen to be in the area. It's so *demeaning*.' Tess gave a little shudder of distaste and didn't notice he'd grown rigid with anger. 'I think what you need is a good old-fashioned mistress!'

Abruptly Rafe rolled over onto his side and firmly removed the sheet from her white-knuckled grasp; equally firmly he took hold of her slim thigh and tugged her down until they lay face to face. His eyes burnt with fierce determination as they swept over the slender length of her trembling body before coming to rest on her face.

'What I need is you.'

Heat flooded her belly; tiny red dots danced before her eyes.

'And you need me,' he announced with equal authority. 'I know we didn't go out looking for this to happen, but it has.' He felt the tremor run through her body as he cupped one soft breast in his big hand. 'I certainly wasn't looking to forget my problems in some sort of sexual frenzy,' he admitted hoarsely.

Frenzy! Had he really said frenzy? Tess was having trouble focusing on his lean dark face. She had never thought of herself as the type of female capable of inspiring frenzy in anyone. It was satisfying to have it confirmed that she hadn't been the only one to feel that way. She squirmed and said his name softly as his thumb rubbed gently over her tight, rigid nipple.

His next words suggested that Rafe was equally puzzled by this bizarre occurrence. 'Neither was I expecting to find myself feeling this sort of attraction for anyone so soon—if ever—least of all you!'

Tess looked as though she had a nasty taste in her mouth. She was furious with herself for lying there passively letting him touch her how he wanted. Deep down, the idea of letting Rafe touch her how he wanted—how *she* wanted—was a dizzyingly exciting prospect.

She placed her hands on his shoulders and pushed hard, but to little effect. 'That's where I have the advantage, Rafe,' she puffed. 'I've always known you were shallow, but I can see the discovery has come as something of a shock to you…'

'You could have some great fun exploring my shallows,' he promised with a wicked gleam in his eyes.

Tess gave a worried groan and stopped trying to budge

his muscular bulk. 'Don't you think this is getting a bit…*heavy* for a harmless flirtation?' she worried.

'It got heavy for me about the same time you started to rip off my clothes.'

He had been pretty active on the ripping front, and Tess wasn't about to take the entire rap. 'You were the one ripping.'

'Talking of which.' He reached behind her and clicked free the crumpled bra which had stopped being supportive some time before. He held up the scrap of black lace before dropping it to the floor.

'You're obviously on the rebound' she suggested, trying to sound confident and slightly amused about this. Her failure to sound anything but shakily breathless was mostly due to the fact his right arm had smoothly settled into a possessive position over her hip. His fingers moved restlessly over the soft skin of her modestly rounded behind. Her words might have had more impact if she hadn't responded so enthusiastically to the long, languid kiss he pressed to her slightly parted lips.

'Far less dangerous to rebound in your direction, Tess, than a stranger who might think…'

'It meant anything,' she finished dully, drawing the back of her hand angrily over her just-kissed lips. She couldn't wipe away the taste of him from her mouth.

'Of course it means something.' His fingers moved in a series of graceful, gentle arabesques along the projections of her spine. Desire sharp and sweet clutched deep inside her. 'It means I want you, and you want me.'

'Aren't you presuming…?' Under her half-closed eyelids she watched with a sense of helplessness Rafe examine her aching breasts as they visibly responded to his statement. Small wonder he looked pretty smug!

'Am I?'

It was an inconvenient time to discover she couldn't look

him in the eye and lie. 'You make it sound uncomplicated and simple…'

Even while she was protesting, she had the feeling they both knew she was just going through the motions. Some things in life were inevitable and she'd discovered pretty late on in hers that one of them was when Rafe said he wanted her she was a lost cause! Could this be a genetic flaw? she wondered.

'It's nothing of the sort. So far all we've done is argue and fight…'

'We *always* argue and fight.'

'And normally I don't give a damn.'

She saw a thoughtful expression drift into his eyes. Stifling a cry of vexation, she bit her tongue until she tasted the tang of salt. 'Listen, Rafe,' she said, grabbing a pillow from above her head and pushing it between them. It hurt her sensitised breasts and it made a puny defence, but it was better than nothing. 'I value our friendship, but it'll never survive us…'

'Being lovers? Aren't you being just the tiniest bit perverse? One minute all we do is argue and fight, the next our friendship is worth preserving at any cost…including my sanity!' he growled.

Shock made her forget how imperative it was not to look directly at him. It took about two seconds of exposure to that dark, smouldering glare to almost paralyse her with desire.

'You should go visit your grandfather.' She found it hard to form the words. 'I should…'

'Sit here all alone and brood. I think my idea is better. You know how to wound a bloke, Tess. Here I am offering you my body and my not inconsiderable expertise…'

He might have made it sound like a joke, but Rafe was deadly serious. He knew she'd enjoyed their first frantic coupling; her reactions had been more eloquent than any lavish words of praise. Rafe found he wanted to teach—to hell with want! He *needed* to show her the finer subtleties, show her how good restraint could be. He'd be so damned restrained that she'd be begging him to take her, he decided, smiling with grim determination into her flushed, aroused face! He might do a bit of begging himself, just to show her there wasn't a damned thing wrong with it.

Just when his own was climbing to explosion-point, the strain faded from Tess's face and she burst out laughing. 'Why, you...!'

Rafe grabbed the pillow she'd just whacked him over the head with. 'That wasn't just an idle boast.' Tess found the combination of warm laughter and smouldering awareness in his eyes tremendously potent and attractive. The smile faded from her face.

'I'm sure you've been around, but spare me the details.'

'Compared to you, Tess, a newborn kitten has been around, but I'm here to change all that.' He took her chin between his thumb and forefinger and refused to let her look away.

'I don't think I want anything to change.'

'What are you going to do—pretend we didn't make love? Pretend you didn't enjoy it? Pretend you don't want to repeat the experience just as much as I do?' He shook his head reprovingly from side to side. 'Too much pretending for one woman. Break the habit of a lifetime, Tess. Live for the moment, lover...'

'That's a very dangerous philosophy.' Attractive and extraordinarily tempting, she didn't add.

'You're a warm and sensual woman, Tess.'

She knew it wasn't true, but Rafe had a very authoritative way with words. The fact his hand was expertly caressing her breast again probably helped the illusion along slightly too!

Tess felt as if she were dissolving along with her doubts. 'Was it *very* obvious, Rafe?' she whispered, unable to restrain her curiosity any longer. His thumb moved across her nipple and she moaned.

'It was obvious you were made to do this to me,' he responded huskily. 'God knows why I never realised it before.'

'Do what?'

'This.' He took her hand; Tess got the drift straight away.

'You feel…'

'Overdressed.'

'That too,' she conceded huskily.

'You could do something about that. Would you like to?' he asked, brushing the heavy swathe of hair from her hot cheek.

'I want to so much I can't breathe.' Her confession came in a rush and with much heavy breathing. His reply was music to her ears.

Rafe inhaled deeply, drawing the female fragrance of her deep into his lungs. 'You can do all the things you want to.' He continued to kiss her face and neck, sliding his fingers deep into her hair as he angled her chin first this way and then another until there seemed hardly a centimetre of skin his lips hadn't touched.

All she wanted to do was love him, this person she'd known almost all her life but had never really *seen* until today. Had she changed…? Had he…? Tess thought it didn't really matter. It mattered that she'd never been as sure of anything in her entire life. Not that it does me any good, she thought bleakly, when it's the one thing I'm not allowed to do.

'I'm not sure I know how.'

Rafe stopped playing at kissing and did it properly. Rafe's casual was way better than most people's best; his best was very good indeed! 'I know how, I'll show you. All you have to do is tell me what you want.'

'I couldn't do that,' she whispered.

'You've never run scared of telling me what's on your

mind before.' His thumb moved rhythmically over one tight, swollen nipple.

Tess gave a tortured moan. 'That's different.'

'Beautifully different, just like you.'

It was.

CHAPTER SEVEN

RAFE sat at the opposite end of the long table from his grandfather. The arrangement wasn't exactly intimate. You could have comfortably seated at least twenty people between them along the gleaming mahogany surface. In the past he'd frequently seen it accommodate at least that many people. The atmosphere had been convivial on those occasions; tonight it was not.

He toyed with the empty crystal goblet beside his plate. 'Do you eat in here when you're alone?'

'Some of us like to maintain standards.' Edgar Farrar looked with thinly veiled disapproval at his grandson's casual attire. His grandfather's disapproval had stopped bothering Rafe a long time before. 'What would you have me do—eat on a tray in front of the television?'

Rafe's lips twitched. What a scandalous thought! He had noticed the old man's colour had got progressively darker through the meal as he'd accepted the wine his grandson had refused…drinking for two? Rafe wondered how the old man's blood pressure was behaving these days. He didn't ask—he didn't think his concern would be well received. He supposed the ironic thing was that he did actually feel concerned.

'Yeah, the dreaded telly, it's really killed the art of conversation, hasn't it?'. Rafe drawled, his sarcasm pronounced. They'd sat through four courses and not exchanged more than half a dozen words before the coffee stage.

I'd have been better off staying at the cottage with Tess, he thought, not for the first time. Actually he would have stayed if she hadn't forcibly expelled him, insisting she wanted to cope with Chloe without any distractions.

'Heard from Dad lately?'

His father had been living in luxurious exile with his wife in the South of France since he'd been caught with his fingers in the till. Actually, the embezzlement had been a little more sophisticated than that—Guy Farrar might be greedy and impatient, but he was also clever. Not as clever as his father, though, it turned out.

When he'd discovered the crime Edgar had used his own money to cover the theft and set about limiting the damage. He'd succeeded. Inevitably there had been rumours but the family honour had survived the incident intact, which Rafe pondered cynically, was all that mattered! This done, Edgar had told his son he was no longer welcome in the country. Guy had known that Edgar had the power to make life very uncomfortable if he hadn't obeyed the edict.

Rafe didn't regret his parent's departure, but he did feel a twinge of remorse as the older man's ruddy colour intensified.

Despite all the odds, he felt an affection for the bigoted, intolerant old despot which he had never felt for his own father or, for that matter, his brother. His mother had been tearfully delighted to see him when he'd sought her out just after his eighteenth birthday, but you couldn't turn back the clock. Rafe didn't resent this. He knew she had a new family to consider, and he was genuinely happy she'd found someone to make her happy. No, he and Edgar were stuck with each other.

It was probably cruel to bait his grandfather, but then, he reflected wryly, the old man always had been a lifelong advocate of blood sports!

'I hear from your father. He worries I've disinherited him.' Edgar's heavy-hooded lids lifted and he gave a thin-lipped smile.

'And have you?' Rafe wondered casually.

'You'd like that, wouldn't you?' Edgar accused.

'If you think I give a damn one way or the other about

your money and this estate, you couldn't be more wrong,' Rafe told him without heat.

Edgar Farrar's face betrayed the frustration he felt knowing the boy only spoke the truth.

The shrill buzz of his mobile interrupted Rafe's thoughts, which had already wandered in the direction of Walnut Cottage.

Under his grandfather's austere gaze he fished the phone from his pocket.

'Tess.' He could see her so clearly she could have been standing here in front of him. His nostrils twitched; he could almost smell the soft scent of her body. Taking into account the fact his imagination had failed to supply clothes, it was probably just as well—for his grandfather's continued mental well-being—that the image remained a product of his fertile, not to mention erotic imagination.

Rafe was shocked by the degree of pleasure he felt at hearing her voice. He was even more shocked by the way his body reacted lustfully. The pleasure rapidly faded as he registered the anxiety in her voice.

'Blood group…?' His brows drew together in a perplexed troubled line as he supplied the information she requested. 'You know I have. As rare as hen's teeth, so they tell me.' He recited parrot-like the constituents of his rare blood group. His expression darkened as he listened to the babbled explanation. 'The infirmary—I'll be there.' He glanced at the metallic watch on his wrist. 'Twenty…no, make that fifteen minutes.'

'Did you know…?' he rapped, surging to his feet. Struggling to contain his anger, he towered over the older man looking forbidding.

'Know what?' Edgar Farrar wasn't used to being looked at as if he were a particularly nasty bug; he didn't like it.

For once Rafe could find no redeeming humour in the old man's sneering attitude; the joke of being the object of his grandfather's distaste had abruptly vanished.

'Know that your precious Alec had fathered a bastard of one of the local maidens.' One of the only things he'd ever had in common with his deceased elder brother was an extremely rare blood group. It seemed his brother had passed that same blood group on to his son Ben, who was now awaiting surgery in the local city hospital. Tess must be beside herself... He wanted to be there with her; he didn't want to waste time here with the old man.

Edgar Farrar shot to his feet, his arthritic knee forgotten. His eyes blazed. *'How dare you?'*

'Sure,' Rafe drawled, throwing his jacket over his shoulder. 'You shouldn't speak ill of the dead and he was worth ten of me, but don't say you didn't know my sainted brother habitually cheated on poor Annabel.' He laughed harshly as fresh colour suffused his grandfather's already ruddy cheeks. 'Sure you knew, but he cheated with such exquisite discretion and good taste you turned a blind eye.'

'Where do you think you're going, boy?' Edgar yelled at the ramrod straight back of his only remaining grandson. 'Do you think I'd have ignored a child of Alec's if I knew he existed!'

The quaver in the old man's voice made Rafe pause. He slowed and turned back. 'Any heir would be preferable to me, is that right?' He searched the old man's face. 'I thought so.'

'Rafe!'

'Shut up! If I don't get to the hospital soon you won't have an heir at all!' he flung angrily over his shoulder.

It was the first time in his life that anyone had ever told Edgar Farrar to shut up. It took him several moments to recover from the shock, but recover he did.

'You really can't get up yet, Mr Farrar,' a young nurse protested weakly as Rafe swung his long legs over the side of the narrow bed.

'No, he can't,' the older and coolly imperious uniformed

figure who had escorted Tess into the cubicle agreed. 'I've no desire to spend my evening filling in accident forms in triplicate after you fall flat on your face.'

After a short pause Rafe, whose head had done some spectacular spinning as he'd sat up, complied with a rueful grin.

'Right, I'll send along a nice cup of tea and biscuits and you'll feel yourself in no time,' she said briskly, withdrawing with the younger nurse in her wake.

They just looked at one another. Tess knew she had to do something…say something… You couldn't tell a man what she had told Rafe and leave it like that.

'Fancy meeting you here,' Rafe drawled as Tess moved awkwardly forward. 'Any more secrets stored within that delightful bosom?' His eyes lifted from the heaving outline and he saw colour suffuse her face.

Tess sighed regretfully. 'I'm sorry I hit you with it like that, but things were a bit urgent.'

'How's the boy?'

He sounded as if he cared… What am I thinking? If he didn't care he wouldn't be here, she chided herself. 'He's in the operating theatre,' she explained huskily. 'They'll probably have to remove his spleen…' she caught her lower lip savagely between her teeth and continued huskily '…but he should be all right; thanks to you.'

'And the others?'

'Chloe had a nasty bang on the head, but it's only concussion. She should be able to go home in the morning. The driver of the lorry is suffering from shock, which isn't surprising. It must be a nightmare having your brakes pack up on you like that.'

'Sit here.' Rafe rolled onto his side, lifted his head and patted the side of the narrow bed he lay on. 'You look all in.'

Perhaps it was the trauma of the past hour or so, but the

gentleness in his voice brought an emotional lump to Tess's throat.

'Did they take much…?' She glanced warily at the plaster mark on his arm and took him up on his offer.

Actually she was glad to sit down. Her metabolic rate had been in a head-spinning, upward spiral ever since she'd received the phone call from a distraught Ian telling her about the accident. While she'd had something to do, namely get Rafe here to donate his all important blood, she'd been able to cope. Now all that was left was the waiting and she felt so tense a sharp word might be enough to make her crack wide open.

'The odd armful or two. Do I look pale and interesting?'

Actually he looked so devastatingly handsome that her heart had almost leapt from her chest the instant she'd seen him lying there.

'More pallid and pasty.' Tess heard the tremulous quiver in her voice and decided she might leave the sparkling repartee until she was more than one step away from being a basket case. She raised a self-conscious hand to her cheek. 'That probably makes two of us. It was lucky I remembered about your odd blood group.'

'I prefer rare, actually.'

'You had your blood frozen in case it was needed when you had that knee surgery a few years back, didn't you?'

'They do keep some in cold storage for me,' Rafe agreed.

'When they told me about Ben's I realised straight away it must be the same one…'

'Considering our close relationship,' he put in quietly.

'I knew you'd be mad with me.' Worriedly she searched his face and discovered he was searching hers just as diligently.

'For not mentioning in passing that I'm actually Ben's uncle?' The truth was he'd been planning on demanding an explanation from her, but one look at the wary, worried expression on her pale little face and his rancour had vanished leaving an urgent desire…no, actually, *overwhelming* came a lot closer to describing his desire to enfold her in a comforting embrace that would wipe the lines of worry from her brow.

'I don't know what I am with you, angel,' he admitted abruptly. 'I know I'm mad with Alec. Lucky for him he's dead,' he reflected, his eyes glowing with contempt as he thought about his late and unlamented brother. 'He always was a randy sod, but I didn't think even he would stoop that low…*my mistake*,' he added drily as Tess rested her forehead against his.

With a sigh Tess slipped off her shoes and cuddled up properly beside him. It was a relief to her he had taken the accuracy of what she'd told him for granted. He could have got understandably irked if he'd just thought she was bad-mouthing a dead man who couldn't defend himself. But then Rafe knew better than most that his brother had not been a nice man; in fact it was pretty obvious to her that she couldn't despise Alec any more than Rafe obviously did.

Her perfume was a pleasant change from the antiseptic hospital smell. Rafe inhaled deeply; he wasn't sure if she found it soothing to have her hair stroked, but he found it soothing doing the stroking.

'There's probably a rule about this sort of thing.'

'Considering the overstretched state of the National Health Service, bed-sharing could well be the way forward.'

Tess smiled weakly and rubbed her cheek against the hand he'd lifted to brush her hair from her eyes. 'Perhaps I'll just lie here for a moment. I can't actually do anything just now and they'll tell me if…'

'Sure they will,' he agreed in a soothing voice.

'I shouldn't have let him out of my sight.' Her voice was muffled against his shoulder.

His hand went to the back of her head. Rafe took a deep breath. How were you meant to console someone who sounded pretty damned inconsolable?

'I expect every parent thinks that when anything happens to their kid…and don't start with that "I'm just a distant relative" routine!'

'I just wish it was me lying…' Her voice cracked, before she ruthlessly stilled her trembling lip. She saved the luxury of tears for later when Ben was well again.

'I don't!'

A vision of Tess lying crumpled and broken like a rag doll on some roadside flashed before Rafe's eyes; he felt physically sick. He became conscious that some of his revulsion must have shown in his voice—Tess was staring at him oddly. He cleared his throat.

'Exchange isn't a solution in these cases,' he informed her drily. 'What the hell had Chloe seen in Alec anyhow? Silly question—the same as all the others did, I suppose.'

'She was very young and you can't deny he was *extremely* good-looking.'

'God, not you too!'

Tess had always disliked intensely the elder Farrar for trying to belittle his younger brother on every possible occasion. Even back then Rafe had been remarkably self-contained. It must have infuriated Alec that Rafe had risen above his sly jibes; it had also made him more vicious. Some people had seen the charm when they'd met Alec; Tess had seen that streak of viciousness.

'I thought he was a first-class sleaze,' she responded indignantly as she lifted her head from his shoulder. 'And you have to take your share of the blame in this.'

'Me!'

'Well, Chloe only turned her attention to Alec when you didn't co-operate. Don't tell me you didn't know she fancied you something rotten.'

'I knew, all right,' he conceded, looking uncomfortable as he recalled some of her attempts to gain his attention. 'And I'd sooner—! Well, shall we just say she's not my type?'

Tess couldn't let this assertion pass without comment. 'I'd have said she was *exactly* your type…tall, leggy and blonde.' She suddenly felt acutely the lack of all these attributes.

'You seem to have made an in-depth study of the subject,' he mused, taking her chin in his fingers and turning her face up to him.

Tess didn't want to expand further on that theme; she tugged her head away. 'Actually, I'm pretty sure Chloe imagined he'd leave Annabel and marry her,' she explained grimly.

'At least his death spared her a very nasty wake-up call,' Rafe rasped. A puzzled frown puckered his brow. 'Knowing Chloe's big romance with materialism, I'm just amazed she hasn't been milking Grandfather for money.'

'Chloe isn't *that* avaricious,' she protested stoutly.

'If you say so.'

'Actually,' Tess admitted awkwardly, 'she thinks she is…well, not *milking* exactly.' She raised herself up on her elbow and tucked a hank of floppy hair behind her ears. 'There's an annuity for her from the capital she *thinks* your grandfather provided…'

'And he didn't…'

'Gran never touched any of the money Mum and Dad left me for my education, and even after the taxman had his cut I did make quite a lot when I was working…'

'No wonder you seem strapped for cash.' Rafe shook his head in astonishment. 'Why the hell, Tess…?'

'My thought exactly. Run away, girl.' They hadn't noticed the two people enter the cubicle. The young nurse, even more overawed by the older generation of Farrar than she had been the younger, vanished like a worried rabbit. Edgar's gimlet gaze fixed on Tess. 'I assumed you were the mother…'

'No…no, I…Chloe…'

'Tess thought Alec was a sleaze,' Rafe explained succinctly, coming to Tess's rescue. 'You'd better make it quick, Grandfather—that poor kid has probably gone for reinforcements,' Rafe predicted, nodding after the retreating student nurse. Tess wondered how he could sound so calm. 'Or maybe it's just tea she's gone for. They did promise me some, not to mention biscuits. Shall I ask for another cup, Grandfather?'

'Spare me your savage wit, and don't get up on my account,' Edgar Farrar drawled as Tess, painfully conscious of how she must appear, tried to scramble off the bed. A strong and determined arm prevented her.

'We won't,' Rafe promised, his eyes coldly derisive as they clashed with his grandfather's.

'Well, girl?' the old man rapped.

'She's not a girl, she's a woman…she's *my* woman.' Rafe made it sound as if it made all the difference in the world, and of course it did—at least to Tess's world…or it would have if he'd meant it.

Tess knew Rafe's retort had really been intended to wind up, aggravate and generally provoke his grandfather—he never could resist an opportunity. Despite this, his words hit Tess just as hard in their own way as the lorry had hit Ian's car earlier that evening. The dramatic impact swept away the last wispy doubts she'd managed to retain; she wanted to be Rafe's girl, his woman, his *love*.

She wanted it for real because she loved him just about as much as it was possible for a woman to love a man. Strange that, even though she had very little personal experience of such things, Tess knew in every cell of her body that this was the for ever sort of love… Or, in this case, the hopeless, unrequited sort of love, she reminded herself brutally.

His grandfather's narrowed eyes moved over the two figures entwined on the bed. 'I'm not blind, boy,' he snapped. 'And I don't care who she is, I still demand to know what she thought she was about denying me my great-grandson.

I won't bother asking why you're conniving with her...' he drawled contemptuously.

His contempt made Tess's face harden; she suddenly felt purposeful, not embarrassed. Rafe was worth a hundred of any Farrar alive or dead, and yet they all persisted in treating him appallingly! She touched the side of Rafe's face; it felt different somehow to look at him and know she loved him and always would.

'It's fine,' she murmured, wondering if she looked as different as she felt.

'Sure?'

Tess nodded firmly. This time he allowed her to rise.

She faced the figure who even now was much feared and revered in financial circles with a militant light in her blazing eyes.

'I didn't tell you for several reasons. Firstly I liked Annabel.' Alec's wife had been a sweet woman who had obviously thought her husband had been perfect. Even before his death she'd been devastated by her inability to supply him an heir; to learn Chloe had been expecting his child would have been one blow too many for the grieving widow.

A lot of people apart from Annabel seemed to think Alec had been perfect, Tess reflected, glaring at Rafe's grandfather as she angrily compared his attitude towards his two grandsons.

'She was always nice to me and I didn't want her to be hurt. Secondly—' her voice shook as she glared contemptuously at Edgar Farrar '—I'd seen how unhappy your household had made one young boy...' Her eyes softened momentarily as she looked back quickly over her shoulder at Rafe, before narrowing to emerald ice-chips again as she squared up to his grandfather. 'I'd no reason to believe you'd do any better the second time around,' she announced scornfully.

Rafe looked on in amazement as his grandfather flinched

and looked away from those critical, unforgiving green eyes. He doubted Tess realised what a rare thing she was seeing.

'Rafe was…is my son's responsibility,' he blustered uncomfortably. 'It wasn't my place to interfere with Guy.' This statement lacked his habitual assurance and it seemed from his expression he was conscious of the fact.

'Can I have that in writing?' Rafe muttered. He wasn't surprised when both combatants ignored him.

'I don't know who I despise more,' Tess announced, her clear voice ringing with scorn. 'Those people who beat children or those who know about it and do nothing!' She thought maybe she'd gone too far when Edgar gasped and clutched at his chest. 'Are you all right?' she cried anxiously.

'Sit down, Grandfather,' Rafe instructed sharply, rising from his sickbed with an athletic bound and taking charge of the situation. 'Shall I call a doctor?'

'Don't be stupid, I just need my pills!' Edgar drew a bottle from his breast pocket with tremulous fingers. 'That's better,' he breathed a few moments later.

Tess was relieved to see the blue discoloration had faded from his lips.

'Your father is a weak fool,' he wheezed. 'When I found out what Guy was doing I told him if he ever laid a finger on you again I'd break every bone in his body.'

'And they say violence breeds violence,' Rafe remarked. Underneath the sarcasm Tess could see he was looking thoughtful.

'You've brought up this boy alone, I take it.' The shrewd old eyes moved momentarily towards Rafe. 'There is no husband, live-in lover…'

Tess shook her head before he came up with another phrase to describe her solitary state. 'So far there's just been Ben and me,' she confirmed cautiously. She wasn't sure she liked the way Edgar Farrar's thoughts were heading. 'Shouldn't you lie down?' she fretted, watching as Rafe be-

gan to pace about the tiny space like a caged animal.
'You've lost a lot of blood.'

'I didn't lose it, I gave it away.'

'And I'll never forget it!' she told him, her eyes shining
with gratitude.

He'd be finding out just *how* grateful later; Rafe felt
ashamed of the thought. 'Don't worry, I won't put up a fight
when you want to get me into bed later,' he promised. He
grinned unrepentantly as heat flooded her indignant face,
leaving it prettily pink. 'Only just now I feel like being on
my feet…'

Not if…*when*… The arrogance of the man was astounding. Almost as astounding as his scorching sex appeal. She
made a last-ditch effort to tear her bemused eyes from his
face.

'There's plenty of time for courting later, boy,' his grandfather remonstrated, listening to this interchange with a critical frown. 'Right now I've got more important matters to
discuss than your love life…'

'Talking about important matters.' Tess gave a distracted
frown and patted the pager they'd promised to activate when
Ben was out of theatre. 'It shouldn't be long—perhaps I
should go and wait upstairs…' She turned with a frown to
Rafe.

Edgar Farrar stared in startled disbelief at the slim young
woman who had so summarily dismissed him.

'I'll come with you.'

'You should be resting, and you can't leave your grandfather…'

'I'm not an invalid, I don't need a keeper!' Edgar Farrar
exploded. 'And in point of fact I'm not your grandfather
either!'

Rafe's lip curled in a sneer. 'Isn't that taking wishful
thinking too far?' he asked, pointedly tapping his distinctive
aquiline nose. An almost identical feature adorned his grand-

father's weather-worn features. 'This sort of evidence is kind of hard to deny.'

'I'm not trying to deny anything.' The old man pulled himself to his feet with difficulty; his eyes didn't leave the younger man's scornful face for an instant. 'I'm your father.'

Tess realised by a process of elimination that the startled gasp had emerged from her mouth; neither man had moved or made a sound. Rafe's face looked as though it were carved from stone, except stone didn't have a pulse and she could see one in his blue-veined temple pounding away like a piston as he stared fixedly back at the older man.

'My father is living in the South of France with his charming wife.'

'Guy isn't your father.'

Rafe shook his head. 'Is this some bizarre attempt—?' He broke off, his eyes on the older man's face. 'You're telling the truth, aren't you?' he grated. 'My God, you *bastard*, you slept with your own son's wife! You slept with my mother…' He closed his eyes and shook his head as though his brain just couldn't deal with the information. 'I was always convinced that you were behind her going away, but I never suspected why!'

Edgar visibly recoiled from the white-hot animosity that glowed in the younger man's eyes.

Tentatively Tess touched Rafe's arm. 'His heart…'

'What heart?' Rafe grated, dismissing her concern with a harsh laugh. 'Did—?' He stopped on the point of saying *father*. A humourless grin pulled at the corners of his mouth. 'Does he know?'

'Guy…?'

'Well, I'm not talking about Prince Charles.'

'Nobody knows but your mother and I. It would have destroyed him.'

'Is it just me, or does your concern come a bit late in the day?'

'You have to understand that we did what we thought was best.'

'Best for who?' Rafe blasted. 'I know now why she went away, something that I've never been able to understand, but why the hell did she leave me behind where nobody wanted me?'

'I wanted you with me.'

'Don't make me laugh.'

Edgar gritted his teeth and persisted in the face of his son's acid scorn. 'You were…you *are* a Farrar, it's your birthright. Your mother understood this. Eventually it became untenable for her to stay with Guy.'

'I didn't need you, and I didn't need a birthright, I needed my mother.'

His words pierced her heart. Tess wanted to go to him, but she knew that for now she had to remain a bystander.

'I've told you we only did what we thought was best at the time. If Guy had found out there would have been a terrible scandal. Your mother knew that, she wanted to protect you.'

Rafe's cynicism deepened. 'Scandal! Now that sounds like something I can believe.'

'You don't understand, boy…we…we fell in love,' Edgar blustered awkwardly.

Tess winced at the scathing expression on Rafe's dark, unforgiving face. 'Pause for ironic laughter?' he suggested. 'Some things are just not possible and making what you did sound noble and virtuous definitely comes under that heading!'

'It was only the once. She was lonely and desperately unhappy.'

'And you were a bastard. I forgot—that's me, isn't it?'

'I'm not proud—'

'Of fathering such a disappointment…yeah…I'd sort of gathered that over the years.'

'I'm not proud of what I did to your…to Guy…to your

mother…to you. I felt guilty. I can see in retrospect that in trying to compensate for what I did I might have indulged Guy, and Alec. I didn't want to show you any preferential treatment.'

'You succeeded.'

'Alec wasn't the sort of boy who could forgive a younger brother who was better and brighter in every way than himself. If I'd shown you any favouritism it would have only made his resentment worse. I might have gone overboard,' Edgar conceded gruffly, 'but you were never a team player,' he accused. 'Always so damned headstrong, you never gave an inch. I exerted a lot of pressure to keep you at that damned school, called in several favours, offered to build them a new library. All you had to do was say you were sorry—not a lot to ask considering the fact you were responsible for two dislocations, one fracture and several missing teeth!'

'I didn't emerge exactly unscathed.'

'Would you apologise? You wouldn't budge an inch! You've never needed anyone,' Edgar accused harshly.

Tess watched as the heavy eyelids drooped protectively over Rafe's eyes. Her heart bled for him. When the extravagant sweep of dark lashes lifted there was absolutely no expression in those dark, shining depths.

'I don't need you,' he told his father with cold deliberation.

Tess found she actually felt sorry for the proud old man. She looked at his lined face; for the first time it was obvious that he really was old—old and tired.

'Why now?' Rafe asked.

'I could die and you wouldn't know… I couldn't let that responsibility fall on your mother. It suddenly seemed important for you to know.'

The pager vibrated in Tess's pocket. Torn by her conflicting desire to be in two places at once, she placed her hand on Rafe's arm and spoke his name. He looked at the small hand and then her face with an expression that suggested he'd forgotten she was there.

'I've got to go.'

'I'm coming with you.'

'But...' One look in his eyes made her bite back her response.

'We should be able to transfer him to the ward in the morning.'

'I'm so grateful,' Tess said for the hundredth time. She was, though. She was pathetically grateful for the people whose skill had saved Ben's life.

'You'll be welcome to stay on the ward with him, but he isn't going to wake up here until we reduce the sedation. What you should do is go home and get some sleep.'

'I couldn't possibly—' she began.

'I'll see she does, Doctor,' Rafe interrupted her.

Tess looked up at him indignantly as the doctor responded to a fresh call on his attention. 'I'm staying.'

'So that you're falling asleep tomorrow and the next day when Ben actually does need you?' When it was put like that, she was forced to concede that her all-night vigil didn't look like a practical solution. 'It's up to you, I suppose, but...'

'All right, all right,' she conceded crossly, casting one last look at the small sleeping figure. 'But they'll call me if...'

'Haven't they said they would, ad infinitum?' He sighed. 'Come on, Tess, you're only getting in the way,' he told her brutally.

'Thanks a lot!' Deep down she knew what Rafe was saying made sense, but she resented hearing him say it all the same.

'I'll take you home.'

She nodded reluctantly.

Tess inserted her door key into the lock and discovered that in her haste she'd left the door ajar. 'Are you coming in?'

she asked tentatively, turning to the tall figure standing just behind her.

'That was the general idea, but if you've got any objections…?'

The moon was bright but the flagstoned path was overhung with a thick canopy of heavy branches and his face remained a slightly paler shadow amongst many shadows.

'After what you've done for Ben, you think I'm going to slam the door in your face?'

'I was sort of hoping your welcome might be motivated by something other than gratitude.'

Flustered by his unfriendly tone, Tess pushed her fringe off her forehead. 'I didn't mean…of course I want you…that is, I don't *want* you.' Liar, liar… 'I want you to come in.'

He waited with apparent patience for her to finish tying herself into knots and subside into embarrassed silence. 'If you're worried I'll try slaking my lust at an inopportune moment, I'll take the couch.'

Despite the debilitating exhaustion invading just about every cell of her body, the prospect of lust-slaking didn't sound so awfully bad to Tess.

'Actually,' she told him, blinking against the harsh electric light in the narrow hallway, 'I thought it might be nice to hold someone and be held.' She didn't much care if she sounded forward and pushy, she didn't want to be alone.

'*Just someone?*'

Tess gave an exasperated sigh. 'No, not just someone…just you, actually. Happy now?' What a silly question—of course he wasn't happy! 'Do you want to talk about—?' she offered gently.

'No!' he cut in savagely. 'I don't want to talk to or about my grandfather…sorry, *father*.' Tess winced at the palpable bitterness in his voice. 'I suppose this makes my father my half-brother…?' He gave a bitter laugh. 'Talk about happy families.'

She knew he should talk; she knew he had to talk—she was equally sure that now wasn't the time for her to point it out. Taking his big hand in hers, she led him upstairs to her bed.

Tess slept straight away. She wasn't sure if Rafe did; she suspected not. When she woke some time later it was still dark and she could tell from the light shallowness of his breathing that Rafe was awake too. In the shadows she could see his back was turned to her. She'd fallen asleep in his arms—it didn't feel right not to wake up in the same place.

She felt the quiver run through his lean body when she placed her hand on his back, but he didn't move or protest when she leant across and started to massage the smooth flesh across his broad bare shoulders. She could feel the tight knots bunched under the silky surface. Tess was breathing hard from a combination of exertion and excitement by the time the tension had eased.

'Better?' she whispered softly, pulling herself closer until her front was hard against the strong curve of his back. His deep sigh was the sort of confirmation she'd hoped for.

She slid her arm over his shoulder and ran an exploratory hand down lower over his hard torso.

'What are you doing, Tess?'

'Touching you,' she told him, widening her area of interest. 'Do you mind?'

Suddenly the idea of payment for services rendered didn't seem so attractive. In fact it left a very sour taste in his mouth. He wanted her to do this because she needed to—needed to as badly as he did.

'You don't have to do this because you feel you have to repay me.'

Tess wished she could see his face. 'Is that a polite way of saying you're not in the mood?'

'I only want you to do this if—'

Her voice, high and unsteady, cut across his. 'If I can't think of anything else but the taste and smell and feel of you. I can't think about anything but having you kiss and touch me…feeling you move inside me.' A wild little laugh bubbled up inside her. 'Is that enough wanting for you, Rafe?'

She felt the growl vibrate deep down in his chest as, with a breathless display of speed, he turned over and pulled her on top of him.

'It'll do for now,' he confirmed, his dark eyes moving hungrily over the pale image of her face. 'It'll do just fine!'

He kissed her like a man starving for the taste of her lips. Tess responded with wild enthusiasm and deep relief. For one awful minute she'd thought he didn't want her. Rafe was a man whose life was being turned upside down. He was seeking an outlet for his frustration and she was more than willing to provide it. She pushed aside the depressing thought that his present need was only transitory.

CHAPTER EIGHT

TESS heard the taxi arrive just as Rafe, his sleeveless tee shirt wet with sweat, entered the kitchen. Breathing hard, he bent forward and braced his hands against his muscular thighs. His legs were dusted with a fine mesh of dark hair. Like his skin, they were dampened and glistened faintly. She swallowed and averted her gaze.

'I've been for a run,' he explained somewhat unnecessarily as he straightened up.

'So I see.' She checked she had put her mobile in her bag before snapping it shut and swinging it businesslike over one shoulder.

Her insides were mush and she felt about as businesslike as a limp stick of celery. She was driven to cast a furtive fleeting glance in his direction and instantly regretted it as, heart thudding painfully, she immediately withdrew her glance. How could you know someone for so long and not notice how simply *magnificent* they were?

'It helps me think.'

Tess nodded vaguely; she'd given up on sensible thought about five heartbeats earlier.

'I tried not to disturb you.'

Tess found herself praying he'd never appreciate the profound irony of that statement.

'About last night…' he began.

'Not now, Rafe, I need to get to the hospital.' To avoid looking at him, she opened her bag and pretended to be searching for something significant. She didn't want to hear him say that last night had been a mistake…not now—not ever, actually—but she was trying with limited success to be realistic.

131

Waking up alone had been enough realism to last her for the rest of the morning! She gritted her teeth against the deluge of loneliness that engulfed her when she recalled reaching sleepily out towards him only to find an empty pillow beside her.

'My taxi's waiting.'

'I can take you,' he said, peeling off his sweaty top in one elegant motion.

Tess took one look at his bronzed rippling torso and almost ran from the room. 'No, it's fine, the taxi's here,' she babbled before she put as much distance between her and Rafe as humanly possible.

Ben had already been transferred to the brightly decorated children's ward by the time she arrived. Chloe, one bruised side of her face an interesting multi-coloured rainbow of colours, sat beside him. She looked up when Tess walked in and got to her feet.

'How is he?' Tess asked, her eyes on the tiny, vulnerable figure in the bed.

'Doing even better than they expected.'

Tess gave a sigh of relief. 'They don't tell you a thing on the phone, do they? Don't get up on my account,' she said, feeling awkward. Who am I to come between mother and son…?

'No, I was just going to join Ian for a coffee. Tess…?'

'What, no aunty—?'

Chloe gave a sheepish smile. 'You're not actually much older than me, are you?' she said as if realising it for the first time. 'Could we talk a little later?' she asked, displaying a surprising amount of diffidence.

'Sure,' Tess agreed, trying not to sound as worried about the prospect as she felt.

It was Ian who came along a little later and suggested that she meet Chloe in the coffee shop while he sat with Ben. She didn't really have any legitimate excuse not to co-operate as Ben was dozing again, so reluctantly Tess agreed.

Ian touched her on the shoulder as she got to her feet. 'I know...' An impatient expression flickered across his handsome face. 'Who am I kidding? I don't begin to know how you must have felt when Chloe said she wanted to take the boy away.' His hand tightened on her shoulder. 'But I've got an imagination.' His eyes were warmly compassionate.

'I have to support Chloe in what she decides to do. Whatever that is,' he explained half apologetically. 'For what it's worth, I don't think she thought it through, and if it's any comfort,' he added thoughtfully, 'I think she's beginning to realise that too.'

Tess looked up at him and smiled. 'You really love her, don't you?'

Ian shrugged. 'For better, as they say, or worse.'

Impulsively Tess reached up and kissed him swiftly. 'I think Chloe is a very lucky girl,' she said huskily. She turned and almost walked slap bang into Rafe.

'What are you doing?'

He didn't reply immediately, just continued to glower furiously down at her, apparently in the grip of strong but dumb emotions.

'I'd ask you the same thing,' he replied eventually with a distinct lack of originality, 'if it wasn't so obvious.' He cast a particularly vicious glare towards Ian's back. Tess could almost visualise the daggers protruding from between the older man's shoulder blades.

I'll be damned if I'm going to apologise for an innocent peck on the cheek, she decided, lifting her chin defiantly.

'I'm going to see Chloe,' she explained, waiting impatiently for him to move. He didn't.

'I thought they were discharging her this morning. Has she had a relapse?' He didn't sound too devastated by the prospect.

'No, she hasn't, I'm meeting her in the coffee shop.' At last he moved to one side but, unfortunately from her point of view—she couldn't think straight with him around—he fell into step beside her. *'Alone,'* she added pointedly. Experience told her there was very little point being subtle with Rafe.

'Are you trying to tell me I'm not wanted?'

'I think Chloe might find your disapproving presence intimidating.'

'And do I intimidate you?' The idea seemed to startle and intrigue him.

'You irritate me.'

'It's mutual,' he came back immediately. 'I expect Chloe might be irritated herself if she knew you'd been kissing her boyfriend,' he sneered nastily.

His bizarre dog-in-the-manger behaviour flabbergasted Tess. 'Are you going to tell her?'

Rafe's dissatisfied sneer deepened.

'Have you any idea how silly you sound, not to mention look?' she wondered.

Rafe looked struck by her barbed comment. Twin bands of dark colour stained the sharp angle of his cheekbones as he mentally reviewed his behaviour. 'And whose fault is that?' he complained testily.

'I take it I'm meant to throw up my hands in culpability at this point.'

'You can do what you like with your hands, although I could put forward some interesting suggestions,' he mumbled in a dark velvety undertone that made Tess's insides melt, 'so long as you keep them off that actor guy!'

His sentiment was so unexpected and so belligerently unreasonable that Tess momentarily lost her powers of speech completely. When they returned she was sizzling mad.

'If I want to grope the entire county cricket side I won't ask your permission!' she announced somewhat ambitiously.

'Since when did you know how many were in a cricket team?'

She tossed her head. 'The more the merrier, as far as I'm concerned.' It occurred to Tess that for someone who had not so long ago accused Rafe of sounding silly she wasn't doing so bad herself! 'Why don't you go away?'

'You want me to?'

The question stopped Tess in her tracks; her righteous indignation fizzled away. 'Not really,' she conceded huskily. It had been bad enough waking without him this morning—the idea of Rafe vanishing off her personal horizon left her experiencing profound panic. Maybe she was only delaying the inevitable, but for the moment that didn't matter. To her relief Rafe didn't milk her admission—it was probably worth several pints of humiliation. He appeared happy to accept her reply at face value.

'If you feel the need to kiss men, I'm available.'

A small superior smile curved her lips as she raised her face to him. 'You call that a kiss,' she mocked.

'No, I call *this* a kiss.' He proceeded to demonstrate the difference. Rafe's persuasive powers were quite remarkable.

'Yes…well…' Tess remarked vaguely when her head stopped spinning. 'That was…' his politely quizzical expression invited her to elaborate on the theme '…completely unnecessary,' she announced severely.

His dark eyes crinkled deliciously around the edges as his expression got all intimate and personal. 'But quite nice?'

Tess cleared her throat. '*Very* nice, actually, but I still don't want you to come with me.'

Rafe seemed prepared to accept her decision this time. 'Fair enough,' he drawled, giving a good impression of a reasonable, fair-minded individual he wasn't! 'I'll see you later.'

'You will?' Tess frowned. The words had emerged far too breathlessly hopeful for her peace of mind.

'I'll be around,' he assured her, heading off in the opposite direction with a casual farewell salute.

For how long? she brooded, trying to turn her thoughts to Chloe and what she might want to say. It turned out Chloe said a lot and almost all of it surprised Tess.

'Children, they're a big responsibility, aren't they?' Chloe fretfully toyed with the bracelet around her slender wrist.

'It was an accident, you can't blame yourself,' Tess soothed.

'I don't,' Chloe responded immediately, looking puzzled. 'I suppose you've felt like this every time he's been ill. I couldn't bear it!' she choked.

'I try not to be overprotective, but it's an uphill battle,' Tess admitted. 'There are compensations, you know,' she added quietly. 'Children give a lot more than they take.'

Chloe looked unconvinced. 'I…I'm not used to worrying about anyone but myself,' she confessed in a rush.

Tess hadn't thought Chloe was capable of such self-awareness. She felt quite dismayed by the maturity it implied—maturity she'd always been happy to believe Chloe lacked. Perhaps she could make a good mother, given support and an opportunity. She forced herself to consider the unpalatable possibility that she wasn't the best person to take care of Ben—not if he had a real mother with a loving partner ready and willing to take on the role.

'That's perfectly normal. Neither was I before I started taking care of Ben.'

'That's not true, you were always taking care of some stray or other,' Chloe interrupted with an impatient gesture. 'I'm selfish, and I *like* being selfish.' She threw out the words like a challenge and waited for Tess to supply the condemnation; when she didn't Chloe's expression grew frustrated.

'I know you think it's pathetic, but I like being the one everyone fusses and worries about. I don't like sharing Ian with anyone.' She bit her lip and lowered her eyes. Tess had to strain to hear what she said. 'Ben called for you after the accident. Ian told me.'

'Well, he hardly knows you…' Tess swallowed and silently cursed the overdeveloped scruples that wouldn't permit her to take advantage of the situation '...*yet*,' she added, softening the blow.

'Why are you doing this?' Chloe wondered, lifting her head jerkily. Her eyelashes, for once undarkened, were wet. 'You don't want me to take Ben away. All you had to do was tell me what an inadequate, awful excuse for a mother I am, and we both know it would be true. Why are you being kind to me?' Unwittingly she echoed the question Tess was asking herself.

'You are Ben's mother.'

'I gave birth to him.'

'What exactly are you saying, Chloe?'

'I'm saying he should stay with you.'

Tess didn't know she'd been carrying around the leaden weight until it magically lifted off her slender shoulders. 'For how long?' she asked when caution and common sense overcame relief. She wasn't sure if she could go through all this in another few years when Chloe once more changed her mind.

'Permanently. We'll make it legal, if you like.'

'Are you sure? Perhaps you should wait.'

'I've made up my mind. There isn't any room in my life for children, not for years and years... Maybe not ever.'

'How does Ian feel about that?' Tess wondered.

Chloe looked surprised by the question. 'Ian wants me to be happy,' she explained simply.

The student nurse permitted herself a second backward glance as she moved away from the tall figure who was now bending solicitously over the child sleeping in the cot. She wondered if it would be unprofessional to ask for his autograph.

Tess's eyes narrowed cynically as she noted the backward glance. 'Did she call you...?'

'*Daddy?* Yes, she did,' Rafe admitted, looking a little startled by the experience. 'That's a first.'

Probably not a last, though, Tess reflected, nibbling at her neatly trimmed fingernails. Rafe could produce as many babies as he wanted in the future.

'I feel I should be wearing slippers…a pipe might be pushing it…' he conceded.

'If it's any comfort, I don't think little Miss Nightingale was regarding you in the cosy dependable light.'

'Really!' He made a point of looking around hopefully for the trim white-clad figure. The acid in Tess's glare increased tenfold and he grinned widely. 'You haven't done that for years,' he observed, taking the spare chair beside the sleeping boy's bed.

Tess snatched her hand self-consciously from her mouth. 'It's been a stressful day.'

Rafe's deep sigh suggested he agreed with her. 'He's asleep, then.'

He made it sound as though this peaceful state of affairs had been achieved without a great deal of patience and persuasion.

'Small thanks to you.'

'You asked me to amuse him,' Rafe protested.

'Save that hurt, bemused look for the nursing staff!' she advised tartly, allowing her glare to include the slim figure in an attractive uniform who was once more drifting past. 'I've already had to suffer gushing reports of how much nicer and better-looking you are in the flesh.'

Her eyes moved of their own accord to the small V of olive-toned flesh revealed by the neckline of the knitted polo shirt he was wearing. Don't think flesh—don't think flesh, she instructed herself firmly.

'She's back again,' she muttered in a tight-lipped undertone. 'Call me a cynic, but are we getting more attention now you're back?'

'You're a cynic,' he repeated obligingly. 'Is it my fault I have fatal charm?'

Tess snorted. It was less easy to treat his lethal charm

lightly when you'd fallen victim to it as irrevocably as she had. 'I asked you to amuse Ben. If I'd known you were going to overstimulate him I wouldn't have bothered taking a break.'

'You wouldn't have bothered eating either.' He subjected her slim figure to a thoughtful, narrow-eyed inspection. 'And you can't afford to lose any weight.'

Tess's sense of misuse increased. 'I didn't notice you being so picky last night.'

'I'm always picky, Tess,' he assured her soothingly.

The way he was looking at her made her heart beat wildly against its confinement in her chest. She swallowed. 'You've no idea how flattered I feel,' she drawled sarcastically.

'You've no idea what sort of personal interest I take in how you feel,' he came back smoothly.

Tess decided a swift change of subject would be a good idea. 'He was pumped up so high I thought he was going to self-combust,' she grumbled. The student nurse bustled by yet again and Tess's expression grew pained. 'Why didn't you tell her you're not?' she demanded in a pained whisper.

'Not what? Irresistible…available…?'

'Ben's dad. She already thinks I'm his mum. If she thinks you're his father she'll think…think we're…' Under his interested innocent gaze, the colour bloomed darkly in her cheeks.

'Intimate…?' His voice was a seductive rasp that made all the fine hairs on her nape dance. He folded his arms and settled further back in his seat, smiling with malicious pleasure at her hot cheeks. 'Having carnal relations? Doing *it*…? What a *shocking* thought!'

'Must you be crude and vulgar?' she choked.

'Must you worry about what people think?' he came back with equal distaste. 'Besides, I would have thought that you of all people would have appreciated that it's easier not to say anything sometimes. People in glass houses, my pet…'

'I'm not your pet!' she snapped, her eyes flashing green fire.

His eyes dropped to her heaving bosom. 'No,' he agreed softly. 'More feral than domesticated...but definitely feline.'

'Will you stop talking nonsense?'

'Yes, it probably is about time we got serious.'

She didn't like the sound of that at all. 'It is?'

'We can't talk here.' He gave a dissatisfied grimace as he looked around the quiet, dimly lit ward. 'Let's go somewhere more private. I've been trying to talk to you all day, only you keep running away.'

And if there were anywhere left to run she'd still be doing so. 'I don't want to go anywhere private with you, so will you kindly stop manhandling me?' she hissed. 'You're making us conspicuous.'

'I think gentle encouragement is nearer the mark, but have it your own way.' Ostentatiously Rafe removed his hand from her shoulder. 'Anyone would think I'd flung you caveman-style over my shoulder—a method, incidentally, I don't see much wrong with.'

'That comes as no surprise to me, but I can think of a few other people to whom it might. If only those dynamic lady politicians you have eating out of your hand could hear their charming, politically correct host now!'

'Is that a threat?' he asked, not sounding particularly bothered.

'Depends on how far you push me,' she grumbled.

'I'm prepared to push you the whole way if that's what it takes,' he explained cryptically with a pleasant and spine-chillingly ruthless smile. 'However, for the present this ought to be far enough. Good, it's empty,' he announced briskly, after poking his head around the door of the small sitting room reserved for parents. 'In my capacity as your lover—you'll probably say I was exceeding my authority.' It was hard to miss the fact he didn't actually look or sound particularly apologetic.

This was a description that she couldn't let pass. 'Your capacity as *what*?' It was the wrong time for a stab of sexual hunger to tie her stomach in knots.

'You prefer boyfriend?' He appeared to give frowning consideration to the option. 'A bit tepid, don't you think? Anyhow, leaving my official title to one side for the moment, I refused entry to a visitor for Ben earlier.' He looked as if the memory afforded him a considerable degree of pleasure.

'Who?' she managed weakly.

'My grand... Sorry about that.' His lips formed a humourless parody of a smile. 'My father.'

That explained the pleasure part.

'And he went away...just like that?' That didn't sound like the Edgar Farrar she knew.

'Not just like that exactly—you could say he needed a bit of convincing. He queried my right to eject him, too.'

Tess was striving for philosophical but it wasn't easy. 'But you managed to convince him.'

'I just explained how things were,' he announced airily.

'Perhaps when you've got a moment or two you might do the same for me...only not now!' she begged drily when he opened his mouth to oblige. 'There's a limit to the number of shocks my nervous system can take in one twenty-four-hour period. Did you get around to asking what he wanted?'

'Ben, I should think...wouldn't you?' Rafe watched the colour retreat, leaving her marble pale. The hand she raised to her lips was visibly shaking.

'You're not serious.'

'Forget me,' he advised. 'It's the old man you have to worry about and he's deadly serious. Ben's his grandson and, as far as he's concerned, a Farrar. He's taken one Farrar from his mother,' Rafe reminded her grimly. 'You don't honestly think he'd have any scruples about doing it again?

Sit down,' he said softly, pushing her down into one of the soft easy chairs.

'But Chloe is Ben's mother and she wants me…'

'Will Chloe remain resolute if Edgar waves a dirty great cheque in front of her sensitive nose?' He waved an invisible bribe before her nose and, on the point of removing his hand, seemed to have second thoughts. 'You've got a kind of cute nose.' He allowed the tip of his thumb to gently graze the tip of her small neat nose. The action had all the hallmarks of compulsion about it. 'Has anyone ever told you that?' His voice carried a degree of intensity that didn't match the joking frivolity of the comment.

'That's a horrible thing to imply.'

'That you've got a cute nose?' Despite her defence of her niece, Rafe could clearly see the doubt in her troubled emerald eyes. He withdrew his hand but let his fingers slide down the curve of her cheek as he did so; he felt the vibration of the quiver that involved her entire body. He was glad about that quiver; if a man was going to get obsessional about possessing a woman's body, it made it less worrying if she felt the same way.

Tess pulled her eyes from the dark, mesmeric hold of his unblinking regard. I am, she decided forlornly, addicted to the man.

'You know what I mean,' she protested huskily.

And I know what you're feeling. 'Don't shoot me, angel. I'm only the messenger.'

'You could try not to look as though you enjoy your work.'

'It might be different if you were married and financially solvent. The old man would find it hard to prove you're not a fit person to care for Ben then.'

'Would he take things that far?' she asked dubiously.

'You could wait and find out, or you could take pre-emptive action.'

'I'm not a military unit!'

'You might be a military target, though. You forget Edgar was the younger son before his big brother took a bullet in the war. All younger male Farrars do their obligatory stint...officers and gentlemen, one and all...' He gave a mock salute.

'Except you.'

'Except me,' he conceded. 'The old man is particularly fond of pointing out that I'm not gentleman material. He's also fond of saying that his military background always gives him the edge over competitors. Nothing like honing a man's natural homicidal tendencies to equip him for life in the financial jungle.'

When it came to survival techniques Tess doubted there was anything anyone could teach Rafe—mind you, he would have made a uniform look as good as humanly possible.

'Anyone would be excused for thinking you're trying to panic me. I'm a respectable, responsible person.'

'A pillar of the community,' he agreed obligingly.

'And I'm *not* in debt,' she gritted.

'Maybe not, but you don't have much put aside for the odd rainy day.'

Tess chewed her lips as she silently acknowledged the truth of what he was saying. 'There are more important things than money.'

'Not when you haven't got any.'

Tess gritted her teeth. Why was it Rafe *always* had an answer? 'Ben's older now, and I'll be able to go back to work soon.'

'A latchkey kid—that should go down well.'

'I was talking about a nanny, not neglect!'

'There is a simple solution...'

'Sure, I could win the lottery. *Well...?*' she prompted when his dramatic pause got too lengthy for her impatience. 'I'm a captive audience—what are you waiting for?'

'Marry me.'

Tess's eyes widened to their fullest extent and a tiny choking sound emerged from her parted lips as she shook her head.

'Strange—you don't look mad.' Then again, he didn't look like a man proposing either.

There was a distinct lack of tender emotion in his hard, unflinching gaze. He looked more like a man determined to push through a particularly unpopular business deal against all the odds—maybe that wasn't such a bad analogy... Tess didn't think for one minute he actually wanted to marry her. He just wanted it *more* than he wanted Edgar to have any control over Ben's future.

'You'll laugh about this,' she continued, stifling a strong urge to weep loud and long, 'but for a minute there I thought you said—'

'I did.' There was a definite note of impatience in his voice. 'Marry me, Tess.'

'I knew I was imagining it, because not even you could come up with such a crazy idea.' Tess managed a slightly shaky laugh to demonstrate how amusing she found the entire notion.

'Why is it crazy?' There was a note of belligerence in his deep tone.

'Listen, even if there was a possibility of your...of Edgar trying to get custody of Ben—which I don't think for one minute is going to happen—there's no way I would even consider marrying you.'

'You're sleeping with me.'

To her intense frustration and growing desperation, he showed no signs of having heard her at all—the man had the flexibility of a steel bar! She decided to appeal to the rational side of his nature.

'There's a big difference between casually sleeping with someone and marrying them, Rafe.'

Rafe clenched his even white teeth until she heard them grind—it wasn't the most *rational* sound she'd ever heard.

'Meaning any convenient body would have done as well as mine!'

'Of course not!' she responded indignantly. 'I couldn't possibly sleep with anyone else but you!' she told him in a voice that throbbed with conviction.

Any male could be forgiven for looking slightly complacent when a woman made that sort of announcement—Tess suspected her candour was going to cost her dear this time.

Rafe visibly relaxed. If he didn't actually preen himself, he came remarkably close. 'Then that's a good start.'

'I meant that...' Go on, Tess, what did you mean? 'I'd have to stop sleeping with you before I...I...' Until she'd actually put it into words, Tess hadn't really given much thought to how hard the transition back to a less intimate relationship was going to be. The prospect was one of the most depressing scenarios she'd ever contemplated.

'Move on to pastures new?' he suggested delicately when her hoarse voice dried up completely. 'I think on the whole that's probably wise. It can be hell trying to keep too many balls up in the air at once.'

'You'd know, I suppose,' she choked.

'I thought I'd already established that I'm strictly a monogamous sort of guy.'

Tess gave a soft moan of pure exasperation and tried to formulate a single sentence that would put paid for good to his flights of fancy. All she managed to come up with was rather weak and tremulous.

'You know I can't get married.'

He shook his head and ruthlessly pushed aside her objection. 'I *know* you can't have my children.'

It was true, but it hurt to hear him say it all the same. 'It amounts to the same thing.'

'Ben would be our family.'

There was something awfully seductive about his logic and his air of complete certainty.

'Stop trying to hustle me, Farrar,' she growled. 'I know

you want to thumb your nose at Edgar, but isn't this going a bit far?'

Rafe didn't deny her accusation, but then he wouldn't because basically he was a decent, honest man. If he weren't he would have been telling her the sort of things she wanted to hear—things such as he loved her—but he hadn't.

'It was only a little while ago you were going to marry someone else.'

'That was entirely different.'

Of course it was; he'd loved her—still did. 'Yes, *I'm* not already married.'

'That really bothers you, doesn't it?'

Tess bristled, resenting the implication her attitude was prudish. 'Call me a freak—'

'I wouldn't do that—'

She loftily ignored his interruption, and found it harder to ignore the warmth in his eyes. The starch went out of her spine and she sighed.

'Yes, as a matter of fact it does bother me. I happen to think that if you make vows you should stick by them. If you don't...'

'If you don't, things like me happen.' He met her confused look with a thin-lipped sardonic smile. 'If it hadn't been for marital infidelity I wouldn't be here...but maybe you don't think that would be a great loss?' he teased. 'I won't cheat, if that's what is bothering you, Tess, and I know ignorance is no defence in law, but I was sort of hoping you'd be a little more flexible? I honestly didn't know Claudine was married when we met and when I did find out she swore to me her marriage was over in all but name.'

She'd sworn a lot of things that had turned out not to be true—things such as she wasn't sleeping with her husband, she still loved Rafe, she just loved her husband as well, or, as it had turned out, *more*—and he'd believed them all because he'd wanted to believe them. He'd wanted to be needed, not just for his looks or his money, but needed for himself. It had finally got to the point where self-deception hadn't worked any more.

'And it wasn't?' Tess persisted masochistically. Nothing showed in his eyes but she had the impression a lot was going on behind that enigmatic façade.

'She's pregnant and it's not mine. Does that answer your question?'

'Are you sure?' she blurted out without thinking.

'My dear Tess, do you think I'd have had unprotected sex with you if there was the *remotest* possibility I could have passed anything to you?' he asked her incredulously. 'The baby is *definitely* not mine.'

'Are you saying you've never *not* used…with anyone else…*ever*…?' She'd been more articulate in her life but it seemed Rafe hadn't had much problem following her.

'A first for us both, angel.'

She drew a shaky sigh. 'I suppose it was because you knew I couldn't get pregnant.'

'I wasn't thinking of consequences at the time…*were you*?'

Tess's stomach muscles spasmed. She tore her eyes from his dark intense gaze and fixed them on her hands, which lay white-knuckled and tightly intertwined in her lap. How could she forget that primal need to surrender, to be possessed, when she felt the same way, give or take the odd ache every time she looked at him? Hell, look nothing—every time she *thought* about him!

'I met Claudine when her marriage was going through a rough patch,' she heard him recall. 'She admitted to me at the end that the only reason she slept with me originally was to pay her husband back for an indiscretion.'

Tess winced. 'Not good for the ego, I grant you, but that's a position a lot of men must fantasise about finding themselves in.' Contemplating the shallow nature of the male of the species, she gave a cynical smile and flexed her stiff fingers to encourage the circulation to return. 'Especially if the vengeful wife happens to be drop-dead gorgeous, of course.'

She wasn't shocked when he didn't jump in and explain that Claudine had been nothing to look at—since when did men make fools of themselves over a sweet nature?

'It just so happens that I'm not one of them...or,' Rafe conceded with a shrug, 'not on this occasion, I wasn't. Ironically, when she told the husband about me it seemed it revived his interest. I must have put the spark back in their sex life—quite a feather in my cap, don't you think?'

Under the circumstances Tess wasn't surprised that there was an air of suppressed violence about him. The husband's interest had resulted in a baby, without which Rafe might be with Claudine at this very moment...?

'Hard luck.'

Some of her feelings must have shown in her voice because he looked up, the bitter, distracted expression gradually fading from his face.

'How did we come to be talking about that?'

'Let's see,' she mused, pressing a finger to the tiny suggestion of a cleft in her rounded chin. 'You asked me to marry you, then to clinch the deal you started pointing out the plus points of marital infidelity, and for good measure finished off going into painful details about your ill-fated love for the much-married and embarrassingly fertile Claudine.'

'Hell, Tess, you make it sound—'

'Boring?'

A thoughtful frown creased his forehead. 'You don't sound bored.'

He was too sharp for his own good—or hers!

'I'm polite.'

He permitted himself a wry grin at this assertion. 'I'll let that one pass.' His expression sobered. 'You sound angry.'

'Would it be so unreasonable if I was? You were mad when you caught me innocently kissing Ian. You don't have to be in love with someone not to like the idea of them slobbering over someone else!' she finished shrilly.

'I didn't say you were in love with me.'

Panic raced through her tense body. No, he didn't, but if I don't keep my stupid tongue still the whole world and his neighbour will know. It was too late now to retract her words—she'd just have to tough it out.

'Of course you didn't. You're stupid and vain, but not *that* stupid and vain.' She saw there was still shadowy suspicion in his eyes and her bolshiness faded; it wasn't getting her anywhere. When she managed to compose herself there was the unmistakable ring of authenticity to her words. 'If you must know, the idea of you touching me while you're thinking of...' She broke off and covered her mouth with a trembling hand. 'It makes me feel ill,' she revealed in a tearful whisper.

Rafe swore and dropped down on his knees before her. There were some things which everyone but a totally insensitive fool would realise! One of them was that there were some things you could discuss openly with your best friend that you couldn't discuss if she unexpectedly became your lover. Top of that list was other women.

Did this mean that the price of intimacy would be a loss of the closeness they'd always enjoyed? He'd no longer enjoy the freedom to say exactly what he felt around her? He hoped not.

'Of course it does, angel, only I wouldn't...I haven't.' He took her face between his hands and looked into her tear-filled eyes. The slight quiver of her soft pink lips drew his attention to the full passionate curve...actually his appetite never had run to sugary confections, and Tess was definitely more spice than sugar.

'I honestly can't think of anything or anyone but you when we're in bed together.'

A man would have to be crazy to admit his mind wandered while he was making love to a woman, especially if that wandering took him in the direction of another woman. It struck Rafe forcibly at that moment that he didn't need to seek refuge in prevarication—loving Tess had not left room for any intrusive thoughts. There had been nothing and nobody for him but Tess—his senses had been saturated with her. A flicker of confusion passed over his face before he continued.

'I fell in love with Claudine...' he heard the odd defensive note creep into his voice and his frown deepened '...but what did it get me? Nothing but a short stint in hell! I *never*,' he told her in a voice that came straight from the heart, 'want to feel like that again. No,' he explained to her warmly, 'what we have is much *much* better. We have incredible sex. Admittedly,' he conceded realistically, 'that might not last.' Experiencing a sudden flashback of her slender, sweat-slick body arched beneath him, Rafe determined to do everything within his power to keep their passion alive.

Now there, Tess thought bitterly, was a prospect to keep a girl warm at nights.

'But we'll still be friends; we'll *always* be friends. What could be a better basis for a lasting marriage? Sometimes the solution is so simple you don't notice it.'

So long as he doesn't have any more revelations! The longer he remained oblivious to things like the neon sign above her head saying, 'I love you, you idiot' in great big letters, the better!

Maybe he was having second thoughts. His enthusiasm sounded a bit forced to her—almost as forced as the smile she responded to his concern with.

'It's all right if you want to talk about Claudine,' she lied bravely. 'I was being silly.'

Her tolerant generosity seemed to go down like a lead balloon.

'I don't want to talk about her.'

Tess caught his hands as they fell from her face and gave them a comforting squeeze. 'I understand.'

'Lucky you.'

'I can also understand why you want things to be simple after what you've just been through, but don't you see if we get married things won't be simple any more? The way things stand you...either of us can just walk away at any time.'

'So you're willing to lose Ben to the old man just because you want to keep your options open in case a better prospect in bed happens along!' Rafe shook off her hands and she watched his own ball into fists.

Tess shook her head in disbelief. 'Only you could turn this around so that I'm the selfish one.'

Rafe pressed his face into his hands before lifting his head and dragging them through his dark hair. 'You're right.' His ready retraction did more to sap her resolve than all the moral blackmail in the world. 'I'm sorry, Tess. It's just I know what it's like to be brought up in a house where you feel nobody wants you. Together we could make sure that Ben knew he was wanted every day of his life.'

His conviction was deeply compelling. Tess found herself reaching out to touch the side of his face. His jaw was vel-vet-rough under her fingertips.

'That's a truly lovely thing to say, Rafe.'

He looked embarrassed. 'I mean it.'

'I believe you, Rafe, it's just...' She felt too emotional to continue.

'We can make it work. I *know* we can.'

'For Ben's sake?' It would make all the difference if she didn't already know the answer to that question.

His eyes slid from hers. 'You know me, Tess, I'm not big on self-sacrifice.'

'You're not trying to pretend you *want* to marry me!'

His broad shoulders lifted as he captured her small hands in his. 'Should I?'

She pursed her lips and grated her teeth in exasperation. 'You've started to pick up a lot of nasty habits from the political types you interview. You're getting as slippery as they are.'

'I don't know what you mean.' He was the picture of injured innocence.

Tess snorted. 'Don't come the innocent with me, Rafe. I'm not saying another thing to you if you continue to respond to everything I ask you with a question.'

'Was I that obvious?'

She nodded.

He shook his head. 'I must be slipping. You're *really* not going to say another word.' Another nod. 'You promise?' Rafe gave a slow, wolfish grin. 'In that case...' The long, curling eyelashes lifted and Tess watched transfixed as the sizzling desire stirred smokily in his spectacular eyes.

From where he knelt their heads were almost level. A long, soundless sigh emerged from her slightly parted lips just before Rafe threw his rigid control to the winds and took full advantage of her self-imposed silence.

Tess melted into his embrace and with a tiny lost whimper wrapped her slim arms around his neck. Weakened by a flood of scalding desire, she shamelessly clung onto him. There was blind urgency in the long, hungry kiss which went on and on until Tess thought she'd simply melt.

When his lips left hers they didn't go very far. His nose pressed against the side of hers, he stayed there breathing hard. Even the touch of his warm breath against her skin aroused her to the point of babbling delirium.

'I love—' she only stopped herself just in time '—the way you kiss.'

There was a slight uneven catch in his deep warm laugh. Her skin was moist where tiny pinpricks of moisture had exploded across the surface; she could feel that his skin was damp too. Without thinking of the consequences she dabbed her tongue against the salty sheen across his jaw. His splayed fingers were pressed against her back. They spasmed and for a moment the pressure was painful. The moment passed swiftly and the hand that continued to move up and down the length of her spine became almost soothing. It also effectively prevented her drawing back; as it happened the last thing on Tess's mind was escape.

'You've absolutely no idea how much I've been wanting to do that,' he groaned, taking her chin in one hand and pressing another urgent kiss to her soft, inviting lips. *'Last night…'* The muscles in his throat visibly worked as he swallowed hard. 'Oh, God, Tess, it was…' He gave a hoarse cry. This time his kiss was tender, lingering.

'We shouldn't be doing this…here.' Tess made a token protest even though she was exactly where she wanted to be.

'Doing what?' he asked indulgently as he brushed back her fringe to reveal a shapely broad forehead. 'Kissing?'

'I'm leaning on you.' She made it sound a shameful thing to be doing. Leaning seemed somehow more significant to her than kissing; it implied trust, dependence, reliance, vulnerability—things that Tess had no practice displaying.

What am I doing? The man hasn't just offered me his soul, just a marriage of convenience, she reminded herself brutally. It was crazy and dangerous to lower her defences and respond like this.

Rafe seemed to understand instinctively what she was saying… I suppose it's just as well one of us does! she thought.

'That's the idea, Tess, that's what I'm here for. You don't have to shoulder the responsibility alone any more.'

Oh, he'd like that, wouldn't he, if she got all meek and compliant? Tess tried to ignite the dregs of her resentment and failed miserably.

'You've told your grandfather we're getting married, haven't you?'

'I knew I couldn't pull the wool over your eyes.'

She dug her fingers deep in the thick hair that curled against his neck. 'But you thought you'd try anyway. I suppose the theory is that this makes it even harder for me to say no.'

An irrepressible grin split his lean features. 'I knew you wanted to say yes!'

Tess's eyes widened. It wasn't just his audacity and arrogance that drew an outraged gasp from her, it was his perception. Her fingers twisted tighter in his hair until he held up his hands in mock surrender.

'You...you manipulative...'

'You know me so well, angel.' There was no laughter in his eyes as they ran over her face. 'And I'd like you to get to know me even better. I want you to be able to forget where Tess ends and Rafe starts.'

The erotic rasp in his voice made her shiver as his hands moved to either side of her slender shoulders. The pressure he exerted drew her body upwards.

'I wish you weren't staying here tonight... It's all right, I know you have to,' he soothed as she opened her mouth to speak. At that moment a distant cry made her stiffen.

'It's Ben!' she cried, pulling away from him. She pulled a shaking hand firmly across her tender lips and tried to compose herself. 'I have to go.' She stated the obvious for his benefit as she leapt urgently to her feet.

For a moment he stayed where he was, on his knees. It seemed strange to see Rafe of all people in the position of a supplicant. Rafe didn't plead—he might go as far as to coax, cajole and generally confuse the issue, but not beg.

'How do you know?' He frowned. 'Know that it's Ben?'

Tess looked at him as though he'd just said something extremely stupid. She'd know Ben's cry if you hid it amongst another hundred others.

'I just *know*,' she announced impatiently.

Rafe reached the boy's bedside about the same time as the nurse. Tess was already soothing the fretful child.

CHAPTER NINE

TESS felt miserable that they'd argued before he'd left for town. She knew it was unreasonable to feel mad with Rafe for leaving in the middle of a sizzling row, but she did anyhow.

Nursing her rancour, she chose not to dwell on the fact he hadn't had much choice in the matter. It was quite a coup to get an interview with the latest high-profile political casualty. The higher they'd climbed, the more spectacular the fall and the greater the public interest—so far this chap had refused to speak to anyone but Rafe.

She couldn't even legitimately complain that Rafe put work ahead of everything else. He'd taken loads of time out of a crammed schedule when Ben had been in hospital and newly returned home.

He must be wondering what he had to do to make her happy...pity she couldn't tell him! The thing was, her emotions were all over the place. The emotional see-saw of dramatic mood swings was exhausting, which probably accounted for the intense, bone-deep fatigue she'd been experiencing lately.

She wasn't the only who looked less than bright-eyed and bushy-tailed. Rafe was displaying signs of strain too, but it was probably pretty tiring living with someone when you were never very sure if they were about to burst out crying or demand urgently to be made love to!

She gained some comfort from the fact Rafe always seemed happy to oblige her where the love-making was concerned—their communication problems didn't extend as far as the bedroom, where things remained several degrees better than blissful!

That initial anger she'd felt was now tinged by a steadily growing conviction that she might have overreacted slightly when she'd found out he'd put the announcement of their impending marriage in *The Times*.

Rafe's casual response when she'd waved the offending item under his eyes had transformed her shock into simmering anger.

'I meant to tell you, it must have slipped my mind.' Rafe slid the last item into his holdall. 'The old man might actually believe we're serious now,' he added, fastening the bag and heaving it over his shoulder.

His explanation didn't fool her; *nothing* slipped Rafe's mind!

'Edgar isn't the only one who will see it.'

Rafe's eyes narrowed suspiciously. 'And that bothers you?'

'It bothers me that people will expect me to act like a blushing bride,' she snapped.

It bothered her that she couldn't tell him she loved him. Part of her wanted to take the risk; she'd been on the point of blurting it out a hundred times. Sometimes she literally ached from wanting to tell him. If he'd ever given a single hint that he wanted anything more from her than sex, she might have.

'I can make you blush.' He used the soft intimate purr that acted on her like an instant aphrodisiac. His words reawakened the memory of the things he'd said to her when they'd made love that morning, things that had made her whole body burn.

Her stomach muscles contracted violently. Looking in his eyes felt like drowning…drowning in desire.

'God, I wish you didn't have to go!' she wailed hoarsely.

'Then come. Come with me,' he responded immediately.

A brilliant smile lit her face, then just as dramatically it faded. 'I can't—I'm not packed, neither is Ben. It isn't really practical.'

He shrugged as if it didn't matter to him anyway. 'But you're all right about the announcement?'

He didn't even care enough to try and persuade me... 'Does it matter?'

'A formal gesture might not be necessary if you were wearing my ring,' he drawled, his glance skimming her bare left hand.

Tess's hand curled into a tight fist. 'Not that again! I've told you...'

'That a ring is an outmoded symbol of ownership,' he recited in a monotonous monotone. 'Yes, you have, Tess—on numerous occasions, and if those were your genuine views I'd respect them, but we both know they're not.'

'You can't leave after saying something like that!' she cried, slamming the door he had just opened and leaning her back against it.

'Let's face it, Tess, you threw the ring back in my face because you're determined to act as if this marriage is some sort of cosmetic affair. A ring, an official announcement, it all makes it seem too real for your taste. When the vicar asks if you will, you'll probably say *maybe*!'

His accusation was so close to the mark she naturally got a lot madder.

'It may have escaped your notice, but this marriage *is* a cosmetic affair.' Her dulcet tone concealed desperate pain.

'This marriage,' he bit back, 'will be what we make of it. For Ben's sake...'

Does he think I'm likely to forget this is all for Ben's sake? she wondered miserably.

'We were talking about this,' she interrupted coldly, shaking the offending newspaper, 'yet another example of your high-handed behaviour and—' She stopped abruptly. 'Did you say vicar? I thought we'd agreed that a register office would be more appropriate?'

'I didn't agree with anything.' His gentle smile was provocative in the extreme as he opened the door with her still attached to it and calmly stepped through.

Her fury and frustration bubbling over, Tess followed him into the hallway, almost running to keep up with him as he made his way towards the front door of the cottage. Of all the stiff-necked, self-righteous, *stubborn*...

'You really are your father's son, aren't you?' she flung wildly at his broad-shouldered back.

That got his attention. He stopped and turned so abruptly that Tess had to dig her heels into the worn tread of the mellow-toned carpet that covered the oak boards to prevent herself catapulting into him.

'Did you just say that for effect, or have you actually got a point to make?'

Rafe had remarkably expressive eyes—had she been allowed she could have covered several sheets of A4 with adoring descriptions of those sensational velvety orbs—and right now they weren't saying anything flattering about Tess. A lesser soul, or possibly a less furious soul, than Tess might have been intimidated by the austere sneer that drew one corner of his mouth upwards at exactly the same fascinating angle as one quizzically haughty eyebrow.

'You're just as anxious to keep up appearances as Edgar is!' she told him, her lower lip quivering with disgust and disillusionment. 'I always thought you were more honest than that.'

If she'd thought for one second Rafe's extravagant plans had been inspired by anything other than a desire to make their marriage plans look authentic for the benefit of the world in general, and his father in particular, she'd have rejoiced and been more than happy to wear his ring. Hell, she'd have worn an elastic band if the reason he'd offered it had been that he loved her!

There had been no mention of love when he'd produced the ring; in fact his manner had been insultingly offhand. She would have happily been married in a cupboard, and by the same token would have walked down the aisle in a cathedral if the man who loved her wanted to shout about their love to the world! Knowing Rafe didn't just made her more reluctant to go along with his plans.

'I'm sorry if my integrity falls short of your standards.' The frigid silence lasted for a handful of seconds before he turned on his heel and left. Tess wanted to run after him, but she didn't.

During the miserable twenty-four hours since he'd been gone Tess had come to accept that she couldn't carry on punishing Rafe for not loving her. She ought to feel glad that at least when it came to important things he'd never pretended.

She was going into this marriage with her eyes open, it was Rafe who wasn't, which in her eyes made her the worst sort of hypocrite! The more she thought about it, the more convinced she became that she couldn't go through with the wedding without telling Rafe the truth, which was why she'd caught the train up to London and, with a holdall under one arm and a baby under the other, was now standing outside the building where Rafe lived.

Rafe's flat was on the top floor of the old warehouse conversion, a minimalist's paradise with acres of polished wood floors, lots of industrial chrome and light streaming in through vast windows that overlooked the river.

It made her feel even guiltier to recall that at a word from her he'd made it clear he was willing to sacrifice this bachelor haven for a more child-friendly environment. She wouldn't even wear his stupid ring!

Perhaps she'd feel better once she'd told him the truth. The flip side of that coin was that she could feel a lot worse if he reacted badly to the news his reluctant fiancée was actually wildly in love with him!

Tess opted for the lift. Stairs might be the healthier option, but not when you were carrying a sleepy toddler. Ben was making up for lost time—he seemed to have put on several pounds in the weeks since he'd been discharged from hospital.

I just hope that after all this Rafe's at home. Who are you kidding, Tess? she mocked herself. You're praying he won't be home. Just in case her prayers were answered and the inevitable was delayed, she'd brought the key he'd given her. Spontaneity was all well and good, but with a baby in tow it paid to make contingency plans.

As it happened she didn't need a key—the front door was ajar. Tess frowned. People—Rafe included—just didn't leave their doors open or even ajar in the security-conscious city. Either Rafe had had burglars or he'd been spending too much time in their crime-free village.

Not burglars, she decided, walking into the scrupulously tidy open-plan living area. The first thing that hit her was the absence of baby clutter. She pictured some blonde draped across the soft leather sofa and the bile rose in her throat. She'd never suspected that jealousy could be such a physical emotion. Along with the nausea, her throat was dry and her heart was palpitating as if she'd opted for stairs.

The anticlimax was tremendous when her call produced no response.

She wandered through to the bedroom, looking about her curiously. It had been a long time since she'd been here. The Japanese-style decor in the bedroom was new. With relief she knelt down and laid the sleeping child on the bed. Relieved of her burden, she flexed her aching shoulders.

Out of the corner of her eyes she caught a flicker of movement. It came from outside on the balcony that ran the length of the flat linking the living area to the master bedroom.

Don't think, just do it, she instructed herself firmly. The door slid silently across, and Tess was just about to step outside when she realised Rafe wasn't alone. She hastily drew back into the bedroom. Once she'd heard the voice was female there was no question of her closing the door and waiting.

'I knew when I saw the announcement in the paper what a terrible, *terrible* mistake I'd made, darling!' The unseen person pleaded in a breathy, little-girl whisper. 'You must know you're acting on the rebound. Don't do it, *please*!'

There was the sound of sobbing. It wasn't the sort of no-holds-barred sobbing that made a girl's eyes red and puffy; it was a delicate, restrained, eye-dabbing variety, designed to melt susceptible, protective male hearts.

Tess, her eyes closed tight, could visualise the sort of comfort going on during the nerve-racking silence. There was a scream building up somewhere in the tight confines of her chest.

'If it wasn't for the baby...we'd—'

Tess wondered how the other woman managed to make a laugh sound bitter and sexy simultaneously.

'I know it's not easy for any man to take on another man's child...'

'I might have agreed with you once. We live and learn.' There was a note of joyous discovery in Rafe's voice as he warmed to his theme. 'I could take on another man's child. If I loved the woman, Claudine, it wouldn't matter...nothing would matter! And as a matter of fact I do love a woman...'

There came a point when enough was enough and Tess was way past that point. With a keening sob aching to escape her tight throat, she turned, picked up Ben and ran. She didn't stop until she ran slap bang into a tall figure dressed in an exquisitely cut dark suit that shrieked of expensive bespoke tailoring.

She placed a soothing hand on Ben's head as he stirred in his sleep. Wiping the moisture from her cheeks, she lifted her downcast head to mumble an apology to the stranger.

Her tragic tear-washed eyes seemed to fill her entire face. She summoned a weak smile.

'I'm sorry... Oh, it's you!'

'Good afternoon, Miss Trelawny.' Edgar Farrar's gaze slid from her tear-stained face to the child asleep in her arms.

'He's got Alec's colouring,' came the terse verdict after a moment of intense, apparently unemotional scrutiny.

Eyes wide and fearful, Tess took an automatic step backwards.

A sneer appeared on his lined, lean face. 'Don't worry, child, I'm not about to snatch him away.'

Tess wasn't too keen on playing Little Red Riding Hood to his big bad wolf. Her mouth firmed as she looked him straight in the eyes and declared in a clear voice, 'I wouldn't let you.' She didn't want him having any doubts on that score.

'No, I don't suppose you would.' A thoughtful expression accompanied this response. 'Is Rafe at home?'

At the mention of Rafe she was plunged straight back into the depths of despair.

'He's got company.'

Edgar hadn't mentioned her tears, but it was unrealistic to suppose he hadn't noticed and put two and two together. His next words confirmed her suspicions and his interrogator's keen eye.

'The sort of company that makes you weep?' With a lordly gesture he brushed aside Tess's mechanical rebuttal. 'You don't strike me as a young woman who weeps easily'

Another second and he'd see exactly how easily she could weep. 'If you'll excuse me.' She tried to brush past him but he moved to block her path.

'No, I don't think I will.'

'Pardon?'

'I won't excuse you just yet. Where exactly are you going?'

It was easier to reply than argue, so she did. 'I'm going to catch the first train home.'

A crowded train on a hot and sticky day—what better way to round off a perfect day? she wondered sourly. What was I thinking of, imagining even for one minute that Rafe might admit he felt anything other than lust, and possibly pity for me? She flinched away from the mortification of her own stupidity. At least she'd had her eyes opened before she'd made a total fool of herself…the thought of her lucky escape didn't do much to improve her frame of mind.

'I think we can do rather better than the train.'

Edgar moved—quite nimbly for someone of his years—to one side and Tess saw the large sleek Rolls illegally parked at the kerbside.

At a gesture from the owner the driver leapt out and opened the nearside passenger door. She glanced nervously over her shoulder, half expecting Rafe or his lover to emerge from the building. Deliverance had never looked so fraught with danger to Tess, or so luxurious.

She didn't imagine for one moment that Edgar's gesture had been motivated by concern for her welfare. On the one hand her nose was detecting the unmistakable odour of an ulterior motive, but on the other there was no denying that railway travel with a tired toddler was no picnic, especially when you'd been stupid enough to leave behind all the toddler's favourite foods and toys. She wanted to be well clear of here when Rafe discovered the bag of baby things in his bedroom.

'I thought you were going to see Rafe.'

The elder Farrar didn't deny this. 'As were you…' her determined rescuer pointed out.

'I changed my mind.' About a lot of things.

'Not the sole prerogative of women. Now get in, Miss Trelawny…' his shrewd eyes scanned her pale face '…this is becoming tiresome.'

What was it about the Farrar men that made them automatically assume she was there for them to bully?

'I should explain that I react very negatively to intimidation tactics.'

'The last time we spoke you were far more decisive. Despite what you might have been told, I don't eat babies.' He gave a thin-lipped smile.

'I suppose,' she conceded ungraciously, 'that you're the lesser of two evils.' Actually it was the realisation that her wallet had been in the holdall along with Ben's things that tipped the balance. She sat back in the air-conditioned luxury and sighed.

'Would I be correct in assuming that the greater evil is tall, dark and at present entertaining another woman?'

It would seem that Rafe had inherited his irritating habit of reading between the lines from his father. Aware that she was being observed for any response, Tess willed her expression to remain impassive.

'We'll be going home, William,' her host told the driver.

'You'll be happy to know the wedding won't be going ahead.' Somehow she didn't think that Rafe was going to be too sad when she explained she could no longer consider marrying him.

If this news gladdened the elderly financier's heart, he hid it well. 'You know, you look very like your grandmother.'

Tess was momentarily diverted from the gloomy contemplation of the rest of her life. 'I didn't know you knew Gran.'

'A remarkable woman. When it came to my attention that Rafe was making nocturnal visits to your home, I confronted her.'

'*You knew!*'

'So did your grandmother. She assured me that when the time was right she'd put a stop to it. I trusted her judgement.'

'Put a stop...' Tess puzzled.

'I believe she had a word with Rafe when she considered it to be inappropriate.'

'*Oh!* I didn't know...' Tess's cheeks began to burn. 'It was all perfectly innocent!' she protested.

'I never doubted it, but youthful hormones being what they are...' He gave an expressive shrug. 'Actually, I was glad that there was somewhere that Rafe felt at home.'

The expression on his hard, autocratic face hadn't altered,

but something in his tone made Tess forget her own embarrassment and stare.

'You knew Rafe was unhappy, yet you didn't do anything about it,' she accused.

'My hands were tied,' he told her stiffly. 'I regretted it, but…'

'Your regret didn't do Rafe much good,' she told him bluntly. 'The way I see it, he suffered for your mistakes!'

'It seems to me that Rafe is most fortunate to have so loyal a friend.'

'I don't want to be his *friend*!' she wailed. 'Oh, God!' She gulped, covering her mouth with her hand. 'I'm sorry.' She sniffed and found a large, beautifully laundered white handkerchief thrust in her hand.

'I was under the impression that Rafe desired more too,' Rafe's father murmured drily.

'That was all an act,' she admitted miserably.

'My, my, the boy's talents are limitless, it would seem. You probably think I was extremely…*clumsy* when I told Rafe about his true parentage.'

'I think your timing was a bit off, say by twenty years or so,' she told him resentfully.

'I loved Natalie, you know.' He glowered at a startled Tess as if she was about to dispute this surprising confession.

'I don't really remember her. Rafe has a photo…' Rafe had inherited her dark colouring.

'You'll find as you get older that there are pivotal moments in life. You don't always recognise those decisions for what they are at the time. You don't realise there's no going back… There are so many things I'd do differently, though loving Natalie is not one of them,' he growled. 'There hasn't been a day since she left I haven't wished I'd had the guts to create a scandal and say to hell with family honour! I shouldn't have sent her away, we should have gone with her, the boy and I...but it's too late now. Do you think me a very selfish man?' he wondered.

There was an intensely sad expression in Edgar's pale blue eyes as he contemplated what might have been. Tess felt some of her hostility dissolve towards this powerful, driven old man.

'I suppose it makes me think of you as human...which I have to admit,' she told him with a tiny spurt of mischief, 'comes as something of a surprise to me.' Her expression sobered. 'Have you explained to Rafe how you felt about his mother? It might help.'

The old man's dark scowl was back. 'I tried...you heard me...Rafe isn't interested in listening.'

'Since when did you take no for an answer? Not that it's any of my business,' she added, uncomfortably aware that, just when she ought to be distancing herself from the Farrars, she was getting sucked in all over again.

'While you're bringing up the youngest Farrar—and, if I may say so, doing an excellent job of it...' this unexpected commendation stilled her alarmed protest '...I would think that it's as much your business as anyone's.'

'Does that mean...?'

'Give me some credit! I'm stubborn, girl, not blind! I can see that you're an excellent mother to the boy. I would, however, like to get to know my great-grandson. How do you feel about that?'

'If you must know, relieved.'

'Excellent! Then, if you're not too tired, why not bring Ben here over...he does wake up occasionally, I take it?'

'Oh, he wakes up, all right,' Tess promised drily.

'Bring him over to the house for afternoon tea. I'll send the car for you. It would be an opportunity for us to discuss financial arrangements.'

The smile vanished from Tess's face. That would teach her to remember not to lower her defences with a Farrar. 'I don't want your money.'

Regarding the mutinous jut of her soft chin with a thoughtful expression, Edgar leaned forward in his seat and spoke softly.

'I've never been a big fan of this modern compromise nonsense either, but then look where stiff-necked pride has got me... I'm a lonely old man with one son who would stab me in the back for my money, if he thought he could get away with it, and another who hates my guts and wouldn't take my hand if he was drowning. Let me do something for Ben, Tess?'

Despite her natural inclination to view everything he said with cynicism and hostility, she was impressed by his obvious sincerity. Even allowing for the fact the 'lonely old man' part was a little bit hard to swallow, Tess was sure that this was as close to pleading as Edgar Farrar had ever been and it was close enough to amaze her.

'We'd like to come to tea.'

It wasn't a major concession, but to judge by Edgar's expression he was satisfied with his progress.

'You mentioned that you're no longer engaged to my son...'

Her spine stiffened until her back was barely brushing the deep upholstery. 'That's right.'

'Did you come to this conclusion as a couple, or was this a unilateral decision...*your* unilateral decision?'

'Rafe won't fight me on this,' she assured him dully.

'If you're sure...? You accused me earlier of not taking no for an answer. I think you'll find when it comes to obstinacy Rafe is in a class of his own. Think about it,' he advised when she didn't respond.

Tess was treated to a first-hand sample of Rafe's stubbornness later that day when she'd secured a freshly scrubbed and refreshed Ben in the back of the chauffeur-driven Rolls and was sliding in beside him.

'Where the hell do you think you're going?'

She slammed the door in Rafe's face. 'Drive on, please!' Tess appealed to the impassive-faced driver.

'Don't move!' Rafe barked, banging his hand on the roof of the Rolls and poking his head through the open rear window.

The driver was obviously at a loss to know what to make of his conflicting instructions. Rafe took advantage of his indecision.

'You do know who this car belongs to, don't you?'

'I'd hardly get into a stranger's car, would I?' she announced carelessly.

'I've not even been gone forty-eight hours. You've got to hand it to the old man, he's a fast worker.' He sounded anything but admiring. 'How did he work the magic? A slick line or have I misjudged you—did it just take a nice fat cheque?' he jeered nastily.

'If I didn't know it would frighten Ben,' she snapped, glancing protectively towards the small boy fastened into his brand-new child restraint before bestowing a contemptuous glare on Rafe, 'I'd slap that self-righteous smirk off your face.'

It was the fact she obviously considered he could be a threat to Ben rather than the threat of physical violence that really made him mad!

'Would you care to explain to me exactly what's going on? I found your bag complete with credit cards, cash and cheque-book on my bed. You, however, were noticeable by your absence. You haven't been answering my calls—as far as I knew you could have been lying on a morgue slab!' He bowed his dark head and she saw his knuckles whiten against the window rim.

'Don't be so dramatic!' she advised him scornfully.

His head lifted sharply; his dark eyes were burning. 'I've been *frantic*!'

Tess sniffed with deliberate disdain, but her feelings overcame her.

'Was that before or after you'd finished rolling around on the bed with Claudine?' she spat, abandoning her dignified contempt in favour of green-eyed—in more ways than one—fury!

Was there no end to his deceit? she wondered, conveniently ignoring the fact he'd never denied being in love with Claudine as she viewed with growing contempt his superb display of bewildered confusion.

'Will you please drive on?' she pleaded urgently.

Her desperation must have swung the day because the driver managed to overcome his reluctance to leave his employer's heir standing ignominiously at the side of the road and started up the engine.

Tess had a last glimpse of Rafe's furious features just before the car drew away. Her sigh of relief turned out to be premature; the car was still gathering speed when the door beside her was yanked open and Rafe almost landed on top of her.

'How dare you?' she gasped, putting as much space between her and Rafe as was humanly possible given the confined area—the confined part was already inflicting major damage to her nervous system! Her senses were so finely tuned to him that the barely detectable male scent that emanated from his warm, lean body made her stomach muscles go into a series of seriously disturbing spasms. A wave of sexual longing so powerful it literally robbed her of breath for several terrifying moments swept through her.

He grinned coldly through gritted teeth. 'There are few things I don't dare when it comes to getting what I want.'

And am I supposed to believe that's me? 'What am I supposed to do now...applaud?' She dealt him a look of withering scorn. 'Go flex your ego somewhere else!' She raised her voice. 'Will you stop the car, please? Mr Farrar is getting out.'

'Actually,' Rafe drawled, 'I'm not. Short of physical

force, angel, what do you suppose you can do about that?'
He smiled with grim satisfaction.

He had her there and they both knew it. The chauffeur
didn't look able or willing to eject Rafe, and, considering
the dangerous light in his eyes, she didn't altogether blame
him.

'That was such a stupid, dangerous thing to do, you could
have slipped and…' Her scolding tone faded as an image of
Rafe under the wheels of a moving vehicle popped into her
head. She had to close her eyes until the waves of nausea
passed.

'Are you all right?'

Tess felt his hand on her shoulder. His arm lightly grazed
her breasts, which had been curiously tender of late. The
contact made her nipples burn; she winced and pulled away.

'So now you can't stand me to touch you!' he thundered
in an outraged voice that suggested he'd do his utmost to
make her retract it if she was foolish enough to confirm this
accusation.

Tess opened her mouth to contradict him when it occurred
to her that she'd be better off letting this false impression
stand, though, she reflected bitterly, he couldn't be nearly as
intelligent as everyone thought he was if he could think she
didn't like his touch… It was weak, it was pathetic, but she
was dying inside for his touch!

Head on one side, she subjected his sternly handsome face
to an apparently objective scrutiny. 'Sulky doesn't suit you,'
she concluded after a short silence.

'I'll try and remember that,' he promised grimly.

'What's your next trick going to be?' she rounded on him
with brittle sarcasm. 'Wing-walking or jumping from a ten-
storey building? I know all *little boys* like to pretend they're
James Bond.' She gave a superior smile as he coloured self-
consciously. 'But I'd be grateful if you could restrain yourself while Ben is watching. He tries to ape everything you
do—for some reason he thinks you're marvellous.'

'And you don't?'

'I think you're…' She took a steadying breath. 'I won't repeat in front of Ben what I think of you.'

Rafe tore his unresponsive eyes from the heaving surge of her bosom. 'This isn't about that damned announcement, is it?'

'Oh, you're so quick,' she admired. 'No, it isn't about the announcement, which, incidentally, you'd better retract. It's about the fact you met up with Claudine and told her you still loved her.'

'*I what?*'

'Don't bother denying it! I heard you.'

'You heard?'

'Yes, I heard. For a man who makes his living asking questions, you sound like a parrot.'

The driver pulled the car over onto the grass verge as they finally cleared the section of hairpin bends in the road. He cleared his throat discreetly.

'Will this do, miss, for Mr Farrar to get out…?'

'Mr Farrar isn't getting out,' Rafe contradicted flatly.

'Fine, then we are.' Her trembling fingers were making heavy weather of the baby harness. 'I'll walk.'

Rafe sat for a moment watching the slender, rigid-backed figure stalk along the road ahead. He sighed.

'Thanks, we'll *all* walk.'

'What shall I tell the other Mr Farrar?' the driver yelled worriedly after Rafe.

'Don't tempt me,' Rafe muttered as he broke into a jog to catch up with Tess. 'Slow down, woman. Let me carry Ben.'

'We can manage without you.'

'Maybe you can, but I sure as hell can't manage without you,' Rafe ground back forcefully.

Tess tried to blink back the tears and almost tripped over. Forced to come to a halt—there was no way she was outrunning him—she kissed the top of Ben's head apologetically.

'Why are you saying this to me?' she asked in an agonised whisper. 'Why are you being so cruel? There's no need to pretend any more. I know how you feel—'

His bitter laugh cut her off. 'If that wasn't so tragic it would be funny!'

Bewildered by the biting note in his acrid observation, Tess didn't put up much of a fight when he took her hand and drew her off the road and into a small grassy picnic area. The car, which had been crawling along behind them, came to a full stop several yards away.

'Edgar isn't going to try and take Ben off me.'

'I don't know or care just now how you happened to get cosy with *Edgar* all of a sudden.' He proceeded to take Ben from her. 'You play here, mate,' he said, putting him down on the floor.

Ben appeared perfectly willing to co-operate with the big man who made him laugh.

'*Now…!*' Grim determination was etched in every intriguing plane and hollow of his tense, lean face.

'Don't use that tone with me!'

'You're not leaving here until you tell me what the hell you're talking about.'

'You're in love with Claudine and you don't care if her baby isn't yours.'

Comprehension flickered into his eyes. 'So *that's* what you heard.'

Her shoulders sagged. One tiny part of her had still been hoping against all the odds that there would be some sort of last-minute reprieve. No wonder he sounded so relieved—he was probably just grateful he no longer had the onerous task of explaining the state of play to her.

'Are you going to wish me well?' He might have bent down to add a stick to Ben's growing collection, but his watchful regard was still reserved for Tess.

Tess knew she'd bite off her tongue before she could bring herself to mouth meaningless platitudes—if that made her a sore loser, so be it!

'I just hope you know what you're doing. I hope you'll forgive me for talking frankly,' she said earnestly, 'but we've been friends for a long time and I…I…care about you…' she mumbled.

He rose to his feet and her stoic, pain-filled gaze slid uncomfortably away from his alert glance.

'That's nice,' he said softly, taking her chin in one hand. 'How much?' he asked huskily, tilting her face up to him.

Rafe's face was a dark silhouette as she squinted against the strong early evening sun. 'How much what?' she whispered.

'How much do you care about me?' His fingers trailed down her cheek as, eyes wild with panic, she tore herself free.

'Ben, Ben…' She suddenly developed an uncharacteristic concern about the grass stains on his clean pale blue shirt. 'You little grub!' she chided softly. 'And look at your hands,' she fussed, bending down to turn over his chubby little baby hands.

'Leave him be, Tess, there's no harm in a little dirt.' Firmly Rafe took possession of her own hands and pulled her to her feet. 'You didn't answer me,' he reminded her, running a finger down the curve of her cheek.

'That wasn't an accident.' Her mouth wouldn't form the smile to accompany her flippant response. 'What do you want me to say?' she asked him angrily.

'I want you to say that you've been enduring seven kinds of hell since you *discovered* I'm so besotted I'd even take on another man's child…that the obstacle hasn't been created that could stop me loving my woman! I want to hear that I'm not the only one who's been suffering. *You little fool!*' he groaned hoarsely as he hauled her unceremoniously into his strong arms and kissed her.

It was the sort of kiss that went on for a long, *long* time. She emerged panting hard, one shaking hand on her heaving bosom. Ears filled with the pounding of her heartbeat, she stepped back a pace and struggled to gather her fatally scattered thoughts.

A deep frown puckered her smooth brow; her head spun. 'It felt like you meant that.' Which meant what, exactly...?

He grinned tautly in response to her breathless observation.

'Did you come up to town because you wanted to spy on me?' His blazing eyes held the definite suggestion he'd go to any lengths to extract a reply.

She could still feel the sensuous impression of his warm lips on her tender mouth, still taste him; preserving her pride no longer seemed particularly important.

Pretending that they could go back to their old cosy relationship was obviously a non-starter, and why should she be ashamed of loving him anyhow? It wasn't as if things could get more strained or awkward than they already were!

Bravely she lifted her head and tossed back her hair. 'I felt guilty because I was marrying you under false pretences. I didn't want to marry you because of Ben, I wanted to marry you because I'm in love with you. When I overheard...' Her brave voice faltered and she bit her quivering lip. 'I realised there wasn't much point. Why did you kiss me like that, Rafe?'

'Like I couldn't get enough of you?' He continued in the same hard, driven tone, his eyes boring mercilessly into her. 'Like you're as essential as oxygen? Like you're just as intoxicating as a twenty-year-old bottle of fine brandy? Like I want a Tess hangover for the rest of my life? Like you're the woman I love enough to marry no matter what?' His voice dropped with each successive question until it was a deep, impossibly sexy growl which made her receptive pulses leap crazily.

It finally clicked! And with a great leap of faith Tess

stepped off the precipice that had opened at her feet with a smile on her lips. Joy imploded in her head.

'Even if *I* was carrying another man's child!' She gasped, raising shining eyes to his face.

'I knew you'd get there eventually,' he drawled. 'Claudine got the point I was trying to make straight off.'

'Oh, I wish I could, Rafe!' Tess sighed.

His eyes were impossibly tender. 'Wish you could have another man's child?' he teased softly.

Her eyelashes fluttered protectively downwards. 'No, I wish I could carry yours,' she explained gruffly.

'Look at me!' She'd never heard Rafe use that precise tone before; she responded to the command without thinking. His eyes bored down into hers. 'I don't want to hear you talk like that ever *ever* again. I've got you, that's all I need. I have got you, haven't I?'

She could hardly believe that Rafe was seeking reassurance from her! The troubled expression faded from her face as she vigorously nodded. With a grin on her face, she opened her arms wide.

'I'm all yours!' she carolled.

A fierce grin split his lean features. 'Hold that thought for a more private occasion,' he pleaded with a groan.

She shook her head in blissful bemusement. 'You were talking about loving *me*, not...' Self-consciously she stopped, unable to bring herself to say the name of the other woman.

'Not Claudine,' he said it for her. Gathering her face tenderly between his hands as he did so. 'Never Claudine. She was always acting a part—the Claudine I convinced myself I loved never even existed. She turned up uninvited on my doorstep today and I didn't feel a thing. After living with the real thing I've lost my taste for insipid imitations.' His eyes were fiercely tender as they drank in her lovestruck features. 'You're simply, superbly *amazing*,' he choked huskily.

'I am?' The imbecilic grin just wouldn't budge from her face, but Rafe didn't seem to mind. 'It must have come as a shock to her,' Tess intoned piously, while struggling to suppress an unladylike urge to punch the air triumphantly.

'She had her chance,' Rafe murmured heartlessly. 'Lucky for me she didn't take it. Hell would be falling in love with you and not being able to do anything about it.'

'Well, you can do something about it,' she promised, smiling blissfully. 'You can do anything you like.'

'You know what I like,' he growled, drawing her close. She shivered as his lips moved sensuously over the sweet curve of her neck. He pressed his mouth to her ear. 'I like,' his dark, wicked whisper explained, 'finding you wet and warm every time I touch you. Every time you pushed me away I reminded myself of that.'

Her legs sagged, and she whimpered as a wave of longing almost washed her away. She clung to him. 'I never pushed you away.'

'Not physically.'

She buried her head against his shoulder. 'This must be a dream.'

Rafe tilted her head firmly up to him. 'Oh, no, angel, this is the real thing,' he contradicted firmly.

'I've been so naggy and horrible,' she fretted.

'It's called frustration, angel. The sooner we get married, the better.'

A loud baby chuckle came from the ground beside them.

Laughing, they both looked down. 'That settles it!' Rafe announced. 'The baby has the clinching vote.'

'Let's just call it a unanimous decision,' Tess suggested happily.

CHAPTER TEN

WITH Ben between them they strolled towards the big house. To Tess, who was seeing things with the benefit of love-enhanced vision, the mellow stone facade seemed to be smiling benignly down at them.

'There's Edgar,' she said, spotting a tall figure beside the reed-edged lake. She lifted her hand in greeting. 'Now be nice,' she admonished sternly.

'I'm hurt you think me capable of being anything else.'

She threw him an exasperated, but loving glance. 'And don't sneer,' she instructed, lifting her hand to coax his curling lip back in place. 'Let's go and meet him halfway.'

'Subtle symbolism.'

'I thought you were going to be nice?'

'Nag…nag…' Rafe kissed her conveniently placed finger, drawing it into his mouth; his eyes darkened with male satisfaction when he saw the tell-tale tide of heat travel over her exposed skin.

'I'm serious, Rafe!' she told him hoarsely as she snatched her hand away.

'Angel, for you I'd have tea with the devil himself.'

'The way you were going on I thought we were.'

They were only a hundred yards or so away from Rafe's father when there was a loud creak followed by a sickening groan as the hand-rail on the far side of the old wooden bridge that was suspended across the narrow end of the lake broke off and landed in the lake with a loud splash. They watched in horror as it took Edgar with it.

'Hell!' Rafe hit the ground at a flat-out run.

Hampered by Ben, Tess was much slower. By the time

she reached the reed-choked bank of the lake, Edgar was crawling out of the muddy shallows.

She bent down beside him. 'Are you all right?'

Edgar dragged an unsteady hand through his sodden head of silvered hair. 'I always meant to learn to swim.' He looked around. 'Where's the boy?'

At first Tess thought he meant Ben, who seemed interested rather than distressed by the unexpected turn of events. Then she realised who he was looking for.

'Rafe!' she yelled out loudly as panic and alarm began to set in seriously. 'Rafe, where are you?'

'He was right beside me in the water until we got to the shallows.' Edgar staggered to his feet and, eyes shaded with his hand, looked out at the still, silent water.

The intense coldness started on the inside and worked its way outwards until Tess felt like a solid block of ice. 'No, this isn't happening!' she mumbled indistinctly from between bluish lips. Desperately she continued to call his name.

'Watch Ben!' she told the shivering and shocked figure beside her. 'Don't let him near the water!'

Tears were running unchecked down her cheeks as she ran towards the water's edge and began to wade in. Later she wouldn't be able to recall the exact sequence of events that led to her being thigh-deep in the inhospitable lake, her voice hoarse from crying his name.

'Please let him be all right, please let him be all right!' she repeated like a mantra. 'So help me, Rafe, if you do this to me I'll never forgive you,' she yelled out. 'Do you hear me? *Never!*'

'I hear you.'

With a cry she spun around in the direction of the voice and he was standing there looking pretty terrible, with a deep, gaping gash that began at cheekbone-level and disappeared into his hairline. Dizzying relief hit in a vast tidal wave. Terrible didn't matter—he was in one piece. He was alive!

'Tess...Tess...?' She could hear her name being repeated over and over with some urgency, then the darkness closed in. She didn't hear or see anything else until some time later.

'Where am I?' Part of her brain proceeded to supply her with the necessary information while the other part cringed at the corny predictability of her question.

'In hospital!'

'Rafe?' With a gasp she pulled herself into a sitting position.

The white-coated figure pushed her back down. 'Your companions are fine. The elder Mr Farrar was in the middle of discharging himself the last time I saw him, the little chap is with him. The gash on your other friend's head required stitches.'

'How did he...?'

'He collided with a submerged piece of bridge apparently and was dazed. We'll keep him in overnight just to be on the safe side, but he'll be fine.'

'What's wrong with me?'

'Been feeling a bit off colour lately, have we?' came the cagey response.

'I don't know about you,' she responded testily, 'but I have. Sorry,' she added, ashamed of her churlish response. The man was only trying to help her, she reminded herself.

The medic stopped being enigmatic and told her. She didn't believe him; she didn't believe quite loudly. But when he performed the tests to confirm his diagnosis she had no choice but to accept what he was saying was true. It wasn't easy—miracles never were easy to believe.

She was still lying there in a state of euphoric shock when the door opened. She sighed—not again. Had the staff here never heard of neglect? If she had her blood pressure taken once more she'd scream—Tess wasn't the best patient in the world.

The scowl faded from her face when she saw who it was. Greedily her eyes drank in the details of his bruised and battered but beloved face.

'Well, don't just lie there, move over, woman,' her grumpy lover mumbled.

'They,' she predicted, meaning the uniformed medical types who were far too bossy for her taste, 'won't like it.' The possibility of their disapproval didn't stop her throwing open the covers invitingly and shuffling to one side.

'I don't give a damn what they like,' Rafe muttered, displaying an arrogant disregard for the wishes of the medical establishment.

'They'll make you leave.' She snuggled closer and discovered that under the badly fitting hospital-issue dressing gown Rafe was wearing a thin cotton gown like her own that was open to the elements—or, in this case, her questing hands—all the way down the back.

'Not if they don't find me. Innovators are never appreciated,' he mourned. 'I'm a fearless pioneer of the bed-sharing scheme.'

'Your poor, poor face,' she crooned gently, touching the bruised side of his face tenderly. 'Talking about fear, don't ever, *ever* do that to me again!' Her eyes darkened as the memory of those awful few moments when she'd thought she'd lost him for ever surfaced once more. 'I think I've accumulated enough material to keep my nightmares supplied for the foreseeable future.'

'Poor baby, I'm sorry. If we're talking fear...' He drew a ragged breath and pulled her head down onto his chest. Tess lay there, content to hear the steady thud of his heartbeat. 'When you collapsed like that I went totally to pieces. If it hadn't been for Edgar I might still be standing there with you in my arms like a great useless lump of wood!' His uneven voice was laden with bitter self-recrimination.

'Remind me to thank him,' she said, arranging her curvy bits with catlike pleasure around his hard masculine frame, a frame which didn't feel any the worse for his experience.

'I already did; in the ambulance after you came to.'

Tess, who had been diverted by the promising news that Rafe had actually been speaking with his father, lifted her head abruptly. 'I came to?'

'Don't you remember?' He smoothed down her feathery dark brows with the square tip of his thumb.

'I just remember waking up here.'

'But you are all right? What did the doctor say?'

She could almost feel his alarm growing. 'I'm fine…'

'I can hear a but, Tess.' He took her jaw between thumb and forefinger and left her with no choice but to meet his interrogative gaze. 'I thought we'd done with secrets, but I can see them in your eyes,' he reproached.

'It might be inconvenient having a husband who can read me so well.'

He ignored her weak attempt at levity. 'So I'm right; something is wrong.'

'Not *wrong*, exactly…at least, I hope you won't think so…I don't…but I suppose it depends…'

He placed a gentle but firm finger to her lips. 'You're babbling.'

'You know how I told you I can't have babies.'

Compassion was swiftly replaced by determination in his eyes. 'It doesn't matter. I want you, not babies.'

'What if we come as a package deal?'

The hand that was massaging her scalp through the dense covering of shiny hair stilled suddenly; his expression froze mid-smile.

'Are you trying to tell me…?'

Tess nodded vigorously. 'I'm pregnant.' It felt strange thinking it; saying it was proving to be an even more wonderfully peculiar experience.

'You can't be.'

'That's what I said,' she agreed. 'But they did all the tests, I even saw the heartbeat on the scan…' The special memory brought a sheen of emotional tears to her wide, wondering eyes. 'Apparently there's all the difference in the world between impossible and improbable. They explained it all scientifically, but I still think it's a miracle,' she announced, a dreamy expression of wonder drifting once more across her face. 'I had all the symptoms, but it just didn't occur to me…'

The glazed expression faded from his face as he grinned. It was possibly the least intelligent expression she'd ever seen on his lean face, and perhaps the most satisfying. She'd thought he'd be happy, but it was good to have it confirmed.

'We're going to have a baby, Tess.' He sounded incredibly complacent about the fact.

'I know, darling.'

'A brother for Ben…'

'Or a sister,' she felt impelled to add.

'Whatever,' he agreed with vague good humour. He gave a sudden whoop of unrestrained joy and sat up. Eyes burning with a stunned kind of enthusiasm, he planted his hands on the pillow and leaned anxiously over her.

'Is everything all right? Are you…? Is there anything you should be doing…resting…?'

'This is resting, Rafe,' she pointed out. 'And I've been given a complete clean bill of health by the doctor. So you can relax.'

'Do you think the baby would mind if I kiss you?'

'I've not the foggiest, but I'd mind very much if you didn't,' she announced firmly.

The nurse continued to stare at the crumpled bed. 'He should be here,' she said for the fourth time.

'You mean you've *lost* my son?' The notion of his six-feet-four son being mislaid made Edgar's lips twitch. He had his own ideas about where the boy was.

'Well, not *lost*, exactly…we just don't know where he is,' she admitted miserably.

'A fine distinction, the significance of which escapes me at the moment.'

'He can't have gone far; he doesn't have any clothes. People with head injuries can sometimes do unpredictable things,' she admitted unhappily.

'I feel very much better knowing that.' His stern expression faded. 'Don't worry too much, we used to lose him all the time when he was a boy. Do you mind telling me where Miss Trelawny's room is? I take it Miss Trelawny is in her room, not wandering around…?'

'I don't know if Miss Trelawny is allowed visitors. I'll check…' Two seconds' exposure to the hard Farrar glare and her uncertainty had the good sense to vanish. 'I'll show you straight away, sir.'

'I thought so!' Edgar, pleased to have his hunch proved right, boomed as the door to Tess's small room opened.

'Oh, dear!' the nurse beside him gasped in a scandalised tone as she stared in disbelief at the two figures entwined on the narrow hospital-issue bed. 'You can't do that sort of thing here.'

'I think a little flexibility is called for here,' Edgar announced authoritatively. 'It's not as if they're having an orgy or anything. Stands to reason, the boy's in pain.'

'Not that much pain,' Rafe responded in defence of his libido.

Tess choked and pulled the covers over her head.

'Besides, it would be useless telling him he can't share her bed, my dear, he's been crawling into it since he was fourteen years old.'

'Thirteen,' Rafe corrected with an appreciative gleam in his eyes.

'I don't think you'll ever break him of the habit. Nor,' Edgar added, his eyes gravely holding Rafe's, 'would I want to.'

'Tell her I'll keep an eye on Ben tonight,' she heard Edgar say in a loud voice, for all the world as if she'd left the room. 'She's not to worry.'

'I will,' Rafe promised, with a quiver in his voice as Tess viciously pinched the non-existent spare flesh across his belly. 'Would you mind feeding the dog too?'

'Have they gone?' Tess asked after the room had gone quiet.

Rafe lifted the covers. 'It's safe, you can come out now. I'd have joined you, but I thought it wiser not to invite smutty speculation.'

Tess gave a horrified croak and emerged, her hot cheeks glowing and her hair wildly tangled. 'They didn't think I was...?' she began in a horrified whisper, then she saw the devilish laughter dancing in his dark eyes. She swatted playfully at his chest. 'You rat! Did you see that girl's face!' she groaned.

'Why would I look at another woman when you're around?'

'I'd prefer it if you restricted your *looking* to a minimum when I'm not around too. How could Edgar say those things? And you egged him on,' she accused indignantly.

'Actually I thought he was talking a lot of sense. Perhaps I will invite him to our wedding after all,' he mused thoughtfully.

'Well, if he doesn't come neither do I.'

'In that case, angel, he's top of the list.' The covers muffled her giggles and anxious squeals of protest as he pulled the covers over both their heads.

'It looked interesting when you did it...I was wondering...'

'Rafe, you can't do *that*!'

She rapidly discovered that Rafe *could* do that! Being Rafe, he did it very well indeed.

A CONVENIENT MARRIAGE

by

Maggie Cox

To Ruth and Graham –
I feel so blessed to know you both – and Jean,
who loved to read romance. I miss you still.

The day **Maggie Cox** saw the film version of
Wuthering Heights, with a beautiful Merle Oberon
and a very handsome Laurence Olivier, was the day
that she became hooked on romance. From that
day onwards she spent a lot of time dreaming up
her own romances, secretly hoping that one day
she might become published and get paid for doing
what she loves most! Now that her dream is being
realised, she wakes up every morning and counts her
blessings. She is married to a gorgeous man, is the
mother of two wonderful sons and her two other
great passions in life – besides her family and
reading/writing – are music and films.

Don't miss Maggie Cox's exciting new novel
Public Mistress, Private Affair,
out in November 2007
from Mills & Boon® Modern™.

CHAPTER ONE

'FAT lot of good *you* did me!' Disparagingly, Sabrina Kendricks glared at herself in the tailored burgundy suit she'd splashed a couple of hundred pounds she couldn't afford on, and knew she'd have to be clean out of every piece of clothing she possessed before she could bring herself to ever wear it again. Dressing to impress had sadly failed to have the desired effect on Richard Weedy—the pompous, halitosis-afflicted excuse for a bank manager whom she had met less than an hour ago. Weedy of stature and weedy by nature as far as Sabrina's assessment was concerned. Spineless, in fact.

'You're not a good risk, Miss Kendricks,' he'd whined. *Not a good risk?* She'd run East-West Travel for fifteen years now, so what was he talking about? What did he want—a cast-iron guarantee? Business was all about taking risks, surely? Good job she didn't have a cat because right now she'd kick it.

Instead, she padded into the kitchen in her stockinged feet and peered hopefully into what she already knew was an empty fridge. Empty because she hadn't had time to shop, and because food seemed to be low down on her list of priorities when she was in dire need of some proper investment to bring her small company in line with twenty-first-century technology. The mere thought of the task that lay ahead haunted her into the early hours. She wasn't going to let the business she'd worked so hard to establish get swallowed up by the big boys who were currently monopolising the travel industry.

Thinking back on her recent interview, she wondered if she'd come across as too hopeful or just simply desperate? She made a face at the bereft shelves, slammed the door shut and went across to the sink to pour herself a glass of water instead. She thought she'd pitched it just right, but maybe her smile had been too forced? Maybe the way she'd pinned back her hair had been too severe? Maybe Moroccan-red lipstick had come across as somehow intimidating? And maybe Richard Weedy just had a thing about pushy career-woman types, as her mother referred to women who didn't permanently wander round the house with a pinny on and a duster in their hands.

Thinking about her mother gave Sabrina indigestion and made her realise that not a morsel of food had passed her lips since six-thirty yesterday evening. It was now just after eleven-thirty in the morning and she was beginning to feel quite nauseous. Maybe it was time to change her bank? Could she do that? One thing was certain, no pinch-faced, patronising, woman-resenting bank manager was going to stop her from making East-West Travel the unalloyed success she knew it could be. She'd sell every pair of shoes she owned and go barefoot before she let that happen.

'Don't go, Uncle Javier! Please don't go!' The slender eleven-year-old with the liquid brown eyes and plaited black hair held on tight to her tall, broadshouldered uncle, her tenacious grip surprisingly powerful for a child so slight, the plea in her voice and the pain in her expression cutting Javier's heart in two. Above the child's head, his own dark gaze sought out her father, and, looking back at him, Michael Calder's face was nothing less than haunted.

'Hush, Angelina, hush, my angel,' Javier crooned against his niece's hair. 'I was only going to make a phone call to cancel my meeting. I will stay with you as long as you want me to, if that is all right with your father?'

Michael's silent nod was curt but hugely relieved. Both father and daughter were facing a situation that was possibly going to tear the little family apart, and Javier shared doubly in their turmoil because Angelina's mother had been his beloved sister Dorothea, who'd died eight years ago when Angelina was only three. Now the child was facing the possible death of her father. How cruel was that? Just yesterday Michael Calder had been diagnosed with a particularly devastating form of cancer and his prognosis was not good. Tomorrow he would go into hospital for some radical treatment and only God knew how long he would be staying in…maybe he would never come out again. Javier bit back the black thought and concentrated on the weeping child instead. Around her, his embrace tightened. Michael should not have to bear this burden alone. Javier vowed he would do everything in his power to ease their suffering. He would try and bring some stability to Angelina's young life when all around her were shifting sands, as well as being a good friend and support to her father. But first he had to find a way of staying in the UK permanently because as an Argentine national he would need permission to reside.

'I'll get Rosie to make you up a bed.' Unable to bear the sight of his daughter's distress any longer, Michael went in search of their friendly Welsh nanny, clearly thankful for the distraction.

'Let us go and find a video to watch together, hmm?' Holding his niece slightly apart so that he could furnish her with a smile, Javier wiped her tears away then took her gently by the hand into the family's sumptuously furnished living-room.

He woke up to rain. It was pelting his bedroom window with a vengeance, like a hundred small boys firing missiles from catapults. But it wasn't the sight of grey skies and rain that made Javier's heart feel heavy. Angelina had cried herself to sleep. At eleven years of age, she already knew what losing a parent meant. Her uncle had stayed with her long into the night just listening to her breathing, praying with everything he had in him for God to send her peaceful dreams—dreams that weren't possessed with darkly terrifying images of grief and loss. He had left Michael in the living-room nursing a thick glass of single malt whisky—too mentally shattered himself to suggest his brother-in-law should lay off the drink, considering the circumstances. They couldn't go on like this. *Something was going to break if they didn't find a solution soon...*

The smooth tanned lines on his forehead puckering into a scowl, Javier got swiftly out of bed and headed for the bathroom. Once he'd showered and dressed, he would have a cup of Rosie's exquisitely made coffee, then go and rouse Michael with a cup. The man would have one hell of a hangover, that was certain, but then wasn't he entitled? How would *he* feel if he were facing such a bleak future? Scowling again as the family's problems seemed to mount in his head, Javier turned the shower dial to hot then quickly stripped off his clothes.

'OK, so he turned you down, it's not the end of the world.'

Only her sister could come out with such a throw-away remark in the midst of her sibling's disappoint-ment and worry, Sabrina reflected in exasperation as she got down on her knees to play 'peek-a-boo' with the baby. Sometimes she wondered if motherhood had somehow blunted Ellie's perception of how it really was out there in the working world. Once a high-flyer herself, now mother to three lively children under the age of five, Ellie seemed to wrap every problem in a soft-focus cloud of pink, and her adoring husband Phil did nothing to disillusion her.

'Maybe not to you.' Sabrina tickled baby Tallulah under the chin then reached for a baby-wipe to clean the drool off her fingers. 'But it's my livelihood we're talking about here. If I don't get the investment I need then I'm never going to be able to bring the business up-to-date. It will just be a matter of time before we have to fold. And what about Jill and Robbie? They'll be unemployed. Great thanks that would be after all their years of service!'

Ellie stopped her ritual picking up after the two toddlers to shake her head at Sabrina.

'I can't see the fascination myself. It's a dog-eat-dog world out there, Sabrina. Haven't you had enough of the treadmill after fifteen years? You're what now, thirty-seven? Soon you'll be too old to have children, then what? Cold comfort your business is going to be when you have nothing but an empty flat to come home to.'

'You're beginning to sound just like Mum.' Picking up Tallulah, Sabrina nuzzled her affectionately behind her ear, the scent of talcum powder and six-month-old baby giving her heart an unexpected squeeze.

'She only wants you to be happy.'

'I *am* happy, for God's sake! Why is it both of you can't see that I'm doing what I want to do? I'm not like you two; I'm just not the maternal type.'

'No?' Grinning widely, Ellie absorbed the picture of her pretty older sister cuddling baby Tallulah to her supple, willowy frame as if she'd been born to the task.

'Anyway,' Sabrina retorted defiantly, 'I haven't the hips for it.'

'Oh, no? I've seen the looks you get from men when you walk down the street, and believe me—you go in and out in all the right places. What I can't quite believe is that you haven't had a date for at least a year now, maybe more. Are all the men you come into contact with blind, as well as dead from the waist down?'

'I don't have time to date. The business takes up practically every waking hour.'

'Now, that's a sad indictment of a young woman's life.' Wagging her finger, Ellie scooped up a handful of soft toys that littered the carpet and dropped them into the baby's playpen. 'Forget the business for a while. Get yourself a date and go out and have some fun. That's my answer to your present dilemma.'

'Is that the time?' Grimacing at her wrist-watch, Sabrina got hastily to her feet, plonked the baby back into her mother's arms, paused to kiss each of the toddlers sitting in front of the TV, and headed for the front door. 'I'll ring you later. Sorry I've got to dash but I must get back to relieve Jill for lunch. The woman's been in since eight and hasn't had a bite yet.'

'Well, I'm giving you my advice whether you want it or not!' Ellie called after her as she hurried towards the compact gun-metal-grey car parked in the drive. 'Find yourself a date and soon!'

With her sister's undoubtedly well-meant advice ringing in her ears, Sabrina reversed out of the drive into a wide avenue and headed towards town. 'Get myself a date,' she muttered irritably as she fiddled with the radio dial. 'Like I don't have enough problems already without adding a man to the mix!'

Wrestling with her umbrella as well as her now soggy packet of sandwiches and her shoulder bag, Sabrina didn't see the man standing in front of East-West Travel's shopfront peering in until she was almost on top of him. As a strong arm reached out to steady her, she was engulfed in the lingering fragrance of expensive male cologne and a surprising heat that seemed to tinglingly transmit itself right through her body from the brief but firm exchange of contact.

'I'm so sorry. I didn't see you there—I don't normally try to mow people down with my umbrella.' When she'd folded it, transferred her damp packet of sandwiches to her shoulder bag and brushed her brown hair from her eyes, Sabrina gave the man her full attention. Something inside did a funny little flip when she did. *He was gorgeous.* That was the only adjective that came to mind. Tall and Latin-looking with jet-black hair and eyes to match. Eyes that were so dark they glimmered back at her like perfect onyx jewels. When he didn't reply she felt suddenly foolish—foolish and unprepared…but unprepared for what? To cover her embarrassment she gushed, 'If you're looking for somewhere warm at this time of year, Tenerife is always a good bet. I can put you in touch with some wonderful little family-run hotels, or if you wanted something a little more upmarket I could personally recommend some stunning places.'

When he still didn't reply, Sabrina had a couple of bad moments of sheer panic. Perhaps he didn't speak English? Perhaps he was looking at her wondering what this mad woman with the dripping hair and soggy sandwiches was blathering on about?

'Oh, well.' Thinking she'd better make a hasty retreat before she made a complete twit of herself, she shrugged good-naturedly, delivered one of her sunniest smiles and pushed at the shop door to go inside.

'Wait.'

Funny how one softly enunciated little word could convey such innate command. 'I beg your pardon?'

'I would very much like to come inside and discuss a vacation with you.'

'Well, great. Why don't you follow me inside out of this rain?'

Jill had her coat on and her umbrella at the ready behind her desk. The blonde's keen gaze positively lightened when she saw the dazzling specimen of manhood who walked in behind her boss. 'Hi. It's all been very quiet since you've been gone. I sent Rob out to lunch fifteen minutes ago—was that OK?'

'Sure, Jill. You go out and get something yourself now. I'll be fine here.'

'OK. You be good, now.' With a brief conspiratorial wink, the blonde swept past them both and the doorbell jangled behind her.

'Take a seat. I'll just get rid of my coat.' Silently appreciative of the fug of warmth that enveloped her after the cold outside, Sabrina smiled again at the man as she made to dash into the little office at the end of the room. Javier hesitated, his astute business sense automatically kicking in as he scanned the small but neatly presented room with its three old-fashioned desks planted side by side, with an equally old-fashioned computer terminal positioned on top of each one. What was that word the English liked to use when describing something traditional rather than modern? 'Quaint', he thought it was. Yes, quaint. He smiled back at the woman who'd careened into him with her umbrella and registered that her eyes were startlingly blue and guileless...almost untainted by life.

'You must eat your lunch as we talk,' he instructed, and the guileless blue eyes shone back at him in surprise.

Sabrina could hardly believe a stranger was capable of such consideration. A little burst of warmth spread inside her. 'I'll make some coffee,' she replied. 'Would you like some?'

'Black—no sugar. Thank you.' Javier positioned

his tall frame in a padded chair nearest to the office. Silently he watched her through the open door, marking her hurried movements. He saw her remove her coat and hang it on an old wooden coat-tree, saw her hand pat the back of her golden-brown hair encased in its slightly awry knot and registered that she was very pleasingly built beneath the rather plain blue suit and white blouse. Even several feet away from her, her light floral perfume lingered, insinuating its way past his defences and making him feel surprisingly at ease. Astounding when his heart and head were in such turmoil over Angelina and her father. Michael had insisted the child attend school today and at three-thirty Rosie would pick her up and take her to a friend's for tea. 'Best keep everything as normal as possible,' Michael had instructed him. Javier intended to be back at the house to greet her when she came back from her friend's—by which time he would surely have had news of the outcome of his brother-in-law's treatment?

'There you are.' Registering the slight rattle of the cup in the saucer as she placed the coffee carefully down in front of him, Sabrina noted there were no rings on his fingers and his hands were very slender and very brown. And that accent of his—she couldn't quite place it; South American perhaps, but which country?

Sliding behind her desk, she drew her own mug of steaming coffee towards her. Self-consciously unwrapping her sandwiches, she gathered up the cling film into a little ball and jettisoned it into a nearby bin.

'I hope you don't mind?' she checked again before

taking a ladylike bite of her chicken sandwich. 'I didn't actually have any breakfast and to tell you the truth I'm starving!'

'Go ahead. One cannot properly conduct business on an empty stomach.' His lips parted in a brief smile. His teeth were very white against his tan, and movie-star perfect. For the first time she noticed he had a dimple in his chin…a very sexy little dimple. Somehow her morsel of food had trouble getting past her throat.

'So…any ideas where you'd like to go?'

'Excuse me?'

'On holiday? I presume you're thinking of taking a break somewhere?'

Javier shrugged his broad shoulders and wondered what the perfectly English Miss—he squinted at the name on the small gold badge on her lapel—Sabrina Kendricks would think if she knew he had travelled the globe more times than she'd find it easy to believe. As a man who'd built up a successful one-stop travel business on the internet, he spent a large majority of his life travelling. No, he didn't need a holiday. What he needed right now was a little more complicated than that…

'Are you usually this quiet?' Ignoring her question, Javier posed another one. As he did so he glanced curiously around him, noting the colourful posters of varying exotic locations on the walls behind her, the two tall potted plants that resembled miniature palm trees by the door, the once rich maroon carpet beneath his feet that was more than just a little faded. The whole business had an air of regal deterioration about it. Rubbing his hand round the back of his neck,

Javier sighed. Her computer system looked badly out of date, too. How on earth were they making a living?

Sabrina took a hasty sip of coffee, nearly scalding her mouth in the process. 'It's raining,' she explained as if he should understand the unspoken meaning without her elucidating further.

'That puts people off?' His lips quirked wryly. The woman was blushing and it intrigued him as to why.

'It's a slow time of the year.' Shrugging, she glanced quickly away from his too knowing black eyes.

'I should have thought many people would be booking vacations leading up to Christmas. The prospect of getting away after such a hectic time would appeal to most, no?'

He said it as if he knew what he was talking about and Sabrina felt herself grow prickly and defensive. She could hardly tell him that the bigger travel chains that dominated most high streets nowadays naturally took most of the business. But then they couldn't offer the very personal, specialist, highly skilled service that Sabrina and her colleagues had perfected over fifteen years, could they? The chains didn't have time to devote to planning sometimes elaborate itineraries for their wealthier, more established clients—not when they wanted to shift as many cheap package holidays as possible. If Sabrina wanted to compete, it looked as if she would have to go that way too.

'It's not always as quiet as this.'

'I have offended you.' Javier heard the slight quiver in her voice with genuine remorse, saw the wave of pink that shaded her cheeks.

'No.' Putting down her half-eaten sandwich,

Sabrina patted her lips with her paper napkin. For some reason a picture of the loathsome Richard Weedy floated into her mind and she heard him say again that she wasn't a good risk so he wouldn't be recommending the loan. She'd walked out of the bank feeling as if she'd gone to him with a begging bowl. Ugh!

'I'm just not having a very good day. Nothing to do with anyone else but my own sorry inability to rise above my disappointment.'

Inexplicably, Javier's gaze went to her fingers. Her hands were pretty and small but minus a ring of any description. 'Someone hurt your feelings…a man, perhaps?'

It took only a couple of seconds for his comment to click. 'Not in any romantic sense, no.' She was smiling now, her blue eyes shining with humour, and Javier realised that, with her high cheekbones and generous mouth, she was really quite exquisite. *She'd be even more exquisite if she let that hair of hers down…* Now, where had that thought come from?

'Anyway. Back to business. If you don't want a holiday, Mr—er—?'

'D'Alessandro—Javier D'Alessandro.'

He said it so beautifully that Sabrina was instantly transported to another time and place; somewhere very different from chilly, dreary London, somewhere with a landscape of burnt sienna and hot sun, a place where conquistadores ruled the land, conjuring up pictures of glamour and adventure. A place where her current concerns and worries disappeared like magic beneath the hypnotic gaze of a dark-skinned, dark-eyed lover…

'If you don't want a holiday, Mr D'Alessandro, then what can I do for you?' Unconsciously her tongue wetted the seam of her lips. Javier's eyes seemed to grow darker still as he registered the fact.

'I'd like to take you to dinner.' How long had that little thought been going round in his head? Javier wiped his palms down the thighs of his expensive Savile Row suit. He concentrated for a few seconds on her name badge. 'Can I call you in a few days, Sabrina? Right now I have some important business to take care of.'

'Dinner?' For a crazy moment she wondered if she'd heard him right. Good-looking strangers didn't usually just walk in off the street and ask her for a date. Her shoulders stiffened slightly with suspicion.

'Yes, dinner. What do you think?'

'Not a good idea.' Picking up her pen, she scanned the loose papers on her desk for something that needed her attention—anything that would distract her from the quiet scrutiny of those disturbing dark eyes. 'I don't date people I don't know, Mr D'Alessandro.'

'Ahh.' His smile was fleeting yet uncomfortably knowing. 'You're not a risk-taker, then, Sabrina?'

She thought about the business; about the fact that her bank manager thought she wasn't a good risk. Now this handsome stranger in front of her seemed to be implying she was lacking in courage too. It was suddenly all too much. 'All right, Mr D'Alessandro, I will accept your invitation to dinner…whenever that may be. Thank you.' She scribbled something inde-cipherable on a piece of paper and hoped he didn't notice that her hand was trembling slightly. 'Get yourself a date!' Ellie had called out to her only a short while ago. Well, it looked as if she'd got herself one…whether she'd planned for it or not.

CHAPTER TWO

HE DIDN'T call and she shouldn't have been either surprised or disappointed but perversely Sabrina was both. Ever since she'd set eyes on the handsome and intriguing Javier D'Alessandro, she'd been oddly unsettled and discontented. Which wasn't like her at all. Sighing heavily, she gave her make-up one final check in the bathroom mirror, flicked off the light and returned to the living-room to collect her suit jacket and raincoat. The force of the rain outside was rattling the window-panes and a helpless wave of despondency washed over her. Yesterday, she, Robbie and Jill had been practically fighting over customers, they were so few. The day had dragged endlessly on, and when six o'clock came Sabrina had actually been glad to put on her coat and head for home. In fifteen years of running East-West Travel she had rarely been so eager to leave the office. Maybe Ellie was right? Maybe she should call it a day as far as the business was concerned. Concentrate on other things instead. Like finding a potential 'Mr Right' and perhaps having a child of her own before it really was too late. She really loved her sister's kids and she probably wouldn't make the worst job of raising her own. Would she?

'Sabrina Kendricks, where is your head?' Amazed at the winding and not entirely welcome path her thoughts had taken her down, she donned her jacket

and coat, retrieved her prized umbrella that she'd
bought from an exclusive Knightsbridge store in the
sales, then slammed the flat door behind her with
enough force to rattle every window in the whole
house.

'Call for you, Sabrina! And I've left your coffee on
the side; don't let it go cold, will you?'

Waving the receiver at her, Jill waited patiently as
Sabrina made her way into the cramped little room
that served as general 'all-purpose' filing cabinet and
was also a repository for foreign exchange, petty cash
and stationery. They also kept a small fridge for milk
and juice, and the most essential item of all—the kettle.

'Thanks, Jill.' Not many people called her on what
she thought of as her private line. Just a handful of
people had the number, namely her parents and Ellie
and an old schoolfriend who she kept in touch with
from time to time.

Spying her coffee, she lifted the mug to her lips
and took a sip before speaking. 'Sabrina Kendricks.'

'Miss Kendricks, this is Javier D'Alessandro.'

She couldn't prevent the breathy little gasp that
came out of her mouth. She'd forgotten that she'd
given him this number as well as her home one.
Carefully, she placed the mug back on the cluttered
pine shelf that was crammed with box files, fearful
she would spill it because her hand was shaking.

'Mr D'Alessandro...what can I do for you?'

'A short break in Tenerife perhaps? Los Christianos
maybe. In one of your charming little hotels that guarantee rest and relaxation and salve to the spirit...'

Oh, my. He could read the Oxford English Dictionary *out loud and it would sound sexy.*

'Really? So you changed your mind about a holiday, then?' Perversely, Sabrina didn't want to talk to him about holidays. She chewed at her fingernail, grimacing at the flaked pearl nail-polish that she'd been too tired to replace last night; another uncharacteristic decision.

'I make a jest with you, Miss Kendricks...Sabrina. I don't want a holiday. I asked you out to dinner, remember?'

'Three weeks ago,' she blurted unthinkingly, then cursed herself for perhaps revealing too much. Now he would think she'd been counting the days.

'I am sorry it has been so long. There were things—family concerns—that I needed to take care of.'

'I understand.' Was he married? Going through a divorce? Did he have kids? A thousand questions backed up in her brain—after all, she knew nothing about this man except that he was too gorgeous for words with black eyes that made her think of things she hadn't considered in a very long time. And young. Don't forget that, Sabrina. He probably wasn't even thirty, and here she was, fast approaching thirty-eight. The whole thing was ridiculous. Best keep her mind on work and not let herself be so foolishly disappointed.

'Would this evening be too short notice?' Javier was suggesting. 'If you give me your address I could pick you up at, say, eight o'clock if that is convenient?'

Sabrina swallowed hard. 'Perhaps it wouldn't be such a good idea for us to meet, Mr D'Alessandro; I—'

'Javier. Please call me Javier.'

'All right…Javier, I don't want you to feel obliged to ask me to dinner just because it seemed like a good idea three weeks ago. I understand how things can change.'

'Then you are a very tolerant woman, Sabrina, but I seriously would like to take you out to dinner and I do not understand this "feeling obliged" you talk about. My only motivation is to see you again. I sense that we may have more in common than you think.'

She heard the faint thread of humour in his voice and let out a long, slow breath. 'All right, then. You've talked me into it.' *As if I needed to be persuaded.* Sabrina allowed herself a grin and told him she would prefer to meet him outside the designated restaurant. Once she got the details, he bid her a slightly formal goodbye and told her he was looking forward to their meeting. As Sabrina replaced the receiver on its rest, she went mentally through the contents of her wardrobe and—apart from that disastrous burgundy suit—tried to remember the last time she had bought herself something really nice to wear. The sort of 'something' that would be suitable to wear to a very elegant restaurant in Knightsbridge with a man who would make Hollywood stars look plain.

'I wish you weren't going out tonight, Uncle Javier. I wish you were staying in with me and Rosie.' Angelina glanced up from the television screen as her uncle came into the room, her dark eyes noting how handsome he looked in his suit and tie, his black hair gleaming beneath the soft lamps that lit the room. The slender blonde in her faded jeans and pink sweatshirt, sitting on the luxuriously thick rug beside the child, also marked his entrance with appreciative china-blue eyes.

'Your uncle deserves a night out, Angelina,' she said softly. 'He's stayed in with us every night since your father went into hospital. If you're good you can stay up half an hour longer and watch the end of the film with me.'

'Thanks, Rosie.' Javier flashed her one of his most dazzling smiles and Rosie couldn't help wishing that she was the lady he was taking out tonight. She'd gleaned that his dinner date was a woman named Sabrina because she'd heard him explaining to Angelina. *Lucky Sabrina.*

'I won't be late. I'll look in on the little one here before I go to bed. If you hear anything from the hospital…anything at all, you've got my cellphone number, haven't you? I'll keep it with me.'

'Of course.'

'Now, you be a good girl for Rosie, *mi angel.* Tomorrow after school I will take you to the movies to see that film you have been longing to see. We will eat popcorn and ice cream and forget about everything else but having a good time. *Sí?*'

'Yes, Uncle.' Angelina angled her cheek affectionately for his kiss and at the last minute flung her strong little arms around him and gave him a fierce hug. Javier's heart went 'bump', as it was apt to do every time his beloved niece demonstrated her love for him.

'Sleep well.'

'Tell Sabrina I said hello,' Angelina quipped as he reached the door. Javier smiled.

'I will be sure to tell her,' he promised and left the two females to their television programme, feeling just a little more at ease than he had for the past few nights.

'So you started up the business fifteen years ago?' Javier concentrated his full attention on his dinner companion. How could he not when she was looking animated and beautiful in her scoop-necked scarlet blouse and slim-fitting black trousers, her gorgeous golden-brown hair rippling unhindered to her waist, every bit as lovely as he'd imagined it would be?

'I know, fifteen years…makes me sound as old as Methuselah.'

'But you don't *look* as old as Methuselah,' Javier charmingly assured her. Was she sensitive about her age—this woman with her smile as bright as sunlight and eyes the same stunning blue as a summer sky? She could be no more than thirty-four or thirty-five, surely, and even if she was, what did he care? A woman with a past was always far more interesting, he found, than some inexperienced twenty-year-old who didn't know her own mind.

'I feel it sometimes.' A cloud seemed to slide across the dazzling blue irises. Pouring some more wine into her glass, Javier frowned. 'Something is troubling you. Want to talk about it?'

Sabrina hesitated. Should she burden this charming, good-looking man with her problems at work? The trouble was, he was so easy to talk to. Already she felt as if she'd known him much longer than the two occasions they'd met. After a generous sip of wine to fortify her blood, she decided to go with her instincts. 'I promise not to let my troubles dominate the evening.' She smiled and Javier leant forward, intrigued, his own profound concerns about his family momentarily suspended.

'My problem is that the business needs to expand, come fully into the twenty-first century, and I can't raise the capital to do it. We're even losing some of our oldest customers because they've been lured by the tempting promises of all kinds of incentives by the chains, incentives we can't possibly match. Our equipment is outdated and old-fashioned and the day we met I'd just been turned down by the bank for a loan. At this point I've got two very loyal staff members who've been with me practically since I started and I feel so bad that, unless I can raise some money to modernise soon, they'll both be out of a job.'

'I see.' His eyes were impossibly dark, Sabrina reflected, her heartbeat racing suddenly. It was the wine, she told herself. She'd better take it easy. More than a couple of glasses and she might—just might—make a complete fool of herself…

'If I owned a house I'd put that up as collateral but, as I only rent my flat, that isn't a possibility.' Shrugging, she tried to dismiss her worries and focus on the man in front of her instead. She'd come out to enjoy herself, not bring everything down by talking about work. Ellie was probably right. She was too fixated on her job. She'd almost forgotten how to have fun.

'This wine is delicious. Thank you so much for

asking me out for the evening. I'm really enjoying myself.'

'You are very passionate about your business…and loyal to your staff. I admire that, Sabrina.'

'And what about you, Javier? What are your passions in life?'

'Don't you know you can't ask someone from my country such a question without the same answers?'

'And that is?'

'Argentina. I'm from the capital city—Buenos Aires—and my passions are football, politics and— until very recently—living life in the fast lane.' One corner of his beautiful mouth hitched slightly upwards as if the confession pained him. Even with the wine heating her blood, Sabrina couldn't fail to pick up on the sudden sadness in his voice. Immediately she felt guilty. They'd spent most of the evening so far talking about her. She wasn't usually such selfish company— at least she prayed not.

'So.' She fixed him with such a direct gaze that Javier suddenly experienced a very disorienting feeling of light-headedness. 'Something must have happened to change that? Life in the fast lane, I mean.'

Brought back to earth with a bump, Javier felt his stomach muscles knot painfully as he remembered Michael in hospital, Angelina crying herself to sleep and his own life thrown into the worst kind of personal turmoil yet again in the space of eight short years.

'You are right, something happened,' he said heavily, loosening his tie. 'But it is not something I care to talk about right now.'

'I understand.' Her voice was softly concerned. 'I

just want you to know that if you felt the need to share what was troubling you, I would be a good listener.'

'Of that I have no doubt.' Raising his glass, Javier gave her a small toast. 'I am wondering why you are alone, Sabrina, or am I being too presumptuous? Is there a man in your life?'

'Apart from my horrible bank manager, my colleague Robbie and my lovely brother-in-law, Phil?' Her laugh was uninhibitedly melodic and very, very sexy. The kind of laugh a man didn't easily forget. 'No, Javier. I am footloose and fancy-free…whatever that means. Most of my time is taken up by the business. When I'm there, work just takes over, and when I'm not there I spend most of my free time worrying about it. Boring, aren't I? I don't think many men would put up with that.'

'Men who do not welcome a challenge, perhaps.'

What was he saying? Sabrina thought in fright. Would *he* welcome such a challenge? Her heart did a crazy little dance.

'And what about the future?' he wanted to know, dark eyes speculative. 'Do you see yourself perhaps getting married and having a family?'

It would be too crude to make some flip comment about her biological clock ticking, Sabrina thought, suddenly depressed. Suffice just to tell him no—such a future probably wasn't on the cards for her personally.

'Not really. The business is my baby. Oh, it's not that I don't love kids, I do. It's just that—well, I'm not twenty-something any more and, anyway, I'm probably far too set in my ways for any man to want to take on. How about yourself; do you have a lady in your life? Perhaps at home in Argentina?'

Javier thought about Christina, the 'twenty-something' beautiful Brazilian model he'd been dating up until a couple of months ago—when he'd come home unexpectedly early one afternoon and found her in bed with his twice-married, chain-smoking neighbour, Carlo. He shrugged. 'The lady in my life is eleven years old.' Inevitably a smile found its way to his lips when he spoke about Angelina. He wondered if there was any news from the hospital. He prayed she would get to sleep without tears wetting her pillow tonight.

'You have a daughter?' Blue eyes widening with surprise, Sabrina leant towards him across the table, unknowingly treating him to a very tantalising view of her creamy breasts down the scooped neck of her blouse. Heat raced into Javier's groin and for a moment he was stunned. It had been such a long time since the sight of a beautiful woman could do that to him spontaneously.

He blinked. 'A niece. My sister's child, Angelina.'

'What a pretty name.'

'Yes.'

The waiter interrupted them with their meal. As he bustled about, laying plates on the white rich linen cloth and replenishing their wine, Sabrina sensed there was an air of sorrow about her companion that tugged at her heartstrings and made her want to know what distressed him so. Right now those impressively broad shoulders of his looked weighed down with the worries of the world and she longed to be able to offer even the smallest crumb of comfort.

'Everything looks wonderful.' Picking up her fork, she tried to lighten the mood a little.

Javier smiled that destroyingly slow, thoughtful smile of his that made something in her innermost core clench and tighten with shivery anticipation, and simply said, 'Eat. Enjoy. Then we will talk some more.'

He accompanied her in a taxi home but didn't come in when Sabrina offered him coffee, a nightcap or both. Instead he told her how much he'd enjoyed her company, advised her not to worry about the business because he felt sure something good would turn up, and politely kissed her hand. What threw Sabrina completely was that the charmingly old-fashioned gesture was so unbelievably erotic that her legs were shaking when she finally let herself into her flat and closed the door. Dropping down onto her softly patterned couch with its fading beige and green flowers, she briefly closed her eyes and sighed heavily. He hadn't suggested they see each other again and no doubt she'd blown it by wittering on about the business. A cool, sophisticated, urbane man like Javier D'Alessandro probably thought she was totally boring and one-dimensional, and who could blame him?

When she opened her eyes again she was dismayed to feel tears running down her cheeks. She'd tried so hard to be a success. *So hard.* And all her parents and Ellie were concerned about was when was she going to settle down with a man and have a brood of kids. The fact that she'd successfully run a business for fifteen years meant nothing to them. Suddenly her life seemed all those things she'd accused herself of being and more and she was very, very sorry for it indeed.

Michael rallied after his latest treatment but the doctors told Javier and Michael's mother, Angela, that they mustn't be too hopeful. Too hopeful? The fury Javier experienced in his gut burned him like fire tearing through dry tinder, his Latin temperament rising up in rage against the expected conformity that was supposed to be the acceptable Western reaction to such news. Angela Calder simply squeezed her son's pale, listless hand with her own beringed elegant one and smiled in calm acquiescence. Too ill to notice, even though he'd been much better all day, Michael too seemed to have resigned himself to what he thought of as the inevitable. When Angela briefly quitted the room to go in search of a cup of tea, Michael gestured Javier to his side and told him he had something important to discuss.

'Angelina.' The sick man leant back against the plumped-up white pillows on his hospital bed and forced a smile. Javier immediately felt his throat tighten. It was hard to look at his brother-in-law with all the tubes and medical equipment attached to him without wanting to rip them out and take him home.

'What about Angelina, Michael?'

'I want you to adopt her. You're her closest link to her mother and me. I'd ask Ma but she's not equipped to take care of a child of eleven. She's not strong…a worrier. She let my father do everything until he died. And Angelina doesn't know her that well—she's not exactly been a constant in her life. Not like she knows you, Javier. Will you do that for me, my friend? Will you be a father to my little girl until she grows up?'

There was a burning sensation in his throat and on his lap Javier's knuckles squeezed white. 'It would be an honour, Michael. But you are not going to die…you will get well, *sí*? The hospital, they are doing everything they can to make you well again. Please, do not give up so easily.'

'I'm not giving up. I just know what I know, Javier. Please take care of Angelina and don't take her away from her friends, from all she knows. There must be a way you can stay here. I know it's a lot to ask…your home is in Argentina, but you have a home here too. You've always had a home with us. You know that.' Michael coughed and went deathly pale. Jumping up beside him, Javier gently squeezed his shoulder.

'Michael! Shall I call someone?' He was already turning away, hurrying to the door, pulling it wide and glancing up and down the thickly carpeted corridor for a nurse.

'Javier.'

He returned to Michael's bedside, his heart pounding.

'What is it? I am here.'

'Promise me. Promise me you'll adopt Angelina? I've got to know if you will do this for me.'

Taking the other man's hand in his own, Javier squeezed it as hard as he dared. His chest feeling as if it was in a vice, he managed to dredge up a smile, thinking, *This is too hard, too cruel for anyone to bear; first Dorothea, now Michael.*

'I promise, Michael. I give you my word.'

As the nurse bustled into the room, pushing the drugs trolley ahead of her with a cheery smile that made Javier want to curse, he excused himself, telling his brother-in-law that he needed to get out and get some air—to walk and think and come up with some kind of a plan.

He'd hardly known where his feet were leading him until he found himself outside East-West Travel. There were two other customers in the shop today, one seated opposite the young blonde woman he'd seen on his first visit, and the other engaged in conversation with a man who appeared to be in his late thirties. His brown hair was thinning on top and he wore pale steel-framed glasses that made his colourless face seem even paler. There was no sign of Sabrina. Perhaps she had gone to lunch? Glancing down at his watch, Javier saw that it was just past eleven in the morning. Coffee break, then? He'd never know until he went in and asked.

Jill glanced up in surprise as she recognised the incredibly good-looking male who walked through the door.

'Hello there,' she said cheerily. 'Looking for Sabrina?'

'*Sí.* I mean yes. Is she around?'

'She's in the back.' She pointed vaguely in the direction of the little room at the end. 'Busy doing paperwork.'

'Then I won't disturb her.' Frustrated, Javier went to walk away.

Jill waved him to a stop. 'Don't be silly! There's nothing Sabrina likes better than to be distracted from her paperwork. Go on through. She might even have the kettle on.'

His first glimpse of Sabrina was her back. She was wearing a formal blue skirt and jacket, her delightful hair caught up in some intricate tortoiseshell comb, her stockinged feet bare. At the moment one small, slender foot was easing its way up and down the back of her calf as if to soothe the strain that was there. He heard her proffer up a very unladylike curse beneath her breath as she studied some papers on top of an antiquated steel filing cabinet, and couldn't help but smile.

'Hello there. Your colleague said it was all right if I came through.'

Her heart knocking wildly against her ribs, Sabrina spun round, took one look at Javier D'Alessandro and found her greeting jammed in her throat. Wearing a stylish black coat over black jeans and a navy-blue cashmere sweater, the man looked like a million dollars. The citrus, woody tang of his aftershave wafted round the room, tightening her insides, instinctively making her want to retreat behind her professional mask for protection.

'It's nice to see you again.' Smoothing down her skirt, she smiled. *She was the first good thing that had happened to him all day,* Javier acknowledged. Perhaps it would make it easier to broach the subject he had come to talk to her about? He hoped so.

'You too. I was wondering if we could talk a little?'

Taken aback, Sabrina tucked a stray glossy strand of hair behind her ear. 'Of course. Is here all right? I know it's a bit cramped but I don't really have anywhere else to—'

'I noticed a park across the road.' Javier jerked his head vaguely in that direction. 'Can we take a walk?'

'Why not? I could do with some fresh air, to tell you the truth. I'll just get my coat.'

The winding concrete path into the ornamental gardens was littered with the colourful debris of autumn leaves. As they walked along side by side, Sabrina shivered inside her warm camel-coloured coat, wishing she'd thought to add her scarf to the hastily donned outer clothing. A tremendous gust of wind whooshed past her ear just then, and she shoved her hands deep into her coat pockets and turned her head to grin at the man beside her.

'Tenerife is sounding more and more attractive by the minute, wouldn't you say?' she announced cheerfully. 'Coming from a warm climate, this weather must seem positively Arctic to you!'

'My country has an amazing diversity of climates and landscapes. Don't forget we've got the snow-capped Andes as well as acres of hot, humid jungle. But yes, I do agree, by my home city's standards, it is pretty cold.' As he smiled back at her with something like pleasure in those deep, dark eyes with their straight black lashes, it was still clear that Javier had something on his mind other than the weather.

In for a penny… Sabrina decided to bite the bullet. Best clear the air and get whatever it was he had to say out of the way, then maybe, just maybe, she could suggest they meet for lunch later on in the week? She could practically hear Ellie cheering on the sidelines. Sabrina had *never*—not even once—asked a man out on a date. Well, there was a first time for everything, so they said…

'You wanted to talk. Was it something in particular?'

Spying a weatherworn bench near a thick clump of hedgerow, Javier jerked his head towards it. 'Perhaps it would be better if we sat down?'

For some reason, Sabrina's heartbeat thundered in her chest as she sat down beside him. Where previously they'd been companionable, something in the air had shifted perceptibly and there was a new tension emanating from the big, handsome man sitting next to her. Once again Sabrina shivered, but this time not with the cold.

'I can help you with your business,' he said without preamble.

'What did you say?' She'd heard but couldn't begin to make sense of such a statement.

'I will give you the money—whatever the amount—as well as my expertise and knowledge to help you modernise the business and bring it into the twenty-first century.'

Sabrina's pale hand curled tightly round the wrought-iron arm rest of the bench. 'What's all this about, Javier? I don't understand.'

CHAPTER THREE

His expression couldn't have been more serious. Dropping his head briefly into his hands, he drew them back and forth through his thick, dark hair. 'I am also involved professionally in travel. I have a very successful internet business that I have been running for the past six years. I believe I know exactly what it is you need to do to turn East-West Travel around. If you will let me I would like to help you.'

'I'm sorry but you'll have to give me a couple of minutes here.' Completely bewildered, Sabrina considered Javier with stunned blue eyes as if he had suddenly grown fangs and an extra head. 'Am I hearing you right? You are in the travel business and you would be willing to lend me money and your expertise to expand my company? Why? Out of the goodness of your heart? Forgive me if I sound cynical, Mr D'Alessandro, but I'm not as green as I'm cabbage-looking!'

Frowning, Javier tried to make sense of her words. 'I'm afraid you have lost me.'

'You are no more lost than I am, that's for sure!' Her heart beating wildly inside her chest, she folded her arms tightly across her coat and glared at him. 'Is that why you were looking in the window that day? Did you already know about my circumstances? Were you hoping to buy me out for a song, because if you are I can tell you right now, you're on an awfully sticky wicket!'

Javier groaned. His head hurt trying to keep up with her colourful outpouring of injured pride.

'I do not want to buy you out, Sabrina. That is the first thing. It was pure chance that had me standing outside your window that day. I had a lot on my mind and needed to walk and think. I'm staying at my brother-in-law's house, which is not so very far away from you. I suppose I naturally gravitate towards anything to do with travel—like you, I am passionate about it. *That's* why I happened to glance in your window when you ran into me.' He paused to gaze into her pale, anxious face, hoping that his words had reassured her that he wasn't some opportunistic shark waiting to snatch her beloved business out of her grasp.

Her heartbeat returning to a more normal cadence, Sabrina released an audible sigh. 'OK. Go on. I take it there's more?'

He nodded briefly, his long brown fingers linking together on his lap. 'If you agree to let me help you, there is something I would ask of you in return. Something that is not altogether an easy thing for me to ask.'

He didn't have to tell her that. Sabrina guessed whatever it was was causing him great concern and difficulty. As for his incredible offer—the answer to her prayers, no less—well, she wasn't about to jump up and down with joy just yet. She had a natural tendency to be naïve about a lot of things but not this—not her precious livelihood.

'Ask away. I'm listening.' Two pigeons landed a

few feet away, picking hopefully around in the leaves for a bite to eat. When they found nothing they simultaneously flew off into the trees in a brief flurry of wings and foliage. Sabrina pulled up the lapels of her coat around her ears and prayed she wasn't going to be crushingly disappointed by whatever Javier had to say. Already she was beginning to like this man too much for her peace of mind and she couldn't pretend she wouldn't be sorry if she never saw him again.

'I told you I have a niece? Angelina.' Sabrina heard the love in his voice and something warm stirred in the pit of her stomach, something that her heart suddenly ached for. 'She means everything to me. Especially since her mother—my sister, Dorothea—died eight years ago. Now her father, Michael, is ill. Dangerously ill. His prognosis, they tell me, is not good. I would do anything to help Angelina, to keep this terrible hurt from her, a hurt she has already experienced once before in her young life.

'Michael would like me to adopt her. There lies my problem. I do not have permanent residency in this country and, although I can more or less come and go as I please, the courts will not be favourable to my application if I cannot offer Angelina a permanent home here. She is too anglicised to want to live in Argentina, though of course she has grandparents there, family. Plus she would not wish to be separated from her friends. To get straight to the point, Sabrina, I need a British passport to stay here and adopt her. The only way I see I can get that quickly is to marry someone from this country.'

Frowning as the meaning of his words began to

sink in, Sabrina let out a long, slow breath and tucked some windswept strands of honey-brown hair behind her ear. 'You're asking me to—to marry you?'

He unlinked his hands to push his fingers through his hair. 'It would be—what do you call it?—a marriage of convenience. Only on paper, no more. Of course, we would have to live together for a reasonable amount of time to please the courts, but after that…' He shrugged as if it was the most reasonable proposition in the world. 'After that I would, of course, not contest a divorce. You would be a free woman once again.'

'And if I agree to this—this "marriage of convenience"—you agree to help me with the business?' Her whole body felt suddenly terribly cold. A wave of vulnerability settled on her shoulders like a heavy coat. The first man she'd met in the longest time that she'd felt even remotely attracted to and all he wanted from her was a cold-hearted business proposition. Well, that just about summed her personal attributes up nicely, didn't it?

'*Sí.* Yes. You have my word.' Of course. He had to be a man of honour—young as he was. Even on such brief acquaintance, that was never in doubt in Sabrina's mind.

Feeling ridiculously like crying, she got slowly to her feet, turned to Javier and smiled in spite of the fact that her face felt like a block of ice with no movement in it at all.

'I'm sorry, Javier. I couldn't do it.'

'What is it you want in return? How can I persuade you to change your mind? I will double any figure you care to come up with. I am a very wealthy man,

Sabrina. You can check me and my company out on the internet. You say you rent your flat? I will buy you a house of your own for you to keep after we are divorced.'

He was only making it worse. Her heart ached at the thought of that possibly soon-to-be-orphaned little girl—Angelina—but Sabrina couldn't agree to such a bizarre proposition for her sake only...could she? Even if what he had offered her in exchange seemed like the solution to all her worries.

Recognising the anxiety on her face, Javier told himself to ease back—not to push. She would need time. He could see that. She was not the sort of woman who would grab at such an opportunity with no thought of what it might mean to her personally other than the help she needed to expand her business. No. Sabrina Kendricks clearly had a lot of good qualities. Qualities like warmth, tenderness and integrity... He cut himself off short. He wasn't looking for a lifetime partner so such qualities hardly mattered. Nor was he in the market for the kind of marriage that his parents and grandparents and—up until eight years ago—his sister and Michael had enjoyed. What was the point in setting yourself up for potential disaster and misery? He'd seen what love could do. Love could rip away your soul just as soon as your back was turned. That wasn't for him. Instead he would pour all the love he had in his heart into caring for Angelina. If he could do that, then his life wouldn't be wasted.

'I'm really sorry about your niece. It must be terrible to be faced with losing both parents—at any age, never mind eleven years old. But I couldn't do it,

Javier. Please understand. I'm just—I'm just not like that.'

'But you are an astute businesswoman, no?' Pushing himself off the seat, he towered over her. 'How could you throw away the perfect opportunity to save your business? You already told me the bank manager turned you down for a loan. Where else are you going to get the money from, Sabrina?'

'That's my problem.' Flinching from the cold whipping round her ankles, she seriously wondered if it *was* the perfect opportunity. Surely she owed it not just to herself but to Jill and Robbie to do all she could to save their jobs? If Javier D'Alessandro could look on the whole thing as purely a business merger, why couldn't she?

Sensing the conflict that was raging behind those bright blue eyes, he shook his head and decided to go for broke.

'It wouldn't have to be a problem at all if we agreed to make a deal. I'm not asking you to engage your emotions here, Sabrina. It is an emotive issue, I know that, but I am speaking to you as one business-man to another—we have both something to gain; it makes sense, *sí*?'

'I'll think about it.'

Without another word she turned on her heel and hastened back down the path, through the sea of dead leaves, back the way they had come.

Javier stayed where he was for a long time after she had left. He returned to the park bench and stayed there with his head in his hands, his mind working overtime and his gut churning until finally the raw bite of the increasingly cold wind made it impossible for him to stay there any longer. *She would think about it.* It didn't mean she would agree. His heart heavy, he headed back to the house, preparing himself to hear the worst and cursing every fate known to man for the predicament he found himself in.

'I've been ringing you for two days now with no answer. Jill told me you were home with a cold. Why haven't you been answering your phone?' With baby Tallulah on her hip, her light blue eyes unusually fierce, Ellie McDonald barged her way past Sabrina, only noticing that her sister was still in her dressing gown when she plopped herself down on the couch and settled Tallulah against a pile of velvet cushions with her rattle. Not only was Sabrina in her dressing gown but also the room was almost unbearably hot, with the radiators obviously turned up to maximum heat.

Slowly Sabrina came towards her. Pressing her handkerchief to her reddened nose, she smiled uncharacteristically feebly. 'I *have* got a cold,' she said defensively. 'I've been in bed. That's why I didn't answer the phone.'

'But you never get colds!' Ellie sounded cross. 'You're usually disgustingly healthy. What's up, Sabrina? Something must be wrong.'

'Nothing's wrong, other than I've got the mother of all colds.' Crossing to an armchair littered with books and a half-eaten plate of toast, Sabrina weakly cleared away the mess and flopped down, her blue eyes watery. She'd been suffering for a week now, ever since she'd left Javier in the park, contemplating the fate of his beloved Angelina. Racked with guilt and remorse, she'd had three badly sleepless nights before waking up one morning with a head that seemed as though every bell in Canterbury Cathedral was clanging through it, and a mouth so dry it felt as if it were stuffed with straw. Every muscle ached when she moved, and throbbed when she didn't move, and it was all she could do to struggle out of bed and get herself something to drink. She was sick and miserable and, if it was true that there was light at the end of the tunnel, right now she couldn't see anything but a very big black hole.

'Sounds more like flu to me.' Ellie's voice softened. 'Got any paracetamol?'

'In the cupboard in the kitchen.'

'When was the last time you took some?'

'About seven.'

'This morning?' Ellie tucked a couple more cushions around the smiling Tallulah and jumped up, glancing at the clock on the wall as she did so. 'Did you know it's nearly five o'clock? If you're going to get better you need to look after yourself properly.'

'Stop behaving like my mother.'

'Well, here's news for you, darling. In her absence I *am* your mother. She'd kill me if she knew you were in such a state and I did nothing. Don't worry, I don't have to rush back. I've left Henry and William with her and promised I wouldn't come away until I was sure you were all right.'

A hot drink cupped in her hands and the cold medicine duly taken, Sabrina leant back in the armchair and smiled at the gurgling baby nursing in her mother's arms.

'Thanks, Ellie. I'm not usually so disorganised. It's just that this thing has knocked me for six.'

'I can see that! In a minute I'm going to heat you up some chicken soup. Thank God you had some tins in the cupboard—but not much else, as far as I can see. I'll have to do you a shop before I leave.'

'You don't have to—'

'I *do* have to! Stop pretending you don't need any help, sis; it's not a sign of weakness, you know. Sometimes we all need a bit of help.'

Javier needs help…my help, Sabrina thought bleakly. What could it hurt to agree to his proposition? There was no one on her side to object, after all. No adoring boyfriend waiting in the wings to protest. Her family—Ellie and her parents—might have something to say about it, but at the end of the day it was her decision. She was thirty-seven years old and answerable to no one but herself. Just as soon as she was better she would get in touch and tell him. But how? She had no telephone number for him. But there was always the internet. Maybe if she got in touch with someone at his company, they might have a mobile-phone number for him? She could only pray they had because unless he contacted her there was no other way forward. Her mind made up, she made a cooing noise at the baby, then paused to sneeze several times in quick and noisy succession so that Ellie sighed and told her to go back to bed; she would see to everything while she slept. Too weak to disagree, Sabrina did as she was told.

It had rained at the funeral and not for the first time that day Javier heard someone make a pithy comment about it 'only raining on the just.' Whatever that meant. If it meant that Michael Calder had been a good man then they were right. He'd been a doting father and a skilful surgeon and his sister had adored him from the moment she'd set eyes on him. Initially reluctant to let their beloved only daughter settle in a foreign country far away, Javier's parents had eventually come round to the fact that Dorothea was head over heels in love with her new husband so what could they do? There was still a strong thread of chauvinism in the culture, and they believed emphatically that, when all was said and done, a woman's place was with her husband.

A week after the funeral, Javier was never far from Angelina's side, Michael's mother Angela and the distraught Rosie doing their level best to run the house around them. At night, when Angelina at last fell into an exhausted but troubled sleep, Javier continued to monitor his business from the UK, using Michael's office and computer. Although exhausted by grief and worry himself, he welcomed the distraction of work to help him get past the ever-present problem of gaining a British passport and starting adoption proceedings. In spite of the fact that she was obviously unwilling, Javier found he couldn't regret the proposition he'd made to Sabrina. Maybe one day she would understand what had driven him to make such a desperate request. Perhaps he should send her some flowers with a brief note of apology? He truly hoped he hadn't offended her. She was a nice woman. A *good* woman. The kind of woman he was sure could help Angelina smile again, given time. Sighing, he switched off the computer and sat drumming his fingers on the desk. Staring down at the cup of coffee that Rosie had made him an hour ago and was now congealed and cold, he picked up the phone without further thought and dug around in his wallet for her telephone number at home.

On the third ring, Sabrina forced herself out of bed on leaden legs, clicked on the light in the darkened living-room and pushed her dishevelled hair out of her eyes. Glancing at the clock on the wall, she blinked in disbelief at the time. Ten to midnight. What the—?

'Hello?'

'Sabrina.'

'Javier?' She blinked again as her heart started to race.

'I know it is late.'

'What's wrong? What's happened?' She knew it had to be his brother-in-law. Something heavy settled in her stomach.

'I owe you an apology.'

'No, you don't.' She was surprised at the strength in her own voice, taking it as a sure sign that she was well on her way to recovery despite the woolly feeling in her limbs.

'I would have been in touch sooner but Michael died over a week ago and things have not—well, I'm sure you can imagine they are not good.'

'I'm so sorry. I really am. How is Angelina?'

'Devastated. Lost. Frightened. I keep telling myself that there must be a reason for everything that has happened but it is hard to see what it could be. Anyway, I am forgetting my manners. How are you?'

The man could ask after her welfare when he was going through personal hell? Her fingers went white where they were clutching the receiver. 'I'm fine. Just getting over a cold as a matter of fact, but Javier, I—'

'You are keeping warm and eating well?'

She frowned. 'Honestly, I'm fine. I just want to—'

'I would like to see you again before I go back to Buenos Aires. Perhaps I can take you to lunch?'

'You're going back?' Sabrina caught her breath, glanced round helplessly for a tissue to press against her itching nose and wished her mouth didn't feel as if something had died inside it.

'I have to,' he replied heavily. 'I cannot stay indefinitely. Angela—Michael's mother—is going to look after Angelina until I return again, which I hope will be soon. It will have to be this way until I can think of some better arrangement.'

In her mind, Sabrina saw those riveting dark eyes of his deep with pain and she foolishly wished she were with him so that she could offer him solace. Perhaps put her arms around him and ease some of his hurt in the way that only a woman could. Who was she kidding? He didn't want that kind of comfort from her. The only kind of comfort he needed was her agreement to marry him so that he could settle in the UK and get a British passport. At least she could offer him that. Her breath tight in her lungs, she swallowed hard before speaking.

'No, Javier. You don't have to go back. Not if I agree to marry you.'

The sharp intake of breath at the other end was audible. 'What exactly are you saying, Sabrina?'

'I'm saying I agree to your proposition. The one

you made the other day in the park. I'll be your wife, Javier, if that will help.'

'You do not know what this means to me, Sabrina. From the bottom of my heart I thank you.'

'You're welcome.' With a sad little smile flitting across her face, Sabrina knew with certainty that she was doing the right thing. The *decent* thing. As her parents had always drummed into her from an early age. If nothing else, she could surely take comfort in that?

'You do realise I'm almost thirty-eight years old, Javier?' she blurted out suddenly, for God only knew what reason. Maybe to put him off?

To her consternation he chuckled, the warm sound rippling over the telephone lines like a physical caress and sending her temperature even higher than it already was.

'And I am thirty; so what of it? Age is—how do you say?—nothing but a number. It makes no consequence.'

Of course not. Why should it? It wasn't as if they were contemplating a whole future together, was it?

As she gripped the receiver even tighter, Sabrina's voice dropped to a barely audible whisper. 'I just thought you ought to know,' she told him.

The little bunch of freesias looked slightly wilted where she clutched them in her lap in the back of the taxi but their soft, elusive scent was intoxicating and somehow added to the sense of unreality about what she'd done. As Sabrina glanced out of the window past reams of shoppers and office workers on their lunch breaks, she reflected that normally she'd be one of them if she hadn't taken the day off to get married.

Married. She studied the slim gold band encircling her second finger, left hand, and sighed. It seemed so final. Somehow incontrovertible. Which was ridiculous when it wasn't really a marriage at all. Not really. Just a paper contract so that Javier could stay in the UK with his beloved Angelina. What her parents and Ellie were going to say about it all when they found out, she hardly dared imagine. Whatever it was, 'congratulations' probably wasn't going to feature.

'You are cold?' Sensing her shiver, Javier turned to his new wife with a concerned gaze, searching her vivid blue eyes for confirmation. He owed this woman so much—he didn't intend to let her down in any way. He started to remove his coat to give it to her but Sabrina shook her head quickly and smiled.

'I'm fine, really.'

In spite of the unusual circumstances of their marriage Javier had felt a spurt of pride pulse through him as he'd stood by her side in the register office listening to her strong, clear voice repeat her vows. In her cream suit and white silk camisole, her make-up understated but becoming and her honey-brown hair lifted off her nape into a stylish chignon, she looked pretty and sophisticated. His heart beat a little faster when he thought about introducing her to Angelina, knowing he would have to play it very carefully so as not to cause his niece even a moment's anxiety that this unknown English woman might replace her in her uncle's affections. Distracted by thoughts of the child, he silently acknowledged that he was getting used to walking very warily around her. Every day since the funeral had been like a time bomb ticking away, potential disaster looming at every corner. Both her doctor and the children's grief counsellor had told him to give her time, plenty of time to express her emotions or simply keep them to herself. He shouldn't expect too much. It was early days yet and the loss of her father had hit her hard.

With everything he had in him, Javier prayed that one day he might bring a smile to her face again. Maybe Sabrina could help? Glancing back at his new wife, he allowed himself a brief moment of ease. He didn't know her well—how could he on such short acquaintance? But already he had the feeling that those slender shoulders of hers would prove a more than worthy ally if the situation called for it. In return, he would make certain that she got everything she wanted.

'Is this the house?' Sabrina was craning to see out of the window as the taxi pulled up in front of an impressive Edwardian terrace in a very exclusive part of Kensington. Her teeth worried her slightly fuller lower lip as she absorbed what it meant. This was to be her new home for the time being—until Javier found them another, more neutral residence, where he, Angelina and Sabrina might make a fresh start away from the ghosts of yesterday and the tragedy of all that had happened. *At least until he and Sabrina got divorced.* Her stomach lurched a little at the thought. Already she was becoming dangerously attached to the idea of becoming more than just a 'temporary' wife—a thought she'd better quickly divest herself of if she knew what was good for her.

'Come and meet Angelina,' Javier instructed quietly, sliding his hand over hers.

Electricity shooting through her at his touch, Sabrina managed a husky 'OK' before preceding him nervously out onto the pavement.

CHAPTER FOUR

ANGELA CALDER had offered her a cup of tea and been cautiously welcome. Now Sabrina sat with Javier in the bright modern kitchen—some original features from such a dignified old house not withstanding—and sipped at the brew in the delicate porcelain cup feeling as if her equilibrium might be as easily shattered any moment now. The tension between them all was tangible, enforced politeness making Sabrina emit a silent scream of protest somewhere inside her head. She knew they'd suffered the worst tragedy but shouting and crying was surely better than this frozen veneer of coping?

Beside her, Javier had loosened his blue silk tie, removed his coat and jacket and commandeered the sturdy ladder-back chair with his tall, hard-muscled frame as if silently taking stock of all that had happened. Just what was going on behind those brooding, faintly weary dark eyes of his? Once again Sabrina had an almost uncontrollable urge to reach out and offer him comfort—but here, in front of his niece's grandmother? It was easy to sense such a display would go down like a lead balloon. *They* were family and she the interloper, in Angela Calder's eyes an unknown quantity—a loose cannon that could potentially blow them all apart.

'This is a wonderful cup of tea,' she said out loud,

breaking the silence that had fallen round the table. 'Just what I needed.'

'Thank you, dear.' Angela's eyes flicked across to Javier. 'When you're both finished, perhaps you might like to show Sabrina her room, Javier? She might like to put her feet up for five minutes.'

'I'd like her to meet Angelina first. I let her take the day off school so that she would be here when we came back. Why didn't you tell me that Rosie was taking her out to the park?'

It was the first time she'd heard his disapproval and Sabrina studied the handsome, almost sculpted profile of her husband and felt a small shiver run down her spine.

'The child hadn't said two words all morning, just sat in front of the TV watching one of those daft pop-music programmes. Both Rosie and I thought that some fresh air might do her good.'

'No doubt you are right.' Dragging his fingers through his sleek black hair, Javier pushed away from the table and stood up to his full height. He looked deliberately at Sabrina. 'Let me show you your room. Angela is right; you must be tired. You have only just got over a cold.'

I'm not an invalid! Sabrina wanted to reply but bit back her unexpectedly angry retort out of deference to the situation. If anyone was showing the strain of the morning it was Javier—not her. Those broad shoulders of his were presently carrying the weight of the whole planet if his expression was anything to go by.

In the large, bright, decidedly feminine bedroom with its huge canopied bed, flowing voile curtains and walnut furniture, Sabrina perched on the edge of an antique Edwardian chair and glanced up at the man currently pacing the floor. Restless energy was pouring off him in waves, like a trapped tiger prowling its cage.

'Javier?' she ventured quietly. 'Are you having second thoughts about all this?'

Immediately he stopped pacing. A muscle flinched in the side of his smooth, recently shaven cheek.

'No. Are you? This is a big thing for you to have done, Sabrina. I understand you must have many doubts but I will try and ease them one at a time. Will you ring your parents today and tell them what has happened?' In truth, it worried him that she had ventured into this arrangement without apparently telling a soul. He knew it was in reality a temporary arrangement, a marriage of convenience, but it still bothered him that she wouldn't share the news of their union with the people closest to her. What would they think when they found out? Would they believe he had some kind of hold over her? Would they distrust his promise of help with her business? He sighed and rubbed a hand round the back of his neck.

'Of course I'll tell them…my sister too. I can hardly keep it a secret when I won't be at the flat any more. I know this is how it has to be to satisfy the courts that our marriage is bona fide but is this arrangement going to work, Javier? I mean, living here in Michael's house—his daughter's home? What did you tell Angelina about me?'

'I told you. I said that you were a very nice woman who had agreed to a marriage with me so that I could get a British passport and stay in this country. I explained that you would be living with us for a while so that the courts would believe our marriage was real; that it was important for us to be able to convince them.'

Sabrina dropped her gaze to the floor, to the rich powder-blue carpet that she knew her feet would disappear into if she kicked off her shoes. Everything about the house spoke of luxury and wealth. Michael Calder had been a highly skilled surgeon with a practice in Harley Street. It followed that the family had money. She knew that her husband was wealthy too because she had done as he had suggested and found his company on the internet. There had been newspaper and magazine articles posted on the site—'Javier D'Alessandro, young internet entrepreneur—multimillionaire by the age of twenty-eight.' What had he thought of her small, cramped little flat when he'd come to collect her suitcases, with its faded wallpaper and mish-mash of colourful rugs that covered up a carpet that was threadbare and old? She would have liked to perhaps decorate more but because of her devotion to work, barely ever had the time. Oh, well, too late now for recriminations. As she glanced up, her anxious blue eyes careened helplessly into his. 'At least you told her the truth. She won't expect me to…to—'

'Act like a real wife?' A flash of pain stole into his suddenly hard gaze. 'Let me reassure you on that score, Sabrina. I have no intention of holding you to anything other than a purely business arrangement. I have neither the aim nor the desire to infringe that in any way whatsoever, so you can relax. Now I have to go and make some phone calls. Rest or unpack, I don't mind which. I'll bring up your suitcases then leave you in peace until Angelina returns.'

He walked out of the room with a purposeful, almost angry stride, leaving Sabrina bewildered and hurt at the unexpected coldness in his voice.

'Hello there. I'm Sabrina. You must be Angelina.'

The child was drinking a glass of milk, a plate with a sandwich on it next to her elbow. She glanced up at Sabrina's voice, marking her entrance with huge, doe-like brown eyes, watching her for one or two anxiously assessing moments before concentrating once again on her drink.

Wiping her hands down the front of her trousers, Sabrina cautiously approached the table. She hadn't wanted to stay confined to her bedroom any longer and, when Javier hadn't come back for her, decided to show her face without him. At the sink a petite blonde in jeans and blue sweatshirt was rinsing some fruit beneath the tap. 'Hi. I'm Rosie; pleased to meet you. Sit down—I'll get you a cup of tea in a minute, or would you prefer coffee?'

'Coffee would be nice...thanks.'

She pulled out a chair two spaces down from Angelina. 'Did you enjoy your walk in the park?'

'It was OK.' The girl didn't look up from her sandwich. Sabrina's stomach lurched. Oh, God, this was going to be so much harder than she'd even imagined. All she really wanted to do was gather the child into her arms and hold her close. Just as she did with her nephews Henry and William and baby Tallulah when they were scared or hurt.

'Near where I work there's a wonderful park where

I sometimes go to eat my lunch. It has a bandstand and squirrels and a small playground with swings. At this time of the year you can barely see the grass for all the leaves covering it. When I was little I used to love to run through the leaves in the park. I thought it was the greatest fun. Do you ever do that?'

Angelina seemed to consider the question. 'You're not like my uncle's last girlfriend—Christina. She was much skinnier than you.'

And what exactly was she meant to glean from that? Did the child resent Sabrina for marrying her uncle when she would maybe have preferred the skinnier Christina?

'I won't ever be skinny,' she admitted with a smile. 'I like my food too much.'

'But you have a nice figure. Like my dance teacher, Holly. She teaches me ballet and tap.'

The unexpected compliment completely threw Sabrina. 'Really? I'd like to be able to dance but my dad always said I was about as graceful as an elephant!' She grinned at the memory and tried to ignore the little stab of hurt that always accompanied the thought. It was Ellie who had been the graceful one. The one who all the boys had whistled at on the way home from school.

Angelina nodded. 'My daddy loved to watch me dance.' At the drainer, Rosie paused in arranging the newly washed fruit into a thick glass bowl. Sabrina's heart beat a little faster.

'I'm sure he did. He must have been very proud of you. Very proud.'

'You married my uncle today.'

'Yes.' Her face flooded with heat. 'Do you mind?'

Considering the question for what seemed like a lifetime, Angelina eventually shook her head. 'No.'

'No what?'

Newly showered, his black hair glistening sleekly, Javier strolled into the kitchen, his gaze immediately alighting on his niece.

'I said no, I didn't mind you and Sabrina getting married. Can I be excused now, Uncle? I want to go and listen to some music.'

'Sure. Do you like pop music, Sabrina?' He asked the question as if he was genuinely interested in her answer. Perhaps he thought she was too old to enjoy that sort of thing? Willing herself to stop being so damn sensitive about her age around him, she summoned up a grin instead. 'Yeah, I like pop music. I confess I have a real soft spot for some of the boy bands.'

'Me too!' Angelina's eyes lit up at the news and, catching his expression above her head, Sabrina felt Javier's gaze melt thankfully into hers. It gave her heart a real jolt—as if she'd been plugged into a new, mysterious source of power.

'How many CDs have you got, Angelina? I've got a small collection of my own I could let you look through if you'd like?'

'Sure.' She glanced up at her uncle as if to search for his approval. 'If that's all right?'

'If Sabrina says it is, then it is.' Javier walked across the tiled floor to a worktop. He examined the kettle for water then plugged it in. 'Maybe you'd like to show Sabrina your room later. I think she'd be impressed by your own music collection, don't you?'

'OK.' The girl took a bite of sandwich, seemingly satisfied by her uncle's response.

Had she unknowingly jumped a hurdle where Angelina was concerned or was it far too early to tell? Arms folded on the table top, Sabrina sought out Javier as though drawn by some invisible connective cord. What was it about the man that made a room light up when he entered it? No wonder his niece adored him. Had the skinny Christina adored him too? It was none of her business, she decided unhappily. Not when her own presence in his life was destined to be merely the most temporary of arrangements.

'Run that by me again.' Jill was regarding Sabrina as if she'd just told her she'd won the jackpot on the lottery. 'I thought you said you'd got married. Was I hearing things?'

Clicking some papers into place in a large ring-binder, Sabrina paused, flustered, and instinctively knew that her colleague's reaction to her announcement was going to be a mere bagatelle compared to her parents and Ellie. Yesterday she'd been so on edge anyway, what with the ceremony, settling into the house and meeting Angelina, that she had deliberately avoided ringing them, and now the prospect of their disapproval loomed like a collection of stormy grey clouds on the horizon.

'No, you weren't hearing things. I got married. Please don't make it into a big deal, Jill. It's not a love match or anything like that.'

Jill's eyes grew even wider. 'It's not?'

'I've done it to help someone out.' So why was she having palpitations at the mere thought of the man?

'Someone?'

'Javier. He needed a British passport.'

To her consternation, Jill cracked a wide, knowing smile. 'You're talking about that gorgeous hunk who came in here looking for you a couple of weeks ago? Oh, Sabrina! You dark horse!'

'Before you leave tonight, I'll give you my new home telephone number, just in case you ever need to reach me there.' Heaving another large ring-binder onto her lap, Sabrina pushed her hair out of her eyes and mentally made a note to take more time with her appearance tomorrow. This morning she'd woken in a strange house with unfamiliar voices and unfamiliar sounds and had lain in bed feeling dazed at what she'd done. In a bid to give the family space and not get in the way, she'd hurriedly washed and dressed and raced out of the house without so much as a cup of coffee. Then she'd spent half an hour in one of those popular coffee chains, nursing a frothy cappuccino and feeling as if she'd burst into tears if someone so much as glanced at her the wrong way. Had Javier been surprised that she'd left for work so early? Or was he too concerned about his own activities once he'd delivered Angelina safely to school? He'd explained to Sabrina that he took the child in the morning and Rosie picked her up at three-thirty. And what did they do about dinner? Should Sabrina get something for herself on the way home, just in case she worked late?

A heartfelt sigh escaped her and she took a moment to absorb the fluttery feeling in her stomach. There was so much she didn't know. So much they hadn't had a chance to discuss.

'I'm sure *I* wouldn't be looking half so glum if I'd just got married to someone as seriously sexy as him.'

'Please, Jill.' Pursing her lips, Sabrina picked up the phone. 'Can we just get on? I really don't feel like discussing this right now if you don't mind.'

'All right, but don't think you're getting off as lightly as all that. And I'm seriously miffed you didn't even have a hen night.'

Rolling her eyes, Sabrina put down the receiver without making her phone call. 'I told you, it wasn't like that. We only got married to—'

The little bell over the door jingled and both women glanced up to see Javier D'Alessandro step inside. He acknowledged Jill's presence with a brief nod of his head but his gaze—deep, dark and intense—gravitated almost immediately to Sabrina. Her anxiety increased tenfold.

'Hi. This is a surprise.' Feeling Jill's scrutiny beside her, Sabrina strove to keep her voice light, but everything inside her was going crazy at just the sight of the man. He looked like the successful young entrepreneur he was in his effortlessly elegant suit and expensive overcoat, his sexy masculine fragrance leaving an indelible presence on the room.

'A pleasant one, I hope?'

Sabrina dipped her head. 'Of course. What can I do for you? Did Angelina get off to school all right?'

'She's fine. You left without having breakfast, without joining us.' Was that reproach in his voice?

'I'm sorry, I…' She turned and looked at Jill, who clearly had forgotten why she was there. 'Don't you have some clients to ring this morning, Jill? I'm just going to take Mr D'Alessandro…' Flushing, she realised her mistake and stood up in a rush. 'We just need to have a talk. If there are any calls for me, please tell them I'll call back just as soon as I can.'

In the back room, she busied herself putting the kettle on to boil and sorting out the makings of tea and coffee. For several seconds Javier just watched her, his brain working overtime with the effort to fathom her out. Was she regretting marrying him? Was she too unhappy and uncomfortable in Michael's house? As soon as he could look for somewhere for them all to move to, he would. But he still wanted to know why she'd felt the need to escape so early this morning, without so much as even bidding them goodbye. On the way to school Angelina had asked curiously if they had had a row.

'Sabrina.'

She jumped at the sound of his voice, spilling a little of the hot water from the kettle onto her hand. 'Ouch!'

'Let me see.' Before she had a chance to guess his next move he was at her side, taking her throbbing hand into his, turning it over for examination then leading her to the old-fashioned sink by the back wall and turning on the cold tap. The water barely cooled her heated skin, she was so unravelled by his touch. Feeling all her blood roar in her ears, Sabrina tried to pull her hand free, and when she managed it and turned off the tap Javier put one hand on his hip and rubbed at his temple as if he had a severe headache.

'Have I offended you in some way, Sabrina? Because if I have I wish you would tell me.' She smelled so good, he was thinking. Flowers and honey with a subtle undertone of musk. A warm, sexy fragrance that was making him feel things he had no business feeling towards a woman who had only agreed to marry him because of a business arrangement. Her soft, dewy complexion was highlighted by two bright spots of pink and her silky honey-brown hair was slowly working its way loose from her tortoiseshell comb. And her eyes... *Dios!* Her eyes! They were so blue he thought he could drown in them—like an ocean.

'You haven't offended me, Javier. Why would you think that?'

'Why did you run away this morning?'

'Run away?' What a curious thing to accuse her of, even if it happened to be true.

'We wanted you to join us for breakfast, Angelina and I. We all need to get to know each other better, yes?'

'I didn't know what you expected. I didn't want to intrude,' Sabrina confessed, flushing again.

'Intrude? How could that be when I asked you to come and live with us? I do not expect you to hide yourself away or creep around the house like a mouse! It is your home as well as ours.'

'Perhaps we need to talk about some ground rules. It's an unusual situation, Javier; right now I don't know how to play it.'

'Just be yourself, Sabrina. If we all just try and relax it might make things easier for all of us. Angelina will come round, given time. It is early days yet. Already she has expressed interest in you.'

'She has?'

'She told me you had a much better figure than my

ex-girlfriend.' He chuckled and the sound made goosebumps chase across her skin.

'Christina.' She bit her lip.

His eyes seemed to grow even darker. 'She told you about Christina?'

'Just in passing. Do you mind?'

'No. I don't mind. I have barely even given the woman a thought, so much has happened lately.'

What did that mean? Sabrina worried. Was he still in love with her?

'And Angelina is right. You *do* have a nicer figure than Christina.' Javier smiled and the impact of that simple gesture caused all sorts of complications in Sabrina's heart. Not least—how was she going to live with a man who bothered her more than she cared to acknowledge? Her husband who wasn't really a husband at all.

'I'll make us some coffee. Or perhaps you'd prefer tea?'

'Coffee is fine, thank you.' To Sabrina's surprise he took off his overcoat and laid it over the back of an old office chair. 'When you have made the coffee I thought we could begin work.'

'What do you mean?' She stopped spooning coffee grounds into a mug and spun round to face him.

'It is time I started to fulfil my part of our agreement,' he said smoothly, 'to help you with your business. If we can spend today going over your books et cetera, then tonight I will devote some time to working out modernisation costs. The sooner we start, the better—yes?'

'Javier, you don't have to do this.'

'What?' He was frowning, dark eyes suddenly troubled.

'If you want to give me some advice I'll accept it gratefully but anything else...' She shrugged and went back to making the coffee. 'I was happy to do what I did for you. I don't need repayment. Honestly.'

If someone had dropped a brick on his head right then, Javier couldn't have been more stunned. Sliding his hands into the pockets of his tailored black trousers, he shook his head. 'You would do this thing for me...for nothing?'

'Lending me your expertise and your business knowledge would be more than enough payment.' Blushing, Sabrina added a little milk to her own drink and stirred it. 'As for modernisation, I'll find the money from another source. I haven't given up yet.' *Nor will I.*

His tanned brow furrowing, Javier wasn't appeased. 'I do not want you to find the money from another source. We have an agreement. An agreement I intend to fulfil.'

'All right,' Sabrina conceded reluctantly, wondering what it would mean to be under such an obligation to a man like Javier D'Alessandro. And, although she'd married him and fulfilled her own part of the agreement—what exactly would marriage to him entail? In the middle of all this was a sad, hurting eleven-year-old girl who would need care and attention from both of them. If Sabrina's heart got involved, what then? Weren't the lines of their so-called 'agreement' going to get dangerously blurred?

'I'll agree to your financial help as well—but only

if we work out an instalment plan for me to pay you back.'

'No.'

'Yes. I insist.'

'You are a stubborn woman, you know that?'

'Some people call it tenacious. I'm used to facing mountains and finding a way over them.' Wincing, she mentally pushed aside the sudden cloak of weariness that descended on her shoulders. She'd always worked hard. She didn't know any other way. Was it because from a young age she'd always felt she had something to prove? Ellie was their parents' blue-eyed girl. Whatever she did was praised to the skies. And when Ellie had given up her phenomenally well-paid City job to stay at home and become a full-time wife and mother, well…her parents were ecstatic at her 'selflessness.'

'I did what I did to help you out, Javier. I don't regret it.'

She meant it. Dear God, the woman barely knew him or Angelina and yet she had already done so much to alleviate their predicament. Now she was telling him that if she allowed him to help her, she insisted on paying him back. Such nobility was a rare commodity indeed in the circles he had moved in. Life in the fast lane had not exactly paved the way for lasting friendships with the kind of friends who would immediately help you out if you were in trouble or even pay you back if they borrowed money. His mother would bless the ground Sabrina Kendricks walked on, he realised—the thought making him warm. Or should he say Sabrina *D'Alessandro*?

Marriage of convenience or not—this charming, generous woman was his wife now.

'We are going to turn East-West Travel into a thriving modern business,' he declared, suddenly fired up at the thought. Sabrina couldn't yet know he was a man who thrived on a challenge. He didn't give up easily—not even on so-called lost causes. She would discover that about him.

'I notice your other employee is not here today.'

'You mean Robbie. He's on a couple of days' leave.'

'Then I may use his computer?'

'Of course, but Javier—' her hand curled round his arm and they both reacted strongly at the contact, a flash of something Sabrina couldn't discern in Javier's dark Latin eyes and a leap in her own heart that made her words get caught in her throat '—you don't have to do this.'

Her hand dropped away, and to her shock Javier tilted her chin and smiled into her anxious blue gaze. 'That is where you are mistaken. It is a point of honour for me and I never go back on my word. Bring the coffee and we will get to work.'

Bring the coffee? Normally she would have bristled at such a chauvinistic-sounding command but for some reason today Sabrina didn't seem to be operating on her usual wavelength. As soon as Javier had walked through the door she'd been functioning on a different frequency and she got the feeling it was one she was going to have to get used to, whether she liked it or not.

CHAPTER FIVE

FOR two days Sabrina worked side by side with Javier, going through accounts, client lists and schedules, meticulously sifting through everything that would give him a good picture as to how East-West Travel was currently being run. She'd discovered that when his mind was on work his concentration was unequalled, and, apart from when it was necessary to ask pertinent questions, he kept his head down—barely acknowledging whatever else was going on around him. To Sabrina's irritation, in between dealing with customers, Jill had taken it upon herself to keep him furnished with regular offers of tea and coffee and even popped out to the most expensive deli in the high street to get him the sandwiches he asked for. It was obvious that he had acquired a fan in her colleague.

That first evening when she returned home on her own, Javier having left earlier to see Angelina, she'd arrived back at the house to find that they'd waited dinner for her. Angela Calder had returned to her own home in the Cotswolds, promising to be back in a week or two to see her grandchild, and Rosie had cooked a wonderfully fragrant lamb tagine for them. After Sabrina's initial hesitance at joining Angelina and Javier at the dinner table, she tucked into the food with relish. If they were a little light on conversation she didn't mind—it was the child the adults were concerned about. Angelina hardly ate a thing. In the end Javier suggested to Rosie that perhaps she could make some sandwiches and put them in the fridge, in case his niece wanted something later. Excusing herself from the table, Angelina disappeared into her bedroom and shut the door. Minutes later pop music rang out and Javier glanced at Sabrina with a faintly weary look and shrugged.

'She'll be all right,' she softly assured him, wishing she didn't feel so hopelessly inadequate to help. 'Perhaps I can ask if she'll let me see her CD collection later.'

'Why not,' Javier agreed, pouring them both a glass of wine. 'Right now all we can do is take one day at a time. By the way, have you rung your parents yet?'

'I was going to do it tonight' she replied, a pang of guilt stabbing through her. Truth to tell, she'd barely given the matter another thought—especially when her head was swimming with thoughts of work and the kind of improvements Javier was going to suggest.

His dark brows came together in slight disapproval. 'Please, Sabrina. Do not put it off any longer. Your parents should be informed.'

She sat back in her chair, her cheeks flushed. 'You make me sound about five years old.'

That elicited a rueful grin. 'Forgive me. I am just concerned they would find out by accident and that would not be good.'

'No. I see what you mean. Well…' She got to her feet and brushed back her hair with her hand. 'There's no time like the present, then, is there?'

Her announcement didn't go down well. Her

mother cried because 'after all this time she still hadn't seen her eldest daughter married' and her father interrogated her on just about everything to do with Javier. He could have had a job with Interpol, Sabrina reflected without humour. By the time she came off the phone, all Sabrina could face was a shower then bed, but she did fulfil her intention of dropping by Angelina's room and asking to see her music collection. After spending just over an hour with the little girl, listening to music, Angelina bade her goodnight but not before tentatively suggesting that Sabrina might like to listen to some more tracks the following night. Eagerly, Sabrina agreed and she went to bed feeling a little lighter than when she'd come off the phone to her parents.

The following evening after their meal, Sabrina was heading for her room and a shower when Javier waylaid her in the corridor. He'd taken off his tie and undid the first couple of buttons on his shirt, and Sabrina caught an intriguing glimpse of strongly corded neck muscles and a smattering of the dark hair that covered his chest. Heat invaded her limbs. 'Tomorrow we will visit your bank and deposit some funds for the modernisation programme,' he informed her without preamble, 'then we will have lunch together.'

'Lunch?' Her voice had turned unwittingly husky. Javier seemed to concentrate his dark gaze even more.

'There is a need to discuss how we are going to proceed.'

There was something inexplicably sensual about his almost formal use of the language—every word carefully considered.

'With modernising the business, you mean?' She was feeling somewhat overwhelmed at the idea that, with Javier's much-needed help, she was finally going to be able to realise her dreams for the company.

'That and other things.' He smiled. 'I will book somewhere.'

'I haven't yet thanked you for all you're doing.' She twirled a button on her blue linen jacket and felt the thread loosen. 'I can't tell you how much it means to me. It's been such a worry for so long…'

'It is a small thing compared to what you have done for me and Angelina,' he replied sincerely. 'And I am excited by it too. I think you will be amazed what can be achieved.'

'Anyway…' Glancing almost shyly up at him from beneath her honey-brown lashes, Sabrina wondered what had happened to the single-minded business-woman who was so certain she neither wanted nor needed a man in her life. She was sure that even her mother would detect the difference in her since she'd met Javier D'Alessandro. Her hard edges had been somehow softened. In his presence she was discovering new aspects to herself all the time. Worrying. Especially when one day soon she'd have to walk away and maybe not even see him again. 'I'm going to take a shower.'

His reaction staggered her. Leaning back against the wall, his arms folded across that incredible chest, he smiled lazily. 'Let me know if you need my assistance.'

'What?' Her stomach fluttering crazily, Sabrina blushed like a schoolgirl.

'Scrubbing your back.' He smiled again. 'Relax, Sabrina. I am only teasing.'

Teasing or not, his suggestive tone had all but turned her bones to jelly. 'I knew that.' Hoping her face didn't reflect the turmoil that was churning her up inside, she turned to walk with as much dignity as she could muster down the corridor to her room.

Madre del Dios! Rubbing his hand across his forehead, Javier wasn't surprised to find that he was perspiring. The sexual charge he had received from his new wife simply by spending a few minutes in light conversation had completely thrown him. Her scent had been taunting him, the dimples at the corners of her lush mouth fascinating him beyond reason. If he had spent a minute longer with her he was almost certain he would have reached out to touch her in some way. That most definitely hadn't been part of his plan. Theirs was a paper marriage only—sexual favours weren't part of the package. Unfortunately he hadn't been able to transmit that fact to his body. Just the brief thought of Sabrina naked beneath the warm spray of a shower, soaping that shapely, sexy body, had heat rushing to his groin like fire. What was he supposed to do? He was a young, virile man with more energy than he sometimes knew what to do with and right now a hot, sweet tumble in bed with a beautiful, warm, willing woman was the only thing he craved. And not just *any* beautiful, willing woman either—it was Sabrina he wanted, rightly or wrongly. Cursing harshly beneath his breath, he turned towards his room to seek a shower of his own—a very icy cold shower that would drive away the suddenly rampant desire that was hijacking his body, before being confronted with the temptation of her smile again.

Ellie didn't mince her words. She flung into the room with Tallulah on her hip, her champagne-blonde hair dishevelled by the fierce wind outside and an expression like a storm cloud on her face. 'You must be out of your mind!' Dropping her bag onto a nearby chair, she ignored Jill and Robbie and stared angrily at Sabrina, who up until a moment ago had been concentrating on the screen in front of her.

'Nice to see you too, Ellie.' Scowling at the unwanted interruption, Sabrina started to get to her feet. 'Hello, Tally, are you going to give Auntie a kiss?' She reached out her arms for her niece and was foolishly hurt when Ellie didn't pass the baby to her as she normally would have done.

'I couldn't believe it when Mum told me you'd gone and got married to a perfect stranger! Have you completely taken leave of your senses, Sabrina Kendricks?'

'Let's have some privacy, shall we?' Sabrina put her hand beneath her sister's elbow and guided her reluctantly into the back room. Closing the door, she flicked her blue eyes angrily over her. 'How dare you just walk in here and start yelling at me? This is a professional business, in case you had forgotten. What if there'd been a room full of customers?'

'I don't give a—' She bit back the curse word and jiggled the baby, who had started to whimper. 'What do you know about this man? How do you know he isn't out to take you for every penny you have? Did you check him out before you married him? And why didn't you tell me you'd met someone?'

'Take me for every penny I have?' Sabrina's laugh was harsh. 'If only you knew the irony of that remark.'

'For God's sake, what were you thinking of?'

'Drop it, Ellie. I'm thirty-seven years old, damn it! I don't need your permission to live my life the way I choose. And if you knew Javier D'Alessandro you wouldn't have to ask me such questions.'

Ellie transferred the baby to her opposite hip and glared. 'But I don't know him, do I? That's the whole point! None of us do. I know I told you that you needed to date more but I didn't expect you to go and marry the first man who asks you!'

'You're making it sound ridiculous.'

'It *is* ridiculous! What's the matter, Sabrina? Did you suddenly get scared of growing older and not having a man in your life? If that was the case, why didn't you just join a dating agency rather than marry a complete stranger off the street?'

Hurt welled in Sabrina's chest. She knew it was because Ellie had inadvertently touched a nerve. Had she been scared about getting older and being alone? Maybe not consciously, but she couldn't pretend that the thought hadn't ever crossed her mind. However, she'd married Javier to help him get a British passport, so that he could stay and raise Angelina as his own. She didn't kid herself it was a real marriage. He was only thirty. One day he'd want to marry someone his own age and add to his family. God! She didn't even know if she was capable of having children.

Seeing the sudden strain on her sister's face, Ellie

shook her head in remorse. 'I'm sorry, sis. I've just been worried out of my mind since Mum told me. He—he hasn't tried anything, has he?'

'You mean, has he attempted to get me into bed?'

Ellie had the grace to flush. Tallulah smiled, her chubby, grinning face catching Sabrina on the raw.

'He's not interested in me that way. I explained to Mum it was purely a business arrangement.'

'I'll believe it when I see it. When can I meet him? What did you say his name was?'

'Javier.' Sabrina took a shaky breath. 'Come on Saturday if you like. Mum's got the address.'

'Saturday, then. Look after yourself, sis. You know where I am if you need me.'

'You seem...preoccupied today.'

Javier's voice broke into Sabrina's thoughts. Glancing down at her coffee, she picked up the spoon in the saucer and gave it a stir. The smart little restaurant in an exclusive Knightsbridge thoroughfare was full of deliciously mouthwatering smells, but she hadn't been able to do full justice to the wonderful pasta she had ordered.

'Do I?' She raised her shoulders in a slight shrug. 'I'm sorry. Understandably I've had a lot on my mind.'

'Are you happy with my suggestions for the business?'

'Of course. But Javier—so much money... I really am going to have to insist on paying you back, you know.' Richard Weedy would surely never dare to look down his nose at her again after the outrageous amount Javier had paid into her bank just an hour ago.

'You have already paid me back. We have an agreement and I am merely honouring my part. The matter is at an end. The money is yours to make the improvements we discussed and whatever else you want to do with it.'

'The matter is not at an end, Javier. I won't be easy in my mind until we work out some kind of repayment plan. I mean it!'

'It has become clear to me that you find it difficult to accept help of any kind, Sabrina. It is not so good to be too independent, I think.'

His stern tone made her bristle slightly. Her chin came up. 'We have a very different culture here, Javier. Women are encouraged to have their own careers, make their own lives, without men dictating what they do.'

A flash of anger crooked his mouth. '*Sí*. You think it an achievement to bypass marriage and family? You are setting yourself up for a very lonely existence, I think.'

'I've never been lonely in my life! I enjoy my work—the challenge, the achievement. It gives me all the stimulation I need.'

The tension between them grew. 'Forgive me, but I think you need more than that. Men and women were meant to be together in mutual partnership. It is not something to shy away from because you are frightened you will be surrendering your independence. A clever woman allows the man to think he has all the power, but really *she* is the one in control.'

'So how come you haven't got married until now?

Not forgetting that this is just a temporary arrangement. No doubt you've been pursuing your own career with a vengeance, otherwise how could you be so successful?' Her heart was beating a little too fast and she wished she'd never started this conversation. She didn't want his antagonism...she wanted something much more *dangerous* than that.

His hand reached for his tie and loosened it. With one arm resting on the table top he scooped some sugar into the little silver spoon in the sugar bowl and watched the grains slide gracefully back in. He did this twice more before speaking.

'I didn't consider marriage before because I had seen what can happen when you give your heart to someone. Divorce, bereavement... I didn't want to set myself up for so much pain.' A shadow stole across his handsome face. 'Perhaps I am a coward.'

Impossible. Swallowing hard, Sabrina slowly shook her head. 'I don't think a man who would risk asking a relatively strange woman to marry him so that he could get a passport to stay in the country and adopt his niece could ever be deemed a coward in any way. You *should* marry properly some day, Javier. You should marry someone your own age and have lots of children to give Angelina brothers and sisters. You would make a wonderful father.'

The conviction in her voice shook him to his innermost core. Pinning her with a darkly brooding gaze, he smiled briefly. 'We will see. Let us change the subject and talk about the business. Tomorrow I will start ordering the new equipment. You will be upside-down for a while in the office but I am sure your staff will be able to work around that.'

'They're as excited as me about it all.' As she felt another rush of gratitude, her blue eyes shone. 'And you don't mind giving us all a little training in the new programme?'

'It will be my pleasure.'

'You seem to know so much. I feel like such a dinosaur in comparison.'

'Stop putting yourself down.' With a small sigh, Javier considered her so intensely that every nerve she possessed snapped into full and immediate attention. 'You have fifteen years' experience of running a successful business. There is much you could teach me, I'm sure.'

Why did Sabrina get the feeling it wasn't just her business technique he was talking about? *Wishful thinking,* she concluded disparagingly. Thinking about her husband in bed was becoming an obsession. She gulped her coffee and returned the cup noisily to its elegant green and gold saucer.

'I had a visit from my sister yesterday—Ellie. I invited her to the house on Saturday to meet you. Was that all right?'

'That is good, yes.' His lips parted, showing those perfect white teeth, and for a long moment Sabrina just basked in the pleasure of his smile.

'I hope you still think it's good after she's gone. I'm afraid my sister isn't one for standing on ceremony. Neither does she pull her punches.'

Javier frowned.

'She says exactly what she thinks,' Sabrina explained. 'I just thought I'd better warn you.'

'No doubt it is because she cares about you.' Signalling the young waitress for more coffee, he stayed silent while she refilled both their cups. When she'd gone, he leant forward towards Sabrina and snagged her hand. His touch electrified her. All she heard was the wave-like pounding of her blood in her ears. 'It is good to have family who care.'

'The way you do for Angelina.'

'*Sí.*' He released her hand to sit back in his chair and Sabrina didn't miss the flash of concern his dark eyes exhibited. 'I have already talked to the authorities concerned about adoption. I have been advised there should be no problem. It is a big relief, yes?'

'Yes, it must be. That little girl deserves something good to happen. She seemed a little brighter yesterday, don't you think?'

'I am glad you noticed. I thought so too. This evening I thought we might all go out for the evening—to the movies perhaps?'

'Javier, I…'

'What is it, Sabrina?'

'We need to talk about us…about—about our arrangement.'

'You are unhappy about something?'

'No! But…where do we draw the line exactly? I mean, I want to help you with Angelina but this marriage of ours isn't real, is it? And I—'

'Isn't real?' He was scowling heavily, immediately alert. 'We said our vows in front of the proper authorities, no? We signed the papers. Of course this marriage is real.'

'You know very well what I mean.' She rubbed the side of her temple and wondered why the room suddenly felt so unbearably hot. 'We agreed it's a formality—a business arrangement. That understood, I can't be so involved in your life. There have to be lines we absolutely don't cross. Do you see what I'm getting at?'

'You do not like spending time with me and Angelina?'

Mortified, Sabrina rushed to reassure him. Without thought she automatically reached out for his hand, covering those fascinating brown fingers with her own pale ones. Heat immediately made its presence felt but she couldn't let go. 'How could you ever think that? I care about you both.'

Her words warmed Javier like a deep draught of brandy stealing into his blood and he couldn't help but smile. 'We are fine as we are, Sabrina—wouldn't you say? As far as I can see, nothing has to be changed.'

Oh, this was getting complicated. Biting her lip, Sabrina slid her hand away from his. She stared down into her coffee, feeling as though all the control she'd assumed over her life for the past fifteen years was slowly but surely slipping away.

'I will order you some dessert. You hardly ate any of your lunch.' Before she could stop him, Javier had summoned the pretty young waitress and ordered some rich-sounding sweet that Sabrina knew under normal circumstances she'd be sorely tempted by. However, her current circumstances weren't normal at all and the pudding would no doubt go to waste.

'You shouldn't have done that.'

'You need to eat. In my country, men look after their women.' He said it so matter-of-factly that Sabrina didn't know whether to hit him with something or simply submit to the inevitable. She'd been taking care of herself for so long now that the mere concept of a man assuming any kind of responsibility for her welfare was completely alien.

'We're back to that again, are we? Have you even heard of feminism in Argentina?' she retorted, rattled.

In return he gave her one of those slow, deeply sexy smiles that made her insides dissolve like melting sugar. 'Some of it we younger men embrace—some we don't.'

'I don't think I should get into this argument.' Her face flushed, blue eyes resentful, she sank back into her chair with a sigh and folded her arms across her chest.

'You think I mind you arguing with me? I like a woman who knows her own mind. I have no problem with you expressing your views, Sabrina. Even if I don't happen to agree…'

So much for establishing where we stand. Staring down at the incredible chocolate concoction the waitress placed in front of her, Sabrina picked up her spoon and defiantly tucked in.

Javier paused outside his niece's door. Was that laughter he had heard or had his foolish, hopeful heart just imagined it? He knocked briefly at the door and his shoulders automatically tightened as Angelina called out, 'Come in, Uncle.'

The sight that met his eyes had him staring in stunned disbelief. CDs and tapes spread out on the floor all around them, Angelina and Sabrina were lying front down on the carpet, propped up on their elbows, sifting through discs like two giggling schoolgirls. Although with Sabrina dressed in tight denims and a little pink T-shirt that was riding above her waist, her long hair loose down her back, she was most definitely all grown up. Javier's breathing felt suddenly laboured. 'What's going on?' he asked lightly, feeling oddly excluded.

'We're just listening to some music and talking about girl stuff.' Angelina's small shoulders shrugged as if it should be perfectly obvious. 'Sabrina said that her sister got my favourite singer's autograph at a concert and she's going to ask her on Saturday if I could have it.'

'That's nice.' Moving to the bed with its bright pink Barbie duvet, Javier sat down, his gaze helplessly gravitating to Sabrina's long, slim legs in soft, hugging denim and the sweet curve of her sexy rear end.

'Did you want something, Javier?' she asked him, smiling. Was it his fevered imagination or was there a more intimate invitation in that smile of hers?

'Yes, Uncle, because if you don't, we'd really like some privacy—wouldn't we, Sabrina?'

'I was just going to offer you both a drink of some kind. How about some fruit juice or a glass of milk, Angelina?' Rising to his feet, he dug his hands into his trouser pockets, irked that he suddenly felt superfluous to the needs of the women in his life.

'Juice is fine, Uncle. How about you, Sabrina?'

'Sure. Thanks.'

'OK. See you in a minute.'

There was a wildlife documentary on the TV about tigers in India he'd wanted to see but, once settled in the big luxurious armchair, the remote control at his elbow, Javier couldn't work up an interest. Not when

Angelina had actually bid him goodnight with a smile on her face for the first time in weeks and Sabrina was taking a shower. Did the woman tell him she was going to take a shower just to taunt him? He shifted against the cushions at his back, cursing softly at the discomfort of having his blood head south with a vengeance.

He flicked off the TV and raked his fingers irritably through his hair. Almost of their own volition his feet took him out of the room, down the thickly carpeted corridor to what was now Sabrina's room. He rapped briefly on the door.

He heard movement from within, the sound of something thunking to the floor and her muttered curse. His heart beat a little faster.

'Hi.' Her face pink from the shower, dressed in a thick white towelling robe and with her long hair scooped up into a loose topknot, she looked deliciously feminine and warm. Javier knew he was playing with fire. *This isn't part of the plan,* he told himself. *I don't want to care about this woman. I don't want to desire her the way I do…*

'Is everything all right?' he asked after a long moment spent just gazing at her as a starving man gazed at a banquet.

'You're too late if you've come to scrub my back,' came her rejoinder, blue eyes issuing a challenge that hit him square in the solar plexus.

'My bad luck, I guess.' As he stepped into the room, Sabrina heard the soft 'snick' of the door closing behind him with a thundering heart.

CHAPTER SIX

'WHAT are you doing?' Her hands went to her robe, fingering the soft collar, absently stroking the material. Seeing the small pulse beat at the side of his temple, she got the strangest sensation that she'd been waiting all her life for his answer.

'Looking at you,' he replied. 'Do you mind?'

Sabrina had heard of being stripped naked by a man's eyes, but her husband was way ahead. He was shamelessly making love to her with that slumberous dark gaze of his, heating her blood with a potent mixture of fire and pure masculine chemistry, making her skin prickle with the sensation of being physically touched in the most intimately erotic way. Inside her robe her nipples peaked, the intense, aching throb bordering on pain. Moisture spread between the juncture of her thighs as her knees literally started to shake.

'You should go.' Finding her voice, she silently acknowledged it had no real conviction. How could it when she craved him the way parched land needed rain?

'We never kissed when we exchanged vows.' He took a step nearer until her startled gaze was in direct line with the second white button on his shirt. The exposed V of his skin appeared very bronze and all the more appealing because of it. The heat they were engendering between them turned up the temperature in the room another notch.

'I would very much like to remedy that, Sabrina.'

When his hands settled possessively around her upper arms, his breath drifting feather-light touches across her face, Sabrina focused on his mouth. That perfect, strong impression of everything that was Javier D'Alessandro—courage, honour, strength and enough sizzling personal attraction to melt all the ice in a glacier.

When that same mouth slanted possessively across hers, she leaned into his kiss as if the decision had been totally taken out of her hands and she might as well bow to the inevitable. With a husky sound of hungry need, she willingly opened to the invasion of his tongue, welcoming his hotly intimate exploration as if it was the Christmas gift she'd always dreamed of but never had. Her fingers curled into the hard, iron strength of his shoulders beneath the silkiness of his shirt, even as he hauled her urgently against the granite wall of muscle and sinew that was his chest. Deepening the kiss until he could hear the wild roar of his own blood in his ears, his heart thumping with all the force of a blacksmith's hammer, Javier told himself he had no right to hold her like this, to demand so much when she had already saved his life by marrying him. But when reason was weighted against pure, raging desire, it made a poor persuader. The sweet, fresh pine scent of her shampoo, her warm, giving body still glowing from her shower making seductive little asides into his senses, Javier's hands moved from her arms to slide up her back, pressing her closer still. Every one of her delicious feminine curves melded with the harder lean contours of his own proudly male body and he was heavily, almost painfully aroused.

With great reluctance Sabrina forced herself to come to her senses. Her small, elegant hands sliding down his shirt, she pushed against him, staring up at him with blue eyes that were dark with longing and regret. She shouldn't be doing this. *They* shouldn't be doing this.

Javier let loose a muffled curse in Spanish. *'Madre del Dios!'*

'We can't. This wasn't part of our agreement.' She shot him a nervous smile.

'No.' Stepping away, ostensibly to put temptation out of reach, he reluctantly agreed. Then, changing his mind, he shook his head, hands dropping angrily to his hips. 'Is it wrong that I should desire you? I know we have an agreement but I am a living, breathing man with hot blood running through my veins! Am I supposed not to notice when you smile at me as if you're pleased to see me, or tell me that you're going to take a shower with an invitation in your eyes? I cannot pretend not to want you, Sabrina. It would be denying my own nature.'

'If we are to see this thing through then you have to! Six months down the line, when Angelina's adoption comes through and we sign the divorce papers, I'll be leaving to take up where I left off, Javier, and so will you. We have to be sensible.'

'Sensible?' Frustration crawling through his skin, Javier glared at her. 'You do not know what you ask. Is the business all you think of? You must have ice in your veins, woman!' Without another word, he turned and exited the room, slamming the door behind him.

* * *

'Good morning, Angelina. What have you got lined up at school today? Something nice, I hope.' Sweeping into the kitchen, dressed in a navy-blue linen suit and carrying her briefcase, Sabrina paused at the work-top to pour a cup of coffee from the percolator, then brought it to the table to join the little girl dressed in her grey and green uniform, her black hair in two neat braids. Angelina acknowledged Sabrina's presence with a slight dip of her head. Immediately sensing something amiss, Sabrina slid her hand across the child's.

'What's the matter, darling? Not feeling well this morning?'

She shook her head without saying a word. The silence was followed by two wet streaks tracking slowly down her pretty face. Sabrina's heart squeezed tightly. Without further ado, she cradled Angelina's head against her chest, stroking down the silky, soft hair, murmuring any words of comfort that came to mind. With a shudder, the little girl leaned deeper into Sabrina's jacket, her hand reaching out to clutch hers. The wave of love that surged through her at that trusting little touch made her eyes sting with tears.

'Oh, sweetheart. I know you're hurting but it will get better in time, I promise. You're being so brave, so brave.'

'Angelina, *mi angel*, what is wrong?' Suddenly Javier was there. Handsome and concerned, he dropped to his haunches beside them, rubbing Angelina's hunched back with firm, soothing strokes, his devastatingly dark gaze meeting Sabrina's, frowning at the tears he saw there.

'I think she's having a bad day,' she explained gently. 'I'll stay with her for a while. I don't have to rush.'

'Would you like that, Angelina? Would you like Sabrina to stay with you?'

The child sniffed and nodded.

'*Te amo.* Everything will be all right.' Planting a kiss at the side of her cheek, Javier smiled tenderly.

'There's some coffee in the pot,' Sabrina told him. 'Rosie must be around somewhere if you want breakfast.'

'She is just drying her hair.' Her small fist scrubbing at her eyes, Angelina hiccuped then leant her head back against Sabrina's chest. Noticing the small, trusting gesture with a thump in his chest, Javier got to his feet, gave Sabrina's shoulder a squeeze, then went across the room to pour himself some coffee.

'Have you eaten?' He directed his question to the both of them.

'I had some cornflakes, Uncle. I don't want anything else.'

'As long as you ate something, *mi querida*. We have to take great care of you. What about you, Sabrina? Can I get you some toast or cereal?'

'I don't usually have breakfast in the morning.'

'Why not?'

'I don't usually have the time.' She was drying Angelina's tears with the pad of her thumb, smiling into the sad little face, still holding her.

Again Javier felt his heart turn over. Was it only last night he had accused this woman of having ice in her veins? Because he had been burning up for her he had let his frustration boil over into an insult when she rejected him—an insult that he deeply regretted. Watching her now with his niece, her beautiful, candid blue eyes too bright, he concluded that his new wife was a natural mother. It was just a shame she didn't know it. 'You should make time,' he admonished, wishing his voice wasn't quite so stern because Sabrina threw him a bewildered look that pricked at his conscience badly. He would make it up to her, he promised himself. Later on today he would go out and buy her a gift of some kind—one for Angelina too. It would, he decided, give him the greatest pleasure to spoil them both a little.

When Sabrina still wasn't home at ten-thirty that same evening, Javier paced the living-room for a further five minutes before retracing his steps to the kitchen to stare at the note that Rosie had scribbled earlier and left for him propped up by the sugar basin: 'Sabrina rang. Said she's going out for a drink with a colleague and not to wait dinner.' Angelina was staying the night at a friend's house. Julie's parents had been good friends with Michael and had been pressing him for a while now to let Angelina come and stay. His niece had been happy to go and so Javier had raised no objections. He understood life had to go on and he wasn't about to curtail even the smallest pleasure if it made the child feel good. But where was Sabrina and what was keeping her? Who was this colleague she'd gone out with? Jill, or Robbie? He scowled at the thought of the young man who worked with her. He'd seen the admiring way he looked at Sabrina sometimes and it made Javier naturally a little cool towards him.

Switching on the radio, he flicked through the stations for something that wouldn't bite on his nerves. As the soothing strains of harp strings filled the room, he turned up the volume a little then poured himself a brandy. Remembering a stack of Spanish magazines he'd bought from the newsagents in Harrods, he returned to the living-room to fetch them, bringing them back to the large pine table in the kitchen. Sipping his brandy, he immersed himself in an article about the compelling virtues of the latest Italian sports car, smiling wryly to himself when he thought about the three similar models he had in his garage at home in Buenos Aires. Once upon a time they'd been his pride and joy. Now they did nothing for him. He would have to ring his cousin Enrique and tell him to take them for a spin.

It was ten minutes past midnight when he heard Sabrina's key in the door. Staring at his long empty brandy glass, the strains of a violin concerto playing softly in the background, Javier waited for her to come and find him. To tell the truth, he needed the extra time to compose his anger. What was she thinking, staying out this late? A woman alone? He hoped her colleague, whoever it was, had either seen her home or put her safely into a taxi.

'Hello. I didn't expect you to still be up.' She put her bag on a chair, kicked off her shoes and undid her jacket. Her honey-brown hair was drifting loose from its clip and there were faint shadows beneath her amazing eyes. Drumming his fingers on the table,

Javier fought the sudden wave of desire that engulfed him.

'Did you think I would go to bed knowing you were still out?'

'Please don't take that high-handed, superior male tone with me. I've had a long day and I'm not in the mood.' Even as she gave vent to the need to reassert her position, Sabrina sensed the tension coil in the man seated just a foot away from where she stood. She threw him a brief glance from beneath her golden-brown lashes, and a prickle of heat radiated all the way down her spine at the sight of him. He was so blatantly, unashamedly male, she thought. With his darkly smouldering good looks, he might have been one of those very conquistadores she had fantasised about. His sleek, midnight hair sexily mussed by impatient, perhaps angry fingers, a faint shadow of beard studding his lean, hard jaw, long, tautly muscled legs in black jeans stretched out in front of him, he was a force to be reckoned with.

'*Dios!*' The noise of his chair scraping violently against the smooth tiles of the floor had all Sabrina's nerves jumping in fright. 'I spend the whole evening worrying about you and all you do is give me this— this "attitude" in return!'

'I didn't ask you to worry about me. *That* wasn't part of our agreement either!'

'Who were you with tonight? Was it Robbie?'

Sabrina told herself she must be imagining his jealous, possessive tone. With her heart rioting inside her chest, she levelled her best glare. 'I don't believe you asked me that. It's none of your damn business who

I go out with, quite frankly. And I think you're taking this whole marriage thing a bit too far!'

Javier saw red. All of a sudden he wanted to show her that as far as he was concerned he wasn't taking it far enough. With enough sexual sparks between them to set the whole street alight, he was tired of pretending he didn't want her.

Taken aback by the hungry flare in his gaze, Sabrina stood rooted to the spot as he advanced, not quite believing what was happening when he pulled her roughly into his arms then crushed her mouth savagely beneath his. All her senses drowning and melting in his heat, at first she started to fight him—terrified of what she was feeling. Never in her whole life had she been swept away by such uncontrollable sensations of lust and longing. Within seconds his devastatingly sensual assault on her mouth was coaxing her into melting submission. She was opening to him, taking as much as she was giving, emitting raw little pleas for more as her hands wound round his neck, her fingers biting into his shoulders as he ground his pelvis into hers. His hands cupping her bottom through the silky linen of her skirt, he dragged the material upwards, running his palms up the backs of her thighs, pulling her in even tighter to his hips. Bending his head, he settled his mouth in the smooth, silky juncture between her nape and her shoulder, kissing her deeply until she felt the hot sting of his teeth in her flesh.

'Javier, please!' She was coming undone badly, past the point of no return, her hair tumbling loose onto her shoulders, her blue eyes a sea of stormy passion. A million miles away from the cool, focused businesswoman she had always striven to be. Javier lifted his head, touched his fingers to her moist, plundered mouth, uttered something husky and indecipherable in Spanish then said clearly, 'We should be in bed, *sí*?'

Trembling as though she would never stop, Sabrina knew she was beyond any pretence about the subject. '*Sí*,' she replied softly.

Above her in the semi-darkness, the breadth of Javier's magnificent shoulders thrillingly outlined in the shadows, he moved up her body, his long, hard-muscled limbs tangling with hers, the faint, spellbinding drift of his aftershave mingling with his elemental male heat, the die well and truly cast to ensure her complete and utter surrender. Sabrina arched her back, pulled him down towards her, drove her fingers through the short, silky strands of his ebony hair, hungrily sought his mouth with her lips—hard, urgent—then broke free, her breathing ragged and her heart wild. 'This can only happen once, Javier. After tonight it can't happen again. We have to be sensible. Ohh...' He stole her breath as he ran his hand across her hip, then trailed it deliberately down to the sweet dark cavern of her most intimate place. Pushing her slender, silken thighs apart, he introduced his fingers, those clever, sensitive fingers, sliding them in and out, daring deeper until she grabbed at his shoulders, urging him upwards, desperately seeking his mouth on hers once again.

He made her wait. He made her ride him slowly, then slid up to capture her breast in the seductive heat of his mouth, his tongue teasing and laving her burgeoning nipple, then nipping with his teeth. Sabrina bit back the sharp pleasure-pain, her fingers grabbing for the sheets to hold on as wave after wave of delicious capitulation shuddered through her.

Breathing hard, she stared up at him in wonder, seeking out those strong, mesmerising features of his in the shadows, biting her lip when he withdrew his hand to place his sex at her entrance, then, slowly but firmly, inserted himself deep inside her. Within seconds her ardour rose to meet his. Weaving her fingers through his hair, she opened to his deeply intimate kiss, then lifted her hips to meet the driving insistence of his as he filled her.

'*Mi esposa hermosa,*' he breathed raggedly against her ear and, although Sabrina didn't know what the words meant, her heart thrilled to hear them just the same.

His own heart beating high and wild, Javier took her hard and fast, his need to possess, to spill his seed in the deep, hot centre of her most feminine core completely taking him over so that every feeling, every emotion, every hungry, impossible hope in his soul played a vital part in his final destination. When he sensed the moment arrive, a cry burst from his throat, mingling with the raw, husky sound of his name on Sabrina's lips as her own journey reached its zenith. Then he fell against her, his mouth against her nape, breathing in her scent and her womanliness, feeling more satisfied and more alive than he had felt in months.

Carefully withdrawing from her body, he raised his head, staring down at her in the dimly lit glow, gently smoothing back her hair and tracing the exquisite line of her jaw with his finger, so that he could focus on her eyes. 'You are all right?' he asked, concerned. Perhaps he had been a little rough? Passion had overwhelmed him and her skin was so soft—easily bruised, no doubt…as tender as a baby's. The thought gave him pain.

'I'm more than "all right," Javier. That was wonderful.'

Her words warmed him all the way through. Almost of its own volition his knee started to manoeuvre her thighs apart. In a few more seconds he would be hard and ready for her again. His skin grew hot at the idea. This time he would take things more slowly, find out what gave her pleasure and make them both a little crazy.

'But it doesn't mean it's going to be a regular occurrence.' Her voice shook a little as Javier grazed his lips at the side of her mouth. 'We have Angelina to think about. We can't risk getting so involved. It's best if we keep things as—as professional as possible.'

Her words fell on deaf ears. Already Javier was positioning himself at her centre, pushing inside her with his satin hard length, making her ache for him all over again.

'Javier!' But her plea for understanding quickly turned into a plea for more of what he was presently delivering, and with a breathless little sigh she wound her arms tightly round his neck and raised her head for his kiss…

Stirring her coffee for the umpteenth time, Sabrina sat at the big pine table in the warm kitchen, staring at the lavishly wrapped gift in front of her as though it were a bomb about to detonate. Its shiny gold paper was topped off with a gorgeous white satin ribbon— also threaded with gold—fashioned into a huge bow, and next to the package was a little card with her name on it, simply signed 'Javier.' He'd told her this morning that he was taking Angelina to her usual Saturday-morning dance class and that he would be back to join her for breakfast.

Glancing at the clock, Sabrina saw that it was a little after nine. She would have to make sure she was showered and dressed before he returned because it surely wasn't a good idea to be sitting around in her dressing gown, considering the highly explosive situation that had now manifested between them. All night they had barely been able to keep their hands off one another. Sabrina had never known a more voracious or experienced lover. Everything they said about hot Latin lovers was true—even if it was a cliché. The man had magic oozing from his fingertips, not to mention more intimate places, and Sabrina's tender skin this morning was more than proof of that. Pulling aside her gown, she bit her lip at the sight of the small pink abrasions on the insides of her thighs. It made her tingle all over to remember where that particular little trail of his mouth had led.

Blowing out a guilty breath, she fanned herself then took a deep gulp of strong black coffee. What had possessed her to be so wild and free with her favours? What on earth had she been thinking of? The fact was, she hadn't been thinking at all. If she'd applied thinking to the situation she wouldn't be in the quandary she was in now. They might have enjoyed being intimate together but Javier wasn't looking to make this marriage real and Sabrina wasn't in the market for a man in her life—at least, not permanently. What needed to take precedence right now was what was happening to her business—the business she'd shed blood, sweat and tears over for the past fifteen years. She wasn't about to throw it all away just because she'd suddenly become enamoured with a man—a very generous, good-looking and sexy man.

'Oh, for goodness' sake, open it. It's not going to bite you!' With an exasperated sigh, Sabrina begin to tear at the wrapping paper, pulling it off in large swathes, her heart racing a little when she saw the smooth silver box inside. Lifting the lid, she stared down at the oyster-coloured satin in disbelief. *He'd bought her lingerie?* Running her fingertips across the sensuous material, she lifted out the exquisitely designed chemise with matching briefs and felt her cheeks burn red. No man had ever bought her anything so beautiful—or so intimate. For some inexplicable reason, tears sprang to her eyes. Then, impatiently dashing them away, Sabrina laid the silky items back against the soft tissue paper in their pretty box, put the lid back on, gathered up the torn gold wrapping paper, and carried the whole lot back into her room.

Minutes later, as piping hot water slooshed down her body from the shower, Sabrina knew that Javier D'Alessandro had got into her blood in a big, big way. It wouldn't be easy to walk away from that realisation when this 'marriage of convenience' of theirs finally came to an end—no matter how strong her resolve. But somehow she was going to have to find the strength and courage to achieve the impossible.

CHAPTER SEVEN

JAVIER was holding the baby and Tallulah was gazing back at him with adoring blue eyes. Beside her, Ellie elbowed Sabrina in the ribs.

'Ouch!'

'That man is dangerous with a capital "D",' said Ellie, dropping her voice low so that only her sister could hear, and grinned.

'Meaning?'

'Well, look at him. He's the answer to a woman's prayer, isn't he? Not only is he tall, dark and amazingly, knee-tremblingly handsome, but he's good with babies and children as well! No wonder you married him!'

Unfolding her arms from across her chest, Sabrina wished that the tight, breathless pain beneath her rib-cage would go. Since she'd slept with Javier, every time she happened to glance at him for any reason at all, she felt it—not to mention the fluttery feeling in her stomach that seemed to accompany it. 'My reasons for marrying him aren't what you seem to think they are, I told you!' Exasperated, Sabrina walked to the living-room door. As her blue gaze swept the room, she paused to smile at Angelina, sitting cross-legged on the floor, helping William and Henry to dress a couple of worse-for-wear soldier figures. Her pretty face was a study in concentration and patience as the two little boys sat beside her, clearly enthralled

99

by her willingness to play with them. In front of the fireplace, Javier was jiggling Tallulah up and down, making her laugh. 'I think I'll go and help Rosie in the kitchen,' she said lightly, catching his eye.

'Rosie is fine. Stay here and talk to our guests with me. Come.' He gestured for her to join him, his dark eyes teasing, almost mocking...*as if he could read her mind*. Inside her chest, her heart jumped at the thought. She was thinking about him, of course—of all the different delicious ways he had made love to her—and wondering when it might happen again. That caught her up short. It wasn't going to happen again. *It couldn't.*

'I can talk to Ellie any time,' she remarked breezily.

Ellie took immediate affront, tossing back her mane of blonde hair with a little huff. 'Thanks. I love you too. See what I have to put up with, Javier?' She lingered over his name as though it were some delicious sweetmeat. Sabrina could hardly believe what she was hearing. Was this the same woman who had torn her off a strip for being so ridiculous in agreeing to marry a man she barely knew? Even little Tallulah was mesmerised by him.

Sighing irritably, Sabrina reluctantly moved to stand next to her husband, her irritation briefly diverted by Tallulah's outrageously gummy grin. Automatically she held out her arms. 'Have you got a new admirer, Tally? Have you, darling?'

As Javier laughed and passed the baby carefully over to his wife, he whispered into Sabrina's ear, 'So has her auntie... Did you know that, sweet Sabrina?'

'Don't talk to me like that!'

'Why not?' His answering chuckle sent goose-bumps scudding crazily all over her skin.

'So tell me, if you please, Ellie—is there anything about your job in the City that you miss?'

Relieved that he had diverted his attention to her sister, Sabrina buried her face in Tallulah's silky, soft blonde hair and breathed in her compelling baby scent like an injection of pure, sweet oxygen.

'Good lord, no!' Laughing, Ellie raised her small glass of sherry and took a sip. 'I know things can be mayhem at home when you've got little ones to look after and I know things don't always run to plan because you've got to allow for so much that's unexpected—but even so, I wouldn't change places for the world. I love being a mum. Phil loves me being a mum too, and quite frankly I wouldn't want some child-minder taking care of my kids just so that I could climb some dreary career ladder in the City! Been there, done that and it's not all it's cracked up to be, believe me.'

In her heart Sabrina knew her sister wasn't having a secret dig at her own choice to run a business, but even so her passionate renunciation of a career as opposed to having children made Sabrina feel slightly inadequate. Something her parents had a knack of making her feel too, if the truth was known. They absolutely doted on their three grandchildren and barely asked Sabrina anything about her day-to-day life apart from the stock, 'How is the business going?' and, 'Isn't it about time you found yourself a nice man and settled down?'

'You are clearly a natural mother.' Javier smiled approvingly and Sabrina was amazed to see the soft pink flush that highlighted her sister's beautiful cheekbones. Did every female between six months and one hundred years old fall under this man's spell? Clearly they did if the evidence she'd seen so far was anything to go on!

'Not *all* women are cut out to be mothers,' she commented defensively.

Immediately Javier's disturbing gaze settled thoughtfully on her face. 'How do you know if you never give yourself the chance to find out?'

'Sabrina thinks she's too old to have children.' Finishing her sherry, Ellie left the glass on a nearby bookshelf. 'Don't you, sis?'

'My mother was forty-two years old when she had me. It didn't prevent her from being a wonderful mother.' Javier was looking straight at Sabrina when he spoke and, riveted, she knew he was thinking about the time they'd spent together in bed making love. Was he wondering if he had perhaps made her pregnant? He hadn't used any protection and he hadn't even thought to ask if she was on the Pill. Which she wasn't—*Oh, God, how could she have been so stupid?*

'I'm not saying it's not possible to become pregnant in your late thirties or even early forties, I'm just saying that I don't think Sabrina sees herself in a maternal role. Do you, sis? She's much more interested in making a success of her business.'

'Why does that sound like a criticism?'

'I think you're being a little over-sensitive, Sabrina.'

'Do you? Well, then, you must be right. You usually are, aren't you?' Plonking a surprised baby

Tallulah into Javier's arms, she swept out of the room, hardly pausing for breath until she reached her bedroom and quietly shut the door behind her.

Her hands shaking, a little shudder of emotion sweeping down her spine, she moved across to the bed and dropped down onto the pale cream counterpane, shocked to find herself inexplicably in tears.

'Pull yourself together, for God's sake!' she scolded herself, then burst into a fresh bout of noisy weeping.

She didn't hear the person who quietly entered the room. It was only when she felt the soft pressure of that little hand on her back that Sabrina glanced up into a pair of sweet brown eyes full of concern.

'Are you all right, Sabrina? Uncle said I should come and find you.'

'I'm fine, Angelina, darling. I'm just being very silly.' Digging into her jeans pocket for a handkerchief, she loudly blew her nose, then smiled brightly at the little girl.

'I don't think you're being silly at all. You're crying. You must be upset about something. What is it, Sabrina?'

'Sweetheart, it's nothing. We've all just had to adapt to a lot of change lately. Sometimes even adults can feel overwhelmed.'

'I was worried when I heard you crying outside the door. Yesterday Uncle Javier was crying too.'

'He was?' Sabrina blinked in shock, her breath suspended. The thought of the strong, capable, sophisticated man who was now her husband reduced to real human tears was like being unexpectedly hit by one of those punch-bags in a gym.

'At first he pretended he wasn't, then he told me he was sad because my daddy had died and he missed him. They were good friends, you know. I told him it was OK to cry and miss my daddy because I do too. I miss him a lot.'

'Oh, sweetheart.' Her heart full, Sabrina pulled the child into her arms and kissed the top of her head. 'I am so sorry you're hurting so badly. It will get better, I promise. You won't forget but you'll be able to deal with it without feeling as if your whole world has come to an end.'

Seemingly satisfied with her reassurance, Angelina straightened and ventured a smile. 'I am glad you're here with me and my uncle. Perhaps you could make him feel better too?'

Out of the mouths of babes. Sabrina's stomach clenched tight. 'I'll try.' What she couldn't explain to the charming eleven-year-old was that her relationship with her gorgeous uncle was testing every single faculty she possessed to the limit—particularly the most threatening one of all: her heart. She hardly knew how to make herself feel better, let alone Javier. Now she had gone and slept with him she'd put herself under totally unnecessary duress in an already highly charged situation. Somehow she had to get it together and regroup, re-establish some of those ground rules Javier was so unenthusiastic about. It wasn't going to be easy, given her current vulnerability, but she would give it everything she had to restore her life to some semblance of normality.

'Rosie is laying the table for tea. I said I would go and help her. Will you come with me?'

Angelina was holding out her hand and suddenly

Sabrina felt mortally ashamed of being so obsessed with her own concerns when the sweet child in front of her was being so astoundingly brave, considering all that had happened to her. Checking beneath her eyes for tell-tale signs of wetness, Sabrina pushed herself to her feet, took Angelina's hand in hers then left the room to go and give Rosie a hand in the kitchen. As soon as Ellie and the children went home and Angelina was otherwise occupied, she resolved to speak to Javier in private and tell him the conclusion she'd reached. Even if he didn't like what she had to say, he would have to hear her out.

'I need to talk to you.'

Standing in the doorway to Michael's office, Sabrina stared at the back of Javier's dark head, at the breadth of those fine, strong shoulders, at the lean, tanned forearms exposed by the rolled-up sleeves of his perfectly white shirt as his fingers used the mouse to scroll up the screen in front of him.

Stretching his arms up high above his head, he swivelled in the chair and almost reduced her to a pile of smouldering embers on the carpet with the long, slow, lascivious look he had in his eyes.

She was only wearing jeans and an old blue and white shirt that she generally wore to do housework in, but she might as well have been standing there in the skimpiest of bikinis as far as the man in front of her was concerned.

'What is it?'

It was a simple enough question, though, annoyingly, the answer wasn't. With her heart knocking against her ribs, Sabrina took a deep breath and snaked her arms round her waist.

'I just wanted to sa—'

'Your sister was nice. I liked her.'

'Most men usually do.' She was thrown by the abrupt change of subject, and her response was out before she could check it. She flushed in embarrassment, knowing she sounded petty and jealous.

'I did not mean her looks—though of course she is pretty.' As he leaned back in his chair, his long legs stuck out in front of him just inches from where she stood, Javier's expression was thoughtful. 'I found her warm, approachable…capable. She is clearly a good mother.'

'Yes, she is.' Unfolding her arms, Sabrina impatiently pushed away a strand of hair that had drifted loose from her ponytail. 'She can do no wrong in my parents' eyes either.'

'That hurts you?'

Now, why did she have to go and tell him that? Nothing seemed to be going to plan today, absolutely nothing. She was like some damned sailing boat, rudderless and cast adrift on an unknown sea.

'I've got used to it. They never thought they'd have another child after me. Ellie is eight years my junior. When she came along I guess they were so happy at their unexpected gift that they simply doted on her. She was probably a much nicer child than me anyway. My mum always says I was too sulky and miserable.'

He laughed softly and all the hairs stood up on the back of her nape. 'You? Sulky? I cannot believe it.'

'Javier, I didn't come to make small talk. There is

a serious purpose to my wanting to talk to you.' She wouldn't let him distract her, she decided irritably. No matter how beguiling his smile or how wicked the look in those incredible black eyes.

'I am listening.' The light went out of his expression. He straightened in his chair and ran his hand through his hair.

'About…about what happened the other night.'

'In bed. *Sí*.'

Oh, boy. This was even harder than she'd suspected it might be. 'I was totally reckless, not thinking straight. I got—I got swept away.' Her blue eyes were so large and shimmering that Javier imagined he could dive right into them. Catching the drift of her scent on the air, he felt the muscles in his rock-hard stomach clench painfully. Ellie McDonald was pretty—but her sister, Sabrina, was beautiful.

'It happens. Passion has a life of its own.'

'You make it sound so simple.'

'It is. Perhaps we are not so repressed in my country in the way that the English are? You seem to want to apologise for everything…even desire.'

His comment completely unravelled her carefully worked-out bid for understanding. Trying to regroup, she shifted to her opposite hip, then folded her arms again across her shirt.

'Whatever. The point I'm trying to make is that it was a mistake. What we have here is a perfectly reasonable—though perhaps not commonplace—business arrangement. If we are both to come out of it intact we need to redefine our ground rules.'

'If we were in a boardroom right now I would be most impressed.' Getting restlessly to his feet, he pushed the black swivel chair right up to the desk then turned to face her. 'You do not have to try so hard to be the perfect businesswoman, Sabrina. Neither do you have to hide who you really are from me.'

'Hide?' Frowning, Sabrina desperately tried to keep her mind on track but it wasn't easy when she had six feet two inches of hard-muscled, devastatingly good-looking male staring back at her as if he wanted nothing better than to redefine ground rules of a completely different kind. The kind that had her pulse-rate rocketing off whatever scale it was measured on. 'I'm not trying to hide anything from you. All I'm trying to do is tell you that what happened between us was a mistake and shouldn't happen again. Please don't pretend you don't understand. I like you, Javier, and that's all to the good, considering our arrangement, but that's as far as it should go. I wanted to tell you that you should carry on as normal—go out with other women if you want to; I have no objection.'

'And that should make me glad?' His expression was forbidding. A muscle jumped in the side of his lean, bronzed cheek and Sabrina dropped her arms and twisted her hands together instead to still their sudden trembling.

'I'm not interested in whether it makes you glad or not!' *He was crying, Angelina had said. Missing Michael.* Probably feeling overwhelmed as well that, as a thirty-year-old successful single entrepreneur with no commitments but to himself, he now had to take on the awesome responsibilities of a child and live a completely different kind of life from the one he'd been used to living. One that no doubt included fast cars, pretty girls and the high-living pursuits of the rich and glamorous. 'All I know is that we need to get on with our own lives. I'm totally happy to help with Angelina, to be her friend if she wants me to—but, other than that, I can't get personally involved with you, Javier. I just can't.'

'*Sí.*'

'Is that all you're going to say?' She was stunned when he swept past her, the air all but crackling with the anger that was rolling off those broad shoulders of his.

Following him out into the kitchen, she watched him fill the kettle and set it to boil.

'All right. Because you have done me this service I will accept your so-called "ground rules". I will pretend that we did not join together as man and woman and I will keep my association with you strictly impersonal. Is that what you wanted to hear, Sabrina?'

Trailing her hand over the cold marble counter-top, she briefly nodded. 'Yes, it would be easier.'

'Easier for who—you? Because you are afraid of life, of really living. Because you feel safer hiding behind a social mask even in your private life. Yes...I can see how that would be easier for you.'

His stark words lashed at her soul like a whip and she actually felt herself flinch. How could he know so much about her when he had only known her for the shortest time?

'I'm not afraid of life; of living. I'm only thinking of the best thing to do for everyone concerned.'

His rage was tangible. 'Do not presume to speak

for me as if you know what is best for me. You clearly do not!'

'I'm sorry to make you so angry. How can we resolve anything if we can't even talk to each other without getting in an argument?'

'You think this is an argument?' His laugh was short and harsh. 'Clearly our cultures are very different.'

Her voice trembled. 'I'm beginning to see that.'

Dropping his shoulders, he seemed to take pity on her. 'Don't worry, Sabrina, I will not make any more "inconvenient" demands on you. We will conduct this marriage like a business merger and that is all. Does that make you happier?'

'Yes.' *Liar!* her heart protested. 'Thank you.'

'As far as I can see, you have nothing to thank me for. *Nada!*' His black eyes blazing, he swept out of the kitchen without giving her so much as a backward glance.

'Well,' Sucking in a deeply shaky breath, Sabrina fought hard to keep her composure. 'That went well…'

Making coffee in the end room, Sabrina heard Javier get up, open the door and tell Jill that he was going out to get some lunch. When the door clanged shut behind him she closed the lid on the milk carton, opened the fridge and popped it inside without releasing her breath. When she did, it whooshed out of her as if she'd been holding it under water and had only just surfaced in time. Since their little 'talk' personal relations between them had been strained to say the least, but here in the office Sabrina could find no fault in Javier's conduct. He was the consummate young professional, guiding Jill, Robbie and herself almost effortlessly round the new programme he had installed with ease, making the difficult seem simple, answering their questions with a display of understanding that belied his mere thirty years on the planet. They quickly learned that he was a natural leader as well as a natural innovator and they were all enthused by his suggestions for making the company more competitive in the marketplace while retaining the long-honed skills they had acquired themselves on the way.

But still Sabrina felt unaccountably hurt by the fact that he'd gone to lunch alone. When he rang half an hour later to inform Jill that he'd bumped into a friend and would be away longer than he'd thought, Sabrina's mind jumped into overdrive.

Who was this 'friend'? Was it someone Michael had known or was it perhaps one of the parents from Angelina's school? Until he returned an hour and a half later she couldn't concentrate on a damn thing and when he did return and looked at her with a cool, almost dismissive glance across the top of the computer monitor, her insides turned to ice. Determined to devote her complete attention to the young woman planning a backpacking holiday in India who was seated in front of her with her boyfriend, she conjured up her best, most professional smile and pretended it didn't matter that Javier D'Alessandro clearly no longer regarded her as a friend.

On her way home later that evening, Javier having left before her, Sabrina found herself heading towards one of the big chain shops that specialised in modern, trendy clothing for youngsters. Estimating Angelina's size, she picked out a couple of nice sweatshirts with the shop logo on and a pair of jeans and hoped the child would like them. Her purchases packed, she then headed towards a favourite bookstore that housed a welcoming coffee-shop and, after browsing for a good hour, finally settled at a chrome table to drink a café latte and flick through the books she'd bought. While she'd been active it had not been so difficult to push thoughts of Javier from her mind, but, once seated, her shopping bags at her feet and her books piled beside her on the table, she felt strangely hollow at the thought that he was giving her the cold shoulder—at home at least.

Sipping her latte, she wondered if she hadn't made things even more difficult for herself by insisting they keep their relationship strictly professional. And why was he so angry with her anyway? The man could surely have any woman he desired in a heartbeat. Why he should want a work-oriented thirty-seven-year-old who hadn't had a decent relationship in longer than she cared to remember, she couldn't begin to fathom. Was it just because she happened to be sharing the same living space as him? After all, wasn't it a given that some men found it easy to have sex without getting their emotions involved? The sooner the adoption went through the better, as far as Sabrina was concerned. Her heart ached at the thought of leaving the child, whom she'd really grown to care for, but ultimately she knew it was best in the long run. One day Javier would meet someone more suited to his age and status, and in all likelihood

add to his little family. Once she'd paid him back the
money he'd given her for the business—and she did
intend to pay it back, every penny—then Sabrina
would be nothing but a dim, distant memory.

Glancing down at the time on her slender gold
watch, she knew she couldn't put off going home any
longer and braced herself for another difficult evening
with the man she had so recently married.

CHAPTER EIGHT

CRADLING his glass of wine between his hands, Javier gazed thoughtfully at the beautiful woman sitting opposite him, her long legs drawn up on the sofa beneath her, her softly tousled black hair drifting across her elegant shoulders in her tight strapless dress, and wished she were miles away in Buenos Aires instead of here.

'I cannot advise you about whether or not you should marry Carlo, Christina. Only you can judge that. If you are asking me whether I think the marriage will last then that is another thing entirely. He is already paying alimony to two previous wives who have six of his children between them, no?'

The sultry woman pouted and picked off an imaginary piece of lint from her leopard-print dress. 'People can change, Javier. You must know that. Look what you have had to do. You have had to leave your luxurious apartment in Buenos Aires and all your friends and come and take up residence in this cold, rainy country and be a father to Angelina as well! Plus you have had to marry some plain, frigid Englishwoman so that you can stay here! I do not know how you can bear it all, *querido*—I really don't!'

'Plain' and 'frigid' were not words that a man could ever use to describe Sabrina, Javier thought, his blood quickening—even if she had withdrawn every bit of her previous warmth towards him in order to maintain the supposedly required distance between them. As Christina was talking he kept glancing at the clock on the mantel, wondering where she had gone after work and what was keeping her. Angelina had been looking forward to her coming home this evening but now the child was tucked up in bed, fast asleep, clearly unconvinced by her uncle's explanation that Sabrina would be home soon, he was sure. She had probably just decided to work late, he'd told his niece. Now he was all knotted up inside, wondering where she was or—more importantly—who she was with. OK, so he wasn't looking to make this marriage of theirs a permanent fixture and God knew he was not in love or anything like that—but he did have certain feelings for this woman who had answered his prayer in his hour of need. And it was his duty as her husband, real or not, to make sure that she was safe.

'*Querido?*'

Snapping out of his reverie, Javier took a sip of his now slightly warm white wine then with a grimace put it aside on the small occasional table beside him. 'I'm sorry, Christina. I have a lot on my mind at the moment. Forgive me.'

'I was so sorry to hear about poor Michael. I only met him a few times but I always thought he was a nice man. It must have been a blow, *sí*?'

It took an almighty effort to force away the heavy black cloak that he sensed settling around his shoulders. Michael's death had been a terrible blow—Christina had guessed right—and Javier missed the fact that he could no longer talk things over with his brother-in-law the way he used to. Instead, whenever his thoughts turned to Michael or Dorothea, there was such an ache inside him that it almost left him breathless. That was why he had vowed never to get too close to anyone he cared about again. Angelina, of course, being the exception.

'I am living in his house.' He shrugged, dark eyes absorbing the family photographs on the mantelpiece, the baby grand piano by the window that Michael had loved to play whenever he got the chance, the bookcases stacked with biographies and medical books— Michael's favourite reading. 'All around me are reminders of him and Dorothea. They were happy here. Now they are both gone. It is hard to be here, I will not deny it, but I have to be strong for Angelina. When the adoption papers come through I will be her father and we will both have a new life.'

'And this woman…your temporary "wife"—she will go?' Christina held her breath. She knew she wanted to be with her darling Carlo but she wouldn't be a woman if she didn't still have a certain attraction to the beautiful man who had wined and dined her in some of the most exciting capital cities in the world. And, looking at him now, his brow creased and his eyes full of sorrow, she had no doubt he was in need of some comfort. The kind of comfort only a woman could supply. Uncurling her long, slim legs from beneath her, Christina padded across the luxurious carpet in her stockinged feet and settled herself next to Javier on the arm of his chair.

'*Sí*,' he said, glancing up at her glossy crimson mouth, 'she will go.'

'*Querido.*' Sliding her long, elegant fingers beneath his jaw, Christina bent her head and kissed his cheek.

When she attempted to bestow a second kiss—this time on his lips—she felt him stiffen and pull away. Shock radiated through her like a slap.

'I have missed you, Javier,' she told him, her voice deliberately low. 'Have you not missed me too? Just a little bit?'

He remembered walking into his apartment, hearing laughter from the bedroom, pulling the door wide and seeing Christina naked against the pillows while the ageing, paunchy figure of his neighbour, Carlo Andretti, lay beside her, smoking a cigarette. The memory made him sick to his stomach. He pushed to his feet to pace the room, glancing again at the clock, feeling impatient and angry because Sabrina hadn't come home yet.

'You are welcome to stay the night, Christina. There is a guest room already made up. But tomorrow you must go back to your hotel. Apart from taking Angelina to school, I have many things to attend to so I will not be able to keep you company.' Not least of all, telling Sabrina and her staff that they would have to close the shop for at least three or four weeks while the extensive refurbishment was carried out. He knew Sabrina was hoping to avoid such a decision but plainly she could not carry on working with workmen replacing windows and ripping up floorboards all around her. The refurbishment was part of the modernisation programme to give the agency a whole new, much more professional look—a look that would hopefully bring in a lot more customers to boost business. If he hadn't stepped in when he had, Javier had no doubt East-West Travel would be trad-

ing on goodwill alone and soon even that would
dwindle to nothing.

'All right. I understand. You are still mad at me
for finding me with Carlo, *no*? But you were always
working, Javier. Working or travelling. A woman gets
lonely for a man when that happens.' Moving across
the room, her small, slim body in the tight fake leop-
ard-skin dress an eye-catching contrast against the
pale, muted colours of the room, she bent deliberately
slowly to pick up her high-heeled strappy sandals,
then, smiling seductively, moved up close to Javier.
'Show me the way to your guest room, then. I am too
tired to wait for a taxi to take me back to the hotel.'

Relieved that she was retiring for the night at least,
even if she wasn't taking his preferred option of returning to her hotel, Javier gladly took her down the
thickly carpeted corridor and up a short flight of stairs
to the guest room.

Careful not to wake anybody, Sabrina tiptoed down
the darkened corridor to the kitchen and, flipping on
the light, laid her parcels carefully on the table.
Stripping off her damp raincoat and pulling the tortoiseshell clip from her hair, she also kicked off her
shoes then crossed the tiled floor to put the kettle on
to boil. After her shopping trip was over she hadn't
felt brave enough to return home to Javier and
Angelina so instead she'd driven to her flat, opened
some windows to let in fresh air, watered her plants
and collected a few more belongings to bring back
with her. When she'd done all that, she'd sat back in
her armchair to rest for five minutes before starting
for home and had promptly fallen asleep. When she'd
woken an hour later, the wind was blowing an al-

mighty draught through the opened windows and the room was freezing. Rousing herself, she'd closed them tight, given the flat one final check to make sure everything was in order, gathered her belongings and got back into her car.

Concentrating on pouring hot water from the kettle onto some coffee grounds in a cheerful pink mug, she almost scalded herself at the sound of Javier's deep, rich voice at the door.

'I will get a towel for your hair. You are wet.' Disappearing momentarily, he returned to the kitchen just as Sabrina was taking a careful sip of her steaming coffee, her pulse accelerating at the sight of him dressed in dark jeans and a black polo-neck.

He handed her the large sky-blue towel and she put down her drink. 'Thanks.' Shivering slightly, either from her damp hair or the sheer tension of sharing the same air space as her husband, Sabrina briskly rubbed her hair, knowing she should really head for a hot shower and dry it properly, but too tired to even contemplate it.

'You went shopping?' He jerked his head towards the various carrier bags and parcels on the table, relieved to know where she'd been but still anxious to know why she had returned home so late.

'It's not something I indulge in very often,' she replied a little defensively, hoping he didn't think she'd been spending some of the money he'd given her for the business. 'Now and again a little retail therapy doesn't hurt.'

His dark gaze lingering on the unconsciously sensual way the silk of her blouse stretched taut over her breasts as she stretched upwards to dry her hair, Javier manfully absorbed the hot sexual jolt that shot through his body and told himself not to forget that Sabrina's new ground rules were now apparently in operation.

'Implying that there is an emotional need not being met, *sí*?'

There was something terribly erotic about the way he pronounced the innocent Spanish word. Folding the towel over the back of a chair, she ran her fingers self-consciously through the tumbled weight of her honey-brown hair, her eyes curiously bright. 'Still playing amateur psychologist, Javier?'

His laugh was low and husky. 'Is that what you think I'm trying to do, Sabrina, figure you out?'

Turning back to the mug of coffee she'd left on the counter-top, she glanced vaguely back across her shoulder. 'Do you want a drink? The kettle's just boiled.'

He hated the knowledge that she was suddenly uneasy with him and wished he knew how to put things right, to make her realise he wasn't going to pounce on her as soon as she let her guard down. A yawn catching him unawares, he stretched his arms high and shook his head. 'No, thank you. I think I will go to bed now that you are home. We have a busy day ahead tomorrow.'

'Thank you for waiting up, but you didn't have to.' Her hands tightened round the pretty pink mug and she wished her spine didn't feel quite so tight every time she looked at him.

'It is my pleasure.' With an enigmatic look at her startled gaze, he smiled. 'Goodnight, Sabrina. Sleep well.'

* * *

Angelina tipped out the smart bag with the new clothes Sabrina had bought her, rifled through them, then excitedly held up a bright red sweatshirt to her chest. 'Thank you, Sabrina. They are lovely. I'll try the jeans on tonight when I come home from school.' With a shy grin, she moved round the table to give Sabrina a slight peck on the cheek.

Flushing with pleasure, Sabrina was almost unbearably moved by the little girl's spontaneous delight. Her gift was such a small thing and she hadn't expected such a warm reaction. Tucking her unbound hair behind her ear, she parted her lips in a relieved smile. Drinking her tea in her dressing gown, she reached out to squeeze Angelina's hand. 'I guessed your size but if they don't fit I can take them back and change them. Maybe you'd like to come with me and choose something yourself?'

'All right, then, but I'm sure they will fit. They look fine.'

'And I'm sorry I wasn't home last night in time to say goodnight.' Sabrina's brow creased guiltily as she silently wished she hadn't let her uneasiness with Javier prevent her from seeing the child.

'That's OK. As long as you came home and you were all right.' With a shy glance back she returned the clothes to the white bag with the famous black logo on it and, at a shout from Rosie to come and brush her teeth, left Sabrina in the kitchen to contemplate the day ahead alone. It touched her more than she could say that Angelina expressed pleasure in her coming home. When the time finally came for her to leave the little girl and her disturbing uncle, Sabrina knew it was going to be one of the hardest things she'd ever done, but surely Javier wouldn't mind if she kept in touch—to see Angelina at least?

She was contemplating all of this and more when Javier entered the room. Already washed, shaved and dressed in an immaculate black suit, the tang of his aftershave wafting seductively round the kitchen, he was the epitome of a rich, successful young entrepreneur, and Sabrina self-consciously pulled the neckline of her terry robe closer together, feeling a peculiar vulnerability around him that she wished would go away.

'Good morning. Can I get you something to drink—tea? Coffee?' Starting to rise from the table, she was waved back down again with an engaging smile that made her suck in a deep breath to steady herself.

'I am fine, thank you. As soon as you are ready we will get going. There is a lot to do today and I am anxious to make a start.'

Javier liked the sight of her clothed in the long white terry robe, her beautiful golden-brown hair rippling softly down her back and her face scrubbed clean of make-up. Right now she was a million miles away from her image as a smart, efficient business-woman, which he sensed she was most comfortable with. By the wide, slightly unsure expression in her beautiful blue eyes, he knew she could not have been more ill-at-ease in being discovered in such a way.

'I'll go and get myself sorted out, then.' Just as Sabrina got to her feet, a woman she'd never seen before in her life swept into the kitchen behind Javier, spun round and demanded he help her do up the zip-

per on her very inappropriate strapless dress. As
Sabrina stared, open-mouthed, Javier obliged without
a word—his movements calm and unhurried as if it
was the most normal request in the world. Her fingers
digging into the table-top, Sabrina's knees started to
shake. It was true she had told him he should get on
with his own life, even see other women if he wanted
to, but, God help her, she hadn't thought he would
actually act on it. The woman in the tight dress was
raven-haired and beautiful, exquisitely made up with
slightly almond-shaped black eyes that gave her an
undeniably exotic look. In her comfortable terry robe,
her face unwashed and her hair not yet brushed,
Sabrina couldn't help feeling like some scruffy bag
lady who'd accidentally wandered in on the perfect
couple from a glossy magazine. Had Javier slept with
this woman last night? Had she been waiting in his
bed when he'd bid Sabrina goodnight?

'Sabrina, this is a friend from home. She's working
in London for a few days and dropped in to see us.
Christina, meet my wife—Sabrina.'

The black-eyed beauty's luscious red lips parted in
a purely fake smile. 'So you are the helpful
Englishwoman who came to my darling Javier's aid?
I am very pleased to meet you…Sabrina.'

Sabrina's head started to throb and suddenly she
wanted to get out of the bright, warm kitchen, where
previously she'd been relaxed, and escape to her
room. 'If you'll excuse me, I have to get ready for
work.'

She was out the door before Javier could waylay
her and, hearing him call her name, Sabrina just
headed straight for her room, barely taking a breath.

Her lungs hurt by the time she pulled open the door and slammed it behind her, and she fell back against the wooden panelling with her heart pounding and an acute pain slashing through her ribs. *Jealousy.* She was jealous, angry and betrayed. How could he sleep with another woman under the same roof as her when the one thing she'd been so sure of was that he was one of the most honourable men she'd ever met?

'Sabrina! Let me in…please!'

He was banging on the door, rattling the brass door handle. Swallowing down the pain in her throat, she took a deep gulp of air before replying, 'Go away, Javier. Just let me get ready for work. Please!'

'It is not how it looks, Sabrina. Christina is an old friend. Nothing happened between us last night, nothing. She came to visit and it got late. She was too tired to go back to the hotel so I let her stay here.'

'Old friend, huh? How old? Twenty-four, twenty-five?' She couldn't believe how pathetic she sounded. *Get a grip, Sabrina, for goodness' sake!*

'Are you going to let me in?'

'No! I'll see you at the office. Don't wait for me; I'll make my own way there.'

'*Dios!*' With a final thump on the door, she heard him stride back down the hall.

She'd frozen him out all morning and as soon as Jill and Robbie had gone to lunch and the shop was empty of customers, Javier followed Sabrina into the little back room, leaning against the doorjamb as he watched her make coffee and arrange some sandwiches on a plate.

'You will have to stop being mad at me very soon.

It is not fair on Jill and Robbie to have to work in such an atmosphere.'

Pouring milk into her drink, Sabrina stirred it vigorously with the little silver-plated spoon. 'I am not mad at you,' she said evenly. 'It's entirely up to you who you sleep with. I just expected you to have a little more class than to do it while I was sleeping under the same roof.'

Javier bit back some curse words in Spanish that sprang to his lips. 'And I thought you had more class than to take out your anger on the people who work for you. I thought you took pride in your professionalism?'

That cut her to the quick, even more so because it was true. That didn't, however, prevent Sabrina from venting her spleen on the man who dominated the doorway. His handsome face deceptively calm, she could none the less see the spit of fire in those devastatingly dark eyes and she resented it. Resented it mightily when she was the one who had so clearly been wronged.

'How dare you?' Before she knew she even intended it, she'd walked right up to him and poked her finger in his chest. 'How dare you talk to me about professionalism when you come home and act like some two-penny Lothario? *I* was the one who was trying to behave with some kind of dignity by striving to keep our relationship purely on a business level only! Then because I tell you I'm not going to make a habit of sleeping with you, you have to go and pay me back by bringing another woman into the house!'

'Madre del Dios!' Fury slamming into his gut, Javier stared down into her accusing blue eyes as

emotion finally got the better of him. He'd done everything in his power as far as he could see to make her see sense, to explain about Christina, why she was in the house, that she was only in London for a few days, that she was flying back to Argentina to be with her lover, Carlo. But none of it had apparently convinced his wife that he would never stoop to such a low act as to sleep with another woman just because Sabrina had withdrawn her favours. And why was she getting so angry anyway when it had been her own suggestion that they keep their relationship strictly professional? *Unless she was jealous.* The thought sideswiped him, made his heart beat a little faster and sent heat heading right where he didn't want it to go.

'Do you want me, Sabrina?' His voice dropped to a much lower, huskier cadence. He saw the shock in her eyes, the perfect blue dilate to almost black. He caught her hand mid-air, on its way to slap his face, no doubt. 'Is that what all this is about?'

'Of all the arrogant, conceited, chauvinistic—' He cut off her stream of words with a hard, savage kiss that had her falling against him to keep her balance. With his hands in her hair he held her fast, his mouth devouring hers, showing no mercy, only satisfied when with a desperate little groan she melted into him, her arms slipping almost helplessly round his neck, her skin hot and her breasts pressed tight into his chest.

He wanted her so badly he couldn't get enough of her. She had him burning up with lust, this woman who presented such a cool façade when inside she was pure fire. *Dios!* Did she really believe he could have another woman in his bed after tasting her?

Dragging his mouth away, he set her aside, with frustration tensing every finely honed muscle in his body, his face set into determined, angry lines.

'I am going out for some fresh air. When I return I expect you to treat me with the civility that—as your husband—I am due. No more of this "freezing me out". Is that understood?'

Her mouth still throbbing with the passion of his kisses, in fast danger of losing her centre of gravity, Sabrina stared at him wide-eyed, her silky hair drifting loose from its clip. 'You have no right to speak to me like—'

'I do not wish to stand here arguing with you. If you want an argument, save it for when we get home and Angelina is asleep. Sí?'

His gaze sweeping over her face with barely controlled fury, Javier turned and walked away, leaving Sabrina feeling curiously as if she'd just survived a cyclone.

CHAPTER NINE

'WHAT am I supposed to do for three weeks? Sit around and twiddle my thumbs?' She was spoiling for a fight and Javier knew it. Sitting in front of the TV, one long leg draped across the arm of the chair, he flicked it off with the remote and sighed. They'd already had this 'discussion' once tonight and clearly Sabrina hadn't come to terms with the idea that her precious agency would be closing for such a long time while the refurbishment got underway. Jill and Robbie, on the other hand, had been delighted.

'Why don't you think about a vacation? When was the last time you took any proper time off, Sabrina?'

Folding her arms across her chest, she walked in front of him, a tense, slender figure in jeans and white shirt, her pretty hair left loose down her back. 'That's neither here nor there.'

'Don't give me one of your enigmatic answers. Tell me the truth.'

'Why? So you'll come to the conclusion I'm such a control freak I'm afraid to take any time off from the business in case something goes wrong in my absence?' It was true. She hadn't taken a holiday in over three years, for exactly the reason she had so eloquently outlined. Ironic when she ran a travel business.

Raising a dark eyebrow, Javier couldn't resist a smile. 'How long, Sabrina?'

'Three years. The last break I had was in Tunisia three years ago. Satisfied?'

Come and sit on my lap and let me unbutton your shirt and I might start to be... Coming out of nowhere, the thought had him instantly hardening. He pulled off his tie, dropped it on the chair arm and adjusted his position. 'You should think about it. That is all I am saying. The work will not take place for another two weeks or so, so you have plenty of time to think about what to do with your time off. If you are so eager for contact with work, I could show you how my business works on the internet. Perhaps you would like to learn, hmm?'

Sabrina felt a ridiculous rush of pleasure, quickly followed by a surge of guilt at being so testy with him, then a wave of anger at the thought that maybe he was just trying to placate her after the Christina debacle.

'It's always useful to learn something new.' Her voice sounded grudging even to her own ears. What was it about this man that had her emotions see-sawing around so crazily? She'd always thought of herself as quite a reasonable person, a *forgiving* person. With Javier she was being anything but. Outrageous when he had already given her so much.

Javier sighed and got up from the chair. 'Talking of work, I have a few things to see to. If you will excuse me I will say goodnight to you, Sabrina. Sleep well.' He had to put some distance between them in order to think. It wasn't going to happen while she was so near. *Sweet temptation with a scowling face.* It didn't look as if she was going to forgive him any time soon for what she believed to be his serious transgression with Christina. Well, he would just have to wait it out. She couldn't stay immune to him for ever, could she? Frowning as he reached the door, he didn't risk a glance over his shoulder at the object of his desire. He'd already had enough provocation for one day.

But Sabrina had no intention of letting the matter lie. Convinced he had slept with his glamorous ex-girlfriend when she'd stayed the night, she had to let him know that, fake marriage or not, she wasn't going to be made a fool of so easily. Returning to her bedroom, she collected the box of pretty lingerie Javier had bought her and swept into his office with it, slamming it on the desk in front of him so that the gorgeous oyster-coloured silk spilled out onto his lap. His broad shoulders visibly tensing, Javier picked up the flimsy items and put them carefully down on top of the silver box without speaking.

Unable to contain her anger any longer, Sabrina glared at him. 'And don't buy me things like this when it's clearly just a game to you! I tell you what, why don't you give them to your girlfriend? I'm sure she could find a use for them when you next get together!'

Slowly, Javier got up from his chair. Sabrina saw the warning flinch of muscle throb in his cheek beneath the smooth, tanned skin and her heart missed a beat.

'They are not Christina's size,' he said, his voice deadly even. 'She is all angles, while you are more...' those deep black eyes of his swept almost insolently down her figure '...more curvaceous. Why are you so angry with me, Sabrina? You are the one who was so certain that this marriage of ours should be—how do you say?—platonic. So why does it bother you that I might have slept with Christina? A man has needs, Sabrina. Is that what scares you so? I can see how that might prove a challenge when you have locked away your feelings for so long. Do you intend to spend the rest of your life pretending not to feel?' When he reached out to stroke his knuckles down her cheek, Sabrina hugged her arms around her waist to stop herself from shaking. She had known him such a short time yet he already knew her so well. Perhaps *that* was what scared her the most?

'We—we had a deal, an agreement.' The words suddenly didn't mean a damn thing any more. Floundering in her anxiety, Sabrina sensed all the fight drain out of her. This man had already been through so much. He had lost his sister and his brother-in-law and was now totally responsible for his niece—so much so that he had given up his glamorous lifestyle in Argentina to move to England and adopt her. What he didn't need was any further grief from Sabrina just because her pride had been hurt. He was a very virile, sexy man. Having been a recent recipient of his lovemaking, she could easily attest to the truth of that. No. She would just have to accept the fact that, as he said, 'he had certain needs' and if she wasn't willing to fulfil them herself, then who could blame him for finding solace elsewhere? Even if it was with his ex-girlfriend?

'I'm sorry.' Her head throbbing, she swung round to leave, surprised and shocked when Javier's hand fastened round her arm to waylay her.

'I did not make love with Christina the other night.

I have no reason to lie to you about that. She is in love with another man back home in Argentina. I found them in bed together and that is when our relationship ended. I have no desire or intention to renew it.'

Her cheeks burning, Sabrina nodded slowly. He was telling her the truth. She knew that now.

'I've made a fool of myself, haven't I?' Her blue eyes looked pained.

'No. It is good things are out in the open. Go and get some rest now. I will see you in the morning.'

When he released her arm and turned away, Sabrina was crushingly disappointed. She wanted... no, *needed* him to kiss her. Her whole body ached for it—to feel that incredibly soft yet sometimes hard-looking mouth sliding across hers, sharing his heat, his passion, his incredible taste with her, as intimate as a man could be with a woman.

'Can I—can I take my things?' Biting her lip, she reached around him to pick up the pretty silk from his desk, the material cool and unbelievably erotic beneath her fingers. Without a word, Javier handed her the box, the ghost of a smile flitting across his lips, gone as quickly as it had appeared. 'Thanks.' Not daring to encroach any further on his good will, Sabrina hurriedly exited the room, her own heartbeat pounding heavily in her ears as she rushed down the softly carpeted hall to her bedroom.

'So what will you do with yourself with three weeks off?' Taking a generous bite of her authentic Italian pizza with its extra topping of Parmesan, Ellie glanced speculatively at her sister across the table.

The popular Italian restaurant was full of lunchtime customers and Ellie had had to book a table so they could eat there. She'd left the children at her mother's and was enjoying her 'me time' enormously, as she told Sabrina.

'Javier's going to teach me a bit about his own business.' Pouring some water from the jug into her glass, she took a brief sip, wishing that her body wouldn't get so inconveniently hot at just the mention of her husband's name. Usually all her concerns were to do with work, how things were going, how to improve things, where she was going to get the money to make some much needed changes. Now that all that was taken care of, all she seemed to be able to think about was Javier D'Alessandro. For someone who had never given a personal relationship with a man top priority in her life, that was unsettling indeed. It was going to make it all the harder to leave when the time came—not to mention leaving Angelina...

'God, you've got a one-track mind, sis!'

'What do you mean?' Terrified that Ellie might have discovered her guilty secret—that she was more than halfway in love with her husband, a fact that she was only just allowing herself to admit—Sabrina stared at her, wide-eyed.

'All you ever seem to think about is work! There you are with that gorgeous hunk of man and the only thing you can get excited about is the prospect of working together! I'll never understand you in a million years, Sabrina, I really won't. And why aren't you eating? Your pizza will get cold.'

She couldn't eat, Sabrina thought miserably. Not when her stomach was so tangled up with thoughts of Javier and Angelina and how empty her life was going to be without them.

'I keep telling you that our marriage isn't real. We only did it to help each other out. When are you going to get that through that thick skull of yours?'

'Don't give me that "our marriage isn't real" bunkum. I know desire when I see it and you two could barely keep your eyes off each other the day I visited. I told Phil. Talk about a match to a fire! Come on, Sabrina, be honest—you fancy him, don't you? If you don't then I really recommend a medical check-up because your equipment can't be functioning properly.'

'Can we change the subject?' Pushing at the pizza on her plate with her fork, Sabrina was blushing profusely. What she felt for Javier wasn't just some sordid little 'it will blow over' sexual itch. Her feelings for the man went so much deeper than that it wasn't funny. Right now it was threatening the very fabric of who she'd imagined she was for the past thirty-seven years. Her chosen course in life had been her career—*not* marriage and children. Now Javier D'Alessandro had her seriously contemplating both and she had no right. He was still young and he deserved to find someone more in keeping with his age and background.

'You care about him, don't you?' Taking a sip of water, Ellie placed her glass carefully back down on the cork mat. 'Is that what's going on? Talk to me, Sabrina. I don't just want to pry into your business. We're family. I care about you.'

'Why wouldn't I care about him and Angelina? I'm not made of stone.' Shaking her head, Sabrina crumpled her paper napkin into a ball. 'I didn't mean for it to happen. It's not the cleverest thing I've ever done.'

'But human, very human. Why wouldn't you want love in your life? Isn't that what we all ultimately want—someone who really cares about us deeply?'

'But he doesn't love me.' Hastening to make that very clear to her sister, Sabrina felt choked just saying the words. 'He might be attracted to me but that doesn't mean it's anything more than physical. And besides, I'm too old for him.'

Ellie looked militant. 'Who says?'

'*I* say! Think about it, Ellie. In a few years' time he'll want children. He comes from a very old-fashioned culture where family is sacrosanct. Do you think his parents would be happy if he married a woman who couldn't bear him children?'

'All this is supposition. You don't even know for a fact that you can't have children. You could pop out at least three or four if you got your skates on!'

Laughing in spite of her anguish, Sabrina reached across the table to cover Ellie's hand with her own. 'You are a nut. But at least you make me laugh. I get so wrapped up in the business sometimes I seem to forget how to have fun.'

'Have that conversation with the gorgeous Javier. I'm sure *he* could teach you how to have fun.'

'Hmm.' Thinking about the beautiful lingerie he had bought her that she had retrieved after her little contretemps the other night, Sabrina didn't doubt that was true. What had he been thinking when he bought it for her? Her insides glowed at the thought. 'Dangerous.'

'Hold that thought.' Attracting the attention of a passing waitress, Ellie ordered a bottle of house red. 'You need to learn to loosen up a little, my girl, and this is going to help.'

'No,' Sabrina wagged her finger, '*this* is going to make me fall asleep at my desk.'

'Why worry? Your husband's there to make sure you get home OK, isn't he?'

Returning to the living-room with two mugs of black coffee, Javier stopped in the doorway at the sight that met his eyes. Curled up on one end of the huge couch, her head on two satin pillows, Sabrina was fast asleep. At the other end, curled up in a similar fashion, was Angelina—also asleep. His insides suffusing with warmth, he took a long, slow breath and, advancing into the room, placed the coffee on a sideboard. Standing there watching them both, he couldn't disown the sudden longing in his chest to hold these two females in the circle of his love and protection for ever. The thought almost made him stumble. It was natural he should feel such tenderness towards Angelina; he'd loved her since she was a baby and soon she would be his adopted daughter. But to acknowledge such feelings towards Sabrina—this woman who had appeared out of nowhere, as it were, just when he needed her? This was something else entirely, something he definitely hadn't planned for. She was a beautiful, vibrant, sensual woman and he desired her with a depth that had surpassed anything he'd ever experienced before, but love? He'd sworn to protect his heart from such a fate. Angelina and his parents had his unconditional love but to fall for a

woman and bind her to him with promises to love her
for ever was something he'd vowed not to do, not
unless he was looking to get his heart badly broken.
He only had to remember Dorothea and Michael to
know that love could also be cruel. At thirty years
old he had had enough tragedy in his life. No. He
made up his mind. He was not averse to enjoying a
warm physical relationship with the beguiling Sabrina
but, as far as anything else was concerned, he would
resist. Gazing at her now, her long, luxurious hair
spilling onto the vivid cerise of the satin pillow, he
knew it was going to take every ounce of will-power
to keep his vow.

She awoke to the gentle sounds of a Joni Mitchell
record, the room bathed in the intimate glow of lamp-
light, and as she struggled to sit up she rubbed her
hand around her neck to ease the tight cramp in her
muscle. Disorientated, Sabrina glanced round the
room, seeing the royal-blue velvet drapes drawn
against the night, the fire hissing brightly in the grate
with its comforting crackle and Javier nursing a glass
of some amber-coloured liquid between his hands as
he stared into the flames from his armchair.

'What time is it?'

'Ten to midnight.' For a long moment he stared
into his glass, then slowly he raised his head to regard
Sabrina's half-reclining form.

'So late?' Rubbing the sleep from her eyes, she
wished her head didn't feel so groggy. 'You mean
I've been asleep here since we came back from
work?'

'Too much wine at lunch, you said.' A flicker of a
smile crossed his handsome face and Sabrina groaned

at the admission. Swinging her legs carefully onto the floor, she tried in vain to tidy her dishevelled hair, instead found her clip buried somewhere halfway down her head, rescued it and silently vowed to be a lot tougher in future when it came to her sister's unwise recommendations.

'I try to make it a rule never to drink at lunchtimes. It's fatal. It always makes me fall asleep when I do.'

'You seemed happy when you came back to the office.' The memory gave Javier a decidedly warm feeling. He had seen a very different Sabrina after a glass or two of wine. She'd spent the rest of the afternoon smiling and giggling at him and the customers alike and finally Javier and Robbie had had to take charge while Jill had led Sabrina safely into the little back room and made her drink a large mug of black coffee.

'Yes, well, I promise I won't make a habit of it. Drinking at lunchtime, I mean.' Getting to her feet, she briefly lifted her hair off the back of her neck then stepped forward towards the fire. 'This is nice.' Crouching down beside the crackling flames about a foot away from where Javier sat, she held out her hands then rubbed them up and down her arms to get her circulation going again because she'd felt chilled when she'd woken.

Her hair was haloed by the light from the fire and Javier studied her exquisite profile and felt heat of a very different kind suffuse his body. Taking a sip of his brandy, enjoying the burn that rippled satisfyingly along his throat to his stomach, he offered the glass to Sabrina. 'Have some.'

'What is it?'

'Brandy. Very good French brandy.'

'I'd better not.'

She watched mesmerised as Javier slowly dipped his finger into the glass, wetted it and offered it to her instead.

For one crackling, electric moment, Sabrina didn't know what to do. Her stomach muscles clenched so tight that she almost forgot to breathe. Her eyes huge, she leant forward a fraction and circled her hand round his wrist. She was aware of his white shirt cuff and the onyx cufflinks outlined with gold, the fine black hairs on the back of his bronze hand, the faint spicy drift of his aftershave as she lowered her mouth to capture his finger between her lips.

She heard the low rasp of his breath as she slowly licked her tongue along his flesh then released him, tasting brandy and Javier, feeling light-headed and so aroused that her nipples were erect to the point of pain against her blouse. Then her fevered brain registered the softly seductive Spanish as he moved off the chair and got down on his knees beside her. His eyes were very dark and completely intense as he cupped her face between his hands.

'What is it about you that makes you so hard to resist, Sabrina?' Lowering his mouth, he kissed her gently, experimentally, making her heart zing and her eyelids flutter closed. Curling her hands round his wrists, she eased back to look at him, knowing she could easily ask him the same question, but maybe it was a question she already knew the answer to? He had the kind of 'sit up and take notice' good looks that made women glance knowingly at each other when he walked into a room and smile at the fantasy of sharing his bed. His bearing was relaxed, confident, bordering on arrogant. But it wasn't an empty, shallow kind of confidence—Javier D'Alessandro more than delivered the goods. Not only was he clever and hardworking, but he also had integrity and honour that would put lesser men to shame, as well as being kind to children and women who needed a prayer or two answered. Everything considered, he was a pretty irresistible package all round.

'We said we weren't going to do this,' she whispered softly. One of the logs on the fire cracked and spat and Sabrina held her breath as Javier stroked down her cheek with the pad of his thumb. His eyelashes were very black—almost with a blue sheen—and she could see the tiny lines that fanned out from the corners of his eyes.

'Rules were meant to be broken, *no*?'

She was about to agree when a child's distressed cry cut through the room, making them both spring apart and jump to their feet.

'Angelina!' Javier was out of the room before Sabrina got her bearings. She found him kneeling beside Angelina's bed—the child's hand in his while his free hand stroked her brow. Even at the door, Sabrina could see the little girl was pink and flushed, her dark eyes shimmering.

'She is burning up.' His voice sounding almost unbearably hoarse, Javier threw her an anguished glance and Sabrina hurried towards the bed to feel the evidence for herself.

'Hello, sweetheart,' she soothed, brushing the

child's hair back from her face, 'aren't you feeling well, darling?'

'My head hurts.'

When Angelina gazed at her as if she was about to burst into tears, Sabrina put her hand on Javier's shoulder. 'Get a bowl of tepid water and a flannel.'

He was already halfway to the door when he stopped. 'Tepid?'

Seeing the confusion in his eyes, Sabrina elaborated quickly. 'Not too cold. If it's too cold it might give her a shock.'

'*Sí.*' He was gone and back again in no time. Taking the flannel and wringing it out gently in the water, Sabrina sponged Angelina's feverish brow as Javier looked helplessly on.

'I've checked her over for any rash,' she said quietly, remembering the instructions for signs of meningitis pinned to Ellie's huge American-style refrigerator. 'And there doesn't seem to be anything untoward. Right now we just need to bring her temperature down. Can you look in the medicine cabinet for any Calpol or paracetamol? And wake Rosie; she might be able to help too.'

'It's Rosie's night off. She's gone to visit a friend at university in Brighton. She won't be back until tomorrow.' Driving his hand impatiently through his hair, Javier stared worriedly down at his niece. She'd thrown off her bedcovers and the pretty pink duvet was bunched round her knees. In the soft glow of the night-light Sabrina pulled it up a little over her nightdress and continued to sponge her heated brow. 'She's very hot. If this doesn't work soon we should call the doctor. You have the number?'

'Of course I have the number. I will ring now.'

He disappeared before Sabrina could say any more.

'You're going to be just fine, my angel. Just fine, I promise.'

'You won't leave me?'

Seeing the anguish in her face, Sabrina squeezed her hand tight. 'Are you kidding? I'm going to stay right here all night if I have to. You don't get rid of me that easily! Once I care about someone I stick like glue, I can tell you.'

Angelina's brief, tentative smile tore at her heart. Silently offering up a prayer, Sabrina smiled back, reminding herself to breathe, to stay calm, not to show even the slightest anxiety to the little girl she had grown so fond of.

'He said about half an hour.' Anxiety creasing his smooth, tanned brow, Javier crouched down beside Angelina then dropped an infinitely tender little kiss on her flushed cheek. 'You are going to get well, *mi querida*. I promise. The doctor will not be long.'

Angelina's eyes fluttered closed. Sabrina glanced at the man beside her, her chest feeling tight when she sensed the worry rolling off him in waves. He had already lost so much—his sister, then Michael. No wonder he looked so gripped with fear. Her hand came down on his shoulder and stayed there awhile. 'It's probably just a bug she picked up at school. It happens all the time. She's strong, Javier—she'll get better in no time. I'll stay with her tomorrow. Jill and Robbie can manage for a day without me.'

'Then we stay here together,' he said, not looking round at her but staring at the sleeping child on the bed instead. 'Nothing matters more than Angelina being well again.'

CHAPTER TEN

AFTER two days of worrying himself into a stupor over Angelina, Javier knew he had to start resuming an iron resolve as far as his feelings for Sabrina went. The woman had stayed home from work on both days to help take care of his beloved niece because Rosie had also come down with a bug and advisedly stayed put at her friend's. In the end she'd ministered to both of them, reassuring Javier with words of comfort and hot soup when he refused to eat anything more, and nursing Angelina the way a devoted mother would her child. It was the latter that had him convinced that she was a dangerous woman to be around. Already, he had more than lost his heart to her and it terrified him to finally realise the state of his feelings.

As for Angelina, after two days of being too poorly to leave her bed—a viral infection, the doctor had proclaimed—today she was tucked up on the big couch in the living-room. By her side on the floor there was a virtual Aladdin's cave of videos and DVDs to choose from, and her uncle had left her laughing at a cartoon with Sabrina, who'd popped home for lunch to see how she was, while he mooched around the kitchen trying to come to terms with his emotions. If his adoring mother so much as suspected her son's growing attachment to the woman who'd married him in name only, she'd be on a flight out of Buenos Aires so fast to make sure he held on to her that his father would be left eating her dust.

His brow furrowing at the thought, he glanced up at Sabrina's soft-footed entrance. In one of her plain but smart business suits, her hair coiled up behind her off her collar, some tiny pearl studs in her lobes, she looked the kind of woman a man could depend on— and not just in a business sense. After the past two days, Javier knew Sabrina was capable of so much more. She was cool and calm in a crisis, and more to the point didn't buckle under pressure—even when it was something she was hardly used to handling. If there was ever a woman who was made to have children, it was she. He was convinced of that much.

'She's looking much better today, isn't she? More like her old self.'

'My heart is glad.' The simple statement carried a wealth of meaning. The child meant everything in the world to him. It gave Sabrina a bitter-sweet pang to know how much, because it made her wonder what it would feel like to have someone care that passionately about her.

'You look better today too. I see you've had a shave.' The corners of her pretty mouth kicked up and so did Javier's pulse.

Grinning wryly, he rubbed his hand around his clean jaw. 'I did not want to frighten you away by looking like Blackbeard, no?'

'Funny, but I could see you as a pirate.' It wasn't funny at all, Sabrina realised with a little jolt of heat in her stomach. It was downright licentious! Javier as some marauding pirate looking dark, dangerous and disreputable—it was a fantasy that should be purely reserved for night-time. It had no business interfering with her thought processes during daylight hours. Not when she had to get her skates on and go back to work.

'Anyway, I have to go. I've got a customer coming in to talk to me about visiting Iceland of all places. Just saying the name makes me shiver. As if it wasn't cold enough!'

She was babbling to hide her discomfort. Did he even guess how hard it was for her to behave normally in his presence? After two days in the closest proximity, sharing the worry and concern of a sick child, both letting down barriers they'd rarely let down before, it was becoming more and more difficult to contemplate leaving—and that was *without* taking the lovely Angelina into consideration.

'We will have a take-out tonight, I think. You look tired and I do not want you worrying about cooking. Rosie will be back tomorrow. I had a phone-call this morning so hopefully things can return to normal. Take care of yourself, *sí*?'

Unconsciously his voice had lowered and, venturing a smile, Sabrina took a step back towards the door. 'You too.'

Poring over the take-out menu for a local Thai restaurant later that evening, Sabrina glanced up in surprise at the sound of the doorbell echoing through the house. Leaving Angelina's bedroom, where he'd just gone to check that she was sleeping peacefully, Javier called out, 'I'll get that.'

As her gaze returned to the menu, Sabrina's hand fluttered to her complaining stomach. She was starving. For the first time in two days she actually felt like eating. Now it seemed her appetite had caught up with her with a vengeance.

'Sabrina. You have a visitor.'

Blinking in disbelief, she straightened to see the bustling, concerned figure of her mother enter the room, with Javier close behind her. Joan Kendricks was smaller and plumper than both her daughters but her eyes were as blue as theirs while her hair, although faded to grey, was prettily highlighted with becoming streaks of ash blonde. She smelled of Chanel No. 5, as she usually did, and Sabrina noted she was wearing one of her best dresses beneath her smart black wool coat.

For a moment, her daughter just stared in shock.

'Mum! What are you doing here?'

She was in the process of laying some shopping bags down on the big pine table, and Joan Kendricks' neatly plucked eyebrows flew up towards her hairline. 'It's nice to see you too, Sabrina. What did you expect? That I'd leave you to your own devices when I heard the child was sick? What kind of mother do you take me for?'

The child? Ellie must have said something, of course. Sabrina had spoken to her sister a couple of times while she was at home nursing Angelina.

'And good of you to introduce me to your new husband as well.'

Her heart in her throat, Sabrina stared wide-eyed at Javier across her mother's shoulder. He shrugged and grinned but did not look half as discomfited as Sabrina felt.

'I'm sorry, Mum. This is Javier—Javier D'Alessandro.'

'You're a brave man, taking this one on.' Joan swung round to survey the tall, handsome man who reminded her of one of those old-fashioned matinée idols of the fifties, and firmly shook his hand. 'She's too independent by half.'

'Tell me about it.'

He was smiling...*smiling*, would you believe? Joan smiled back then proceeded to shrug off her overcoat. Wordlessly, Javier took it and disappeared briefly to go and hang it on the coat tree in the hall.

'Anyway, how is the poor little thing? Angelina, I think Ellie said.'

'She is doing very well,' Javier answered. 'She is sleeping now and well on the way to full recovery.'

'I'm glad to hear it. Would you mind if I took a little peek? Just to satisfy myself.'

'No. Not at all.'

'Sabrina?'

'Yes, Mum?'

'Put away that take-away menu. What the pair of you need is some proper food. I know what it's like to nurse a sick child and it's easy to neglect your own needs. In one of those bags you'll find one of my big dishes with a casserole in it. Pop it in the oven and give it a good twenty minutes' heat-through. In another bag you'll find a bottle of champagne. It should be well chilled because I've had it in the fridge at home all day but pop it in yours anyway, there's a good girl. I'll be right back as soon as I've had a look at the child.'

As Sabrina automatically began to sort through the

bags on the table, she stood-stock still all of a sudden, dazedly shaking her head as if to convince herself that she hadn't imagined the scenario that had just taken place. 'Thanks a lot, Ellie!' she breathed out loud. No doubt Javier was already trying to come to terms with that 'just run over by a steamroller' feeling, a state of mind both Kendricks girls were well used to when it came to their mother.

Ten minutes later, the casserole simmering nicely in the oven and fragrant smells permeating the kitchen to mouth-watering effect, Sabrina sat at the table, sipping her coffee, her stomach in knots, wondering what on earth her mother and Javier were finding to talk about.

'What a beautiful child!'

They returned to the kitchen, Joan pulling out a chair to sit opposite her daughter, while Javier switched on the kettle and sorted cups and saucers from the dresser.

'Now, come and sit down, young man. We'll have tea or whatever it is you're making later. Sabrina, open that bottle of champagne and fetch three glasses.'

About to rise from the table, Sabrina dropped back down into her seat, scowling. 'What's all this about, Mum? What's the champagne for? You rarely even take a glass of wine.'

'Listen, it's not every day my elder daughter gets herself married, is it? Even if I wasn't invited to the ceremony I would still like to celebrate with a glass of champagne. Ellie was right when she said your husband was a lovely young man. As soon as she told me I knew everything would be all right. You'll do very well together, I can see that.'

Her heart sinking, Sabrina dared a glance at Javier. He was leaning against the dresser, his arms folded across that gorgeous chest, apparently as relaxed and at ease as if it were his own mother who had dropped by for a visit. But it wasn't safe to make assumptions about anything, was it? He might be hating every second, squirming inside because her mother had clearly got hold of the wrong end of the stick. Hadn't she explained to her that she'd married Javier simply to help him get a British passport and stay in the country? So what on earth had made her suddenly assume it was some kind of match made in heaven?

'Mum, please!'

'Oh, you think I'm embarrassing your young man?' Joan chuckled as she tilted her head towards Javier. 'He's not embarrassed in the slightest, are you, dear? Besides, he'll have to get used to my ways. He's part of the family now.'

Javier produced the glasses, three elegant flutes, while Sabrina got the champagne out of the fridge and plonked it on the table. Even though the whole thing was farcical, she would have to go along with it for now because she quite honestly didn't feel up to facing a scene after the last few days. All of a sudden she was feeling desperately tired, like a favourite old cardigan that was suddenly looking too worn out to wear again.

'Well.' Her blue eyes crinkling at the corners and looking as though she might cry any minute, Joan Kendricks raised her glass to Javier and Sabrina. 'Here's wishing you both a long and happy married life. I must confess I was always afraid that my beautiful Sabrina would end up alone; all she seemed to think about was that business of hers.' She glanced at Javier confidingly, her glass still poised in the air. 'That's not to say that her father and I aren't proud of what she's achieved, but I did fear it wouldn't be enough, if you see what I mean. Nothing can replace children and a good man. So anyway, lots of love to you both.'

'*Gracias.*' His expression unreadable right then, Javier toasted his mother-in-law and his wife in turn, his dark gaze boring into Sabrina as she felt herself blush what must have been a deep beetroot-red. In her top ten of most embarrassing moments, this surely had to be number one? Here they were, drinking a toast with her mother to a marriage that Sabrina and Javier knew was destined to have a very short shelf life. Both pretending that it was something true and honest worth celebrating, while inside Sabrina feared her heart might break if she had to pretend any longer. The truth was she was desperately in love with Javier and couldn't imagine her life without him. Which was tough when that was the outlook that beckoned—like it or not.

'Now, you two,' rising to her feet, Joan patted her hair, 'I'm going to love you and leave you and let you enjoy your dinner in peace. When Angelina is properly well, I'll come and visit again and bring your father if I may, Sabrina? Having met your charming husband, I'm sure George would also like to have the pleasure of his acquaintance. I'll give you a ring, sweetheart. That OK?'

A bit difficult to say 'no, everything isn't OK now

that you've been and caused emotional mayhem,' Sabrina thought wearily.

'You will be more than welcome.' Flashing her mother one of his delectable 'stop a woman in her tracks' smiles, Javier helped her on with her coat, then walked to the door with both women. Watching Sabrina obediently proffer her cheek for her mother's parting kiss, he was surprised but not taken aback when Joan pulled his shoulders down and kissed him soundly on his own cheek.

'Take care, now. See you soon.'

'Well, that was disastrous!'

Following his wife back into the warm kitchen, Javier creased his brow in bewilderment. 'I do not understand.'

'You see what I have to put up with? The woman wants to run my life! She thinks she can just waltz in here and—'

'Sabrina. Your mother brought us a meal. She brought us champagne and asked to see Angelina. What can be disastrous about that? As far as I could see, all she was doing was behaving like a mother. I saw nothing wrong in that.'

'And what about that ludicrous toast of hers, hmm? What did you think about that? She knows full well this is only a temporary arrangement yet she deliberately buries her head in the sand and pretends she doesn't! I wouldn't blame you if you were furious.'

'Well, I am not.' Picking up his glass of champagne, he took a sip. 'Your mother understands the importance of family, sí? You cannot blame her if she only wants the best for you. My mother would be the same.'

'What *she* thinks is the best for me, you mean. You heard how she alluded to my business? Almost as if it was some kind of failing on my part instead of an achievement. Her only goal is to see me as a contestant for ''mother of the year''. She won't be satisfied with anything else, don't you see? Just because I wanted to make my own way in life and not depend on some man to keep me, I must be lacking as a woman in some way. Ellie already gave up her career in preference for being a wife and mother; don't you think she'd be satisfied with one daughter doing what she wants?'

'Are you so against the idea of being a mother? A wife?'

His question, so reasonably asked, cut through the red mist in Sabrina's brain. Her gaze trapped by his slow, steady perusal, her tongue came out to moisten her lips.

'No. I'm not against it. I just don't think it's for me.'

'Too set in your ways, you said.'

What would he say if she simply confessed she was just too damn scared? Scared of not coming up to scratch, scared of failing, of not being enough. At least with her business she knew where she stood.

'You can still be a success in your chosen career and be a wife and mother. In my opinion something would suffer, but that's only because I think the children's welfare should be paramount—at least while they are small the mother should stay at home if she can and take care of them. A child needs stability.'

Something poor Angelina had lost. Now it was up to Javier to provide the stability and love that had been ripped away so cruelly. There was no doubt in Sabrina's mind he was more than up to the task.

'Why is it that whichever way I turn I feel as if I'm in the wrong?' Stupidly she felt like crying. If only her mother hadn't chosen this particular evening to drop by and toast their marriage, because the experience had left Sabrina wishing with all her heart and soul that her marriage to Javier could be real.

'You are not wrong because you have a different opinion. I know how much the business means to you, Sabrina. That is why I want to help you. At the end of the day you have to do what is best for you.'

'And what *is* best for me, Javier? Do you know what's best for me? Because I sure as hell don't!' She'd flown from the room before he had a chance to stop her and Javier put down his drink, dug his hands deep into his trouser pockets and wished his mother or sister could be here so that he could ask them to explain about women...

As he stood in front of Michael's walk-in wardrobe, Javier's gaze settled on all the tightly packed Savile Row suits and knew he could no longer ignore the fact that they were there and something had to be done. He had no intention of wiping out every sign that Michael had ever lived in the house, but he was certain that as long as there were too many visible reminders both he and Angelina would find it hard to make a new life. So he had to make a start. The first thing he would do would be to pack up all the contents of Michael's wardrobes and drawers, and anything that wasn't obviously personal or that Angela Calder didn't want he would donate to a local charity

shop. That done, he would get some quotes from dec-
orators and think about redecorating both Michael's
and Angelina's rooms. He would, of course, involve
his niece in the design process and hopefully get her
excited about planning a new look for her bedroom.
He had had a little chat with Angelina before she went
to sleep last night and they had both decided it was
too soon to start searching for a new home. They
would stay in the house until the summer at least, and
maybe then they could think about moving.

Javier deliberately didn't allow himself to dwell on
Sabrina's position in all of their plans or even if she
would be involved. All he knew was that she had
cried herself to sleep last night after refusing him entry and he had lain awake in his room down the corridor with his door opened, listening to her muffled
weeping, his chest so tight that his breathing felt im-
peded. When she'd left for work this morning, her
usual peaches-and-cream complexion looked pale and
drawn and there were soft smudges of grey beneath
her dulled blue eyes. Whatever was going on in that
fertile mind of hers she hadn't wanted to share it with
her husband, and Javier had watched her leave the
house with a heavy heart, knowing that sooner or later
it was all probably going to end in tears.

Refusing to think about that now, he started to remove the suits from the wardrobe, glad to have something to keep both his hands and his brain occupied
or else he would definitely go crazy.

'How are you feeling today, sweetheart?' Joining
the child and her nanny in the living-room on her
return from work, Sabrina bent low to the couch to
kiss Angelina on her smooth, plump cheek. The little

girl seemed happy and healthy, tucked up beneath her red tartan blanket watching television, Rosie sitting beside her companionably, munching a packet of crisps.

'Much better, thanks. Tomorrow I'm going to get up properly because my friend Julie is coming over.'

'Good news, eh? And how are you, Rosie? I was sorry to hear you weren't well.'

'I know.' Rosie's eyes rolled heavenwards. 'Bad luck that I was laid up the same time as poor Angelina. Still, it was lucky you were here to help her uncle look after her, wasn't it?'

'It was.' Clutching her bag to her chest, Sabrina forced a smile. 'Where is Javier, by the way?'

'In Daddy's room,' Angelina replied, her gaze fixed on the TV screen in the corner of the room. 'He's been clearing out things so that we can decorate.'

'Oh.'

Having changed into jeans and an old chambray shirt, Sabrina knocked on the door of what was once Michael Calder's bedroom and, hearing the terse 'Come!', cautiously stepped into the room. There seemed to be piles of clothing everywhere, on the chair, on the huge canopied bed, on the highly polished Victorian chest of drawers. From the opened door of a walk-in wardrobe, Javier appeared, his black hair mussed, his blue shirt opened at the collar with his sleeves rolled up, his long legs encased in soft, dark denim jeans with a black leather belt cinching his waist. He was scowling and didn't exactly look pleased to see her but the scowl only served to highlight his inevitable attraction. Inside her chest, Sabrina's heart gave a crazy little leap.

'Need any help?' she asked.

'No. I have everything under control.'

'You are angry with me?'

'No.'

'Then would you like something to eat? I bought some steaks and the makings of a salad. Even *I* can't mess that up.'

He didn't smile at her joke and her stomach lurched. 'What's wrong?'

Even though he briefly turned his face aside, Sabrina didn't miss the flash of pain that passed across his eyes. Michael. How could she have been so insensitive as to walk into the room that had once been his brother-in-law's, see the clothes that had once belonged to the man piled up ready for removal, and not realise that her husband was hurting, missing the man who had once been his friend—the man who had been married to his beloved sister…?

'Nothing is wrong. Leave me. I will come and join you shortly.'

'Javier, I—'

'Go, Sabrina! Can you not understand that I do not want you in here?' His black eyes were blazing, and she felt his fury hit her somewhere in the solar plexus. Swallowing down her hurt, she decided to stay her ground. This wasn't about her. This was about the man who had sacrificed his own dreams, his way of life, to come and take care of an orphaned little girl because she was family.

'What if I don't want to go, Javier? What then?'

He swore in Spanish, shook his head, then started to pull open one of the drawers in the Victorian chest. Her heart pounding, Sabrina walked up behind him, slid her arms around his waist, felt his whole body stiffen in protest, then leant her head gently against his back. Her senses were immediately invaded by the warmth and the scent of the man, making her realise just how much she had been longing to touch him like this.

'What are you doing?'

'What does it feel like I'm doing?' she murmured.

'Dios!' Pushing her arms away, he spun round, his expression furious. 'I told you I did not want you in here.'

She blinked. 'I don't believe you. You need me.'

'I do not need anybody!'

'You're lying.'

'Sabrina, I—'

Drawing level, she curled her hand into his shoulder and drew his face down to hers. Before he could react, she slanted her mouth deliberately across his, coaxing his tongue, drawing his silky heat into her own, then slid her free hand down his shirt, passed the leather belt round his waist, and boldly down to the now bulging fly of his denim jeans.

Moving his mouth from hers, he slid it in a damp trail across her cheek to her ear and Sabrina registered his helpless shudder with a small flare of excitement deep in her belly. Murmuring a destroyingly sexual entreaty against the tender skin of her lobe, he lifted his head to stare deeply into her wide blue eyes. 'Go and lock the door,' he commanded hoarsely.

CHAPTER ELEVEN

WHEN she came back he swept her down onto the soft blue carpet, his hands already on the buttons of her shirt, pulling it aside—feasting his gaze on the soft, creamy mounds of her breasts in her white lace bra.

'So,' he said softly, 'you will not share with me what is in your mind but we will share this, hmm?'

Even as he spoke, he was undoing her zipper, tugging at the heavy denim as he tried to rid her of her jeans. In a fever of desperate wanting, Sabrina helped him, then, urging his mouth down to hers, lost herself in the hot, deep flavours of his kiss, the hard, warm male textures of his skin. Feeling the taut muscles of his shoulders bunching beneath her palms, she realised he was reaching for his own zipper, easing it down, with one firm tug divesting her of the matching white lace panties she was wearing.

Reaching into his back pocket, he sheathed himself with the contents of the small foil packet he withdrew, then, positioning himself more fully on top of her, staked his claim with one sure, deep thrust, emitting a gravel-voiced groan as his hips ground against the firm but soft flesh of her thighs. Sabrina shut her eyes, murmuring words that were more like prayers—words she'd never uttered to any man before Javier. He consumed her; not just with his amazing body, but with his mind and his heart and his soul as well.

He was a good man, the *best* man, and she loved him with a depth of feeling and emotion that had been beyond her experience until now. It was terrifying how much she loved him. But oh, how she craved for him to love her back, craved as much of him as he was willing to give and more. As he thrust deeper, the ache for him growing into an unstoppable crescendo, her fingernails dug into the coiled steel muscle of his biceps as he brought her to climax, her body digging deeper into the soft blue carpet beneath her with the force of his possession. With a harsh, heavy groan, his own release quickly followed, his body pumping harder into hers as she sagged, spent, against the floor, her mind spinning, her body throbbing in the aftermath of the torrid, urgent coupling that had just taken place.

As he dropped his head onto her chest his warm, ragged breath whispered tantalisingly across her breasts in the white lace confines of her bra, and even though she was still dazed from his loving she wanted his hands on her again, skin to skin, breath to breath. Consumed by love, Sabrina pushed her fingers through the short, silky strands of his black hair. 'Are you all right?' she asked him gently.

He lifted his head, his dark eyes glittering back at her with hunger and sorrow and something else that she couldn't quite reach.

'You ask me if I am all right?' His perfectly even white teeth looked even whiter against the smooth bronze of his skin. 'It is I who should be asking you that question. I confess I had planned on a long, slow, sweet seduction some time soon before I completely lost my mind with wanting you—but this?'

Apparently furious with himself, he made a move to detach himself, but Sabrina stroked across the rippling muscle in his arm beneath his shirt and her lips parted in a softly coaxing smile.

'Passion has a life of its own, you said. Remember?'

Nodding slowly, he gazed down at her lovely face, those bewitching blue eyes with their sweeping honey-brown lashes, the soft pink flush on her cheeks. '*Sí*. I remember.'

'Then don't be angry.'

'I am not angry with you.' In one fluid movement he detached himself from her, grabbed a handful of tissues from the box on the chest of drawers, disposed of the condom then pulled up the jeans that he hadn't removed completely. Then, reaching for Sabrina's scattered clothing, he dropped the items gently down across her belly. 'It is the world in general I am angry at—maybe God too. I cannot help wondering what else the powers that be have in store for me.'

'Only good things, Javier. I am sure of it.'

'I am not sure of anything right now. I miss the wisdom of my friend. Michael always seemed to know the right thing to do in a crisis. After Dorothea died, people were amazed at how well he coped; how he was able to soothe others even in the depths of his own grief—me included. But I knew his heart was broken. That is why he never married again. In eight years I think he had one or two dinner dates—that's all. He was not interested in any other woman except my sister.'

Sucking in a shaky breath, Sabrina clutched her clothes to her stomach then slowly started to put them on. 'He must have loved her very much.' Her voice husky, she couldn't bring herself to look at him. The sorrow in his voice made her want to protect him from every hurt that ever came his way again. It made her want to throw herself into his arms and tell him how desperately, how deeply she loved him, that she could understand Michael not wanting anyone else after Dorothea because she felt the same way about Javier. But she couldn't tell him that, could she? Not when they'd made an agreement. And Javier wasn't ready to surrender his heart—she could see that—not when he associated loving someone with losing them.

'I'll make us a nice meal.' Touching his shoulder as she walked up behind him, she sensed his relief that she was bringing this conversation to an end. 'Will you join me in a while?'

'Sí.' For a moment the heat of his gaze scorched her and she couldn't look away, then he lifted his hand, smoothed back a lock of her hair and sighed. 'Thank you, Sabrina.'

But as she left the room, Sabrina wasn't exactly sure what it was he was thanking her for.

'William, darling, don't cover Auntie Sabrina in flour, please! She's got to go back to work very soon.'

With two huge, meltingly blue eyes staring wonderingly up at her beneath a shining curtain of precision-cut blond hair, Sabrina grinned at the little boy who up until a moment ago had been liberally dusting flour from his mother's baking all over the kitchen floor, and wished with a sudden fierce longing that he was hers. The yearning for a child of her own had been slowly creeping up on her ever since she'd met

Javier and the delightful Angelina and there didn't
seem to be anything she could do to put a stop to it.
Consequently when she'd woken early that morning
with stomach cramps that were bad enough to press-
gang her out of bed and into the bathroom, she had
hugged her arms tightly around herself and cried
shamelessly at the visible proof that she couldn't be
pregnant. It didn't make sense. The ordered, tidy, safe
little world she'd so carefully constructed around herself for the past fifteen years had been totally turned
on its head and she didn't feel as though she had a
hope of righting it any time soon.

'He's all right. He's just being creative, aren't you,
William? He might be a top chef one day, you never
know.'

'Just as long as he makes loads of money and keeps
his mother in the style to which she could easily become accustomed, eh, Will?' Reaching for the broom,
Ellie began to energetically sweep the trail of flour
dust into a corner before scooping it up in a dustpan.
From the living-room Tallulah's sudden indignant
wail cut through the house and Ellie pushed back her
hair and rolled her eyes at Sabrina.

'Kids, eh? Who'd have 'em? I expect Henry has
lobbed something at her, as usual. I can't seem to
make him realise she's not some kind of bendy toy
doll that won't break.'

Following her sister into the topsy-turvy living-
room that was turned upside-down by an earthquake
of clothes, books, toys and half-nibbled discarded biscuits, Sabrina watched Ellie stoop to pick up the distressed baby from the playpen while little Henry

plonked himself on the carpet and picked up a rattle, apparently oblivious to his sister's cries.

'There, there, now. You're all right. Mummy's here, darling girl.' With a kiss on the top of her head and a firm cuddle, Ellie's practised ministrations quickly soothed the baby's crying, and as the child pressed her face into her mother's faded green T-shirt Sabrina once again had to hold back the tide of emotion that threatened to overwhelm her.

'You're looking a little peaky if you don't mind me saying.' Her brow puckering, Ellie suddenly narrowed her gaze suspiciously at Sabrina.

'Oh, my God! You're not—?'

'No, I'm not.' Kneeling down beside Henry, Sabrina coaxed the toddler into her arms, sitting him down on her lap with the baby's rattle. 'For goodness' sake, you're as bad as Mum. When are the pair of you going to get it through your thick skulls that this marriage of mine is only temporary? A business arrangement?'

'Who are you trying to kid? It's as plain as the nose on your face, Sabrina Kendricks, you're loopy about the man! And if I'm not mistaken—and I *know* I'm not—he feels exactly the same about you. And if you're telling me that you've spent all this time under his roof and haven't done the deed then either your libido has ground to a halt from lack of use or you're an even slower worker than I thought you were when it comes to men!'

'Thanks.'

'Don't mention it. And by the way, that hurt look doesn't wash with me either. You're in love with him, aren't you?' Her voice softening, Ellie joined her sister on the carpet, carefully sitting Tallulah down in front of her to face Henry.

'What do you want, a signed confession?' Sabrina's blue eyes looked pained.

'Have you told him?'

'Are you mad? Of course I haven't told him!' At Henry's startled glance, Sabrina hugged the child to her, ruffling the top of his baby-fine hair with her fingers. 'Javier doesn't want to get involved with me that way. He's lost his sister and his brother-in-law and Angelina is his priority, and nobody could blame him for that. The last thing he needs is an emotional entanglement with a woman eight years older than him and a workaholic to boot.'

'You're not a workaholic. You *used* to be, but since you've met Javier you've changed, Sabrina. Can't you see it? We were lucky if we got to see you once a month, let alone once a week. Now you drop by fairly regularly and when you do you mainly talk about Javier and Angelina—a sure sign that work is no longer your big priority.'

Ellie was right, Sabrina realised. Of course, East-West Travel was still important, but somehow, without her knowing, her priorities had changed. Javier and Angelina had become her family without a doubt and they *did* take priority in her life. So much so that it was going to be an unbearable wrench to leave them behind—as one day soon she would have to. And somehow she knew that, no matter how successful her business became, nothing would ever compensate for the awful loss of the man and child who had come to mean so much to her.

'Well, it won't do me any good. He's not ready to get involved with me. He's hurting too much.'

'Of course he is. He's not going to get over something like this in five minutes, that's obvious, but with you by his side you can teach him how to trust again, Sabrina—how to love someone without fearing for their life, because that's what's at the root of this, isn't it? It has to be, otherwise he would have told you he wants you to stay.'

Expelling a softly shaky sigh, Sabrina swallowed down the lump in her throat. 'How can you be so sure? Javier could have any woman. He's rich, successful...God knows he's good-looking—why would he want me?'

'Honestly, Sabrina, listen to yourself! Is your opinion of yourself really that low? You are a gorgeous, successful woman in her prime—why *wouldn't* he want you?'

'You've never thought of me as successful—you or Mum.'

'What utter rubbish!' Ellie's arms crossed her chest in exasperation. Both Tallulah and Henry looked wonderingly at their mother. 'Mum tells all her friends how proud she is of you. She's forever leaving your business cards about the place wherever she goes, for God's sake! At the doctor's, the dentist, on the bus, talking to a perfect stranger...and Dad's the same. And how could you think *I* wasn't proud of you? Whenever I glance in the mirror lately I pray I'll look as good as you when I'm your age, and on the days when my clothes are covered in baby drool or I haven't even had a minute to pull a comb through my hair, don't you think I think about you and feel just a teeny bit envious? There you are with your own business, taking care of yourself, meeting new people every day and looking gorgeous while you do it and there's me resembling something that the cat dragged in! I don't regret motherhood for a second, you know I don't—but I wouldn't be human if I couldn't see the benefits of the path you've chosen, Sabrina.'

'Thanks, Ellie.' She felt as if a huge weight had been lifted off her shoulders by the time her sister had finished speaking. 'We should have talked like this before. I've been such an idiot.'

'Being an idiot isn't exclusively your prerogative, sis. We're *all* guilty of that from time to time. Now go home and talk to Javier—or is he at work with you today? Wherever he is, go and tell him how you feel. I think I can safely promise he's not going to pack your bags and throw you out on the street!'

She'd picked up a film she'd wanted to see for the longest time on her way home, and in her brown leather tote bag there was a very good bottle of crisp white Chardonnay along with a box of sweets for Angelina. Not knowing whether Javier had made any plans or not for the evening, she prayed he wasn't going out, that he would want to share the film and the wine with her and afterwards talk with her a little. Whether she'd be brave enough to do as Ellie had suggested and tell him exactly how she felt, Sabrina didn't know, but she'd promised herself to stop pretending their marriage was in name only, and prayed Javier was ready to do the same.

But all her hopes flew out the window when she arrived home to find Javier's exotic ex-girlfriend,

Christina, in residence in the kitchen. Javier was no-where to be seen and, apart from the radio playing softly on the counter-top, the house was unusually quiet for that time of the evening. Had Rosie taken Angelina out somewhere? And where was Javier?

Gazing at the sultry woman seated at the kitchen table, flicking through a magazine, her long, very slender legs encased in soft black leather trousers with a silver knit halter-neck on top, Sabrina was suddenly beset by doubt and fear. 'Hello. Where is everybody?' Removing her coat, she automatically folded it across the back of a nearby chair, then moved across the room to fill the kettle for a drink. Anything to keep her hands busy and her brain from going crazy.

'Rosie has taken Angelina to visit a friend and Javier has just popped out to the drug store to get me some headache pills. Are you making coffee?'

Absorbing the slightly condescending glance of the other woman, Sabrina reached up to the dresser for cups and saucers, biting her lip to stop herself from asking the woman why she couldn't have gone out to get her own pills. Who did she think Javier was—her lackey?

'I can do, but is it a good idea if you have a head-ache?'

'It is not so bad now. I have had a long talk with Javier and am feeling much better. He always knows how to make me feel better. *Always.*'

'He's a good man.' Her back stiff, Sabrina switched off the kettle, spooned some coffee granules into two cups and stirred, all the while her heart thud-ding with indignation and hurt. Javier had told her that Christina had a boyfriend back in Argentina, that he no longer felt anything for the beautiful model who was his ex-girlfriend. If that was true, why had she shown up at the house again?

'Do you take milk and sugar?'

'No.' Christina's dark eyes flashed as if to say 'do you need to ask?'. 'I have to take care of my figure. It is how I make my living.'

'And is that what you're doing in the UK?' Putting the green cup with its matching saucer down in front of her on a place-mat, Sabrina returned to the counter-top for her own drink. 'Modelling?'

'I did a shoot for Paris *Elle* and decided to make a stopover for a few days in London so that I could catch up with some friends. I particularly wanted to see my darling Javier. When I heard about poor Michael I was glad to come and offer him some comfort.'

Was that what she'd been offering Javier the night she'd stayed at the house? *Comfort?* Sabrina's heart turned over. He'd sworn to her that nothing had happened between them but that clearly wasn't what the sultry Christina was implying.

'He is hot, yes?'

'Hot?' For a moment, Sabrina didn't know what the other woman meant.

'Sexy.' Christina laughed, the sound curiously like a cat purring. 'Good in bed.'

At Sabrina's flustered glance, Christina fixed her with a knowing little smile, her lipstick appearing suddenly too red next to her very white teeth, giving her a hard, almost brittle look.

'Let's not pretend, Sabrina. You have slept with him, yes? I would have been very surprised if you had not. Javier is a very attractive, virile man with Latin blood flowing in his veins. He naturally has needs…needs which only a woman can fulfil. The fact that you so readily agreed to assume the role of pretend wife doesn't stop you from being susceptible to his very apparent charms. But I want you to know that you have not been singled out particularly. Any reasonably attractive woman would have done. I am only telling you this so you do not get your hopes up where he is concerned. When he has been here as long as he needs to be, he will return to Argentina and his family. I know them well, Sabrina, and they would not take kindly to an Englishwoman as their son's wife. Look what happened to poor Dorothea when she married Michael…she was forced to leave everything she knew and loved behind to settle in the UK. Her *mama* was heartbroken. Imagine how she would feel if Javier—her only son—did the same?'

Feeling suddenly chilled, Sabrina leant back against the counter-top and drew her fingers through her softly mussed hair. Pulling out the tortoiseshell comb, she gave it a brief shake loose, willing her chaotic thoughts to start making some sense, trying to get a grip on what Christina was saying, wondering if she ought to take it seriously or if the woman was simply suffering from a case of terminal jealousy where Javier was concerned because she was no longer the woman in his life.

'As far as I understand, Javier's sister wasn't "forced" to stay in the UK. It was a choice she made because she was in love with Michael. As for the rest, my hopes or plans are nothing to do with you and therefore not open to speculation or gossip. What's the matter, Christina? Does my being married to Javier pose some kind of threat to you?'

The other woman tossed her head disparagingly. 'Not in the least. I can get any man I wish—Javier D'Alessandro included!'

'Then why did you break up?'

'That is none of your business!'

'Fine. I totally respect your privacy. If you would return the compliment we'll be all square. Now, if you'll excuse me, I've been at work all day and I need to go and take a shower.'

'Well, I'm just letting you know, I may ask Javier to take me out to dinner.'

Pausing at the door, her cup of coffee in her hand, Sabrina threw the other woman a disdainful glance. 'Go ahead. As far as I can see, I don't have the slightest thing to worry about.'

She left the room to a string of Spanish expletives that strangely enough didn't hurt her in the least— even if she had known what they meant.

Relieved to see the back of her, Javier gladly saw Christina into a taxi and waved her a final goodbye. He hoped that he'd made it perfectly clear that she'd outstayed her welcome and there was nothing more between them worth pursuing. When he'd got back to the house with her headache medicine, his heart had almost stalled when he saw Sabrina's bag on the table and her coat over the chair. For all his frantic dash to the chemist and back, he'd been too late to get Christina out of the house before Sabrina's arrival and, judging by the self-satisfied, smug look on Christina's face when he'd asked her if she'd spoken to Sabrina, he knew his ex-girlfriend had probably not missed the opportunity to make mischief. Used to being the centre of attention as far as men were concerned, the beautiful Brazilian model would not like to see another woman have the limelight. Especially when that 'other' woman had ensnared her ex-lover's heart where she had been unable to. Javier had enjoyed their association, as any young man would enjoy escorting a beautiful model around town, but as far as anything else went she left him cold. *Especially* when he'd found her in bed with Carlo Andretti—a man not known for his fastidiousness when it came to personal hygiene.

Drumming his fingers on the table-top, he took a moment to gather his thoughts before going to seek Sabrina out. All day his body had thrummed with the memory of their lovemaking and all day he'd lusted after her in a fever of wanting. She was becoming too important to him for him to simply let her go when his British passport came through and the adoption papers were duly signed, sealed and delivered. What would she think if he told her he wanted to make this paper marriage of theirs real? As real as it could be? Would it frighten her away for good? She was so set on her business being a success, would she find marriage to him and being a stepmother to Angelina too much of a bind or a restriction?

He was willing to recognise that there were no guarantees—the loss of both his sister and her husband had brought that fact tragically home—but he'd put off the moment of truth for long enough and would just have to trust that the outcome would be one that favoured both him and his beloved niece.

That said, he stood outside Sabrina's room for a good two or three minutes before raising his hand to knock on her door.

CHAPTER TWELVE

SHE heard him walk up to her door then...nothing. Pacing the room, her chequebook in her hand, she caught sight of her reflection in the dressing-table mirror as she passed it for the third time, alarmed to see that, yes, she did look as frightened as she felt. Was he coming to tell her that he was taking Christina out to dinner—or, worse, that he and the beautiful Brazilian model were getting back together? Her stomach knotted painfully at the thought. On paper, she and Javier didn't look like the ideal match, granted—but it hadn't prevented her from falling head over heels in love with the man, had it? It didn't prevent her from wondering how she was ever going to take in her next breath if he told her that he wanted nothing more from this marriage of theirs than for her to fulfil her part of the bargain then leave.

Oh, God...what was he doing out there? Why was he taking so long? When the knock on the door finally came, Sabrina still reacted as if a bat had swooped down on her in the dark, and with her heart going crazy she took a deep breath and pulled open the door.

'Hi.'

'Can I come in?' His arms were folded across the impressive span of his chest beneath a dark blue denim shirt matched with his jeans, and his dark eyes roved her face with all the intensity of a man hungry

173

to be reacquainted with his lover. The realisation made Sabrina's world tilt for a disconcerting few seconds.

'Of course. Has your friend gone or have you come to tell me that you're taking her out to dinner?' Presenting him with her back, Sabrina paced across the luxurious carpet to the small padded stool in front of the dressing table, where she turned round again. With anxious blue eyes she waited for his answer.

'Why would I be taking Christina out to dinner?' His hypnotic dark gaze narrowed suspiciously. 'What has she been saying to you?'

'She's very beautiful. I could understand if you wanted—if you wanted to get back together with her.'

'You say this to me when I have already told you she means nothing to me?'

'Then why was she here, Javier? And why were you rushing around getting her headache pills? Is the woman helpless or is it that she's just used to crooking her little finger and the men fall over themselves to do what she wants?'

'*Nada! I* do not come running when she crooks her little finger. She was complaining of a migraine. She said she had left her pills back at the hotel and asked me to go and get her some. I could not sit there knowing the woman was in pain. I would not even do that to a stranger.' Shaking his head, Javier advanced into the room. He looked very big and very angry and Sabrina silently acknowledged that she seemed to have an unhappy knack for igniting his temper. Her legs trembling a little, she dropped down onto the padded stool, folding her hands in her lap and gripping her chequebook.

'I don't want to argue with you, Javier.'

'No?' For a moment there was a glint of humour in his eyes. 'Forget Christina. She is history. Tomorrow morning she will be on a plane home to Argentina. She only came to tell me goodbye. But we need to talk, *sí*?'

'Yes, we do. But first I want to give you this.' She opened the slim grey book, tore out a page and passed it to him.

'What is this?'

'It's my first instalment of our repayment plan. For the money you loaned me for the business,' she explained reasonably.

For a moment he said nothing, just stood staring down at it as if he couldn't comprehend its meaning. Then, lifting his head, staring right at her, he ripped the cheque in two and let the pieces flutter soundlessly onto the floor.

'Why did you do that?' She was genuinely bewildered, her blue eyes widening to saucers.

'I told you I did not want you to repay me. You have already repaid me by agreeing to be my wife so that I could stay and be with Angelina. I do not want your money, Sabrina, so do not insult me by bringing up the subject again. Do you understand?'

'I insist that you take it. I don't want to be under an obligation to anybody. That's not the way I work.'

'No!' His shout almost made her fall off the chair. His handsome face enraged, he stalked towards her. 'Your mother and your sister are right. You are independent to the point of stupidity! While I admire your undoubted ability to stand on your own two feet,

I do not admire this stubbornness of yours to try and prove it at every turn.'

'Well, I don't care whether you admire it or not, it's the way I am, so you'd better wake up and smell the coffee, Javier!'

'Pardon?'

Her bottom lip quivering, Sabrina pushed herself to her feet and swept past him. But she didn't reckon on him reaching out and grabbing her. Nor did she reckon on the hard, hot, punishing kiss that followed. Her heart in her throat, she forgot all about being angry as her breasts were crushed against the warm, impenetrable wall of his chest. Forgot all about obligation and independence and stubbornness and concentrated instead on the feelings and sensations that drowned her limbs like a bath of slow, sweet honey as Javier's mouth took possession of hers and his hands claimed intimate knowledge of her body. Anchoring his fingers in her hair, running them down her back, then cupping her bottom, he moulded her to him with a wild, crazy hunger that tore through them both like a forest fire.

'Dios! How did I ever live without you?' Gazing down at her, he proceeded to drop hungry little kisses all over her face, her eyelids, her nose, her cheeks, her mouth, her forehead, until Sabrina's heart felt as if it would surely jump right out of her chest with joy.

'Javier, we still have to talk. We have to—'

'Uncle! What are you doing?'

Startled, they sprang apart at the sight of that little puzzled face in the doorway.

His heart slamming against his chest, Javier considered his niece with a sense of shock, cursing the fates for pre-empting his chance to talk to her about his feelings for Sabrina. Now she would most probably be frightened that Sabrina had replaced her in his affections. How to explain that there was more than enough room in his heart for both of them?

'Angelina, I...'

But the little girl had already turned tail and run, and Sabrina hugged her arms tightly around her middle and wondered if she'd lost the child's trust for good. She prayed not.

'I have to go to her.' His expression undeniably torn, Javier hurried from the room.

Back in the kitchen, Sabrina made coffee that she didn't really feel like drinking then sat aimlessly flicking through the glossy magazine that Christina had left behind. But she didn't really register anything more than a blur of shiny pages because her thoughts were anxious and distracted, and if her stomach churned one more time she'd have to go in search of the bathroom.

'How did I ever live without you?' he'd asked, not knowing that she could have posed the very same question. Now she wondered if she'd left it too late to tell him. If Angelina was too upset by the idea that her uncle had some affection for Sabrina, would he turn his back on his need for her? Would her hopes for the future now all come crashing down around her? And, worse—would she have to walk away from this marriage without telling Javier how much she loved him?

'Sabrina.'

Her heart knocking against her ribcage, she glanced up in surprise at Javier's tall frame towering over her.

'Yes?'

'I've spoken to Angelina.'

'She's very upset? Oh, God, Javier, I would do anything to stop that little girl from being hurt even more. If she hates the idea of me being with you in that—in that way, I'll just give you both more space. I'll only stay until your passport comes through; tell me what you want me to do and I'll do it.' Her hand trembling, she unconsciously smoothed the shiny pages of the magazine back and forth.

Dropping his hands to his hips, Javier registered her agitation, feeling his stomach flare with warmth at the knowledge that Sabrina would sacrifice her own needs for Angelina. He wanted to hold on tight to this remarkable woman and never let go.

'She's not upset, Sabrina, just the opposite. She's delighted with the idea that we have grown to care for each other.'

'She is? We have?' Swallowing down the lump that had lodged in her throat, Sabrina blinked hard, barely allowing herself to dream, to hope.

'*Te amo, Sabrina.* I love you.'

'Javier.' Rising to her feet, Sabrina allowed him to take her hands in his, felt herself engulfed by his warmth and protection, his love, when he urged her head onto his chest. 'Oh, God, I love you too. I don't know what I would have done if you'd said Angelina was unhappy. It would have been so hard—impossible—to pretend I didn't care as much as I did about you.'

'So we are "real", yes? *Mi esposa hermosa.*'

Raising her head to gaze into his eyes, Sabrina

smiled. 'You said that the first time we made love. What does it mean?'

'My beautiful wife.'

'I like the sound of that.'

'You do?' He kissed her forehead, then her nose, then finally her mouth, his lips moving over hers with exquisite tenderness, leaving her in no doubt that he truly loved her. Releasing a shuddering breath, Sabrina pulled away, a frown puckering the smooth, clear skin of her brow. 'You know what people will probably say?'

'Tell me.'

'That I'm too old for you; that I enticed you with my wicked womanly charms; that I married you for your money.'

'Let them talk. They are all lies...except the part where you enticed me with your wicked womanly charms, *sí*?' His hands on her hips, he was urging her against him, heat simmering in those amazing dark eyes of his. 'And you will give me babies...at least two or three, yes? You can still run your precious business—Rosie will be our nanny. What do you think?'

'What if I can't, Javier? Have babies, I mean.'

'Can't is not in my vocabulary. Besides...' he wound his fingers possessively through the soft strands of her pretty honey-brown hair '...we will practise hard. Night and day...whenever we can, *sí*?'

'Sabrina?' Framed in the doorway, her bright pink tracksuit emphasising her tanned skin, her eyes huge and soulful like her gorgeous uncle's, Angelina glanced from her uncle to the woman he held in his arms and back again.

'Yes, Angelina?' Stepping away from Javier, Sabrina dropped down onto the nearest kitchen chair.

Advancing into the room, the little girl planted herself in front of her. Her teeth chewing on her plump lower lip, for a moment she appeared ill-at-ease and uncertain. 'My uncle told me that he is going to adopt me. He's going to be like my daddy. Did he tell you?'

'Yes, sweetheart, he told me.' As she glanced up at the man she loved Sabrina's expression grew even softer.

'Does that mean that when he adopts me you'll be like—like my mummy?'

Oh, God. What was she supposed to say to that? Her gaze naturally gravitated to the tall, brooding man standing behind the child for guidance. She attempted a smile but barely even moved her lips.

'Would you—would you like that, Angelina? I will never take the place of your real mother but I would love you like my own and never let you down, I promise.'

'I think I would like that very much if it means you'll stay with me and Uncle Javier for ever. Will you, Sabrina?'

'Remember what I told you when you were ill? That when I care about someone I stick like glue? Well, when I love someone I stick even harder. You'll never be able to get rid of me now!'

'What do you say about that, *querida*?' Sliding his hand across the child's slender shoulder, he gave it a little squeeze.

'I'm happy. I'm happy that we're going to be a real family. Daddy would have liked that.'

*   *   *

'I don't care whether you think you know the ending or not, we don't want to know it, do we, Angelina?'

Sitting cross-legged on the floor beside the little girl, her back against the couch between Javier's long legs, Sabrina glanced up at her husband, her blue eyes twinkling with mischief as the television flickered in front of them, the film they were watching well under way. His hands resting lightly on her slender shoulders, he bent towards her head and planted a warm kiss at the side of her neck. A surge of delicious tingling flooded her body.

'No, Uncle, don't tell us the ending. You'll spoil everything!'

'OK, I won't tell you. But only if you let *me* choose the movie tomorrow,' Javier teased his niece. 'This is one of those—how do you call them?—girly films. What I want to see is an action movie.'

'Then I'm afraid you're going to be outvoted,' Sabrina warned him. 'There are two of us girls now so you won't find it so easy to get your own way in future, Señor D'Alessandro!'

'Only in some things, *sí*?' Whispering it for her ears only, he tightened the hands on her shoulders perceptibly. 'When we are alone in our bedroom.'

Sabrina melted.

'Stop whispering all that lovey-dovey stuff to Aunt Sabrina,' Angelina scolded, her face breaking into a delighted grin. 'She's trying to watch the film and you're distracting her.'

'Am I distracting you, beautiful Sabrina?'

Reaching for a handful of popcorn from the bowl on the carpet between herself and Angelina, Sabrina couldn't suppress a happy smile. 'Stop fishing for compliments and watch the film. If your head gets any bigger you won't be able to fit through the door!'

At the sound of Angelina's infectious giggle, Sabrina munched her popcorn and thought with a spurt of satisfaction that family life certainly had a lot to recommend it.

Stepping out of the taxi, Sabrina stood for several moments staring up at the new shop-front while Javier paid the driver, excitement and pride rushing through her with equal intensity. In a few short weeks, East-West Travel had been transformed from a slightly shabby, fading exterior to a smart, up-to-the-minute business that wouldn't look out of place in any modern city centre in the world. Inside, Robbie and Jill were already hard at work and, peering through the window, Sabrina saw that several of the smart easy chairs lined up against the pale cream walls were already taken by waiting customers. It didn't matter that at least one or two had merely come in out of curiosity or to ask for brochures—the point was, East-West Travel had been noticed, and, what with the new equipment and the first-class service both Sabrina and her staff knew how to give, things would soon be thriving. Of that she had no doubt. And none of it would have been possible without the unfailing guidance and support of her wonderful husband.

'Aren't we going to go inside?' Smiling, Javier joined her, automatically enfolding her hand in his. The day was windy and cold but Sabrina was immediately charged with heat at his touch, an occurrence she was happily getting used to.

'I just wanted to take a minute. It's not every day

you have your dream come true, you know.' But she wasn't looking at the shop-front when she said the words. Gazing up into the face of the man she loved, she felt a thrill of dizzying pleasure rush through her body, intoxicating her blood like wine.

'*Mi querido,*' she said softly.

'My Spanish lessons are paying off, I see,' Javier teased in reply. When Sabrina had told him and Angelina that she stuck like glue to those she loved, Javier believed her. He had lost his heart to this incredible, loving woman but he had no fear where she was concerned. Sabrina had taught him that love was as spontaneous as breathing, there was no limit to the amount you could give so therefore there was no danger that that love would diminish—no matter what happened. Love was infinite and they had the whole of the rest of their lives and beyond to prove it.

'Yes, but I'll definitely need lots more tuition.' Dimpling, Sabrina touched his lips with her fingers and somehow Javier knew his beautiful wife was not just referring to his native language that he was teaching her.

'You are an insatiable woman, Señora D'Alessandro.' His voice husky, he squeezed her fingers and bestowed them with a loving kiss.

Her lovely blue eyes wide, Sabrina laughed in delight. 'You're nearly eight years younger than me, Javier—don't tell me you're running out of stamina already?'

'Never! I will never stop giving you pleasure. *Usted salvo mi vida.*'

As she reached up for a kiss, Sabrina's expression grew suddenly serious. 'You saved my life too, Javier, and I'm going to spend the rest of our lives showing you how grateful I am. That's a promise.'

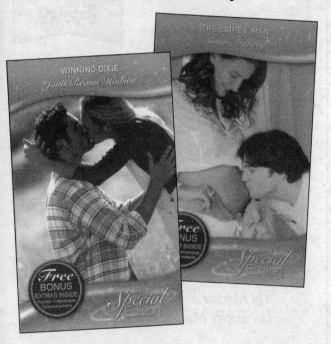

Mediterranean Men

Let them sweep you off your feet!

Gorgeous Greeks
The Greek Bridegroom by Helen Bianchin
The Greek Tycoon's Mistress by Julia James
Available 20th July 2007

Seductive Spaniards
At the Spaniard's Pleasure by Jacqueline Baird
The Spaniard's Woman by Diana Hamilton
Available 17th August 2007

Irresistible Italians
The Italian's Wife by Lynne Graham
The Italian's Passionate Proposal by Sarah Morgan
Available 21st September 2007

THE ROYAL HOUSE OF NIROLI

*...International affairs, seduction
and passion guaranteed*

Volume 1 – July 2007
The Future King's Pregnant Mistress by Penny Jordan

Volume 2 – August 2007
Surgeon Prince, Ordinary Wife by Melanie Milburne

Volume 3 – September 2007
Bought by the Billionaire Prince by Carol Marinelli

Volume 4 – October 2007
The Tycoon's Princess Bride by Natasha Oakley

8 volumes in all to collect!

THE ROYAL HOUSE OF NIROLI

...*International affairs, seduction and passion guaranteed*

Volume 5 – November 2007
Expecting His Royal Baby by Susan Stephens

Volume 6 – December 2007
The Prince's Forbidden Virgin by Robyn Donald

Volume 7 – January 2008
Bride by Royal Appointment by Raye Morgan

Volume 8 – February 2008
A Royal Bride at the Sheikh's Command by Penny Jordan

8 volumes in all to collect!

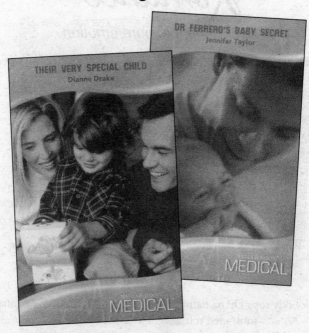

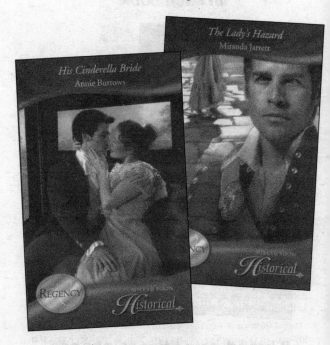

Victorian London is brought to life in the stunning sequel to Mesmerised

London, 1876

Though Kyria Moreland is beautiful and rich enough to attract London's most sought-after gentlemen, she has yet to find love and refuses to marry without it. When she receives a mysterious package, she is confronted with danger, murder and a handsome American whose destiny is entwined with hers...

Rafe McIntyre has enough charm to seduce any woman, but his smooth façade hides a bitter past. Still, he realises Kyria is in danger, and he refuses to let her solve the riddle of this package alone. Who sent her this treasure steeped in legend? And who is willing to murder to claim its secrets for themselves?

Available 17th August 2007